To a D+D Buddy
To morrow you're awesome

David White

More Advance Praise for Heroes of the Fallen

"*Heroes of the Fallen* is a Book of Mormon historical that reads like an epic fantasy. It's not often that the LDS market sees something truly new, but West's debut novel really is different. It was a breath of fresh air and a lot of fun. I read just about every book that comes out of every LDS publisher, and this one feels new. So many Book of Mormon novels get really bogged down in either hyperspiritualism or hyperrealism, and they neglect the one important element: telling a great story. I was impressed."
~**Robison Wells**, author of *On Second Thought, Wake Me When Its Over,* and *Counterfeit*

"David J. West has created a story line filled with excitement, archaeology, treasure and real history. This is a must-read not only for entertainment but also to open new doors and vistas of possibility for the mind. West has intertwined fiction and history in such a way that the reader comes away believing that it might be true. He has used actual archaeological evidence to weave into his story making it more real and exciting. As a novice author, David J. West has done a wonderful job of keeping the reader between the covers of this book."
~**Bruce H. Porter** Ph.D. Brigham Young University religion professor, former Church Educational System institute director

"I found *Heroes of the Fallen* very well composed with a great deal of research and an eye for detail. West's ability to create a story line from historical passages from the Book of Mormon and the history of the Nephite/Lamanite through words of the Prophet Joseph Smith is remarkable. The story keeps one spellbound waiting with great anticipation for what will happen next."
~**Stephen B. Shaffer**, Historian, and author of *Treasures of the Ancients, Of Men and Gold,* and *The Lost Josephine Mine*

"In *Heroes of the Fallen* West tells of an exciting story of Nephites sleuthing the ancient past of America. The question of the peopling of America is no trivial issue; the author skillfully balances historical fact with fiction to bring these characters to life. In the final analysis, the archaeology of America, which has been hidden beneath the canopy of its dense forests, is an adventure story that rivals any main stream

novel—it's a great read for any Book of Mormon enthusiast, searching out the Promise Land of Lehi."
~**Wayne N. May**, Author of *This Land* series and publisher of *Ancient American Magazine*.

"An epic tale of valor and degeneracy where heroes are beset on every side by wicked schemers whose schemes, like a flood, threaten to drown them all. *Heroes of the Fallen* is sure to please any reader who enjoys a multi-threaded plot full of both historical wonders and vicious intrigues which rule the day. *Heroes of the Fallen* will have you praying for the good guys!"
~**Daron D. Fraley**, Author of *The Chronicles of Gan: The Thorn*

"This epic thriller combines meticulous historical and scriptural research with unmatched literary skill to bring into lifelike focus an era of scriptural history that unfolds upon the sacred Promised Land of the Book of Mormon in the Heartland of America. Get ready to live its history!"
~**Rod L. Meldrum**, Author, Researcher and founder of the FIRM (Foundation for Indigenous Research and Mormonism)

"West has included some excellent details in his story. The use of "iron rod" as the name of an irreverent bar typifies his thoughtful attention to detail, and the believable fleshing out of very sparse source material found in the Book of Mormon. The mention of meteoric iron, the incredible body count of individual warriors, scanning the heaven's for auspicious omens, and the balanced devotion to the ways of peace and war are all resonant with historic pre modern societies. In my reading I found the behavior of Chinese officials, Japanese Samurai, Mesoamerican warriors, and other facets from non Western societies mixed in with LDS theological tidbits and even some diffusionist theories. This collection of accurate historic material helps to create an authentic environment for his characters to move through. More importantly, it provides convincing character motivations that propel the story forward and make them more relatable to the reader."
~**Morgan Deane**, military history professor, Trine University

Heroes

of the

Fallen

Heroes
of the
Fallen

David J. West

WiDō Publishing • Salt Lake City

WiDō Publishing, LLC
Salt Lake City, Utah

Copyright © 2010 by David J. West

Cover art by Brina Williamson
Book design by Don Gee
Map created by Jeremy Wilburn

ISBN: 978-0-9796070-3-5

Printed in the United States of America

For my sons and daughter

From the remnants of Zelph's lost map:
The Lands of the Lamanites in the Days of Zelph

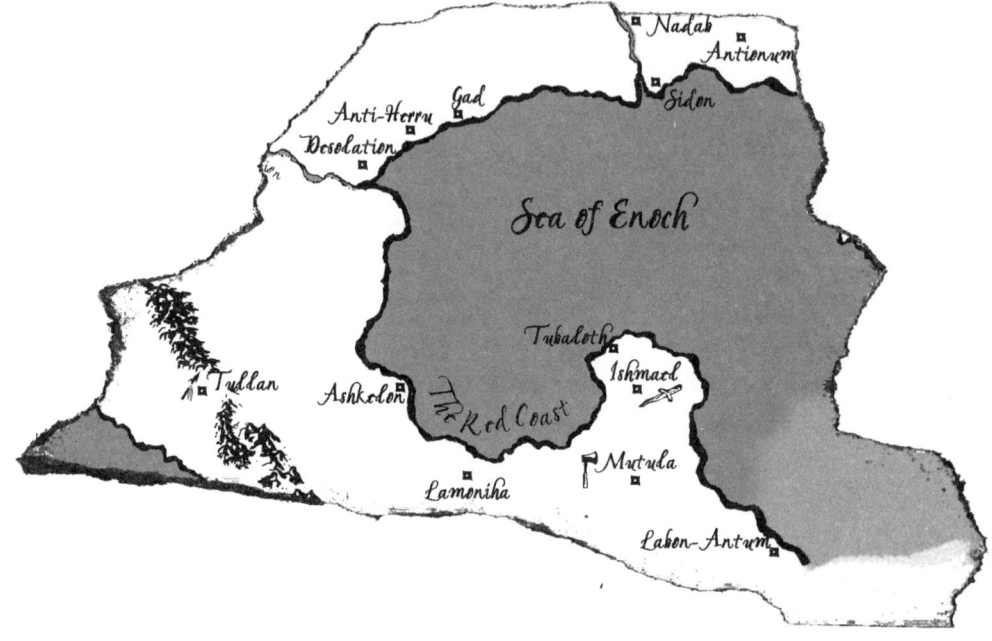

CUMORAH

The mountains womb is gold, the valley's skin is blood.
A dark spirit whispert, bringing the ax and flood,
sending the wicked and righteous back to the mud.

Satan's on his throne, Record is in the ground.
I light the funeral pyres, until it's time be found,
forgotten but by the worms deep in the mound.

I was in the ruin, I was in the shield wall,
I was there to see father Mormon fall,
but none beside could catch him ere deaths call.

Let come the maelstrom, let come the rain,
wash away the memory o' this place once again.
This time perhaps not at all in vain.

—David J. West

From the remnants of Zelph's lost map:

The Lands of the Nephites in the Days of Amaron

AMARON'S LAMENT
The fallen people, how the dream turned round.
And the song ran hard and into the ground.
This saga of those mighty lost souls.
They whose Empire is dust, cold have gone the coals.
Trodden under the foot of revenge and justice. Mercy where art thou?

Sword in hand, darkness sings, on Cumorah's land.
Black hearts and the Hand of God,
kills the King that would stop his work, sing!

Faith trumps doubt but it doesn't mean truth won't bring the pain.
Run cold and hold that inside, words of honor are sound.
Remember, when the torches fade and cannot be found.
Within the hearts that are true, the Lights remain.

—David J. West

CONTENTS

"When the gods wish to punish wicked men for their crimes, they allow them for a time a more than usual prosperity and an even longer impunity, so that they will suffer all the more bitterly when their fortunes are reversed."

—Gallic War Commentaries *Julius Caesar*

"All is not lost—the unconquerable will, and study of revenge, immortal hate, and courage never to submit or yield."

—Paradise Lost, Book One 106-108 *John Milton*

"What was Forgotten will soon be Remembered."

—Book of War, Plate 153 *Nephite soldier's maxim*

Prologue: The End

~Late Summer 385 A.D.
The Land of Cumorah

With the bittersweet music of battle over, I found him at dusk, buried amid the mass of his ten thousand. He and I, the last of his legion. Taking my general back up the great hill, halfway up we surveyed the apocalyptic scene. Twenty-three legions in all, completely decimated in a matter of days. He wept. I cannot, there is nothing inside anymore but a burning sadness. His last son, amazingly still alive, came and helped on the final ascent up the steep palisaded graveyard. We spoke little that night, watching the blood red moon rise and reverberate.

Dawn is breaking. Strange to see how closely the color of the vaulted sky matches the raw ground. Red, black and white, twisted shattered shapes everywhere. The cross guards of swords jutting from the ground, the broken hands that used to hold them. Torn banners, ripped and clutching their rotten fingers at the copper-scented wind. It is the end of a borrowed summer, yet everything is dead like a hard given winter, reflections of our people's collective wicked choice. What else brings this corrosion, this destruction but our own choices? The heroes tried to hold back the tide, but it's we few against the many on the devil's side.

My grizzled old general is wounded, deep in the hip and shoulder. A little more force on the enemy warrior's part and he could have been cut clean through to the heart. But we do not believe in luck. The dead hold their worthless charms, rabbit's feet and lucky golden spoons. Sorceries, witchcraft and magic, does it matter if it works or not? They are dead and can keep their reason, fear and doubt. We are alive, we have our faith. Some say prayers, I say mine.

We stand tall or lie broken, atop the lonely beaten hill, formerly called Ramah, now called Cumorah. All twenty-four of us, the last of a fallen people. These last mighty warriors, all men of indomitable spirit, we will not be beaten, nor defeated. Not yet.

"My lord general, the dawn is breaking." I still clutch my war hammer and Ramevorn, the infamous sword of honor.

1

"Thank you, Amaron. I see it. I was awake, I should have slept, but even with the blood loss I could not. Too much still to record. They will be coming soon for the last of us. Just as soon as that morning star's light fades away," he says, pausing from his record.

"I remember. They abstain from war while the morning star shines out of respect for the Christ; funny how they hang onto some traditions despite all else."

"They're his children too, our brothers. So much has been forgotten...I hope in time they will remember."

"What a life we have led, and here it will end," says Moroni, the general's son.

"Not all of us, not just yet." The general looks upon us, squinting through a congealing gash on his forehead. I can see both the physical and spiritual pain of his heart. An entire people destroyed, countless bodies and bones to bleach upon these hills. The ground will be fertile with life once death is far enough away. This won't be in my remaining lifetime. Yesterday, before the crimson sun had set, the carrion birds blackened the skies, and the white howl of the wolf painted the scene of death.

"Your hair, Amaron, is still long and black as night. You could be mistaken for a Lamanite in the right light. And you the eldest man left," the general laughs before a spasm of pain makes him wince.

"I am only six years older than you, graybeard," I joke with him. His life has taken its toll, he looks twenty years my senior.

"I am only thinking out loud, there is always a purpose, always a way through with the power of the Lord God. Zelph would never let me forget that."

"Yea, I never knew any men so righteous in all my days as you, Onandagus and Zelph. I wish they were with us now," I reflect.

"General, the star is nearly faded," speaks another warrior with a great spear. His name is Gamaliel. The name is ironic to me, Reward of God. Is that what all this is? The reward of apathy, of wickedness, of evil?

With his son's help, our mighty general props against the base of a tree and overlooks the desolate battlefield. "I can hear the call of their horns, the beat of the drums. They will be here very soon," he says before coughing up some blood. Leaning upon his great broadsword, he looks to these last few men under his command. "My son, you will take the record and go. I surmise from the sounds and the last formations of yesterday's

2

battle, that you should go to the southwest. Their lines are weakest there, I know you can get through if the Lion of Wrath goes with you." He points at me. The Lion of Wrath—that had been my grim nickname for years. "Moroni, take the Sword of Laban. It is mine no longer. You must also take the Urim and Thummim."

Moroni, the general's son, takes the valued artifacts with a reserved air, reverent and silent as ever since his own young family had been slain.

"My lord general, my place has ever been at your side. I would go down in battle beside you," I declare.

"The record must get out." The general has a strange look in his eye. "It will get out and be preserved. If the truth is saved and ultimately told, then all will be worth the heavy price paid. It is my final order to you. Assist my son by all means necessary to make sure the record is safe."

"I hear and obey," I say with a grudge on my chin. I have never disobeyed an order from him, not even when he was a pup of a commander at sixteen. He has proven himself since a young boy that he is of God, a rare enough thing anymore. I admit to feeling robbed of my destiny—to go down fighting beside him. But it is true, the record is more important than any man's destiny. Its message will live on for another day, another people. I was to be mentioned once within it, more than I deserve. Much better men than I are not to be found within its heavy gold plates.

Already the son has his skin pack buckled, now heavy with the record, but he is almost as big and strong as his father, still young and in the prime of life though his people are now dust and wind. The father and son must have planned for this all last night when they were writing the outcome of the battle upon the record.

"Let us go," I growl, as I adjust my own sparse pack and heft my great-grandfather Teancum's trusted broadsword. Forged of meteoric iron, it has sent more men to the other side than any judge, any ten judges.

Father and son hug goodbye for the final time, and I clasp hands with the great general. "I will not fail you," I promise.

The general smiles at me for the first time in a long time. "I know that neither of you will fail me. God be with you 'til we meet again. Watch and pray."

"Watch and pray," I repeat.

The wind blows his long gray hair about him in a fury. The drums are close, and the sky is changing from deep azure to mournful red. The morning star fully fading away, doomed like us, by dawn's early light. We bid the fallen Nephite nation a somber farewell.

We, the warrior of renown and the young general, Moroni, make our way down the sharp fortified hillside, hanging low, doing our best to ignore the sickening stench of the battlefield. Already the worms of the earth are supping upon our fallen friends and enemies alike. We know the numbers of our own that have fallen, but the slain enemies could not be counted, a wine-dark sea of bodies stretching out into infinity.

We go a good distance from the Hill Cumorah when I hear the last battle atop it. Looking back like Lot's wife, I am frozen. The scourge of Lamanites wash over the hill in a relentless tide of destruction. I know that even as they slay my general, they venerate him. They will bury him with dignity, as they would honor a great king.

With tears, Moroni says, "Let us not tarry. We must put distance between us."

I am a cold one, dead inside perhaps; I have not shed a tear in years. Not since Adira. I remember all the lost souls I have slain; they call to me. I keep walking, and they keep calling me. If not for my orders, I would go back and face the Lamanite horde and then welcome death's sweet embrace. But we move on.

We keep a good pace while the blood mad howling behind us rises and shakes the earth. Deafening is their rage.

"They have spotted us," says my companion as he drops his heavy, precious pack and draws forth the sword of Laban. It is known as such, for its true name is too sacred to be repeated.

"Pick it up and go on; I will deal with them," I tell him. "Pick it up." I am getting angry.

"There are too many."

"There are never enough for what they have done."

"Your lack of..."

"Forgiveness is my greatest fault, I know; I will work on it. Get moving or it is for naught." I urge him toward the edge of the dark forest.

As the record-bearer disappears into the tree line, dozens of vicious painted bodies charge toward me. The first few bold ones close on me as I grant darkness to swiftly take them on the end of my grandfather Teancum's sword. More pour forth, a river of red flesh and black steel and white bone.

4

I have a sacred duty—the son will escape and fulfill his destiny. The great golden lion shield is hindering me. I drop it and pull my war hammer in my left hand. I swing right and left. The river is dammed. Blade, hammer and claw conquer. I let the smoldering rage boil over me, for what was done to our freedom, our peace, our wives and our children. Yet how much was done by ourselves? We allowed our religion to become a forgotten archaic ship that sank in stagnant waters of neglect.

I swing right and left; I am a whirlwind of devastation as I shout, "Behold, sons of Laman, stay back. My blades know no mercy, my mood is black, and white hot vengeance knows no other."

They refuse the generous offer and charge on. I stand alone, swinging victoriously in a losing battle. The war already lost, I slay for what seems hours. Fierce, painted bodies lie sheared all about me, my arms ache, my heart has already stopped caring. I have lost all strength. I can fight no more.

The Lamanites have stopped as well. A tall, strong Lamanite painted as red death stands before me. His face bears the white death's head grin of a charred skull. "You have always stood beside him. Yet you did not die beside him. We know why. Tell me, where is the record?"

I don't respond.

"I am the mighty Chief Mastema the Destroyer. I am chief servant of the king, True Great Jaguar Claw, and you will tell me," he thunders.

"I will not. You will never take it. Everyone will hear of it and then let them decide for themselves what is truth." They hope to destroy it as King Apophis of old had so wanted.

Mastema snarls like a caged animal, though I am the one surrounded. "Destroy him!"

The waves crash around me once again. As the bloody sword strokes drink my life and my soul is about to flee from this shattered mortal coil, I see the portal of light opening. I see everyone I know there, beckoning me to join them. Adira reaches out for me.

"Come feast in the tabernacle of light! Know you have done your duty! Fulfilled your honor, your mission. Let go and sleep."

Seeing them, I think back to my youth, remembering how it came to this.

Swords of the Judge

~321 A.D.

Amaron saw his quarry. The enormous bazaar stretched on for miles in ever-connecting, tight-knit dirty circles. There were all manner of wares. With senses awake, he could see and smell through the tantalizing scents of salted meats and the perfumes of a dozen dancing girls, to the stench of the open air market where the garbage and filth went uncollected for days on end. He could see beyond the many succulent fruits and shiny trinkets—all meant to dazzle the eye, fill the stomach, cloud the heart and line a pocket.

"Watch and pray," said Amaron under his breath. He made sure the sword was loose in his sheath as he waded through the market.

This was Zarahemla, the white city of peace and light, jewel in the crown of the Nephite confederation. Dazzling sounds filled the air, and sweet-smelling baked goods were arrayed to tempt passersby. Every trade imaginable had something represented here, but Amaron and his companion Helam were looking for only one thing.

When the red-capped little man saw them, he stopped mid-bite with his apple. The two large city guardsmen strode toward him with inexorable purpose, the people of the market parting before them like the waters of the Red Sea for Moses.

"Ho, Ezra," called Helam, sounding friendly while Amaron glared.

"You will sing a song to the chief judge. Come with us," said Amaron, cracking his scarred knuckles.

The thin little man was surprised. He made as if to comply for a moment but then ran. Quick as a cat with its tail aflame, he ducked through the open air markets, hidden almost instantly by the throng of merchants and passersby. Thousands of people bought and sold here daily.

"Baal's devils!" cursed Amaron. "Now we have to chase him."

"Watch your tongue. Which way did he go?" asked Helam.

"He was eating an apple with his right hand, likely he ran to the right down the Avenue of the Ram."

They were young stout men of the guard. Helam was blond and fair-skinned; Amaron dark of hair, his skin bronzed by the sun enough for him to be mistaken for a copper-toned Lamanite, the people of the southlands and the sworn Nephite enemies. That Amaron preferred to wear buckskins instead of fine silks and colorful cottons did not help in differentiating him from his countrymen's enemies. Nephites prided themselves on exotic finery to denote status in their highly class conscious society.

Amaron's fierce eyes pierced the crowded street hunting for the red-capped man. He saw sturdy, mountain people from the Hermounts wilderness with furs and coal to sell, and Phoenicians from across the far eastern sea come to barter for copper and other fine products. Amaron's gaze burned a path through the market as merchants and buyers cleared out of the way.

The guardsmen wore their hair long, as had their captain and teacher, Captain Lachoneus. Captain Lachoneus was a descendant of the Mulekites, people who had crossed the great ocean called Irreantum, ages past. Captain Lachoneus could trace his line back to the Spartan mercenaries who had served King Zedekiah and, according to the oral legend, had saved the little King Mulek from the Babylonian wrath. Only Mulek and his sisters Tamar and Scota had escaped the brutal end of the royal line.

"I see him," growled Amaron, running straight toward the skinny man. He signaled Helam to flank their prey by taking a side street.

Ezra, the pursued, ran headlong into a woman with a cart selling fruit. It tumbled, sending her ripe product to the ground.

"Watch where you are going, vermin," she spat after him. He scrambled to get up and continued running.

The meat market of Zarahemla, the Avenue of the Ram, was the perfect place for Ezra to elude his pursuers. A large stack of turkeys and other fowl in crates would block him for a moment, allowing him to disappear down another path. He took a side street to the right, then left, then right again. The red cap flew from his head and hit the ground. Behind him on the busy market street, people shouted at his pursuers.

"Leave him be!" yelled a turkey merchant.

Amaron scanned the avenue. The skinny little man was hiding somewhere in the alley. Crouching, Amaron picked up the red cap and swore he could hear the man's ragged breathing despite the city's noise. The sound of breathing stopped, and Amaron knew that the little man held his breath, likely praying to Bel, the god of thieves, for escape.

Sending Helam down the adjacent avenue, Amaron came down the alley toward the suspected hiding spot. He could feel the little man's eyes watching him.

Ezra inched back, rustling some debris in the process.

Amaron drew his infamous sword named Ramevorn, 'High Holy Steel' in the reformed Egyptian language of Nephites. Forged of meteoric iron it had once belonged to his great-great-grandfather Teancum. It was second in fame only to the Sword of Laban, now lost.

Crawling backward as quietly as he could, Ezra inched upright and ran down the alley. He knocked some empty barrels and other garbage into the path behind him. He ducked down another alley and found it blocked. He turned around to try another route, but Amaron was already there with his sword bared, glinting in the sunlight.

"On the ground, in the name of the chief judge," snapped Amaron.

"I've done nothing wrong," pleaded Ezra.

"Shut your mouth. Do not speak, dog," came the brutal response, as he threw the red cap into Ezra's face.

"Have you no mercy?" asked Ezra, tucking the cap into his waistband.

"Hands behind your back!" said Amaron.

Ezra did as he was told while the muscular guardsman bound his hands tight.

Helam appeared, much to Amaron's relief. He worried they might have been led into a trap. With their man in custody, they must get him back to the Judgment Hall without incident. Amaron watched the rooftops with a knowing eye. Though he had sheathed his sword, he stayed alert, ready to draw and fight.

"Maybe now we can find out where more are hiding," said Helam.

"I hope so. Move it, scum!" Amaron said, kicking Ezra to move down the alley.

They took a variety of random routes through back alleys and side streets until they came to the wide Avenue of the Eagle. This led from the south gate straight to the grounds of the Judgment Hall.

It was a magnificent building, with a wall over twelve feet tall surrounding the grounds. A squared tower of stone rose up from the hall, and from this tower, one could overlook the entire city and the wide Sidon River basin. The entire complex, except for the stone tower, was made of wood stuccoed with plaster made from crushed shells. The whole of the structure was white. Every few years a new layer of whitewash was added. Rumor was that there was a temple of the ancients hidden somewhere within its walls.

A pair of guards in gleaming copper armor parted to let in Amaron and Helam with their prisoner. They passed through a long, open walkway to a veranda with fruit trees along one side and freshly plowed fields on the other. A fountain splashed in front of them, with the doorways to the courtrooms just beyond. They stopped before the field and a man plowing spotted them and halted his ox. He wore a plain white, long-sleeved tunic. His hair was just beginning to gray at his temples and at the corners of his well-trimmed beard.

"Who's that, eh?" asked Ezra.

"Who do you think?" said Amaron, as he smacked Ezra with the back of his hand.

"Owww. Then why does he plow the fields?"

Before Amaron could strike him again, the man, now within earshot, responded. "So that I am not a burden to my people. I am Chief Judge Onandagus and this is my home, but I work the same as any honest man." Amaron tossed Onandagus the red cap. Catching it he continued, "Unlike you, *Gadianton*."

Ezra shrunk at the mention of his secret brotherhood, those considered robbers or worse by Nephite society.

"Now, Ezra, I know you are a Gadianton apprentice. There is no point denying it. I know what atrocities you commit in your secret oaths and combinations, and for that alone I could have you hanged." Onandagus pointed toward the gallows with the crumpled red cap.

The wooden scaffolding lay bleaching in the noonday sun. Amaron made a soft, ghastly sound behind Ezra, like the sound of a man choking. Ezra looked over his shoulder at Amaron, who made a slicing motion across his neck.

"What do you want with me then, eah?" he stammered to Onandagus, breathing out with a curious gasp.

"I have come to understand that your Gadianton Grand Master is planning something. I want you to tell me all you know of it. And Ezra," he said, as he put his hand on the little man's shoulder and looked into his eyes. "I will know if you are lying."

"How could you know that? Eah," he ended his speech again with the odd exhale.

"With these." Onandagus pulled out two smooth, egg-shaped stones, one light and one dark.

"Interpreters! Eah," gasped Ezra. "I thought the magical stones were only a legend."

"They are real and work for those who know how to utilize them."

"But if I tell what I know I'll be dead. I swore on the Throne of Heaven never to divulge the secrets of the Brotherhood or my blood would be spilt and demons will claim my soul. All brothers take the same vows to slay any who would divulge secrets. There is a whole division established just to ritually kill. I'm sorry, but your sentence would be easier to bear than theirs. Eah."

Onandagus looked him over a moment before answering. "Do you own the Throne of Heaven and have any right to swear upon something you have not? No, you do not. As chief judge I will protect you. Your oath to the order of Gadiantons is forfeit, and no one will ever be allowed to use it against you. Now tell me what you know."

"If only they would honor your word, eah. But they won't, they will take my life if I say anything," insisted Ezra, straining at the ropes which bound him.

"I will find a place of safety for you if you cooperate with us. You have my word on it."

"I don't know much. But with your word I suppose I will talk, but here in the open?" said Ezra, gesturing for his hands to be loosed. He looked at the shadowy doorways off to their right, leading to the courtrooms within this half of the Judgment Hall. His young eyes were full of fear.

"He is right to worry. Let us go to my chambers and discuss this in private," said Onandagus. He led the way, with Amaron still holding onto Ezra's bindings and Helam looking behind to see if anyone followed or watched.

As they went further down the veranda to the hall's offices, they were accosted by a tall, gray-bearded man with a sour face. His black judge's robe had a fine trim of purple silk. A large green stone of the Guild of Judges was about his neck. The jade amulet was a symbol of the judges since the days of Egypt. Onandagus and a few others were the only ones who did not wear the costly ornament. The man had a large pipe on which he puffed regularly, fashioned to look like a bird of prey reclining upon its back. A conical, narrow-brimmed black hat shielded his pale, drawn face from the sun.

"Ah, Chief Judge Onandagus, done with your fields already?" he said arrogantly.

Ezra quivered. "Eah," he mumbled. Amaron tightened his grip on the skinny man.

"Judge Hiram, I have a matter to attend to, if you will excuse us," said Onandagus.

Judge Hiram, grim and contemptuous, was not so easily dissuaded. "Who is this man the guards have detained so vigorously? A thief, I surmise?"

"It is not a case that need concern you."

"You are not taking the law into your own hands again, are you? Why is this man not going before Judge Joshua? It is his time to hear cases now."

"As I said, this is not a case that need concern you. This man has not yet been brought up on any charges," said Onandagus, his voice raising.

"Then why is he bound and held by your pet thug? If you insist on continuing your vigilante-style justice, I will have your seat!" Judge Hiram said, tipping his pipe's ash upon the ground. "This man deserves a lawyer. If one cannot be found immediately I will represent him. Ezra, is it? What are they trying to charge you with anyway? Did you forget to mock a priest or observe the Sabbath?" laughed Judge Hiram.

At the mention of Ezra's as yet unspoken name, Amaron shot an exaggerated eyebrow at Helam. Doing his best to keep his temper under control, Amaron said, "Judge Hiram, this man is not being brought up on charges. He was bound for his own safety. Public insanity." Grinning, he continued, "He needs help."

"If that is truly the case, I can help him," he snapped. Then more calmly, he said, "Give him to me. My doctors can work wonders on him."

"No, eah," murmured Ezra, so soft that only Amaron heard him. "Uh, I am feeling fine now. Let me go, I am feeling much better. Thank you, but please let me go now."

"Well?" said Judge Hiram, looking like an alley cat about to devour a helpless baby bird. "Let him go then. He's fine now, he says."

Onandagus nodded at Amaron, who pulled a colossal dagger from his wide leather belt and cut Ezra's bonds with graceful ease. He put the knife away slow, brandishing it before Judge Hiram, letting the sunlight glint against the striped Damascus blade and flash in his eyes.

Ignoring him, the judge turned to Onandagus, "You go too far, Chief Judge. You push your luck with the people, and they cry out for your resignation."

"*Your* people perhaps, Judge Hiram."

"*I* am not the only one. When the people clamor for a king and wish to do away with the judges, who am I to deny them?"

"Yes, who *are* you?" said Onandagus, implying what they both already knew—Judge Hiram was a Gadianton Master of a high level.

His bonds cut, Ezra rubbed feeling back into his hands. He stood shaking, looking fearfully at Judge Hiram who stood stone-still, his eyes emanating a cold hatred for the scrawny man.

"I uh, must go now," Ezra stammered, trotting away rubbing his numb hands.

"Remember what I said," called Chief Judge Onandagus.

"I do. I mean, I will," said Ezra, almost to the gate.

The copper-sheathed guards at the gate stopped Ezra, then looked inside to Onandagus, who gave them the sign of release. They let the frail man pass and fade into the busy, downtown streets of Zarahemla.

"Good day to you," smirked Judge Hiram. "When the hammer strikes the anvil, where will you be?" He turned and walked away.

Helam spat. "Can there be any doubt that he is a Gadianton Master?"

"Enough. He knows we know, but there is no proof to bring against him. His very arrogance in this will be his undoing. You two must recover Ezra for his own safety and for whatever information we can glean from him. Make haste now, before Judge Hiram sends his own picked men after the poor wretch."

They bowed to the chief judge and turned to go after Ezra a second time.

Amaron pondered, When the hammer strikes the anvil, where will I be? Many times, Judge Hiram and others had tried recruiting him with promises of favors, wealth and women, golden and wanton. Judge Hiram had tried to reason with Amaron, to show by logic how there was no God, no reason for faith.

Amaron's answer was simple—faith moves mountains, doubt moves nothing. Can reason save us? No, it can't.

Where will I be when the hammer falls? I have already made that choice. For good or ill, I am with truth, and faith in the knowledge of things unseen. You can't fight demons without being sure of where you stand; you need to know where they stand, too. In a place like this, they're hard to miss.

Like a Wild Bird

The raven-haired girl, beautiful and shapely, was fearful. She had never gone out dressed as she was now. Father would have forbidden it. The dress was the latest in Zarahemlan fashion, tight across the chest in a crisscross pattern, very low cut leaving her arms, cleavage and belly button exposed. It was expensive blue silk; she had saved for weeks to buy it.

Bethia was leaving Zarahemla. She hated being the daughter of the most important man in the city. She couldn't turn around without people pointing and saying, "That's the daughter of Chief Judge Onandagus. What is she doing now?"

She wanted no more of it. At fifteen years, that young desire to see something of the world called like a siren's song. She could get away and not be missed until nightfall. Her father had been too busy to notice her restlessness for some time now, and her mother had her hands full with the other children. Bethia had left an inked piece of parchment telling them not to worry. Not wanting it to be found too soon, she had placed it under the pillow in her room.

She had not yet decided where to go, when she found herself at the docks of Zarahemla along the River Sidon. The river quarter, or the Bowl as it was known, had been forbidden in the rigid structure of her previous life. It was her choice now.

Ships, of course! Better than riding a wretched horse or some other filthy animal, and better than sore feet from walking.

Wondering which ship to board, Bethia looked upon their various names and cargoes, deciding against the Phoenician ships. Their crews looked too seedy and dangerous. Besides, she wanted to see what this side of the world had to offer.

Bethia looked for kind faces among the sailors and found them hard to come by. She talked to several who seemed amiable at first, until it became apparent that they all had the wrong idea. They liked the dress.

"Come here, my young filly," said a swarthy, grinning man.

She stepped away and turned to go. Several of the sailors laughed while the swarthy one persisted, grabbing her slender arm and tugging. His calloused hand rubbed her arm red as she pulled to escape. "Let go, brute!"

"No, no, no. You can't come down here, flashing the goods and then getting picky on us. My silver is as good as anybody uptown," he slurred.

She could smell the wine on his breath. She jerked away again but only got as far as arm's length. He pulled her in so close, closer than any man ever had. She kicked him in the shin and he laughed.

"Now that's no way to behave," he said, drawing her back.

She kicked again, this time aiming for a more sensitive area, but he caught her shin. He drew back to hit her when a voice interrupted.

"Better let her go," said the huge, blond-haired man standing two strides away. His hard, determined face was accentuated by twin plumes of smoke that exited his nostrils like curling dragons. He rolled his cigar and glared at the sailor, fierce as any predator, his left eye twitching.

"Samson," breathed Bethia.

The sailor let go, and she moved away quickly. As Samson turned toward her, the sailor charged with fists swinging wildly. He caught the first one in mid-air and snapped the wrist back, grabbed hold and pulled the man's face into his fist. The sailor dropped unconscious.

Samson turned to Bethia and asked, "What are you doing down here? And what are you wearing?"

"I bought it from the market. It was expensive, but I like it," she said, examining her reddened forearm.

"Where's the rest of it?" he laughed.

She frowned, wishing she had a cloak to cover herself from the men who were leering at her.

"Your father doesn't want you down here," said Samson. "You know what those other women are?" He pointed at the laughing, painted women lounging around the docks. The knocked-out sailor began to rouse, and

Samson tossed the butt end of his cigar at him.

"I do *now*," Bethia nodded. "Father sent you after me? I can handle myself."

"Yea, I can see that," he smirked.

She turned away. Father must have found her gone already and sent his bodyguard to bring her back. He was her father's age or even older although taller and weighing probably twice as much, all muscle. He was the only man that her father allowed to smoke in his presence. Such a strange man, so unashamed of his vices.

"No, I didn't come here to get you, but you're lucky I was here. You have no idea what the world is like, do you?" He gestured at the sailors and harlots up and down the docks. "They will eat you up. The Bowl is no place for a lady. You don't know what the world is like out there."

"And I never will so long as he keeps me cloistered inside the complex and the north quarter. I go to school, I go to church and I go home, that's all. How will I ever know what life is? You have been everywhere, and father is known from the eastern sea to the great mountains of Nephi in the west. He is known from shore to shore, thousands of trackless miles know the name of Onandagus, the chief judge, the governor, the presiding elder. I need to gain life experience. He always says that we are alive for life experience."

Samson was taken aback at her rant and had to admit she was right about at least some of it.

"You can take me back, but I will run again until I am free," she declared.

His face was impassive. He looked up toward city center and the stone tower that overlooked the city.

"Father speaks of agency and choice. He speaks of the war in heaven where we asked for choice in life, but I have none," she wept, the tears coming quicker with each moment. "You live your own life, why can't I live mine?"

"You're only fifteen and you don't even know where to go, what to do with yourself," he said. "Stop crying, it's going to be alright."

"I need a change, or I don't know what I'll do."

"Alright, that's enough. No more talking like that. You have things to live for," said Samson. His icy exterior melted under her fiery tears. "Please, Bethia, stop."

"Then help me," she demanded, wiping away her tears. "Tell me, how can I make it on my own?"

"Let's go back to the markets. I have an idea."

"You mean it? You will help me?" she beamed.

"Yea, I will help you. But never mention it to anyone that I did," he said roughly.

"I won't, I promise." She hugged him, and he reluctantly patted her back.

They went from the docks up to the bazaars and markets on the Avenue of the Ram. Samson seemed to know right where he was going. He cut through many alleys and side streets until they were near the city's western gate. He spoke to a few caravan people who directed them to a man dressed in bright finery. They soon found him, hard to miss in his orange and green jacket, standing beside a long line of wagons.

"Everyone I know says this Rezon is an honorable caravaner and that you would be more than safe with him, that he would never touch you. He leads a large caravan all over the continent," said Samson. "You wanted to see the world, and this is my best idea for you to do that and still be safe. Are you sure this is what you want to do?"

"Yes. I'll come back when I am ready, when I have seen some of the world. You won't tell father, will you?"

Samson snorted and shook his head vigorously. "Lord, no! I am not about to tell him that I saw you by the docks, or that you weren't wearing enough to fly a kite. I won't say anything, but be careful." He turned and disappeared into the thick, crowded marketplace.

Bethia drew up courage within herself. She felt scared but excited at the same time. She fluffed her long dark hair and went toward the caravan master, an attractive, sandy-haired man about ten years older than herself.

He smoked from a funny-looking pipe; was it shaped like what she thought it was? She turned away in embarrassment at the sight of the vulgar pipe, but she determined to approach him. She trusted Samson, who had said she would be safe with this young man. The smoke rose in circles above his head as other caravan people came to him for directions. This was the right man to talk to if she wanted to leave Zarahemla. Such an oddly dressed man, although quite handsome. She went up to him.

"Excuse me, but where are you going, if I may ask?" she said, giving her biggest smile.

He turned around and returned a lopsided grin. "Why, everywhere. I am Rezon, Prince of Merchants. I trade from the eastern sea to the great mountains of Nephi. Why do you ask? Do you wish to come along?" He seemed friendly enough.

"Yes, how did you know?"

"And why do you want to come with us?"

"I am fettered like a wild bird here. I want to dance and see the world, but there is nothing for me here but a dusty cage."

"There will be work with us, you must understand that. It's not all fun and games. But, yes, there is a certain freedom the caravan lifestyle gives. Wake up in a new town at least every week if not every day, always something fresh to see. Do you want to come?"

"Yes, more than anything! You know what it feels like, don't you?"

"I had that same look in my eye when I first left home over twenty years ago," he said as he blew more rings of smoke from the funny-looking pipe. The smoke rings hung above him like a dirty halo.

"But you don't look much older than I."

"I am thirty summers old," he said, smiling a dashing grin of haphazard teeth.

"That is more than I thought. You left home when you were ten?" she asked, a little surprised.

"Yea, I did. I come from Bountiful, a beautiful city. Much prettier than Zarahemla, I think, though they do not always pay as well. I know your look well. And yes, you may come with us, providing you work hard at the markets with us."

"You have not said where we are going yet." She gave him a coy sideways glance.

"We go everywhere. Our first stop after this is Gideon, and the day after is Manti. Why are you in such a hurry? Are you a thief? You still have not told me your name," he said, feigning frowning.

"I am no thief. I am in a hurry to see something of the world." She hesitated before giving her name, in case news had reached him of Onandagus' daughter running away. She decided not to worry, since hers was such a common name for Nephite women. "I am Bethia."

"That's fair enough. We prepare to leave within the hour, and we cannot wait for you if you are not ready."

"Oh, I am ready. I have everything I need right here," she said, showing her small traveling bag.

"Good. You will ride with Keturah on the wagon with the perfumes and incenses. You will soon tire of their sweet scents."

"That's all right, and I am more than happy to have found you," Bethia beamed.

"So am I," he said. He blew more smoke rings and walked away to inspect the other wagons. The rings trailed after him in a curious pattern of ever-widening spheres. She liked the smell, unlike Samson's cigar that stunk.

"So am I," whispered Bethia, looking after him. She was no longer bound but free, free to see the world and never look back. However, as the wagons departed through the south gate of Zarahemla, she did look back, and it was all she could do to hold back the tears. She would not see her family again for a very long time.

Red Right Hand

Judge Hiram passed down a dim hall and through the gilded doorway of another office. Once inside, he made a gesture with his left hand that only a trained eye could follow. He repeated this sign in four more offices and two courtrooms.

Arriving at his own house, Judge Hiram entered an ornate chamber and sat at the head of a long oaken table. A red-capped servant closed the shutters and drew the dark curtains. The somber room was covered in a thick, dark, ox-blood lacquered wood that absorbed light. His throne had a gruesome death's head grinning from atop the wide peak. He sat there with a nasty headache throbbing upon his wrinkled forehead. An angry worry brewed within.

Nineteen others soon joined him, each standing at an appointed spot around the table. The servant poured crimson wine into goblets of finely hammered silver. He lit black candles of sickly sweet incense that gave off an ominous greenish-hued light, and then he excused himself.

"I call to order this meeting of the Heads of the Zarahemla Order of Gadianton," said Judge Hiram.

"We are here, we are watching, we are listening, we are ready," they all repeated in unison. "We strike!" They each made the gesture of Gadianton.

"The world—ours to fool, ours to rule," they said together and then sat down.

"The time is close, too close for Onandagus to grow wise and to shout our plans from the rooftops," said Judge Hiram, motioning for them to drink.

"Does he know?" asked one.

Another spoke up in response. "You mean of Akish-Antum's plan? If it fails, it need not affect us. Are we not wealthier than we have ever been?"

"I agree. We have more, beyond all other men in the land. We don't need Akish-Antum to be a king over us," said a man with a shaved head and a long, pointed beard.

"You are a fool to say that out loud, Levi," warned Pachus, Judge Hiram's assistant.

"Akish-Antum has killed men for less," said still another.

Judge Hiram broke in. "His plans do not fail. We are all rich because of him."

"Yea, we are indeed," they said.

"Hear, hear!" cried another.

"I meant no disrespect to Akish-Antum," explained Levi, the bearded one. "But Onandagus has a way of avoiding our traps, and he will fight us on appointing Akish-Antum or anyone else as a king,"

"That is why, Brother Levi, he must be killed. No mistakes. He and all his key supporters and his damnable church," said Judge Hiram. "Once the carnage comes, it can be blamed on the Lamanites. No one will care whose dagger is in whose back. Those savages will be blamed for the calamities, and a cry will arise for a leader, a king strong enough to protect us from them."

"Judge Hiram is right. The plans are sound!" cried one, directing his words to another who seemed doubtful.

Holding his hands high, silently calling for order, Judge Hiram spoke, "Is the Order of Daggers here yet?"

"Yea, some of them are here," answered Levi.

"Good, I want only the best on this. Onandagus had a minor apprentice in custody today. I remembered his face from an initiation last fall. Brother Pachus, send a troop of dagger men after one Ezra ben Shem immediately." The man nodded and left. "How many dagger men do we have in the city now?" asked Judge Hiram.

"We have perhaps two dozen in the city already, and two dozen more coming from Bountiful, Desolation, and Jacobgath," said Levi.

"Any from the Secret City?"

"From reports I received yesterday, they are on their way, another dozen at least. Word from the second, Teth-Senkhet, is that Akish-Antum wants this to succeed beyond anything else he has ever done," said Levi, twitching from a shake he had been fighting for weeks now.

"Where are the dagger men now? Will Brother Pachus have any trouble rounding up a few to take care of this apprentice?"

"They have been going over the city carefully, learning its alleys and shortcuts so well that they could do their missions blindfolded," assured Brother Levi. "And Lilith is with them."

"Lilith is with them? May Baal have mercy on the wretches," said Abishur.

"Good," said Judge Hiram. "Our last order of business is to distribute the list of those they are to assassinate."

"Who is on it?" Levi asked.

"Chief Judge Onandagus, Ammaron the Scribe and his barbaric son, Amaron. Mormon the Wise has just recently vacated his seat as governor of Antum, but it matters not. He is but a thorn. Miriam the seeress, Barkos the Fat, Judges Seth, Michael, Alma, Thomas, Pianki, Sinhue, and Sam. All other judges are brothers or can be coerced. A number of the guardsmen loyal to Onandagus—we all know who they are, Gidgiddonah, Captain Lachoneus, Captain Lehonti and so on," said Judge Hiram, as he handed them several leaves of paper. The names of men and women for execution were scrawled across it with a rare red ink.

"Is there anything else then?" asked Abishur.

"Yea, there is actually one more matter of business," said Judge Hiram with a snarl. "Being a part of the Order, we have all taken the oaths, we all bear the scars, we all take risks to get gain and protect one another. Some like this Ezra are worse than the dirt beneath our feet. They abandon that which sets us up above other men and betray us. Our Order has existed for all time. Since the days of Cain's awakening, a Gadianton Grand Master has been on earth to lead and guide us. The Disciples of the Christ," he spit out the name, "say we have a counterfeit of theirs, but I ask you— whose Order was established first? We all know it is ours. We have all foresworn; we all know the penalties and what they are. Zechariah?"

Zechariah, perhaps the youngest man in the room, said nervously, "To have my throat cut ear to ear, to have my belly opened and my entrails thrown over my right shoulder. That I may be unmanned and left to the demons of Abaddon and Asmodeus."

"Yes, of course. Not exactly right but close enough for this room," Judge Hiram said, cold like frostbite as he stalked about the room. He wheeled sharply, holding a long kris dagger in his right hand. The wavy blades were a favorite of the Order, partly for their sinister look, but also for the horrible cuts they inflicted.

"I have asked you, dear Brother Zechariah, because I knew you would remember our laws and penalties unlike another brother who seems to have forgotten them," said Judge Hiram, suddenly bringing the wavy curved blade under the throat of Brother Levi. "You have been taking riches unto yourself from some of the shops under your stewardship on the Avenue of the Cat, haven't you?"

"I beg your forgiveness, brothers. It won't happen again," Levi stammered, his former arrogant attitude washed away with the sweat of his brow.

"No, it won't, will it? Brothers?" said Judge Hiram.

They all looked upon Levi and put their thumbs downward. Judge Hiram ran the knife thrice enacting the penalties in awful exactness.

"Clean this up," he commanded Zechariah, as he shook his red right hand.

✳ ✳ ✳ ✳ ✳ ✳ ✳ ✳ ✳ ✳ ✳ ✳

Along the road to the north, Mormon, a great bear of a man, carried his son. Their wagon had broken an axle, and the boy had broken a leg in the wreck. Lions had chased off their oxen. The man had mended his son's leg as best he could, and they continued on their journey south—to Zarahemla and the boy's destiny.

Ammaron the Scribe had promised the boy a good education and opportunities down in the grand city while Onandagus, the governor and head of the Nephite confederation of cities, had called for Mormon to come and be his advisor of state. It was the right time for both father and son. Memories of a lost wife and mother were still fresh, making it a good time to start over.

The burdens of his responsibilities up north had changed, and Mormon no longer wished to be in such a godless place. Duty, honor and opportunity called, and leaving everything they owned behind did not matter in comparison. What do burnt bridges matter, if you know you are never going back.

Blood is Blood

Beneath the morning sun, mist cleaved away its shroud over the red, hematite-stained pyramid peaks of Mutula, great capital city of the hoary Lamanite king, Xoltec.

Within the grand hall of the old king's court, came the booming deep voice of the chief high priest, Balam-Ek. "Oh, wondrous ruler of the seven kingdoms, blessed of Baal, Kuhtuli, Taloc, Votan, and mighty Shagreel!"

A thick, stout man, he waved his hands to clear away the heavy incense, enough to make the king's concubines choke. "My King Xoltec, most blessed son of Father Laman, I have wonderful news." The barrel-chested priest knelt and looked up expectantly at his king.

Sitting upon a raised platform, the lean, copper-skinned king slit his eyes and sank deeper into his throne. With a wave of his gold-bedecked arm, he ushered away his two serving girls and motioned his dwarf scribe to approach. "Do not lie, Balam-Ek. Chief high priest though you may be, it does not become you to lie. Speak always the truth to me. I have already heard how my general Tzominihah was slain by assassins." The king croaked out the last word.

Getting up, the high priest stood majestic. Strong and stout, he had a wide face surrounded by jet black hair drawn back in a very tight topknot. A short beard came to a sharp point just an inch or two down his chin, done after the style of the Old Ones. Wearing a black cloak and tunic gilded with gold and jade, a brilliant copper face hung upside down across his thick chest. This was the symbol of priesthood dominance over all but the king. "Your Majesty, we have won! The army has taken Lamanihah in

24

a sound victory over your adversary, Madoni. He is gone, he is slain."

A thin smile crept over the old man's face like the clouds parting for the sun. Standing, he cried, "Indeed, it is a good day! I have vanquished the last of the usurpers. We can now look north to Tullan, city of the thieving Ishmaelites and to Bountiful, land of the birthright-stealing Nephites!"

Sitting back down, the king chuckled to himself as he summoned a slave girl to pour him another glass of wine. "Details, Balam-Ek, details," he said, coughing and chuckling at the same time as he slurped down his deep maroon wine.

"Your general, Tzominihah, was slain the day before the battle, but Captain Qof-Ayin rallied the men. He and his son feinted an attack on the southern gate while also climbing the northern wall. They succeeded in slaying the usurper Madoni. Without their leader, all of Lamanihah surrendered."

"Excellent, excellent," murmured King Xoltec.

"They have captured many slaves and set apart others for sacrifice. Captain Qof-Ayin and his son Zelph have returned just as I came to you, my king."

Rubbing his beardless chin, King Xoltec sat and thought a moment. "Qof-Ayin, old Eyes in the Back of His Head, eh? He will be greatly rewarded for this." As he finished off his wine, the slave girl came to refill his glass. He waved her off. Looking to the older of his two sons, who sat on his right hand side, King Xoltec said. "My empire grows for you, my son."

Prince Almek, still young, but tall for a Lamanite, stood and proclaimed, "You should have let me lead the army, father; and then the glory could go to me, your son, instead of going to a dog who has spurned you time and again."

"Nonsense, Almek. You have not the experience. Besides, war is for warriors, not kings, to fight. You are remembered for who you command, not who was commanded. Kings rule, warriors but serve. Never forget that."

"Your majesty," interjected the priest, "you also wanted some new bodyguards after the last queen's *debacle*." He spoke with hesitation as if expecting to be struck down for even mentioning the traitorous woman.

"Yes, yes I do. I need men I can trust, men of valor and integrity, which we seem to lack here of late. What kind of woman, who I made queen no less, who bore my children, would attempt such a thing?"

"Your majesty, she was...touched in the head."

"Enough!" cut off the king with a wrathful glare. "I don't want to hear of her any more, ever again, do you understand me? Tulum, write it down," he barked at the dwarf scribe. The little brown man was surrounded by parchments and a variety of inks to record any and everything the king desired.

"I have the perfect man, your highness, a great hero of the battle. He captured dozens and slew Madoni himself."

The king looked up as he toyed with the neck clasp on his jaguar skin cloak. "Who is he? Where is he now?"

Puffing himself up like a strutting rooster, Balam-Ek announced for the entire court to hear. "His name is Zelph; he is son of Qof-Ayin. Even now, he is with his father training in the courtyard of warriors."

"Training? They have just won a war for me, and they still train to defend me and bring me glory? Take me to them! I wish to congratulate these heroes and bestow upon this Zelph the honor of being in my bodyguard." Rising up from his opulent throne, the king allowed his high priest to lead him.

Close behind was the haughty crown prince Almek, the younger brother Aaron, and their sister, the enchanting princess Sayame. Next came nobles from the various houses of the realm, and these festooned fellows were followed by retainers. Last came the slaves of all those who preceded them.

Outside, the bright sun had cleared away the mist. The tall, red pyramids cast long shadows on the city.

King Xoltec stopped on top of a broad, open atrium that overlooked the warrior's courtyard. A tall skinny nobleman took the opportunity to approach the king, his bright purple tunic and perfumed presence announced his arrival before he even opened his mouth. "Rabbanah," he said, using the polite title of Lamanite kings. "If I might say something not mentioned by the good priest."

"*High* priest," broke in Balam-Ek.

"Ah yes, high priest."

Sniffing and sighing, King Xoltec said, "What is it, Tzichak?"

"Rabbanah, thank you. This Qof-Ayin, if memory serves me right, was not he the one who once refused to be your bodyguard? A great disgrace."

"Silence, you perfumed boy lover!" The king scowled at Tzichak.

Tzichak looked aghast and attempted to slide back into the crowd of courtiers, but the king's interest was piqued. "Well, smelly, what are you trying to say? Come on out with it," he growled.

"Blood is blood, your majesty, and Zelph is his father's son. They are of the bloodline of that traitor, Samuel, are they not? Samuel, that false prophet who betrayed his people to spread the lies of the Nephites," said Tzichak.

The king and his entourage halted immediately. King Xoltec spun about and smacked Tzichak across the face, shouting, "Fool! Qof-Ayin is the greatest warrior in my army. He won Lamanihah for me! And do not cast aspersions on Zelph, the son of Qof-Ayin, who could become the next greatest warrior in my army. If there is one thing I trust among the whole of you who trail after me like dogs following a bloody butcher, it is Balam-Ek. I trust the man who kills for me. Balam-Ek knows more than all of you. Was it not he who told me of my queen's attempted rebellion?"

"Yes, Rabbanah, but you must know that Qof-Ayin and Zelph do not honor nor venerate the gods. I have heard it said that Qof-Ayin even denies the power of mighty Shagreel and scorns the priests of Baal, even Balam-Ek himself."

Furrowing his brow, Balam-Ek admitted, "It is true Qof-Ayin has said such things in the past, and he will not attend the sacrifices of Baal or Shagreel. But Zelph is young, only eighteen springs, and we can mold him as we need him. If he is a bodyguard, he will be apart from his father, and we can return him to the priesthood in the true service of the king."

The old king nodded at the high priest's words.

"But blood is blood," muttered Tzichak.

"Away with you, dog!" commanded Balam-Ek. "Look and see for yourself, my king, how even now after a hard battle they seek not for glory or prize, but train in your service."

The king looked down upon Qof-Ayin and Zelph, his aged eyes squinting to take in the swift movements. Two titanic figures fought with wooden training swords. The younger man was huge and thick-set with strong arms. He stood over a foot and half taller than his tall father. His black hair was cut shorter than the Lamanite style, close-cropped, sticking up only an inch. The long haired, older man was muscular but much leaner than his son and although not as quick, his sword craft experience was the greater. Each wore the standard Lamanite warrior's tunic of reddish brown and sturdy ankle-wrapped sandals. Their feet forever moved as they circled each other before lunging in for a flurry of blows upon one another.

The elder of the two, his hair graying at the temples, spoke softly as they sparred. "Look at them, Zelph. They are watching us. It brings the lesson—the path of the true warrior cannot be learned through pointless contests or sparring to impress someone else. It can only be fully understood when one's own death is possible."

The wooden training swords hammered at one another. As Zelph lunged and swept his sword across and low, his father leaped over it and tapped his own blade lithely across his son's left shoulder. "You must always train with both hands. If this were real, you would have lost use of your left hand. Now switch," said Qof-Ayin.

Letting go with his left and pressing the attack further with his right, Zelph charged ahead, while Qof-Ayin continued, "The purpose of the warrior's path is to win. There can be nothing else. When it is time to fight, to attack, it must be with full resolve. Be absolutely sure of yourself. There is but one purpose, nothing else—to destroy your enemy!" He slammed a flurry of lightning-quick blows down upon the now singly held weapon. Zelph had to step back a pace or two on the defensive.

"When the time comes and you are contained and on the defensive, you must summon up strength from within yourself, the power of the will to explode into your enemy quickly and with true purpose. Think only of destroying them by any means necessary," Qof-Ayin instructed.

Ceasing his retreat, Zelph attacked, ferocious as a cornered dragon. He hammered the swift strokes like a beating drum, though Qof-Ayin blocked his strikes time and again.

"You are obligated to the attack. You are only to draw your sword when you mean to use it. The path is not a game. The only reason to draw your sword is to cut the enemy down. You must continue the attack," he said, as Zelph had slowed to listen. "Not doing so is practicing hesitation, which even for a moment allows an enemy the opportunity to defeat you." The older man's grace and fluidity with a blade was remarkable. He could almost dance around his son's defenses. Zelph parried and pressed the attack again, now pushing Qof-Ayin onto the defensive.

"Good. The true path of the warrior does not allow you to be inferior to anyone. You are the best and will win, or you are not and you will die." Trading positions yet again Qof-Ayin slapped Zelph across the leg and almost tripped him. The quick older man brought his wooden sword down and Zelph narrowly blocked it, but the elder had overextended his balance ever so slightly and the son knew it. Heaving the crossed swords away, he swept his own dull blade across Qof-Ayin's chest. A slight amount of breath was lost at that instant, but a smile beamed from his father's face.

"Excellent, you have won this time; you are beginning to understand the path. Now tell me the true purpose of mastering the sword."

The son nodded and bowed to his father and spoke. "I understand the necessity in mastering the sword. We master the violence to best combat it. It is the only righteous and sane answer."

The father nodded. They each drank deeply of the cool water a servant brought from the reservoir. Another servant put the mock swords away on a rack that held a variety of other exotic weapons.

"Exactly," Qof-Ayin continued. "The only honorable reason for mastering violence is to abolish it. A warrior must also understand the ways of peace and the arts. To not do so would make one shortsighted and stiff-necked. It would keep you from growing outward. Now, let us see what the king and his pretty birds have to say to us."

With the tournament over, the king and his entourage came down the broad stone steps in a wide procession of radiant color. Most of them beamed; but Almek, behind the king, frowned.

"Marvelous, wonderful. Truly, all I have heard of young Zelph is true. I will give you gold and honor for this victory at Lamanihah," said King Xoltec. "You as well, Qof-Ayin. The strategy for the victory was yours, was it not?"

"Yes, indeed it was, Rabbanah."

Strutting about on the courtyard of warriors as if it were newly conquered territory, the king said, "I am well pleased. And your son, Zelph...is he now your better on the battlefield as well?"

"Nay, I am not, Rabbanah," answered Zelph before his father could speak.

King Xoltec gave Zelph a curious stare. "Still, I am well pleased. Tell me, Zelph, where is your umbilicus buried?"

"Here in Mutula, under the hearthstone of my father's house."

"And how old are you now?"

"I am eighteen summers."

"Good, good. Now down to business. I would have you for my chief of bodyguards. Balam-Ek!" he barked.

The stout priest stepped forward. "Yes, my king?"

"See to both their rewards personally. Zelph, thank you for slaying Madoni. I did not even wish to see the worm grovel in my dungeons, I so despised the man." The king turned and left with his entourage in tow.

Zelph thought he saw Prince Almek give him a dark frown, while Princess Sayame smiled at him. The high priest, Balam-Ek, remained.

"For your services beyond the call of duty, you are each to receive an extra limnah of gold beyond whatever loot was personally taken from Lamanihah," Balam-Ek said.

"That seems like too much to me," broke in Qof-Ayin. "It is not fair to the men I led that I should be given more. I could not have done it without them."

Balam-Ek frowned. "It is your choice to take or refuse it, I suppose, but you would take nothing from anyone living. It would come from dead General Tzomin's share. You will also be given access to a woman from the king's harem, a rare privilege."

Zelph blushed at this. "That will not be necessary," said his father.

"Very well, that is your loss. There is something else which cannot be refused, Qof-Ayin." The father and son stood with absolute attention to the high priest. "Times have changed since your younger days, when you refused to be a bodyguard. This comes not as a request but a command. There will be no debate on this and no appeal. You will comply, or you will both be treated as traitors. Do you understand me?"

Both Zelph and Qof-Ayin looked at each other and then at Balam-Ek who continued, "Zelph, you are to be the new captain of the king's bodyguard. You will be given a room in the palace—as commander of the bodyguard such is your privilege. I expect you to report in three days, no longer. Enjoy your own time now." He turned on his heel and walked away.

"Father, have times changed?"

Qof-Ayin looked away before answering. "When I was young, I refused by convincing King Xoltec I was needed in the field much more—to fight and win battles for him rather than standing beside him in the palace all day. He agreed, but later thought I had made a fool of him. Such could not be further from the truth. His advisors, a den of vipers, whispered that I had insulted his judgment. Still, he had given me his word and could not go back on it. From then on, he seemed to resent me. It has taken years for him to go beyond it."

They continued to converse in private. "Now, King Xoltec controls all the southernmost known lands and has ambitions for Tullan and the Nephite lands to the north and east. He is getting to be a very old man, and he knows it. I doubt he truly expects to wage war on the Nephites or Tultecs. King Xoltec fears the growing influence of the power hungry Gadiantons, and he knows that I would never join them and neither would you, as my son. Therefore, being incorruptible, you make a very desirable bodyguard."

"Father, I will not let them change me, nor will I forget the many things you have taught me."

"The palace is not for you, my son. It is not that I doubt your heart, but I know the many evils of their lives. Tell me this—do you wish to serve him?"

"I would rather stay with you and serve as a warrior. But if I must do this duty, I will."

"Listen to me, Zelph. The palace is more treacherous than any battlefield. The snakes and worms within feed on each other. If any favors you, beware, for jealousy abounds along with all manner of revenge. Many will try to use you, to have access to the king, or hate you for doing your duty. And it is not unheard of for a king to take his bodyguard and his harem with him to the grave."

Zelph looked aghast at that.

"King Xoltec is an old man with few years left. I saw how his son Almek looked at you; I fear on his ascendancy, he would do just that."

"Is that one of the reasons you refused years ago?"

"No, I refused because I wanted my own home, not an apartment in the palace. I wanted to be with your mother and you. Bodyguards are not allowed to have families."

Zelph sat down on the cold stone steps. "This gets worse with every moment we talk about it. Let us go home and forget the day."

Qof-Ayin put his worn, calloused hand on his son's shoulder. "I will pray for an answer, my son. I will think of something. Let us go home."

✳ ✳ ✳ ✳ ✳ ✳ ✳ ✳ ✳ ✳ ✳ ✳

"So blood is blood, after all." Dark eyes glistened and watched just around the corner. Balam-Ek, the chief high priest, bristled at the thought that these valued warriors had such disrespect for the king's wishes.

Returning to the Temple of Baal, he instructed an acolyte, "Watch the father and son. If anything suspicious happens, alert me as well as the captain of the palace guard immediately. You are my eyes and ears. Do not fail me." Nodding, the shaven-headed priest departed.

Left alone in his own chambers, Balam-Ek pondered what to do with Zelph and Qof-Ayin. If they were to refuse the king, he would sacrifice their brave hearts to feed the hunger of Shagreel. He drank some wine from a skin, and then he slept.

"Awake, awake, oh worshipful master!" A strange voice not suited to the voluptuous female figure of his dreams called out to him. He rubbed his face in confusion and disappointment. Rolling off his reed mat, he groggily answered, "What? What is it?"

"Master Balam-Ek, there is a dark omen in the sky, a dark star. The king wants you immediately!"

The high priest roused himself with scented water and donned his sandals. Rushing outside to the palace, he looked into the deep night sky. "How did I sleep so long? What is that?" He looked up to see a pale golden comet blaze across the southern sky.

Dozens of priests were in the courtyard, several wailing about the bad omen. Others argued that it was all an illusion of the trickster god.

"It is like a flaming ear of corn," said one.

A flash of lightning came out of an otherwise clear sky and caught the roof of the temple afire.

"Get to work! Put it out! We cannot have the mighty Shagreel homeless!" Balam-Ek ordered the throng of priests. They ran to fetch buckets of water from the reservoirs, a futile endeavor as the winds flared to feed the flames. The Temple of Shagreel, God of the Sun, was no more.

Somewhere in the distance, a woman wailed. "My children, we must flee far away from this city. Oh, my children, where shall I take you?" Tales of her lament were told for many days to come throughout the city, and the people of Mutula believed she was the Goddess Zilonen trying to warn them of impending disaster.

The priests, desperate to take charge, proclaimed the god's anger at the people for not doing all the priests had asked of them. This backfired since the only structure truly damaged in all the fires and storms was the priests' own temple.

Balam-Ek was angry. Why did this have to happen now when so many things were in motion? He did not want to appear out of touch with the spirit world. But there up above him glowed a dark fallen star that seemed to mock him and his supposed wisdom.

Wolves and Jackals

Amaron and Helam, the two brawny guardsmen, had little trouble finding where Ezra had gone. Here in the south side of Zarahemla, the more undesirable elements of the city gravitated and congealed together. It was as though the dregs of humanity slid downhill into the physical depression of the riverfront called the Bowl, a near lawless stretch of town where anything could be bought and sold.

Many times Onandagus had fought to close down the whorehouses, gambling halls, drug dens, and lascivious taverns but with little avail. Few other judges supported his efforts and most guardsmen would turn a blind eye for a small bribe. In years past, honest guardsmen who ventured into the Bowl often found themselves ambushed by gangs and beaten severely, if not murdered.

As Amaron and Helam approached an infamous tavern, The Iron Rod, they were greeted with catcalls and insults from both the street and balconies.

"Go away, we don't need your law here!" called an ugly old woman, throwing trash into the street.

Helam responded, "Just wait until you are robbed."

"Not me, I'm under protection," she cackled.

"See, they openly admit Gadianton law. What has this city come to?" Helam said.

"She is not our concern right now," growled Amaron. "Our man is inside, according to his sister."

"If we can trust her."

"We don't have to...her fear for him was true enough. He's here all right."

A wrought-iron sign hanging out front of the tavern was made to look like an iron rod as understood from the holy book of Lehi, but then it had the voluptuous silhouette of a woman sitting upon it. A man out front called for any and all to enter. They passed through a beaded doorway beneath the signpost. The scent of cheap incense could not cover the smell of sweat, liquor, and vomit.

A brown-haired, scantily-clad girl in green silks welcomed them. "Greetings, my masters, and how may I be of service?" She cast an especially inviting smile to Helam, swaying ever so slightly as she spoke.

"Have you seen a young man named Ezra, a short weaselly-looking fellow wearing a brown tunic and blue headscarf?" Helam asked. "Thin facial hair, a little bug-eyed."

"Nay, I have not seen such a man," she cooed. "But give me some coin, perhaps a senum or two, and I will help you look for him. We can start up in my room," she whispered up toward his ear as far as she could reach.

"At least someone in the Bowl is kind to us," Helam said, smirking.

"Yea, and pure as the dust off my sandals," Amaron retorted. "Away with you," he barked at her. Sauntering away, she ignored them and began to ply her trade elsewhere.

An old man who sat watching near the doorway spoke to them in a friendly voice. "I have a brother in the city of Desolation. He's a preacher, an' he says this place is a den of iniquity. But I say if you don't like having a little drink once in a while an' lookin' at a pretty girl there's something wrong witcha." He laughed and returned to sipping his ale and watching the dancing girls.

"Tinkling cymbals and sounding brass," said Helam, "and women offering themselves."

Amaron signaled Helam to look around the right side of the tavern as he went left. The Iron Rod was big, full of men and women sitting at dozens of tables. They eyed the two guardsmen suspiciously. The patrons were eating all sorts of spiced meats and drinking the house wines and ales. Small alcoves had private dinners and private dancers. Musicians played bawdy tunes with heavy bass drum beats. Drunken laughter filled the air as women gyrated on tops of tables.

They had circled the entire main floor and not found Ezra. Helam looked disappointed. "Did the sister lie?"

"I think not...there," said Amaron, pointing. Ezra descended the stairs with a worn, woolen bag over his shoulder, packed full.

Helam called out, "Ho, Ezra!"

The thin man looked aghast at the two of them and said, "You have signed my death warrant!" He raced down the steps and back toward the kitchen.

Helam followed quickly, while Amaron had to shove a man out of his way to give chase. The man, falling to the ground, grabbed Amaron's foot, tripping him. Kicking the man to free himself, Amaron got back up and headed to the back door.

Turning first to the left, Ezra changed his mind and ran to the right. The indecision gave time for Helam to close the gap and reach him a few paces away from the door. He grasped Ezra's shoulder, the skinny man wormed away from him, then wheeled about to strike him hard in the face, something Helam didn't expect from such a skinny, diminutive presence. His grip loosened momentarily and Ezra ran free again, leaving his bag lying on the street. He didn't look back.

"Wait! We are here to help you!" Helam called after him. In the darkness of the Bowl, Ezra never heard him. As Helam ran down the alley after him, a number of unseen eyes watched ready to make their move.

Amaron burst through the back door, as empty wine and ale bottles flew toward him and smashed against the outside wall, the good patrons of the Iron Rod wishing him farewell. He scowled at them and put a hand on his broadsword. The bottles stopped coming, and the music of the night began again. Amaron could just make out Helam's blond hair and copper greaves in the distance. He began sprinting after his companion, unaware of the dozen others close behind. The dagger men were dressed in shadowy colors of dark blue, black or deep Phoenician purple, making them almost invisible in the gloom of the Bowl at night.

Helam caught Ezra as he attempted to scale a short wall at the end of an alley.

"Let me go," Ezra sobbed. "Is it not enough that I am a dead man? My masters have seen me talking to you and the chief judge. All is lost."

"We can protect you," said Helam, gripping his arm like a python.

"No, you can't. Most of the judges are Gadiantons, and I am a dead man," he cried. "The sooner, the better to them. I who have only ever served them diligently. Curse the gods that brought you to my door."

Heavy quick footsteps caused Helam to turn, ready to face whoever it was. "Amaron?"

"Yea, it is I." Amaron came forward, but not alone. Whirling about, he heard them as they came up behind. He flashed his sword, Ramevorn, to give space and warning. "Stay back whoever you are. We are on the business of the chief judge."

The dark-cloaked and red-capped dagger men drew a step or two closer. They did not respond but spread into a half moon to contain the alley. "He is the one," said one, a swarthy looking man, gesturing toward Ezra.

"What of these other two?" asked another.

"The traitor has spoken with them, they all must die," said a throaty female voice from somewhere in the murk behind. The dagger men had short scimitars or long, wavy kris knives drawn, and they began to advance slow and easy to best judge how to attack their prey.

Amaron silently mouthed, "Watch and pray," as he stretched his fingers upon his sword hilt. Helam had a brass-studded cudgel out and swung it round once to flex and stretch his arm. Silent, the dagger men charged. Amaron swung wide and hard, cutting one deep across the chest and severing the arm of another. Helam battled, knocking away heads and hands even quicker than Amaron could cut them. Never one who wished to draw blood or end a life, Helam had become quite adept with the cudgel.

With the combatants' attention divided, Ezra seized his chance to escape. Sprinting to the wall behind, he leapt up three times before he had enough of a hold to scramble over the top and disappear into the darkness.

"The traitor is escaping! Get him!" commanded the woman's voice.

Amaron slashed two more of the dagger men as they attempted to flank him, roaring at them, "Jackals of Set! You have never before fought a man with his blade ready for you!" Another assassin went down, clutching his stump, and Amaron cried again, "You dogs have neither courage nor skill!"

Helam knocked one unconscious with a sound hit atop the assassin's unprotected head, receiving a small gash on his forearm from the dagger man's knife as the man went down.

"Enough," said the sinister female voice. "Pull back. These wolves of Onandagus are too much." The six remaining dagger men began to withdraw. They left behind five dead and one grievously wounded on the ground.

"Help me," moaned the eviscerated dagger man before collapsing from his wounds.

Amaron, his blood boiling, was ready to charge after them.

"Do not follow us, you lone wolf of Onandagus," said the woman in the gloom.

In the faint moon light he could see the dark-haired woman's outline as she faded into the night. "Quickly, over the wall, Helam. They will go after him, and we can still catch him." Amaron moved to the wall and grabbed the top.

"I can't," gasped Helam.

Dropping down, Amaron came back to examine his wound. "It is only a small cut, you have had worse shaving."

"It burns as nothing I have ever felt before." Helam exhaled deep and sagged onto the alley floor amidst the carnage. "A foul poison...I'm having a trouble breathing."

Amaron drew his own knife. He cut the tiny wound bigger to let the poison bleed out, then slung Helam over his left shoulder. Sword in his right hand, he began moving down the street. Eyes ever upward and forward, he scanned the darkness with rage at the hidden enemies who had done this.

He felt Helam go limp, the weight of his body relaxed. "Helam? Helam?" Putting his friend down, he felt for a pulse. There was none. Standing up, angry as a heathen god, he clenched his fists and shouted a rage-filled cry of despair.

He heard someone behind him. Wheeling around with his sword drawn, he slammed the figure backward against the wall.

Ezra cried out, "Please don't kill me, you are my only chance. Take me to Onandagus, please."

Glaring at him with hate, Amaron removed the blade which left a faint red line on the man's throat. "Help me with him." They stooped and picked up Helam's lifeless body. Amaron carried the bulk of the weight while Ezra led down the alley.

"Who was that woman?" Amaron asked.

"I cannot be sure, but it could have been Lilith."

"And who is she to command dagger men?" he snarled.

"She is the consort of Akish-Antum, Grand Master of all Gadiantons. She is a procuress, a sorceress who speaks with the dead. A frightening woman, she tortures men for Akish-Antum."

"What was on their daggers to murder Helam so quickly?"

"A poison concocted from scorpions of the west. Out there the scorpion is symbol of the master of the Secret City, the trademark of dagger men from Kishkumen."

"Is there an antidote?"

Ezra was silent too long for Amaron's mood.

"Well, is there or not?"

"No, I am sorry. As soon as he was scratched with that dagger, he was a dead man. I am sorry, eah."

"Shut up."

"I am sorry," mumbled Ezra.

"And I said shut up!"

They continued down the darkened street until they came to a T where they had to choose left or right.

"Which way do you want to go?" asked Ezra.

"You always go right, so we will go left now."

"But that is deeper into the Bowl."

"Those dagger men are expecting us to go straight to the Judgment Hall and the safety of Onandagus, so we won't go where or when they are expecting us," said Amaron. "Their impatience will make them sloppy."

"Where are we going then?"

"I do not even know yet, wherever I feel the spirit leads me."

"The spirit? Which spirit?" Ezra asked.

"Never mind, I am not a missionary, and this is not the time." They moved along silently, ever suspicious of shadows, until they reached a wide avenue.

"Which avenue is this, the Dog or the Ox?" asked Amaron.

"It is the Ox. It runs parallel to the Avenue of the Cat and eventually meets the Avenue of the Eagle in about a half mile," said Ezra, pleased he could help.

Getting his bearings straight, Amaron asked, "Why did you come back?"

"Wherever I run, they will find and kill me. You fought off a dozen of the best the Order has. So, it's safer with you two. I mean you...I am sorry about your friend."

Amaron never stopped scanning the streets, fully expecting to have to drop his deceased brother in arms to fight another attack, but none came. A wagon creaked by, a farmer with a load of hay for market on the morrow.

"You there," Amaron called to him. "We need your wagon."

Startled, the farmer said, "I have nuthin' of value and the horses are old. They are of no worth to such as you." His drawl sounded as if he were from the northeast wilderness.

"Take it easy, we have no wish to rob you. My friend was struck down by robbers. We are guardsmen and would appreciate you helping us get him to the Judgment Hall."

Looking around fearfully at the darkened streets, the farmer said, "All right. Get 'em into the hay in back."

They loaded Helam's body into the wagon, and Amaron covered his body with a fair amount of hay to hide it.

"So there are more out there looking for you two?" asked the farmer.

"Yea, there are. Will you still help us?" said Ezra.

"I am no friend of the robbers. Get under the hay in case they are watching the Judgment Hall then," he said, adding, "I am Jonas."

"We thank you," said Amaron. "But I will sit beside you on the wagon. If something happens I must be ready with my sword, not hiding under the hay."

Jonas nodded at that.

"If you don't mind, I will sit behind you in the back," said Ezra.

"I mind," said Amaron. "Sit to the side there, where I can see you."

Ezra did as he was told, but still hunkered down a little into the hay and covered himself. The wagon began its creaking journey down the Avenue of the Ox as Amaron watched every shadow and trick of light with suspicion.

"You need to tell me where it is we are goin' to," drawled Jonas.

"Straight down this avenue until we get to the next big one, and then we go left to the center of the city to the Judgment Hall. You have never been there?" asked Amaron.

"No need. I usually go to markets north of here, but this year with such a good crop, had me some surplus. So I decided to head on down, get city supplies and something for the wife," he said, puffing on his pipe.

The big guardsmen watched. Something would happen soon.

"Can I ask you something, Amaron?" asked Ezra.

"What?"

"How is it you are the way you are?"

"What are you talking about?"

"You faced a dozen dagger men without backing down."

"So?" came Amaron's surly reply, along with a shrug.

"Dagger men are the worst of the Gadianton assassins. They are cold-blooded, ruthless killers."

"What makes them any different than you?"

"I am only an apprentice, not a killer," protested Ezra.

Amaron sniffed at that.

"You don't have to kill anyone to become an apprentice or middle grade. You do to become a master," Ezra mumbled at the last.

"I care nothing for your false secrets," Amaron growled.

"I'm telling you the truth."

"Your kind knows no truth," said Amaron, glaring at him.

"I know a little about church, the church you and Onandagus belong to," said Ezra, stopping short.

Amaron raised an arched eyebrow at him.

"I know some," he went on.

"What are you trying to say?"

"I joined the Order because I am ambitious. I wanted to be rich, have fine clothes, a fine home, and a fine woman by my side. Why, even your Chief Judge Onandagus has several homes and properties."

"Shut your mouth! That's his business!" Amaron shouted at him. Then realizing he had been louder than he meant, he turned back around and continued watching the road.

Jonas looked at him, then Ezra, but said nothing.

"It just seems that when a man has so much—" Ezra began.

Amaron cut him off. "Well, it is not like that. He works for a living like all the rest of us."

"I'm sorry, I got a little off track," continued Ezra. "How do you face down a dozen dagger men?"

"I never have before tonight."

"A dozen with poisoned daggers, dedicated killers."

Amaron stared hard at him. "Perhaps you have forgotten that my friend is dead." He grabbed Ezra by the scruff of his collar and thrust him at the cold dead face of Helam. "He did not flinch either!" His eyes flashed fire.

"I'm sorry, you can let go." Ezra pulled back a little.

Amaron released his grip so suddenly that Ezra fell back hitting his head against the sideboard of the wagon.

Jonas turned to look at them, but still said nothing. Puffing away on his pipe, he turned back to drive his nags.

"I respect you. I only want to know and understand how you have the courage to face a dozen," said Ezra, holding the back of his head.

Looking from Jonas to Ezra, Amaron was silent for a long time.

"Courage isn't something I see within the Order," said Ezra, still waiting upon the brooding guardsman.

Amaron finally replied. "A dozen swords or one, it matters not. Any fool can kill you; numbers mean little to me. I have a purpose in this life, and I am good at what I do. I have a talent that makes me a leader of men in my chosen profession."

"Which is?" Ezra asked. Amaron smirked again, holding his sword at the ready. "But why do numbers mean little?"

"Because I will not dwell on defeat. I do not think of it. To win, to prevail is the all. If I were to die, I have served my God and it is my time to go with honor, but as I said before, I do not think of defeat. Only victory. If I am positive enough and strong enough, I will conquer."

"They will not give up."

"I know, and neither will I. Had I known Helam was to die this night, I would have run after those dog brothers of yours and slaughtered them all!"

"Please, I'm done with the Order. I'm one of them no more. Onand-agus said you would protect me and..." Ezra trailed off as Amaron glared at him.

"Do you know something that is worth Helam's death? I hope so!"

"I do know something important. Akish-Antum is far to the south inflaming the Lamanite's hatred. He is coaxing them to come and attack us here in Zarahemla." Ezra tried to sound unafraid.

Jonas, still puffing on his pipe, looked back at them and raised his eyebrows, silent as ever.

"If you are just an apprentice as you say, who has not killed a man," Amaron's voice dripped with contempt, "why would you know anything of importance?"

"Every Gadianton knows. Hundreds, maybe thousands, of us are helping along the roads and byways in preparation for the invasion. I was to help in a supply train from the Narrow Pass to here. My worshipful master Judge Ishmael changed his mind about a number of things and made me part of the internal readiness instead. That's all I know for sure."

"How soon is this to happen?"

"In a few months. In time for some holy feast, this summer I think."

Amaron rubbed the stubble on his chin. "But what could the Lamanites hope to accomplish by coming this far? They would be stretching their supply line to say the least...and what is internal readiness?"

"I can answer both. Once the Lamanites attack, they're either victorious and impose a puppet king; or they're repelled, and the people will cry for a strong king to protect us from them again."

"What of those who would not stand for that, such as the chief judge?"

"That is why there are so many dagger men in the city now," said Ezra, looking over his shoulder into the night. Jonas turned the wagon onto the Avenue of the Eagle toward the tall, white-walled building ahead of them.

"Who would be proclaimed king?"

"I don't know...the Grand Master Akish-Antum, maybe Judge Hiram. I was never sure who they had in mind."

Amaron laughed. "How convenient."

"I speak the truth as I know it," Ezra said growing a little indignant.

"Of course you do, and why wouldn't you?"

Angered at his sarcasm, Ezra declared, "The dagger men came to kill me. Do you think I lie about that? My life is forfeit. If any Gadianton ever sees me, I am to be murdered. My life is over except I help you and Onandagus."

Jonas blew a thick puff from his pipe and said, "I believe ya'. Now anythin' you wanna tell me afore we meet these dagg'r men?"

"They wear red caps, probably black cloaks. Don't let them cut you," said Amaron.

"The dagger men will not stop," said Ezra.

"Put on Helam's breastplate, Ezra. It will stop any arrow or dagger," Amaron instructed.

"No, thank you. It is too big, and I could not run with it on. It would be a simple task for a dagger man to catch me and slide it in around the thing. Dagger men do not use arrows. They don't like bows," said Ezra, watching the side roads.

"They don't like using bows? That's stupid," laughed Amaron.

"Maybe, but the penalties are specific. They want to slit my throat and more. It's personal, so they won't shoot at me...maybe you, though."

Amaron cocked an eyebrow at that, but he had confidence in his well-crafted, hardened-copper breastplate. It was old, forged by the ancient, secret process which made the metal strong as steel. The Nephites called this exalted copper. It had been his great-great-great-grandfather's, as was his sword—all that was left of Teancum the Great. Amaron had always wished he had the infamous spear that had slain kings.

"What did you do before you became a guardsman?" asked Ezra.

"My father is Ammaron the Scribe. He tried to get me to follow in his footsteps, but I was not interested. I can read and write very well, but I have no desire to scribe for judges and lawyers or record the news of the day. I would rather live history than write it," said Amaron, as he held out his sword blade. "My father says a quill cuts deeper than a sword stroke, but I say it depends on which way it cuts."

"What do you mean?"

"Records of some men will outlast the ages, recited for eons, tales of pain and glory, tragedy and triumph. But for others like Helam, it is all done and gone, his torch is extinguished. The cut that took him is more permanent than any eulogy. Farewell, old friend, farewell," cried Amaron, clasping the dead man's hand.

Jonas had driven the wagon to within two blocks of the hall when voices rang out in the darkness. "Death to the traitor!" It was the woman's voice.

Two arrows flew straight to Amaron's chest, hitting him squarely before ricocheting off. His sword was out in a flash as he jumped off the wagon. Ezra ducked into the hay next to Helam's body.

"They got red caps?" remarked Jonas, snickering.

"Get into the hall!" shouted Amaron.

Jonas whipped the reins on his two nags and they picked up the pace somewhat, heading straight to the hall. From the shadows, five men in dark blue cloaks were now trying to run alongside the wagon. With naked blades glinting in the moonlight, one slashed at Jonas who managed to narrowly escape being cut as he slid over and roused the old horses to maximum speed. The assassins were forced to turn and deal with Amaron howling with rage behind them.

Roaring and cursing, Amaron charged the one nearest him with a dragon's ferocity. The dagger man tried to parry the mighty broadsword with his short scimitar, but the wicked blade was broken as was the grinning head behind it. Another arrow flew to Amaron's back but was again deflected. Startled at their foe's resilience, the four now backed up closer to each other.

Savage, like a rabid wolf on helpless sheep, Amaron was upon them in an instant. In his left hand, he had drawn his war hammer, a squared face on the front and a vicious spike on the back. With both weapons, he cleaved into the dagger men, leaving only bodies and broken oaths on the ground. "Dogs! Jackals! I send you to hell," he cried in a red rage.

Cutting the last man asunder, Amaron calmed enough to look for the wagon. It was nearly a block away already, close to the gates of the massive white edifice. He ran at full pace, his heart pumping at an incredible rate. The gate was opened by four guardsmen waiting with Onandagus. Wheeling around, Amaron scanned for threats from the dark avenues of Zarahemla. Finding none, he trotted the last few yards to the gate.

"Are you injured?" asked Onandagus. "You are covered in blood."

"I don't know," Amaron panted in response. "I do not think so...it's just blood of those jackal dagger men."

"Come into my house," the judge commanded. "We will get you cleaned up. Come Ezra."

Two guardsmen reached into the wagon to retrieve Helam's body. Onandagus reached over to clasp the hand of the deceased guardsman. If a tear came to his eye no one else saw it, and his usual stony demeanor quickly returned. He had to be strong, he had to be hard. With his duties he could not afford to break down, the machine had to keep rolling.

"We thank you for your help. And this for your troubles," said Onandagus to Jonas, offering him a senine of gold. "You are also welcome to stay the night here with us. It could still be dangerous out there. Some may be angered with you for having helped us."

"Anything I can do to help against the likes of those robbers, I am happy to do. So you can keep the senine o' gold, but it would be nice to stay here for the night an' perhaps tomorrow you can tell me where I could get a fair price for my crop."

"I will buy all of your hay for the best price possible. We could always use a little more."

The gate was closed and barred for the night, with extra men on guard detail. As they headed to his home within the hall, Onandagus said to Amaron, "We could have used another prisoner or two to glean more information."

"Not these, they would never have surrendered. They were dagger men brought in for the task at hand. Besides, they murdered Helam."

"I am sorry about Helam...he was an excellent guardsman. I know his father, and I will speak to him myself on the morrow," said the judge. "I am grateful to you. You have done us a great service retrieving Ezra. Without him, we would still be in the dark as to the Gadianton plan. Now get cleaned up. Your father would be horrified to see you so bloody."

Amaron smirked. "Yea, he would not understand; he never has. But with a wicked talent like this, what else shall I do?"

A Dark Fallen Star

Balam-Ek!" shouted the old king. "What does the sign portend? Your own priests claim this flaming ear of corn in the sky is a terrible dark omen. What are these unexplainable fires, and this wailing woman mewling for her children? If she is found, I want her flogged." He slammed fist against palm.

The high priest gestured with arms wide open. "I will consult the entrails of sacrificial prisoners to discover what these signs mean."

"I want to know right now!" demanded the king, his voice nearly flaking apart. He stared coldly at Balam-Ek. "Why did you not know of the coming of this dark star? I am disturbed at your lack of vigilance in such matters."

"Your majesty," Balam-Ek chose his words carefully. "The universe is vast. I cannot be properly prepared for all scenarios, and I admit this has caught me unawares. It was not in any known star chart, nor was it scheduled according to the calendar of Tzolkin. We will know what it means very soon."

"Your incompetence is beginning to worry me," coughed the king.

Balam-Ek bristled but wisely said nothing.

Taking a deep draught from a wineskin, the king belched. "Send for all the magicians in the land. I would have an answer soon."

"Yes, your majesty," said Balam-Ek, as he bowed himself out.

A young priest came up beside him outside the hall. "Do we serve an old man who is beyond reason, a stargazer in the noonday sun?"

"You will watch your tongue...still there are many surprises left for that old one," said the high priest. "Have the palace guard bring the prisoners to the altar of Baal. Hurry to it!"

None in the king's court dared speak for a few tense moments after the drunken display of anger at his highly favored priest.

The prince stood and bowed. "Father, may I retire for the night?" asked the young, dark-eyed boy on the king's left hand.

"Eh? Yes, Aaron, you may go. Sayame, see to him," said the king, slurring his words.

Sayame, the princess of sixteen years, took her younger brother by the hand to lead him down the hall to the royal quarters. He pulled out of her grasp; at twelve years of age, he was tired of being treated like an infant. His older brother Almek laughed at him as Sayame tried to grip his hand again. His siblings were day and night of each other. Almek was ugly and cruel, she was beautiful and kind. Aaron hoped he had the best qualities of both.

Why do they always treat me like an inferior child? I am wiser than my elder brother and yet no one sees it. I am more capable. I could rule these grand halls and more, someday.

"Here is your room, dear brother. Do you wish me to read to you until you fall asleep?" asked Sayame with sweetness in her voice. She was the only one who treated him like a person. Dear to his heart she was, even if she did treat him like he was half his age.

"No, not tonight, I would like to be alone."

"Very well, Aaron," she kissed him on the forehead and blew out all but one candle. This sat on an altar covered with small effigies of the main pantheon of Lamanite gods.

Once her thin silhouette disappeared down the hall, he climbed back out of his reed and woolen bed. Kneeling before the altar and the half dozen gods, he whispered, "Tell me, oh mighty gods of my fathers. Direct me and guide me. Show me the path to greatness, show me how to gain the acceptance of my father who dislikes me for my mother's awful, cursed Nephite name. Curse my name and grant me another soon." Head bowed and eyes shut tight in quiet desperation, he felt the wind blow the candle out as coldness entered the room. Though his eyes remained shut, he perceived a presence in the room.

A pleasing voice spoke to him in a musical tone, "Open your eyes. I am here to direct you, Son of the Prophecy."

Slowly opening his eyes, he saw a handsome man standing in his doorway. A bright white light surrounded this stranger. He was as tall and finely shaped as a warrior in peak physical condition, with not a single blemish or scar on his skin. The hair upon his head shone dark like obsidian.

Walking behind Aaron, the spirit said, "I am a guardian sent to instruct you."

Overwhelmed, Aaron asked, "Are you a god?"

"No, I am an angel of the god of this earth. My name is Ahtmar."

"Tell me what I must do."

"A great man is coming to the court of your father. His name is Akish-Antum."

"The Gadianton Grand Master?"

"Yea, it is he."

"Father doesn't trust him, though he did give him the city of Ushmael."

"Are you questioning the will of the gods?" asked Ahtmar, looking menacing.

"No, no I am not," he said, in fear of the spirit.

"Akish-Antum is to be your new master and teacher. Serve him as you would the gods themselves, and your destiny is secure. Tell no one of this charge set upon you." The glow of the spirit disappeared, and Aaron was alone again. Warmth returned to the room.

Aaron could not sleep for excitement. *Destiny begins, the spirit said, and who am I to test a spirit?*

* * * * * * * * * * * *

All through the night, under the fallen star, screams were heard piercing the darkness in agony. Balam-Ek cut out hearts and entrails to read the meaning of the sign in the heavens. Sacrificing over one hundred men, he learned nothing. He had cut man after man, thinking eventually to find something he could use; but there were no secrets in the blood magic to be learned from the bodies of the doomed slaves.

* * * * * * * * * * * *

While his father prayed just outside the front room, Zelph went into the next room and knelt facing east. He was only upon his knees for a moment when a bright light filled the room. The infant in the hut next door shrieked loudly as its mother tried in vain to calm and soothe it.

"Zelph, descendant of Samuel, I am an angel sent to guide you," said a musical voice.

Holding his hand over his eyes, Zelph turned around to face the spirit behind him. Though a little afraid and blinded by the bright light, Zelph asked, "Who are you to instruct me?"

"My name is Ahtmar, I am sent of the god of this earth," he said, appearing as a well-shaped man with dark hair. Zelph sensed that this was not a spirit of benevolence. He remembered his father telling him how to test a spirit, so that he might know if it was an evil spirit sent to deceive him.

Drawing courage unto himself in the cold room, Zelph asked as he had been taught, "Spirit, will you take my hand?" Qof-Ayin had taught him that a disembodied spirit cannot resist touching a living person, although a living person would feel nothing.

"Of course, I will take your hand, just hearken unto me. You are to be a servant of Akish-Antum when he comes hither."

Zelph stepped forward as did the spirit Ahtmar, and as their hands met, Zelph felt nothing. His hand passed through Ahtmar as if he were not there. Zelph felt a greater hint of cold.

"I know you for the devil you are, cloaked in false sunlight to deceive me! Begone, hell spawn! By the power of the Great Spirit, depart and never return to this house!"

"Oh, I will leave. First know that if you heed me not, a darkness will befall you and your father," taunted Ahtmar.

"Begone! Begone, I serve the true Lord!" shouted Zelph.

"I curse you, Zelph. Men will hate you all your days, and you will be a cursed man hunted by your own kind. Those who should venerate you will instead cast aspersions upon your name. You are doomed to be an outcast forever!" said Ahtmar with a fury.

"Begone! Now!" commanded Zelph. Ahtmar turned and walked through the wall, and warmth returned to the room. The child next door ceased crying.

"Zelph, your voice was raised. Who was here? Who could have passed me as I was out front?" Qof-Ayin asked, rushing into the room.

"A servant of the adversary, an evil spirit. He bade me seek out and serve Akish-Antum. Do you know who that is?"

"Yea, Akish-Antum is a Gadianton, a devil clothed in flesh, a shadow across the light. His black magic is strong. I pray you never meet him."

Pausing to look out the window, Qof-Ayin continued, "We live in dark times. You to be bodyguard of the king and now this. It bodes ill. I will think of something to help you, my son. Something."

Zelph could not sleep. He paced through the house, shuddering with each scream from the sacrificed victims of the high priest Balam-Ek. "Father, I cannot stay here. This city bleeds evil."

"My son, it breaks my heart to see how far our people have fallen. The choice is always before the people, and they have taken the evil path. "

"We are not innocent! Those slaves—those men now being sacrificed—we captured them and gave them to the priests. Their blood is on our hands," cried Zelph, brooding into his clenched hands.

Qof-Ayin put his arm around his son. "Those men I gave the priests were prisoners from the dungeons of Madoni. They were murderers, robbers and worse. They are not innocent victims. If I had not given them up to the priests of Baal, Balam-Ek would have taken innocent people to the sacrificial altar."

Zelph looked up. "I apologize for my doubt. You are wise, and I still have much to learn from you."

"If only I were a wise man. I am not, I am only captain of the army in Mutula."

"Then let us leave this place and go to a new land where there is justice and mercy. Let us leave now in the night."

"We can't yet...we are still being watched."

"How can you know that?" asked Zelph, more curious than doubtful.

"My name is Qof-Ayin, is it not?"

"Yea it is—'Eyes in Back of Head.' Where is he who spies upon us?"

"Beside the tree beyond the courtyard, some lesser priest of Baal watches and waits. They are taking no chances with you, my son. I have been too vocal in my disdain for the temple of foolish stone gods. Perhaps Balam-Ek knows our true faith. We are not trusted."

* * * * * * * * * * * *

By morning, the screams of sacrifice had stopped. Balam-Ek was grateful to Shagreel, the Sun God, for banishing the fallen star from the sky. Still, he had no answer for King Xoltec and feared for his current life and station. Unhappy, he trudged back to his abode to ponder something to tell the king next time he was summoned.

A million thoughts raced through his brain as he walked in a daze to his chambers, hoping the king had not been drinking again with the new slave girls. They always made him extra mean. He bumped into his chief scribe, a short thick man, and asked, "Have any magicians or sorcerers arrived to speak with the king yet?"

The wind forced the scribe's thin gray beard to blow into his face as he answered, "No, my master, most have fled as the fallen star was unexpected by all. They have all run away rather than tell the king they are fools who know nothing."

"Strangely, that is good enough news for me. I at least will not have to debate with any other soothsayer what the sign means."

"I am afraid, master, that I have heard someone is coming."

"Taloc! Who is it?" thundered Balam-Ek.

"An enemy of ours—the Gadianton Grand Master, Akish-Antum. His chariot is approaching our lands even now. A message runner just brought the news to me a short time ago. I was about to inform the king."

"How long until he arrives?"

"Mere hours, perhaps less."

"Blast his godless soul. I must have an answer for the king before he arrives. Perhaps I can turn this to my advantage. Tell no one of his coming yet, and see to it that the runner tells no one either," commanded the high priest.

"I will say nothing of it yet then, master."

Thinking, Balam-Ek rubbed his chin, forgetting how bloody it still was. He wiped his face and sat down for a moment to think. Inspiration came, and he quickly rushed to the king's hall. This dark star could still portend something wicked that could be laid at another's feet. Balam-Ek grinned. Akish-Antum would not know he was coming to his doom.

Entering the great hall, Balam-Ek had a stern look on his sinister face as he approached the king, who was flanked by both sons. A jaguar skin cloak hung from the king's gaunt shoulders.

To warm his weak heart, thought Balam-Ek. The sons at least looked awake. Scowling, angry, jealous Almek and quiet, perceptive Aaron— odd that he looks more pleased to be sitting here than usual, as if he is expecting something.

"Your Majesty, King Xoltec, Lord of Mutula, Laban, Midian, Middoni, Lemuel, Lamanihah, Lehi, and Ushmael." The last one was a purposeful jab into the brain stem.

"Ushmael? I do not rule Ushmael. That is the Gadianton city, perhaps won by trickery but his none the less." He coughed from too much wine last night. "Explain yourself, Balam-Ek. Do you incite war with an ally?"

"Ushmael, the city of the Gadianton Grand Master, Akish-Antum, was taken by trickery," said Balam-Ek. "He had told you, my king, that he would build a pyramid in a single night. If he did so, then you were to give him the city."

"I know very well how I lost the city," said King Xoltec. "I thought I had him in a hopeless boast. By morning's light there was a great, oval-shaped pyramid, a strange shape unlike other pyramids, sitting upon the city's outer grounds. I had to give the city and its surrounding lands to the Gadianton Grand Master. I still don't know how he did it. Since then, none but Gadiantons has ever been to the city and lived to tell the tale."

"I know of the Gadianton deceit, the gods have told me," said Balam-Ek, hoping he could bait King Xoltec into betraying the truce with Akish-Antum. "And I have discovered the meaning of the omen in the sky." Balam-Ek paused to dramatize his point, slowly turning to be sure he had everyone's attention. "It is a sign of evil attempting to come over your house, oh King. But it does not mean we are helpless. There is no fate we cannot fight...the gods Shagreel, Baal, and Moloch welcome and reward strength, action and power!"

"What is this evil you speak of?" demanded Prince Almek.

"Oh, Prince, it is an old cunning enemy, our very own neighbor to the direct north in Ushmael—Akish-Antum, the Gadianton Master." A hush fell over the hall.

Aaron sat enthralled, awaiting his new master, as Ahtmar had said. Balam-Ek's rhetoric only increased his hopes.

"You make dangerous accusations, Balam-Ek. Akish-Antum, the Gadianton Grand Master is not to be trifled with. He sees all," asserted the courtier Tzichak.

"No, he does not. My king listen to me...Akish-Antum is an enemy, a Nephite in his heart. That's his blood, the blood of the usurpers. Since our people first came here and the ancient brotherly bond and birthright was broken, their people have sought to dominate us, and he is one of them. There can be no denying it."

"You have seen this in the signs?" asked King Xoltec, now a little more engaged.

"Yea, I have. The sign in the sky was a warning to act," declared the high priest. "We must slay him as he enters our city."

"Enters our city?" asked the king. "What do you know, Balam-Ek?"

"He is on his way here even now to deceive and destroy us. We must act first. Murder him and take back our city of Ushmael. Once this is done, we will destroy the robbers from out of our midst. For this, the Sun God Shagreel will bless us." Balam-Ek paused, confident in his speech and his influence on King Xoltec. "We are the people of Laman, the elder brother, and it is our right to rule over the others, whether they be Nephites, Zoramites, Jacobites, Josephites, Ishmaelites, or even filthy Lemuelites. We must rule and put them all under our feet. This falling star is the sign of our time to rise. Let us begin in our own house and eradicate those treacherous Gadianton dogs of Akish-Antum. Who is with me and the king?" he shouted loud as thunder, praying to dark gods that the king agreed with him.

No one moved or spoke as they watched King Xoltec and waited for his response.

There was clapping, then deep guttural laughing. "Ha, ha, ha, well done...what a performance." The deep bass voice echoed down the hall from the west entrance. Metallic hands clapped a steady primal beat. The shadows extended taller than the man in the doorway. As he stalked in, many turned away, fearing eye contact. The deep ominous laugh continued. "Ha, ha, ha, was that your plan? You pathetic pawn of Shagreel, you worshiper of weakness. The time of sorrow is at hand, and I am here to help you, King Xoltec."

The Gadianton Grand Master had arrived.

Call of Duty

The personal council room of Onandagus was lit warm by the sun. The rays came from windows that reached to the high ceiling. This private chamber was used only by the close friends and family of the chief judge. The walls were stuccoed and whitewashed, giving a bright vibrant appearance. The furnishings were sparse—a desk, a bookcase covered with brass books, scrolls, and dozens of inscribed clay tablets.

Amaron took a spot on the only couch, waiting for the others to arrive. He looked at a glass-covered box containing a tattered remnant of Captain Moroni's original Title of Liberty. Beyond these few things, the room was rather plain and unmarked.

The men began to arrive. As they came in and settled where they could, Amaron recognized many of them. Amon, Stephen, Nephi, Boaz, Nahom, and Isaiah, each from Zarahemla. They were good men, all captains. Simeon from Manti and Captain Tobron of Manti. Amaron knew Tobron slightly, a trusted captain as well. The last was Captain Ahaten from Gideon.

Amaron had talked with the chief judge and Ezra until late into the night, and he was still rather tired. Why had he, only a guardsman, been invited? He would have no more to add to the discussion. They had gone over everything last night.

Onandagus stood before them leaning on his desk, a brooding look upon his drawn face. He seemed much older than his forty-four years. He asked Captain Tobron to pray, and then he began, "You are the ten best men available to me right now for a mission. I understand better than anyone how few good men remain; and yet in your turn I must ask that each of you find the ten best men you can as well. You will each serve as the captain of ten for this important mission, which may entail the next few months."

The men nodded, ready for this responsibility.

"As of today, young Amaron is promoted to full captain of the guard," said Onandagus. Captain Tobron gave a strong slap of congratulations to Amaron's back.

"What about Captain Lachoneus? He is commander of the scouts. He taught me everything I know," protested Amaron. "This does not seem right."

Onandagus went quiet a moment as something inside his eyes moved; but then it was gone, and the stony visage of the chief judge returned. "The dagger men murdered Captain Lachoneus and his wife in the night. I am sorry you had to hear it like this, Amaron. It is in no way related to your promotion, which I had planned to do beforehand."

That was an unexpected blow. Captain Lachoneus was like an uncle to Amaron, the kind that taught you not only survival skills like wood-craft and teamwork but dirty tricks and pranks. When Amaron was a boy, Captain Lachoneus had taken three dozen of the youth out to the north-west edge of the wilderness of Hermounts for a widespread gathering of junior guardsmen. He taught them tracking, camping in adverse weather and other survival skills, and then they had mock battles with youth who had come from other cities as far away as Bountiful and Desolation.

That had been the first time Amaron learned to fight multiple oppo-nents and win. Three much older boys had come to attack him in the dark on a steep hillside. He saw them coming and went low, knocking them down and sending them tumbling down the hill. He was very proud of himself for that. Captain Lachoneus had taught him some of those grap-pling methods, as well as the lesson that there is always a way to prevail. Amaron would never forget him.

"Now to the task at hand," began Onandagus. "The Gadianton Grand Master is manipulating the Lamanites and Ishmaelites for war. The greedy old King Xoltec of Mutula, and the young ambitious King Apophis of Tullan, are the two rulers over all the Lamanites and Ishmaelites. The Gadiantons are inciting these two to attack us, specifically here in Zara-hemla. They are planning to bypass all major roads and sneak in as far as they can without having to fight any other cities, if possible. The plan is simple—a revolution based upon fear. They will slay all known leaders here and abroad. They will instill puppet leaders and rule with as little bloodshed as possible. Far too many of our people could be taken in by this; they would trade supposed security for their freedom. This is a land of freedom, and it must always remain so."

"You are saying this is to be war, after three hundred years of peace?" Boaz questioned in amazement.

"Yea, there will be war. Your part is small for now but crucial. I do not yet know which secret routes these armies will take. Gadianton scouts are going to lead them on little known paths. We must find them while they are still far away from the city. We can then slow them down and fight them where few of our people will be harmed. If they get within a day's march of Zarahemla, there will be too many farms and towns in the direct line of battle."

"So, we are to take a group of men and watch, slow them down and expose them if we can?" asked Captain Tobron, grinning.

"Yea, as much as you can. You will be given horses and carrier birds to best keep me apprised of your individual situations."

"Why not look into your interpreter stones for this knowledge?" asked Boaz.

"They work through the Spirit of the Lord, and they answer things for me that I, as a man, cannot get an answer for myself. Some things the Lord has us figure out ourselves, and this is one of those," said Onandagus, watching their eyes.

Everyone seemed to accept that, except Boaz. His face showed questions but he said, "I do not fully understand that, but I will do as you have asked."

"Good, then here is what I will have you all do." Onandagus pulled out a wide map of all the lands on this side of the world. "Here is the main road from Gideon and Manti. I do not believe they will take this route, as it is too exposed all the way from the Narrow Pass. You could not hope to move even the swiftest of horses through here unseen. Nor do I believe they will come up the Sidon River; the Lamanites are too superstitious a people to travel on water if they can possibly help it. In any case, I do have good people watching the river from below Bountiful."

With ink and a quill, he traced out ten different routes through woods and hills all across the map, denoting the hundreds of miles his captains would soon be traveling. "These are the ten routes you will be leading your squads of ten through. It matters little to me which route each of you take, though I know some of you will have particular specialties. Captain Tobron, I am sure you would like the route to the southwest of Manti where your mother's people live. Amaron, you know the edge of the Hermounts wilderness better than anyone I know. Do you wish to accept that?"

Amaron nodded.

"Good. These others can be divided however it pleases the rest of you. If it comes to battle, do what you can and no more. I believe they will have an army of thousands, so ten men are futile for combat. Gather intelligence and get away; do not endanger your lives. I will not dally words any longer...is this acceptable?"

"Yea!" came the unanimous reply.

"How did you come by this information?" asked Captain Tobron.

"We have a Gadianton that turned for us, who supplied most of it," replied Onandagus.

"What if it's just a Lamanite twist? You trust him?" asked Boaz, incredulous.

"Yes, I do. Don't you agree, Amaron?"

"Yea." Amaron shrugged.

"I want you all to get your affairs in order and be ready to leave within three days. Tell your men that their families can get food and essentials from my personal stores to help care for them while they are away. This is to be a secret mission, so please take care on who you ask to do this. Everyone will know soon enough, but it could draw undue Gadianton attention if too many are talking. God be with you all." He looked upon them, a thousand unspoken hopes in his eyes. "One more thing—my eldest daughter, Bethia has run away. If any of you should hear anything or find her....please, be aware," he pleaded. "Now you may go. Amaron, wait a moment."

After everyone left, Amaron asked, "When did your daughter run away?"

"Yesterday. No one has seen her, no one has any idea. Even Samson, who is usually so good at finding gossip in the streets has found nothing. So far, the prayers of my wife and I have not been answered, but I have faith. I know Bethia will be found. I know God will protect her and watch over her."

"I will do what I can to help. Why did you wish me to stay behind?"

"You need only find nine other men. I have your tenth."

"Who is it?" Amaron asked, puzzled and a little relieved, not sure where he could find ten good men to take with him. Most would not want to leave their families or their crops during the early season.

"I would have you take Ezra with you," he said, watching Amaron closely.

"The Gadianton? He could endanger the mission. What if he has lied to us about some of these things?"

"He has not, I know it absolutely. The interpreter stones do not lie. He is a reformed Gadianton who needs a good strong example."

"Why me then?"

"You have a strong, true heart of the gospel, a rare enough thing in these days. Am I wrong? Think of your dead brother Seantum coming to you and your faith in prayer."

"You're right. My prayers of faith have always been answered. I cannot deny that, not ever. Visited by my brother, Seantum, he an angel and I a child, but still...yes. I know what is true."

"Ezra likes you, and he will need protection for a time. You are the most capable man I have. He may also have more useful information to give."

Nodding to the man he most respected next to his father, Amaron turned and left. He did not like the weaselly Ezra, even if he was reformed. Ezra waited outside Onandagus's office for the burly scout. He wore an ugly blue turban and was doing a poor job of trying to grow a beard.

"That's a terrible disguise," Amaron laughed.

"So did Onandagus-?"

"Yes, you will come with me. But I warn you...no tricks!" he growled, pointing a finger at the skinny man.

"I swear by Isis that-"

Amaron cut him off again. "I want no oath by you. Just do as you're told."

Ezra fell in behind as they left the Judgment Hall.

Does He See Me?

The caravan set up its mobile shops in Gideon and stayed for two days. All the while Bethia was afraid that someone would spot her and drag her back to Zarahemla, but nothing came of these fears. Strangely, here only a day's ride away, no one seemed to recognize her at all. That took some getting used to.

The older woman, Keturah, enjoyed bossing the new girl. "Tell those men how their wives or girlfriends will love these perfumes," she would say any time a man passed. "Speak with your hands, always drawing them back to yourself like so, as if beckoning while you speak. Trust me, it works."

"They do not even look interested," Bethia protested.

"They will be if you smile big like you do at Rezon, and we will have a sale."

Though Bethia felt foolish at first, Keturah was right, and it worked rather well.

By the end of the second day, Rezon counted their take and said, "Here in little Gideon we have made more with Bethia than we did in Zarahemla for a week." The caravan owner was pleased, and she wanted to please him.

Bethia was afraid that her success might make Keturah jealous, but had she not pushed her to flirt and make the sales? As it turned out, Keturah was not the least bit jealous, and they soon became fast friends.

Talking along the road to Manti, the trip seemed to take only hours instead of a good full day. "My second husband was a Zoramite, can you believe it? Let me tell you, everything you have ever heard about them is true," said Keturah, as they passed a man going the opposite direction.

"I have never heard anything about them," said Bethia. "I wouldn't even recognize one."

"That was one, just now," said Keturah, pointing. "They are pigs, it's in their blood, I swear. We were married only a month, and he was gone, out chasing harlots."

"A month? Shouldn't marriage be eternal?"

"Eternal? You are so naive, Bethia, that's why I love you. Eternal, ha! I suppose if men could be trusted it might be eternal."

"I trust Rezon," said Bethia dreamily.

"Yes, I suppose so, because he is of a different breed, as my father used to say. Rezon can be trusted but for all the wrong reasons."

"What do you mean?"

"Oh, you know. Let's just say he is no Zoramite, that's for sure."

"No, he isn't, is he? He is true as the wheeling stars."

Keturah laughed. "You are so funny. You remind me of my third husband's little sister. She was from the city of Helam, and you never saw such a sweet, naive girl."

Bethia wasn't listening anymore. She watched Rezon as he moved up and down the caravan as it rolled along. He made sure everyone was well and the oxen were in good shape, that the wagons' axles were operating, that all in his caravan were happy. She liked that about him—he always smiled and wanted everyone to be happy. When they stopped for an afternoon lunch and to let the oxen rest, she waited for a moment to be alone with him.

When she saw him carrying two large wooden pails from the creek, she hurried to his side.

"Hello, Bethia. How are you this fine afternoon?"

"I am well. May I help you?"

"I have it. Besides, they are heavy."

"I can do it," she said, taking one of the pails from him. It was a struggle as they were heavier than she had thought. He smiled and let her carry it. She smiled back and asked, "Where are we taking these?"

"Peter's oxen need the water, and he has an injured foot. One of the oxen stepped on it."

"That's too bad," she said, realizing she was still smiling at him during the discussion of another man's pain. She blushed and wiped the smile from her face.

"He is alright," Rezon assured her, and she smiled again.

"Do you believe in fate?" she asked.

"I suppose I do, why?"

"My father doesn't, but I think I do."

"We are ready to move again now, so I must hurry. I will talk to you later," he said, taking the pail from her. She watched him, so strong and handsome, as he carried the water to Peter's oxen.

Back at her own wagon, she asked Keturah, "Does he see me?"

"Of course he sees you, what kind of question is that? *Does he see me?*" mocked Keturah. "Trust me, he sees you. But he is too much like my first husband."

"What do you mean? Too wonderful?"

Keturah laughed. "Oh, he was wonderful alright. He just didn't love me."

"I don't think Rezon is like that. He is sincere."

"Yea, Rezon is who he is. No denying that," said Keturah. "But you can't teach a hammer to love nails."

Bethia didn't understand that but no longer cared. She watched Rezon on horseback, riding up and down the caravan again.

"We'll be in Manti, before you know it," he said to her, smiling as he rode past.

She cooed and looked after him, and stuck her head off the side of the wagon to watch him ride down the line. Keturah laughed again.

Bethia enjoyed setting up the tables and booths for the early morning markets in Manti. There was always time to talk to Rezon and visit the other booths as well. How she began to love the smell of his pipe smoke. She used to detest smokers. But even with its odd shape, Rezon's pipe soon became a thing of enjoyment to her every morning. The tobacco and cedar chips became a fragrant staple.

This was fast becoming a life she wanted to go on forever. Someday soon, Rezon would notice what a woman she was, and they could be together forever. She told Keturah about her hopes for him, but the seasoned woman would just laugh and say something about cats and dogs not being able to live together.

What does she know of love? She has never had true love. Not like my parents. They must be worried sick, but this is how it must be. I must find my own way. Keturah means well, but she laughs. She doesn't understand love anymore, she is too old. A good thirty-five summers at the least. Still, she is a good partner for dress shopping, and how can you know what life is like without a good partner for dress shopping?

"Come along, Bethia. If we want Rezon to notice you, you had better get brighter colors. Lots of women have fallen for him, did you know?"

"I am not just anyone," Bethia cut her off. "I am special. He will see that soon enough."

"Alright, you will find your own way," laughed Keturah.

The Bride of Darkness

D eep within an underground passage, a woman's scorn was heaped upon Judge Hiram. "You told me those dagger men were the best! Bah! One Nephite warrior killed ten of them in one night."

Judge Hiram frowned. He was not used to anyone, let alone a mere woman, shouting at him. If this disrespect were in his courtroom he would have had the perpetrator gagged and flogged. In his hidden dungeon, such a person would not come out alive. But this antagonist was no ordinary woman. It was Lilith, wife of Akish-Antum. Beautiful, pale of face with straight, black hair and close-cropped bangs, she was absolutely enchanting until she spoke. Her throaty voice had a contemptuous and malevolent air. Her green eyes shone with an evil, fiery light.

Calming himself, Judge Hiram responded, "I was told by Teth-Senkhet that they were the best."

"What is best in Kish-Kumen obviously is not in Zarahemla," she laughed without mirth. "What? Have you no more dagger men to spare now?"

"I have men out looking for the traitor. They will find and kill him."

"Fool! What's the point now? He has told the chief judge everything he knows, which I hope for your sake wasn't much. One way or another, Akish-Antum always gets what he wants."

"For the sake of the oath, the traitor must be killed. If you were a member of the Order you would know that," he said through gritted yellow teeth.

She stared daggers at him before answering in a violent shriek. "I know more of the blackest of secrets than you could possibly hope to understand! I am the handmaiden of Satan and the bride of darkness!"

Her giant, black Nubian servant entered the room. He was near eight feet tall and rippling in muscle. Naked save for a breech cloth and an Egyptian style headdress, his oiled skin glistened. Mute, he held aloft a wide-bladed scimitar and grinned wickedly at Judge Hiram.

"No, Taharka, not this time. The master wants him to remain in place." She turned to Judge Hiram in disdain. "I should have had my own servant dispatch your guardsmen here. Then we would not be in this mess."

He tried to change the subject. "Perhaps we should move to kill Onandagus now, before anything else can be thwarted."

"You fool! I already told you. Akish-Antum wants to slay Onandagus himself...it's personal. He used to study under him or some such nonsense. No one shall take that away from him. If you try, I will kill you." She stared hard at him until he looked away. She threw a long, needle-like stiletto knife into the wall beside him. It quivered in the wall as he stared at it in horror. She smiled and shrugged her shoulders. "After all, what is a good wife for?" She laughed her awful, mirthless laugh.

"Yes, Mistress Zoreah," he whispered, with a deep contempt.

"Aw, aw, aw," she scolded, waving her long red-nailed finger at him while Taharka grinned absurdly, like a fool. "Not Zoreah, not here. Here, while I am in these lands, you shall call me Lilith."

"Yes, Mistress Lilith," he said through clenched teeth, planning on how he would one day destroy her.

"Thank you. So, if I were Onandagus what would I do now? Knowing just a hint of what the enemy is doing, thanks to a traitor." She sat still a moment and pondered.

Judge Hiram watched expectantly, about to speak.

She shouted, "Shut your mouth, fool. I don't want to hear your ideas. They all fail."

He froze, mouth agape and his finger in the air, about to gesture his thoughts. Working to regain his lost composure and dignity, Judge Hiram pointed out the obvious. "Mistress Lilith, the dagger men were your idea first."

"But not to fail! That was your doing. You should have given me more of them, knowing the big warrior would be too much for them. Why isn't such a man one of ours? And where is my drink? Get me some more wine!"

she shouted, throwing her goblet at him. Taharka looked on amused.

Judge Hiram hurried out the door and remarked to Judge Pachus, who waited outside, "She is deranged, absolutely deranged. Why is she here? Her insane tantrums will only cause problems."

"Careful, master. I heard of others who spoke ill of her. She had them skinned alive."

"I am the regional Gadianton master. I should be subservient only to Akish-Antum himself and his deputy Teth-Senkhet, not his insane wife who models herself after the screech owl of doom."

The door swung open. "Where is my wine?" she asked, eyes burning. She held out her goblet, and Judge Hiram took hold of it as Pachus poured.

Judge Hiram handed her the deep purple liquid. "Here you are, Mistress Lilith."

She drained the cup. "Someone needs to get to the bottom of these troubles. I am going out to the streets to find out what I may. Don't go losing the empire while I am away," she said, laughing as she and the huge black bodyguard walked away.

Travelers on the Road of Fate

Across the city, Amaron and Ezra had recruited three men for the mission. Even with the promise of provisions and food from Onandagus's storehouse, this was not enough to convince many to join in a dangerous, three month journey.

"It is still planting time. I must work hard now, or my family will starve come winter," spoke the latest of several men they approached.

"Please, Jeremiah, if we do not succeed in our task at hand there may not be a harvest," said Amaron.

"No, there may not be a chief judge and governor, is all. The king men still walk the streets and proclaim a change is soon at hand. They have asked me if I would support a king if one should arise."

"What did you say? I thought you a patriot."

"Ha, I told them I deserved to be king. Grandfather claims we go all the way back to the little king, Mulek. So, I ought to be king much as anyone," Jeremiah laughed.

"Maybe you do not understand that if the king men take over, you will lose all your rights, your fields and your home. Maybe even your life."

"Are you threatening me?"

"No, we are old friends. I am talking about what the king men would do."

"Hmmm, you say if I go with you that my family will be given food and provisions while I am away?" asked Jeremiah.

"Yes, they will be taken care of, as well as compensation for lost crops."

"Will this venture be profitable?"

"No, we will live off the land for the most part. It is spring, and it is nothing we have not done before in our youth. We will serve the city and the chief judge."

"I will not go," he said, as he shut the door on them. "There is no profit in it."

They stepped away from his door. Amaron frowned, looking at the list in his hand.

"How many more do you have on your list?" asked Ezra.

"There are seven more that I trust, as I trusted Jeremiah. If we can get six of them, we will have our company of ten. If we cannot, then I will go with less. It's tradition for each captain to have ten men. I don't want to break tradition, but it may be necessary."

They continued on and got four more. They had to settle for the younger brothers of two.

"That's my ten men, eleven total. Let us prepare to leave in three days," Amaron told them.

Three days later they met at the appointed time and place near the southern gate, minus one.

"Jacob told me he could not come and leave his new wife for so long," explained Obadiah.

"But you must have ten," Ezra insisted. "You said it was tradition."

Amaron waved him off. "We need to get going as we will be on foot. I could not find enough horses to requisition for all of us, so rather than have half of us on horseback we will do without."

Near all of the men except Ezra groaned at the prospect of having to march the entire mission. Daniel dropped a heavy pack and began casually tossing items into the street.

"Maybe I can help," Ezra said to Amaron. "I have a young cousin in Manti. I could ask him to join us. Then we would be ten."

"Is he a robber?" asked Amaron, strapping on his pack.

"No, but his father fears he may become one when he gets a little older. So it may please my uncle if we take him with us."

"Our route is not to Manti, it is to the west, past Nephihah and the borders of Hermounts."

"We would lose only two or three days. He's very good with a bow."

Amaron grimaced for a moment before speaking. "Alright, we will go to Manti and get him, if only to make sure he does not end up like you. After Manti, we go overland to Eber then Nephihah."

✷ ✷ ✷ ✷ ✷ ✷ ✷ ✷ ✷ ✷ ✷ ✷

The company began their trek south as the raven-haired woman and her big Nubian bodyguard watched them march out the gate on the southern road. She smiled with devilish white teeth showing behind ruby lips. Hands on hips, she squinted against the sun. "Let us make haste after them. I have an idea."

✷ ✷ ✷ ✷ ✷ ✷ ✷ ✷ ✷ ✷ ✷ ✷

Father and son continued on their own route south. It was a warm spring, and they were covered in sweat and dirt from the road. Forced to carry his son because of a broken leg, the father had left most of their valuables in the broken-down wagon. He still carried his sword, breast-plate and winged helmet, along with a pack containing food and their bedrolls. Passersby ignored them, as though they were loathsome, poor or deranged refugees. The son wished to know why so many people would behave without manners or charity.

His father answered, "The Nephites are a fallen people. They care more for riches and self-importance than the matters of the gospel, of the soul, of the Lord. Many times they gather and flock together like geese, honking and exulting on how they are so wealthy or worldly-wise. It pains me, but I suppose a part of me has grown numb to it after these many years. I care not for the respect of men. What matters is between me and my Lord, not men. Never forget that. I am not half the teacher Ammaron the Scribe is, but I know what it takes to serve the Lord. Never forget your faith and never forget your charity and hope in our Lord. That is the one thing in this world you can always count on, regardless of what the worldly-wise will try and instill upon you. The doubters must always have their say in trying to enlighten you to their way of thinking, of showing you the foolishness of faith. When that happens, just smile and let them talk...let them damn themselves."

"I don't know if I could be that harsh, to let people damn themselves. I want to help people, to teach them."

"Yes, you care too much."

"Like momma?"

"Yes, like momma. You keep being like momma. It will save you as much as any ten things I could tell you," said his father as he stopped and adjusted the weight on his back. He was strong as any three men, but the boy was not so easy to carry day after day. Their progress was slower than he would have liked.

"I want to say a prayer, father, that you won't have to carry me so far by yourself." The father stopped and knelt, letting his son down to pray.

They had only just finished when a farmer leading a slow wagon with two oxen came around the bend. "Hello there, looks like you got a busted leg," said the farmer.

"Yea, it's a clean break though."

"Where you bound for?"

"We are going to Zarahemla. My son has quite a bit of schooling before him."

"I was headin' back up north but great blessin's have been bestowed upon me here lately, and I aim to return it to the Lord an' his people. Climb on in, and I will take you the day and a half back down to Zar'hemla."

"Thank you very much, but I don't want to burden you."

"Father, accept a blessing when it comes," said his son. The father grinned and helped him into the back of the wagon. The farmer then turned the oxen about and began the journey south once again.

"Name's Jonas. Interestin' thing happened to me in Zar'hemla the other night."

Seeds of Evil

Prince Aaron looked up at the sound of the laughter and saw a vile grin within a crimson shadow. The cruel smile revealed sharp teeth. Still laughing his terrifying dirge, the towering man approached. The piercing, volcanic-blue eyes behind the saber-toothed helmet added to his menacing look.

Aaron admired the long sword hung at his side; glyphs decorated the scabbard down its length. It was rumored to be an ancient blade from long ago called Kadar-Lahab, the black flame blade of Coriantumr. Aaron wondered if the Gadianton Grand Master truly had the sword of the last of the Jaredites, the very sword that smote the head from Shiz the Usurper. Aaron had heard the legends of old. Shiz had started a revolution against the Emperor Coriantumr, and these people were now gone off the face of the earth. Now the Lamanites were planning war against the Nephites, the descendants of their father Laman's younger brother Nephi; and soon the hated Nephites would also be destroyed, as were nations of old who lived upon this land.

Girded in bright, copper-scaled armor and a wide black and crimson cloak about his shoulders, the Gadianton Grand Master was a dark golden colossus. A lean, mahogany-skinned Lamanite with a fierce face and tall mohawk followed him, the only one unafraid of the giant of a man.

Looking Aaron in the eye, the Gadianton smiled his horrid smile and stepped forward, alarming a guard who raised a spear toward him. The Gadianton struck and caught the guard's chest as would a great cat and then jerked free, letting the limp body fall. Bringing up his gauntlet, he revealed talons like a fell beast. Gesturing back to the fallen guard he said, "Forgive me, I acted in haste," then laughed in a deep, cavernous tone.

The king cried aloud with the commanding voice of his almost forgotten youth, "Akish-Antum, why do you soil my chambers and slay my guardsman?" His voice betrayed a hint of fear. To portray a virile image he sat upright, pulling himself out of his typical slouch.

"King Xoltec, Prince Almek, Prince Aaron, Princess Sayame." Akish-Antum, the Gadianton Grand Master, greeted them with a bow. "I have come because of the fallen star, the sign in the heavens. I know what it means. It is not a sign of my arrival as some witless wonders would have you believe." He eyeballed the now-shrinking Balam-Ek. "Know this—my city of Ushmael is more than a good week's travel away. That I have come in connection with this star should be proof enough that I am a master of astrology, unlike those who waste slaves to learn nothing." He glanced at Balam-Ek with a smirk.

When the high priest frowned at him, the Gadianton spat at his feet. Balam-Ek stalked from the room, only to return a short time later to watch from a darkened alcove.

"It does seem you know the stars, to be here so soon from so far away," admitted the king. "But can you interpret these signs for me? Or are you as helpless as all the other soothsayers?"

The Gadianton extended his palms out before the king in a gesture of false supplication. "I tell you this. There is no eternal reward or forgiveness for wasting the dawn. We must make haste. Our long enemies, the Nephites, are preparing to move against us to wipe out every man, woman, and child. First, they will strike and take Tullan the Golden, as it is closer. They may even coerce the Ishmaelites to join with them." He left that thought to hang on their minds.

"That could never happen. King Apophis is too ambitious, too proud and arrogant to ever join with the Nephites," said King Xoltec.

"It is possible. I have my second-in-command, a man of Tullan himself, on his way there now to persuade King Apophis of my plan," spoke the Gadianton, low as his monstrous voice would allow.

The king rubbed his jaw. "You have seen this all in the stars?

"Yea, the energy of the planets affects us all. My interpreter informs me of many things," he replied, producing from out of his cloak an infamous seer stone. It was a life-sized crystal skull with a moving jaw. Holding it in front of himself, he swept it in a wide, circular motion toward those in the hall, who responded with gestures warding off the evil eye.

"How soon will the Nephites move against us?" King Xoltec questioned, still skeptical.

"They will come at the end of their growing season, late summer, early fall. We have almost six months to prepare for invasion or to strike ourselves," said Akish-Antum, as he made a thrusting motion with the skull.

"You speak of invading the Nephites upon their own lands?" asked Prince Almek.

"I do," grinned the Gadianton Grand Master, staring into the skull's hollow eye sockets. "I stand to lose my city," he continued. "My Order has always existed, underground if need be, but my city could be lost...your gracious gift." He saluted the king. "But you stand to lose all, if we do not act first."

"It seems I heard another foolish plan of invasion recently," King Xoltec mused.

Holding his crystal skull before the king, Akish-Antum said, "I see much with this. I can show you. Seer stones do not and cannot lie." He moved in closer with the jaw ominously agape.

Recoiling, King Xoltec murmured, "Away with your black magic. I want nothing to do with it."

"What do you see, Stargazer?" said Prince Almek.

"I see your future, Prince," said the Gadianton, deliberately leaving off Almek's official title of crown prince. "King Xoltec, it is truth I speak. The Nephites are preparing soon for war, but together we can defeat them. The instigator is their chief judge and governor, Onandagus ben Nephi, and the disciples."

"Why not send your assassins to kill him and be done with it?"

"If I cut off one snake's head, another always rises in its place. We must burn the neck stumps before any other can rise up. All of them must be slain at once, their church must die. Here is the reality of the situation. This war is coming. Do you wish to fight it on your own lands where your people will suffer many bitter hardships, or in the Nephite lands, where your army can eat from the fruits of your enemy's labors? If we strike quickly, we will catch them off guard. We will win this war together."

The graying king looked the Gadianton over, shuddered and said, "I know you have wisdom beyond the understanding of mortal men, and that you wish for the destruction of our hated enemies, the Nephites!" he spat the name. "They think they have the birthright to rule over us, but they stole it. They call us dark-skinned, barbarian dogs, while their women cover themselves from our father Shagreel. They are the barbarians. They serve councils of fifty in wooden halls and travel everywhere with all they own like thieves. Nephites, bah! I say this, Akish-Antum, the most important thing I have never forgotten is that Amalikiah was a Nephite. He used flattery and wise words to dethrone my great-grandfather of old, to become the king of my people. Therefore, I will not allow you a position of authority in my army, because you are one of them. A Nephite!"

The Gadianton drew himself up, not the least bit perturbed by the old king's ramblings and prejudices. "Amalikiah was an opportunist and a flatterer who received his just rewards at the hands of his enemies. In the long run, we all know he did not and could not end the noble line of the sons of Laman—your line. I may have Nephite blood in my veins, but I also have Zoramite blood and Ishmaelite and Mulekite and even a drop or two of Lamanite. Everyone today is so proud of their lineage, but I tell you this—we go back far enough and we are all the same. Fear the man, not his ancestor. Are we not accountable for ourselves above any that have come before us? We must earn our own keep and make our own legacies. Amalikiah's cursed name is not a legacy I want. Hear me, oh king, if you doubt my word send runners and spies up to the edge of Nephite lands. They will return and verify my word. That is, unless they are slain by the Nephites, further proving their hostile intent."

Standing tall in his own maroon and green-hued elegance, Prince Almek called out, "My father the king, Rabbanah of Mutula, give me the honor of leading our armies." He looked hopeful and hungry as a starved dog with a full table's feast before it.

"You have not enough experience for such a military endeavor," responded his father. King Xoltec rubbed his troubled brow and pondered a long, quiet moment. "There will be no trickery here. Balam-Ek, dispatch runners and spies to verify Akish-Antum's words before we mobilize. I would be a fool not to prepare for disaster when I hear it spoken of so often, and yet I must know I can trust these ill tidings."

"Of course, Rabbanah," said the stout priest, casting an evil leer at the Gadianton.

"What can you offer our possible alliance, Akish-Antum?" asked King Xoltec.

"As I have said, my second-in-command is negotiating with King Apophis for a force to accompany us. There will be a legion of Tultec troops to help accomplish our goals. My Order will guide the army on the best route to Zarahemla, the Nephite capitol city. We will march north, avoiding the cities Desolation and Teancum. Taking secret paths my Order has prepared, we will swing around the narrow passage and come in from the wilderness to the west, surprising them on their own sacred doorstep. My assassins will slay all who oppose us and who oppose the establishment of a new king to rule over them. I have men on the inside who will move into place and declare a surrender. They will take control of the Nephite government in a near-bloodless revolution. This will be effective nationwide. Perhaps a few cities will oppose us, but they would be few. We'll have the rest," he finished with a boastful air. "In the final stages, we shall divide the lands between you and King Apophis."

"Wouldn't this make my kingdom vulnerable to Nephites coming here? If they are preparing to invade as you claim, I don't want my army thousands of miles away."

"No, they would never come here when we hold them captive there. Besides I won't need even a tenth of your army. A government will be put into place to keep the Nephites in line. We will rule them through fear and, with their church dead, no one will oppose us. A new choice land for you to rule, with myself as governor, and I thank you," bowed Akish-Antum.

"I do not wish to split land with that serpent of the dark, King Apophis," muttered King Xoltec.

"There will be a truce only as long as necessary. You shall have greater land and armies to overcome him when you wish. But for now, and only for now, can I have your word on a truce with King Apophis?"

"You have everything ready, do you not? You merely await my word and his word?"

"Correct."

"You have a good plan. We will ally with the Gadiantons and this force of King Apophis as soon as my runners return with word of the Nephite aggression. And there are to be no mistakes on who will command my armies. Perhaps Crown Prince Almek's time has come. General Tubaloth will be sent as my military advisor and direct in line behind my son Almek as commander."

"As you wish," said the Gadianton.

Crown Prince Almek, eldest son of the king, smiled. He had just been given the world on a plate, a sumptuous feast for a starving man.

✷ ✷ ✷ ✷ ✷ ✷ ✷ ✷ ✷ ✷ ✷ ✷

The Gadianton Grand Master was granted a small wing on the south side of the palace. He and his fifty men occupied the entire wing. He kept a good portion for himself at the far end of the hall, where slave bearers carried inside enough equipment for a small house. A small band of fanatically devoted men came to Akish-Antum once his things were situated. The head of these devotees was named Uzzsheol, literally "Strength of Hell."

The deep voice of the Gadianton ordered his most trusted servant on a special mission. "King Xoltec will be sending his runners and spies to confirm the Nephite hostilities. Follow them, slay them all. Let none escape, nor let any find their bodies without a Nephite arrow in their ribs."

"I hear and obey, Evil Eye," spoke the mohawked man without a trace of emotion. Uzzsheol was a man unparalleled in tracking skill. He had watched King Xoltec's runners and spies closely to determine who was the swiftest and the strongest. All of these would fall under his knife and bow.

Left alone, the Gadianton Master began to unpack his many belongings, maps, bottles of various substances that smelled of sulfur and exotic oils, and a huge skull with a double row of teeth, holding a tall, wide candle. The candle put off a powerful light, brightening the open part of his makeshift study, while casting the corners of the room into a deeper sense of darkness. The burning incense of distant lands filled the room. He took off his saber-toothed helmet and his crimson and black cloak, hanging these upon the wall.

The dark stone room was to his liking. With a prepared bowl of ocher, he drew a variety of glyphs on the limestone wall. These were ancient symbols of power from the age of Nimrod and his Queen Semiramis. He liked them for the mystical ambiance they gave his quarters, and for the fear he knew would be upon the Lamanites once he left. Likely they would never inhabit these rooms again and would forever set them apart as his for whenever he might return. His keen ears detected breathing right outside his thin door.

Akish-Antum continued painting the large red glyphs upon the wall then put the bowl away and called out, "What are you looking for, young Prince Aaron?"

The boy was silent, staring through a crack in the wooden door at the symbols which seemed to be drawn in blood.

"If you wish to speak with me, enter. Otherwise, you had best leave. My demon consorts may find you a morsel they can hardly resist," he laughed.

Feeling both brave and curious, the boy pushed the door open to behold the full terror of the room. With awe, he stared at the huge skull. It could have easily fit over the top of his entire head and be worn like a helmet. The ocher glyphs still oozed and ran red down the wall.

"You speak with demons?" Aaron asked.

"Yes, I am beyond the learning of mortal men. If I wish to know anything more, I speak to the long dead masters who have preceded me or to the bodiless servants of my lord, the true dark master."

"Ahtmar?" asked the young prince, thinking of the angel who had visited him in the night.

"Ha! He is a lesser one who enjoys being a trickster. He did well sending you my way."

"They say you are evil," ventured the boy.

"They say, they say. Who are they? Little people in a little world, those who cannot open their minds to the higher consciousness. They are the ones who will not grow. They must obey set rules and limitations in this life. They must have authority and law over them," he spat with disdain. "They believe someone is coming to save them. No! In this life you must save yourself. These types are held in a rotting stagnation that will be their undoing." The Gadianton stared into the dark eyes of the boy. They were wide but unafraid. "Do what you want, that's the true gospel. Don't you think a real God wants you to be happy?"

The boy stared and slowly nodded his head.

The Gadianton continued his tirade. "Of course he does. Look at the old prophets of the Christ, moping and crying. They were burned alive, stoned, fed to beasts, slain by traitors, murdered in the streets...when all along they had power to stop it. What power you might ask? The power of their own free will and choice. They didn't have to choose to follow he who would only bring them misery. No, the real God could save you from this life's troubles. He wants you to be yourself. We are only here for a short while. Before we evolve to the next level of consciousness, we must take advantage of the opportunities here. Stay by me, Prince, and I will show you the way."

Aaron watched him through all this and made up his mind. "You are wise, Akish-Antum. I will have you show me the way. How did you come to this higher knowledge?"

Akish-Antum looked far away through dim eons past, cloaked in the cobwebs and ruin of ages before speaking. "I was born on the sacred cross of waters near to Zarahemla, son of a long line, born to be a priest. I was weak—dead to the world, alive to the spirit. Once I met him, but in my time of need was denied, my prayers mocked, my son drowning. So I turned my back, faced the west, forgot my past, began my future and witnessed the beauty of oblivion. I learned the great secret and I will teach it to you."

"You speak in riddles," said Aaron.

"It is all my past you need to know."

"What is the great secret?"

"Soon...soon I will tell you."

* * * * * * * * * * * *

A strong wind blew in from the west the next morning, bringing storm clouds across a steel blue sky. Aaron sat attentive at his father's side as the Gadianton Grand Master explained more of his plan.

The armies would be guided by the Order on its special route snaking through enemy territory. In this way it could best surprise the Nephites all the way to the center of their land near Zarahemla. There they would be in the best position to take the city with minimal loss, while demanding a nationwide surrender as well as tribute. The Nephites would surrender to the ferocity and omnipotence of the combined Lamanite and Ishmaelite armies.

King Xoltec gloated over this. He had long dreamed of putting the enemy brother's sons under the yoke of bondage and slavery. How he loathed them—they who claimed he was the cursed one, both he and his kin. What gave them the right? His flesh was their flesh; King Xoltec's fathers were the elders. Arrogant Nephites, always portraying themselves as the natural favorites of their god.

Well, now he had his own gods. One for every season, for every emotion and feeling of the senses. Gods of the home and forest, the sea and the sky, rain and sun, blood and death. These gods were easier to appease. You knew what they wanted. A sultry virgin, a warrior's heart, a limnah of gold and the death of the dream of peace.

Akish-Antum continued to flatter the old king and his people, while simultaneously throwing hints of the doom that awaited them if they should refuse to follow his plan of aggression. He told tales of how vicious the Nephites had become and what they would do to captured prisoners, how the Nephites loved to torture and murder. Their sacrifices were embellished to sound a hundred times worse than anything Balam-Ek had ever done.

In many ways, the Lamanites had become unfeeling in the ways of bloodshed. They were numb to violence and had little regard for their own slaves and prisoners. But stories of true warriors being unmanned, robbed of their identities and made to perform women's work appalled them. Better to be sacrificed to gods in a true warrior's death.

"How large an army do you need for this plan to succeed against these fiends?" asked King Xoltec, inspired by the lust for conquest. "You said a tenth of my full army."

"Fifty thousand troops and I can make you king of this side of the world, holding Zarahemla in our collective hands. Then key men will die and other key men will take their places. They will convince the people of the futility of fighting against your armies. The masses will cry out for peace, tolerance, and security. In return for such, they will give you honor and tribute. Your name will be recorded in the sacred books, your face hewn into stone for the ages."

"And you! What do you have to gain in all of this?" demanded Crown Prince Almek. "If these Nephites are as fierce and bloodthirsty as you claim, why would they sue for peace and give tribute with only a single city, even a capital city, falling to us?"

"I have seen the future, and the Nephites will fall. A grateful king will reward his greatest servant and ally," spoke the Gadianton, looking into King Xoltec's and then the boy Aaron's eyes. Heedless of Crown

Prince Almek's smoldering gaze he continued, "It is your family's destiny to prevail. My crystal skull interpreter has seen it. It is going to happen, regardless of what you or anyone else says or does. It is inevitable. This family will rule the entire continent, king of all the lands from the south to the north. I simply wish to be a part of it, to get my share."

"Then what do we even need you for? If I am to be an invincible king, then what are you but a dog? A dog begging for scraps!" shouted Almek.

"Silence, brother," pleaded Aaron.

"I want to know. Tell me, king of dogs!" continued Almek.

Silently, King Xoltec watched, awaiting the climax of the confrontation. True, Akish-Antum was the last person in the world to be trifled with; but to be a strong king, Almek must learn and grow. He must learn to fight his own battles and deal with the consequences.

Stepping closer and bringing his huge bulk right up to Almek, who reached to his mid-chest, Akish-Antum said, "Almek, I am the salvation and guide of your people. Heed me or not. If you don't, it is your choice and your mistake."

The crown prince looked away and mumbled something unintelligible. Then quick as love lost and sharp as slander, he slammed his obsidian dagger into Akish-Antum's chest. Blood poured from the point of impact but not from the man's chest. Almek screamed, clutching his hand.

"You have spirit, I'll give you that. But no intelligence," said Akish-Antum.

Black shards of obsidian lay scattered across the stone floor, in dire contrast to Almek's blood droplets. Only the jade handle remained in one piece...the ebon volcanic stone had shattered in his hand, tearing it apart. Looking stunned, he backed down as the Gadianton stared burning holes into him.

Breathing hard and clutching his hand, the prince muttered, "Impossible, copper armor is not so strong." He ran down the hall, streaking a trail of crimson on the gray limestone.

"You truly are a sorcerer," proclaimed young Prince Aaron.

"Only black magic could have made copper withstand obsidian," agreed King Xoltec.

"No, not magic, just knowledge; knowledge I will share. I can tell you how to make copper armor and weapons as strong as Nephite steel."

"Tell us," King Xoltec commanded.

"Do you believe my warning of Nephite aggression?"

"Show us how to make the miracle metal," insisted the old king.

"It will take a little time for my engineers to show your smiths the process, but it can be done in time to outfit and arm the war machine that we are assembling. Shall we gather your army while we wait?"

"Yes. Tulum, write the royal decree to begin selecting troops," the king called to his royal dwarf scribe. Looking to Akish-Antum, he asked, "By the time the armies arrive will your enchantments be ready as well?"

"Yes, they will be ready. Send all weapons that need to be enchanted to my assistant."

The old king stood and shouted again, "Balam-Ek, send word. Our fifty thousand best soldiers are to report here, and they must bring all possible armor with them."

The big priest went out fuming. This would not bode well for his own plans; the Gadianton was gaining too much. This would upset the plans he had begun some months ago. Something must be done, but the high priest was not sure yet what that would be.

"Akish-Antum," croaked the king.

"Yes, Rabbanah."

"Can you forgive my impetuous son? He is my heir, my hope. I am dishonored at his idle threat to you. It will not happen again."

Akish-Antum smiled his sinister grin. "Of course, my king. Forgiveness will demonstrate our alliance and friendship. By your leave, I will begin arrangements with my engineers to provide for an army of your size. But we will need only a portion of that army."

"What portion do you mean?" asked King Xoltec, suspicious again.

"Only half, twenty-five thousand of the fiercest warriors you have. The other twenty-five thousand will be provided by King Apophis of Tullan."

"I do not trust him," scowled King Xoltec.

"For now we must be united to destroy a common threat. Afterwards, we can deal with King Apophis."

"Very well."

"By your leave," said the Gadianton. The king nodded, and the huge man left the room.

Quickly on his heels was Aaron, asking, "Will you tell me how your armor is so strong, if it is not magic?"

Looking down at the skinny, dark-haired boy, Akish-Antum smiled his awful grin and said, "Do you know how ripples are formed and move in water?"

"Yes, of course I do."

"It is the same with sound, only we do not see it. Using the right sound ripples, I can rearrange the elements within the copper to make it as strong as steel. By rearranging elements a sword will be sharper and stronger than ever before. This one is mine." He drew forth a long, straight, double edged sword. The steel was a deep blue-black with intricate wavy lines, showing that the metal had been folded hundreds of times. "This is my sword, Kadar-Lahab, the Black Flame. It has no equal in the world. It was strong steel before it was treated by the process; now there is nothing on earth stronger."

"Magic!" blurted out Aaron.

"The ancients knew this secret and many others. I am one of a handful that knows this skill. Very few Nephites know of this anymore, yet they retain a larger armory than your people. It is called exalted copper. Whenever possible my Order has taken spears, swords, knives and armor from the Nephites, but there remains a good amount of the exalted copper weapons in the Nephite armies' hands. I want to even the odds should your people have to fight them."

"You amaze me every day, master," spoke the boy, full of awe.

"Good. Because when I no longer do, I will cease to be the master." He laughed and walked on. Stopping mid-stride he turned to Aaron and said, "It begins, Prince. Wrath is coming to the world as never before."

Aaron believed every word spawned from the Gadianton Grand Master, unable to distinguish the truth from the lie. A spark of hate was fanned to flames under the guidance of Akish-Antum that would burn within Aaron all his life, a terrible fire of hate, revenge and wicked knowledge. The seeds of evil had taken full root in the boy prince.

I am Apophis

Venomous black smoke billowed into the sky over the mighty city of Tullan, Kingdom of the Sun. Tullan the Golden it was called, although this afternoon the acrid cloud lessened its gleam. Atop its great pyramid of the sun god stood a copper-skinned king, tall and proud, covered in fine silks and adorned with gold and jade. At once both majestic and cruel, he surveyed his latest handiwork. The king had a dripping blade at his side and blood on his hands.

"Oh, King, this was a mistake," said a man in a blistering hot, black robe, a dusky man with a shaven head and a prominent nose. "Even the Order of Gadianton does not seek to wipe out knowledge."

The king rounded on him. "Teth-Senkhet, second-in-command of all Gadiantons in the north, my childhood friend, my brother in the Order, sharer of the great secret, and lord of the lands of Kishkumen, do not presume to tell me how to run my kingdom. All that you are, I can end," said the tall king, now annoyed at both the heat and the man.

They were alone except for Anathoth, the king's most trusted captain. Anathoth was muscular and tall with dark hair and green eyes, an Ishmaelite, as were most of the people of Tullan; a distinction they were proud of, though to a Nephite they were all Lamanites. For the last generation they had also begun calling themselves Tultecs in honor of their city, which they deemed to be the greatest upon the face of the earth.

"I meant—" said Teth-Senkhet, quickly cut off by the king.

"I am Apophis the King, who makes ashes of my enemies' corpses! I have placed my enemies beneath my feet and made myself their master! I do what I wish," he shouted for the entire world to hear. In his mind, the whole world was listening.

The captain, Anathoth, put his hand to the wide moon-shaped knife ever ready to end the black-cloaked man's life.

"Yes, Rabbanah," said Teth-Senkhet.

"I prefer Nab Narayaw to Rabbanah. Lord of Terror is better than Great King at holding the people in place."

"Yes, oh Nab Narayaw," spoke Teth-Senkhet, the black-cloaked Gadianton.

Stern-faced Captain Anathoth let his hand leave his knife's handle.

The king laughed at the look of sudden terror on the Gadianton's face. "I rule a strong kingdom. Ever since I took the crown from my father's gory head, I have been king. I have ruled wisely these last twelve years, expanding and growing stronger. Your master is right. The time is ripe to destroy our hated ancient oppressors, the Nephites, the usurpers of ages past. My power will be complete."

The Gadianton, Teth-Senkhet, gained a little courage and replied, "Knowledge is power. So why burn and destroy the library, why slay the scribes? Why destroy the records of the past?"

"You think me foolish, don't you? You can find no comprehensible reason I would do such a thing? You should know me better. If the vainglorious records of our forefathers are gone, I can rewrite them. I can eliminate the mistakes and fallacies of the past. History will be my legacy. What I tell the scribes to write and remember will be the new truth. I am the founder of an empire that springs full bloom from out of the dust of ages. I am the god king of darkness, the wisdom from within the chaos. I command the sun to alight each and every day at my whim as a gift to my subjects," shouted King Apophis. People far below the pyramid looked up and bowed when the king looked their way.

"I concede your wisdom and ambition, Nab Narayaw," said the Gadianton. "But what of other peoples and records elsewhere? The Nephites have a vast amount that would dwarf even what you have burned here today."

"All in due time. I begin here with what I can. The library of Tullan was too vast to pick through, with far too many references to Yod He Vau. I am done with him," spoke the king, growing ever more restless. "Where is my pipe?" he asked the captain.

The tall captain turned and held aloft the king's own magnificent pipe of stone carved in the likeness of a long, snorting dragon. The king grabbed it and blew plumes of smoke that merged with the black cloud overhead. His warriors were nearly finished throwing the last of the scrolls and books into the bonfire. He looked on, pleased with himself.

"Very well, wise one. Now, my king, will you consider an answer for my master Akish-Antum?"

"Yea, I will think on it, though I am loath to commit to an enterprise with Xoltec. He has had raiders venturing into my southern-most border kingdoms. Word has only recently come to me of his warriors taking the city of Lamanihah," spoke the king bitterly through his pipe, breathing tubes of smoke out his nose. "The city should have been mine."

"Your southern-most kingdoms? Are you saying you already possessed the city of Lamanihah? Madoni was quite mad and would not be subservient to either you or Xoltec. My understanding is Madoni named himself a god-king and took the city before you could."

"You needn't be coy with me, Senket. Madoni was insane, but I could have taken his throne. I had hoped to fight a hundred weak kings rather than one strong one. I wanted all the Lamanite lands for my own, but now King Xoltec has half and I hold the other half. Something must happen to break the stalemate. Your master's plan to take out the Nephites is a sound one, but I trust not Xoltec and I cannot fight a war on two fronts, one above and one below," growled the king, still blowing scented smoke.

"I understand, oh king, and let me put it this way," spoke Teth-Senkhet. "You want what the Order wants—the end of an independent Nephite nation, and the end of the usurper's priesthood and religion." The lean Gadianton gestured with arms wide open as he spoke with conviction. "The destruction of our enemy and their very way of life is our goal. You are a young king with many years to come. King Xoltec is old and weak, and Almek his eldest son will be heir to absolutely nothing. The old bag of bones will not last much longer, and the heir won't last much beyond that. We shall see to it. We in the Order believe you are the strong one that should lead a united Lamanite/Ishmaelite nation."

"And what of your master, Akish-Antum? What must I give him in return for your help?"

"You will have to acknowledge him as the true Supreme Grand Master of the Order of Gadianton." Teth-Senkhet knew he had struck a nerve with the king. He looked over at the brooding captain warily as he waited for the king's reply.

"No, I was endowed by my father. My line is pure down to Gadianton himself. I can trace a continuous line back more than three hundred and fifty years to the first of the Order. Can your Grand Master do that? No, he cannot. When Yod He Vau came, the Order was broken up and lost among all of the Nephites, but you should know as well as I that one or two of us did survive and kept this forbidden secret. Why should anyone else lay their hands upon me and claim to give me a fullness of the Order which I already hold? I am a Grand Master myself, and regardless of what they say, I hold something more pure and direct than yours can claim. I can count back seven generations, seven direct men who have ordained my father and before him to the beginning. Anything Akish-Antum holds is debased and has passed through countless unnumbered hands. It is a mockery. Did you know that throughout the years under the dominion of the disciples of Yod He Vau, the Nephite Gadiantons did not even administer the rights correctly for over thirty years? You should know and respect these things, brother. You should join me."

"Acknowledge Akish-Antum, and you will be king of the world."

"Ha! King of this half of the world. You have been gone far too long to think me so ignorant. You insult me. I know very well of Rome and Cathy. I know of Thule and Errin, and of course Egypt and Israel. You think me an ignorant savage," laughed the king without a trace of humor.

"It has been a long time since I have seen you. I left Tullan some thirteen years ago," admitted Teth-Senkhet.

"Acknowledge me as your own Grand Master. We were once blood brothers and now you serve a Nephite!" roared King Apophis in grim derision.

"Do not say that; he is a Gadianton. No one living is more dedicated."

"He is a pale, white dog!"

"Even you would not say that to his face. White his skin may be, but his heart is blacker than the abyss of Gehenna."

"But—" King Apophis meant to speak, but Teth-Senkhet raised his hand for silence, and the king allowed him to continue.

"He is my master and what he has chosen to give me, I cannot refuse. He is the head of the Order and he, in his wisdom, has placed me as second over all Gadiantons everywhere, save those under you here in Tullan and its lands." Teth-Senkhet spoke with a calm firmness.

"What of Mutula and the people of Xoltec?" scoffed Apophis.

"Yea, even Mutula is under his dominion. Years ago he brought all the head Lamanites to bend the knee or lose their heads. But now, you are asked to bend the knee only as a member of the Order to Akish-Antum. You would still be king of all the lands."

"I would be king of the earth and Akish-Antum would be my spiritual head. I do not know if I could bear that as yet. I will meditate on it."

"I think you will find it a worthwhile trade.

"Another problem with your plan..." King Apophis began.

"Yes?"

"There is another heir besides the Crown Prince Almek. Another son."

"Yes, there is one more legal heir of Xoltec. Aaron, the one with the Nephite name. He is young."

"That never stopped me," smiled King Apophis, as he recalled his first murder. "At the age of nine, remember? I fought a group of boys within a back alley of Tullan and knifed one. I spoke of it to no one save you, Teth-Senkhet, my best friend. Inside, I was very proud of myself, for they were many and I was one."

"I am no prophet," began Senkhet, watching the king's reaction, "but the other son is of no concern, because there is also a daughter."

Apophis looked up at him sharply and grinned. Senkhet continued, knowing he had captured the king's complete attention. "Her name is Sayame. As your friend and blood brother, listen to me now if ever you would. If and when it is offered to you, accept her hand in marriage. Take her to wife."

"If I took her now, I would be honor-bound to Xoltec as his son-in-law. I would lose my inheritance in all but name. Your plan is insane," grumbled the king, frowning at his strange advisor. "I thought you meant for me to insult the old man one last time, not be subservient to him."

"Nay," cautioned Senkhet. "Not if the old king is dead, along with his appointed heir."

"But the other son, this Aaron..."

"Do not worry. As she is the older sister, the birthright of kingship would fall to you. If you let Aaron survive, he would be a figurehead lord at best."

"I have a large, beautiful harem, what need have I for Xoltec's daughter?" snorted Apophis. "Could we not simply slay all of his children rather than having to sully myself with this intrigue?"

"I have been saving these thoughts, waiting to see what you would do with our other offer of an invasion alliance," said Teth-Senkhet. "A royal union would do you well."

"I have already told you I care not for your intrigues. Out with it, why should I care for this Sayame?"

"She is very beautiful. She would give you fine sons, which none of your harem has been able to do yet."

"True," said King Apophis, frowning. It was the one thing to give him pause to his own superiority, and he was anxious to have relief from his secret shame. "How can I know she could do this for me?"

"Akish-Antum has seen it in his crystal skull. It is an interpreter. It is never wrong."

"I need to know that King Xoltec and Almek will be dead and buried soon. I do not wish to be bound too long to that old crocodile."

"All you need do thus far is supply me with good warriors. I will take them to meet up with Akish-Antum. We will journey northeast and by secret ways take them to Zarahemla to destroy the Nephite leaders. When the time is right, disaster will befall Almek and Xoltec. With the daughter as your wife, you will gain a kingdom without having to lift a sword."

"Who shall I send with you to Zarahemla?" spoke Apophis, grinning.

"We could use your good spearmen that perform the phalanx. They are the best trained of all forces," answered Teth-Senkhet, unable to conceal his pleasure.

Turning to his tall, green-eyed captain, King Apophis commanded, "Anathoth, you will command our forces and accompany Teth-Senkhet. You will also personally make sure that Prince Almek dies by any means necessary once the invasion is under way."

Anathoth nodded and knelt at his king's feet, with one knee almost touching the ground and one arm raised to the square, while the other arm was held tight to the breast in a V shape. He said nothing, for this was the sign of the Henew Rite, a sacred oath, and no words were necessary. The king knew that no matter what happened, Anathoth would follow his orders or die trying.

"It will not be a problem," said the Gadianton. "Akish-Antum has planned how and when all things shall come to pass."

"General Anathoth will see that your promises are kept. When will this Sayame be my bride?"

"Soon enough, I swear it."

"Good. Because if things do not happen as you say, I will burn you as I did these stubborn scribes, friend or no," said Apophis coldly, gesturing to the blazing bonfires far below them.

"I understand, oh king. We are at a crux of ages. Soon enough your dreams of conquest will come to pass."

Now standing upon the raised dais of his throne, King Apophis held his arms high and proclaimed in a loud voice that carried far upon the wind, "That which was forgotten by my fathers of old is remembered in me. My sword will rain fire and blood. Let the world tremble before me. I am Nab Narayaw, the Lord of Terror. I am King Apophis the Destroyer. Soon-to-be king of all our people and even those dog brothers, the Nephites."

✳ ✳ ✳ ✳ ✳ ✳ ✳ ✳ ✳ ✳ ✳ ✳

When night fell on Tullan, the dark was held at bay by leaping red bonfires of oak and sage. Only the ancient sacred tree in the center of the city was safe from burning as King Apophis, the serpentine king of Tullan, declared a holiday for the people. Everyone heard the talk on the bustling streets, that the time was ripe for the conquest over their hated brothers, the Nephites.

Newly appointed General Anathoth was silently inspecting his troops. He knew his men would not be as well armored as the Nephite soldiers, but he had great confidence in their courage and ability. Due to the heat, his people disliked wearing much clothing or armor, but they did weave together a formidable wall of reed and leather shields and long, brazen spears. Such a system had proved to be incredibly efficient whenever they had fought against large numbers of robbers or against the sons of Lemuel, Lemuelites as they were called, the people who lived to the northwest.

Even the brave fighters of King Xoltec could not stand up well against the Ishmaelite phalanx. Anathoth remembered that the phalanx was not originally an Ishmaelite system. His father, Joram-Baal, taught the armies of King Apophis's father, Apep, the system he had learned from the crafty Zoramites. The Zoramites had never been a numerous people but they were very cunning, excelling at business and trading and also in manners of war. True, there were not wars to fight during the golden years of peace under the Christ and his disciples, but the Zoramites kept hold of the records of earlier days. They learned war-craft from the Mulekites which were mingled with Spartan blood, and they knew the way of a warrior society. Modeling themselves both from Sparta and Jerusalem, the Zoramites made either good friends or dangerous enemies.

Zoramite mercenaries were more than happy to have a hand in helping Joram-Baal learn the art of war and he, in turn would teach his people, the Ishmaelites. All of these things were done when the other peoples, the Nephites and the Lamanites, were still ignorantly disputing who produced finer silk or made more costly jewelry. Modeled upon the Spartan warriors of old, the Ishmaelite Tultecs became a force to be reckoned with, conquering vast tracts of land for such a small population, while the Zoramites sat back content with the chaos, and the gold they earned from it.

A typical Tultec warrior carried a shield, a short scimitar or club of razor-sharp obsidian, and a ten foot spear. Most carried slings and short, stout bows as well. If the warrior was designated a full bowman, he would carry a minimum of fifty arrows and all the tools he might possibly need to make more while on the march. A skin pack bore their simple supplies in case of medical emergency, as well as a few days worth of food and water.

They were trained to eat as they marched, devouring whatever food-stuffs they came across in the field, forest or even desert. Water could be harder to find, so each man carried the bladder from a good-sized animal. These had been cured and processed to the point of being very durable. They trained hard for battle, and thus far they had massacred all opposing city states within a thousand miles, with the exception of King Xoltec's. It would be a bitter herb to swallow to now join forces with the Lamanites.

The Lemuelites were deemed beneath notice because of their lack of organization as fighters. They lived like savages and never built cities or stayed in one spot for more than a month. Nomads all their days, they were considered both ignorant and dangerous. If anyone could ever organize them, they would become a frightful host. They had never yet come under the rule of a single chieftain who could lead them in effective numbers.

Even Yeasues, a most capable chieftain, had not been able to unite the Lemuelites, and if he could not, then who could? Anathoth's war-craft was almost exclusively learned by fighting the barbaric Lemuelites in small skirmishes.

Overhearing the conversation between the king and the Gadianton, Anathoth did not think the Lemuelites could ever be organized, which was just as well. Let the Lemuelites stay out of this one, let them continue following the migrating bison in the north. Let them stay a thorn in the Nephite side, at least until there were no more Nephites.

Anathoth's legion looked well; he was proud of his men. They were his men, and he was the king's man, and that was how it went. The drums of the night grew louder as the heavy throb signaled the evening's event almost ready atop the pyramid of the moon. He could remember as a young boy seeing the old King Apep, Apophis's father, burying men alive within the structure as a sacrifice to their dark and bloody gods.

Lost in the past, he was startled by a hideous scream. A man in line to be sacrificed, possibly a Lemuelite from the borders, had awoken from his drugged stupor and realized his horrific fate. The screams of his mortal terror were unnerving to even a hardened warrior like Anathoth. He did not enjoy the spectacle that pleased so many of his people. This was not a way for a man to die, nor a way for a man to kill.

A shaven-headed priest hit the man in the back of the head with the butt end of a spear, knocking the poor fool unconscious. The malevolent rhythm of the drums beat on. Anathoth turned to go, his duties for the evening completed. He went hardly a quarter of the way down the street and retched. The sickness of the scene found its way inside him, and he had to release it.

"You do not care for this, do you?" spoke a voice.

Wiping his mouth on his forearm and hand, he looked up at the shadow before him to see the Gadianton, Teth-Senkhet.

"Yea, the sacrifices and theatrics of Menares, the priest, are not my nail to hammer," said the warrior with a grim smile. He would not want to look weak in front of this Gadianton, but neither would he lie.

"And what would be?"

"Ha, this is no game or show to throw away men's lives for. I am a warrior. I prefer to shed a man's blood face to face, spear to spear, and sword to sword. I have captured many men who have found their way here to die like dogs for the savage amusement of fools and hypocrites. But I have found no honor in it, nor anything to ease the shame at such an end as they have received," he said with both shame and dignity. "The priests would have us believe the sacrifices are necessary to appease the gods in times of drought and famine. I have watched. It makes no difference from year to year. Still the priests say the gods call for more. I have never heard a god say, I want more. They do not listen, they do not hear. I will no longer swear by them, it is meaningless. I no longer believe in gods that want more."

"What do you believe in?"

"Only this," he answered, holding out his moon-shaped knife. "This has never failed me."

"Then why have you served your king to such an end as this?" asked the Gadianton, curious now.

"The only reason I do any such vile work. I have given my word to serve my king. My honor is all I have, aside from my wife and soon to be child."

"What about your loyalty to the priests and counselors of the king?"

"I serve only the king and his word, not the priests. They speak of the traditions of our fathers, how they must be strictly upheld. It is all for naught; in my lifetime alone they have changed numerous things. If there is a god or spirits for them to listen to, the heavens are as brass over these men."

"You are an interesting man, Anathoth. There could be a favorable place for you within the Order," mused Teth-Senkhet.

"I appreciate your interest in me, but I could never go against my king."

"Very well, I understand. Loyalty is something highly revered in the Order. We depart in a matter of only a few short weeks. I will say nothing of our talk to anyone."

"It does not matter. The king knows how I feel. I doubt he cares what the priests say any more than I do. The High Priest Menares, on the other hand, would be outraged if he knew. He would probably claim he could put faith into my heart if only he could cut it out for a little while."

The Gadianton chuckled at that but said nothing more. He nodded farewell to Anathoth and disappeared back into the shadows.

Looking back at the black pyramid, Anathoth was overcome by the stench of burned flesh that threatened to permanently fill his nostrils. "This is wrong," he said to no one.

But another, besides the Gadianton, heard him.

* * * * * * * * * * * * *

King Apophis gloated over the scene of carnage like a hungry demon of carrion. Seeing the bodies heaped up like a dunghill before him made him feel honored. Standing like a dread lord of the apocalypse, he cried aloud in exultation as Menares pulled forth the last beating heart of a hundred lost souls. "Hear me, people of Tullan the Golden. Your king is well pleased, your god is well pleased. The food, the blood of the sacrificed, has sated the hunger of the gods for this season. Soon I shall make the rain to fall and the sun to shine forth upon my everlasting throne of blood. So shall it be! I, King Apophis, son of King Apep and the Goddess of the Jade Skirt, do hereby declare our righteous war against the despicable usurpers, the Nephites!"

The crowds went wild with reckless abandon, filled with blood lust. The mob mentality had them calling for more sacrifices and an even gorier night. Waving his hands about wildly, King Apophis tried to quiet them. "Hear me, my people! Our invincible armies will join with those of the people of Xoltec, King of Mutula."

The crowd was surprised at this. They had been getting prepared for the eventual war with King Xoltec for some time. The shock was too much for some who thought it the joke of a dangerous king. Some shouted in derision.

"Hear me, it is true. We, with King Xoltec and the forces of the northern Gadiantons, will take the Nephite lands. Our cause will be great, our share will be greater. The drum of war is beating!"

Thousands cheered in the bloodthirsty call of doom. The din of the damned rose up to the gates of heaven.

"Your command is incredible. There are few who create such frenzy with people like this," said the Gadianton Teth-Senkhet.

"If it were not, I would cease to be king. Ah, Senkhet where have you been?" asked King Apophis, finally turning his attention back to the top of the pyramid.

"So, with your announcement of war, you have decided to be subject to Akish-Antum?"

"I promise nothing as yet. He must come to me and show me that he is worthy to be my spiritual head. He may be Gadianton Grand Master of the Northern Gadiantons, a vast shadowy kingdom that is true; but I am ruler of the Kingdom of the Sun, I, Serpent of the Dark. My father had grand designs for me, giving me this sacred accursed name. He must have known that someday I would kill him."

"Indeed," said Teth-Senkhet, raising an eyebrow.

"Years ago, as he endowed me within the Order and told me the great secret, he said there were others who would try to steal my birthright. So tell me again, brother," he said, his voice dripping with disdain. "Tell me why you serve a Nephite. You, my cousin, my blood brother, friend of my youth and conspirator of my own coronation twelve years ago, tell me why you serve a Nephite!" He was shouting now.

Menares, the bloody-handed priest, watched with a wicked gleam in his eye hoping for violence.

Teth-Senkhet's dusky face was ashen. "I will tell you why. He has authority, of that I have no doubt." He paused and looked away into the deep black night as if afraid something might come rushing for him at any moment, to carry him off into bottomless gulfs and everlasting torment. "Not even for you would I cross my master, Akish-Antum." The fear in his eyes was real enough.

"Interesting. Can you tell me then, my friend, how such a relatively young man became lord of the Gadiantons? I know others like my father had seniority," said King Apophis with genuine wonder.

"Seniority yes, authority no. The Grand Master can choose any worthy successor, so say the by-laws in the Book of the Law. Any who split and would not recognize the old Grand Master, Jazer Malekite's decision were eventually destroyed and scattered to the four winds, with the exception of your father of course," explained Teth-Senkhet, as he drank from a ceremonial wineskin.

"My spies tell me the northern Order of yours has grown tenfold these last twenty years, since Jazer Malekite's death and Akish-Antum's rise to power."

"Yea, it has. He has initiated all the young, poor, hopeless, and in debt. He has brought many into the Order with a recruiting method he calls the Lost Wolf Protocols. Seeking out the disaffected was easy. He endorsed them to join the Order and thus support him. His down-line of direct followers is greater than almost all other masters combined. He is the youngest grand master ever. I don't believe any before him had the same foresight. None could have anticipated the young former apostle's drive," said the Gadianton proudly.

"Apostle? Was he really one of them? Did he serve under Onandagus the chief judge and governor of the Nephites?" asked King Apophis, now doubting everything Senkhet had told him. This was too outlandish.

"Yea, he did for a time. Something happened, I know not what, but he left Onandagus and Zarahemla behind. Going out into the wilderness, he found the Order. He found the Secret City and became one with us. Even the little I know of his past is more than most, for I am his second."

King Apophis was pleased he had learned more from a few moments with Teth-Senkhet than he had from a dozen spies for a dozen years. "And if I pledged fealty to his authority as my grand master, where would I be?"

"You would remain lord of your kingdom, king of your city and lands. However, within the Order, you would be under him and me. I can promise nothing more. I know you are a powerful man, and I tell you these things not to threaten but to inform you. This is the way the wind is blowing, and ever will it blow."

"Yea, but in my realm, both the sun and moon are stronger than the wind."

"Very well, King of Tullan. I bid you good night and hope that you will think on these matters."

As Teth-Senkhet walked away down the steep, many-stepped pyramid, King Apophis brooded upon his crimson throne, dreaming dark dreams. Menares approached him, but before the shaggy, gray-haired priest could speak, the king waved him away.

No man would take what was his. Teth-Senkhet, his old friend, was now an enemy. All his enemies will burn when the time comes. He would placate them, but he would never bend or break. He would brutalize them when the time comes. With his enemies he would smoke the pipe of peace, while in his heart beat the drum of war.

Sweet like Honey

Bethia folded up her table as Keturah put away the last box of incense. Together they took down the awning that protected them and their wares from the relentless beating of the sun. "Shagreel, my lord, you're certainly beating down on us today," Keturah said.

"Shagreel?"

"Yea, Shagreel. The sun," replied Keturah, surprised that Bethia even needed to ask.

"That's the name of a pagan god. It's not the name of the sun."

Keturah frowned and said, "You have your gods, I have mine."

"You can't be serious."

"Yes, I am serious. Shagreel is my god, so?"

"I am not trying to upset you. I was just surprised. I didn't think anyone...believed in..." Bethia went silent as Keturah's frown grew ever wider.

"We all have to believe in something. For me, I know what rises and sets every day. Nothing else in my life has been so sure. Not my five husbands, my parents, not even the weather! Shagreel is constant, him and the spirits—them you can count on."

"Spirits?" responded Bethia.

"Yea, all the spirits of nature. They are all around us, everywhere. Don't tell me you never tried talking to the spirits?"

"No I never, Father said it was..." Bethia trailed off.

"What? Wicked? I have heard it all before. I can't believe we haven't talked about this yet. Let me read your palm. I can tell your fortune, but if we consult the spirits we could get a far-reaching answer."

"I don't know. I'd rather not," said Bethia, pulling her hand back.

"Don't be afraid, it's safe. How else do you get answers about your day to day life?"

"Well, I pray."

"To which god?" asked Keturah. "Or are you one of those people who believe in that lost book about an extinct people? The Jaredodians?"

"Jaredites," corrected Bethia.

"It's all made up. They weren't real. My fourth husband was a believer, so I know all about it. I used to live down south by the city of Teancum where all the believers said the Jaredodians were, and we never found the slightest trace of them. So it's all a lie," Keturah stated with finality.

"But that's not even where my father said they were; it was north, near the hill called Ramah."

"No, it's all a lie. I know what's real. Shagreel, the spirits, and my own intuition never steer me wrong. We need to have a séance so that you can be in touch with your spirit guide."

Bethia didn't want to offend her new friend so she mumbled, "Alright." Keturah patted her on the back, just as Rezon came striding up.

"Hello, ladies. Another good day for market?" he asked politely.

"I think so, but Keturah handles the till," said Bethia beaming, her discomfort from Keturah's words washed away. "It's good to see you."

"Yes," Rezon said, as he began counting out first the senums of silver and then the seons of gold. The money was exchanged based upon measures of grain. Farmers and other rural people might do an exact rate of change with Rezon at the grain wagon booth for silver and gold, which they then took to his caravan merchants. He always kept his bank wagon towards the center of the caravan so that once people had their coin, they would see his other wagons and spend there first.

Rezon kept meticulous track of what he paid out, and how much he got back from those same customers. He remained focused on his counting while Bethia stood staring at him.

"You know Rezon, some day you should buy a home," she said.

"I have several homes. One in Bountiful, another in Cumeni, and two in Tarshish."

"Someday you may want to settle down and start a family."

He looked up at her grinning, but they were interrupted by a new voice.

"Rezon!" cried out a man with a long curling mustache. He wore a strange hat made of a dark brown fur, and he carried a decorative walking stick with an expensive-looking stone mounted on the top. "Rezon, how goes the markets?"

"Gazelem, good to see you. Sales are good. We are at almost forty-five percent profit for today. No small thanks to the ladies here. You know Keturah, and this is Bethia."

Gazelem nodded to Keturah before taking Bethia's hand. "So you have been doing well for Rezon?"

"I do my best," she said.

"How much is this rascal paying you? It can't be enough."

"Well, I just…" she stammered.

Gazelem didn't wait for her answer but shoved Rezon good-naturedly. "You take care of these girls, or by Set's hoary beard I'll steal them and have them work for me." He laughed louder than Bethia thought necessary.

"Oh, I think they are happy," said Rezon, winking at Bethia.

Bethia blushed and lowered her head, wondering if this meant he would soon be proposing something between them. He was such a gentleman, taking it slow and easy. So kind to think of her feelings and not rush into anything.

"Are you almost done? There is something I wish to discuss with you," said Gazelem.

"Almost, this was my last count of the evening," said Rezon. He was well into the gold seons now.

Bethia couldn't help but blush. He had saved her for last, perhaps to have the best opportunity to speak with her. She looked up just as Rezon finished recording the amounts in his scroll. Keturah had put away their chairs and was pulling out her jug of wine for a quick swig before locking the fragrance compartment.

"Alright, I am done. What is it?" Rezon asked.

"In private, if you don't mind," he replied, dipping his hat to Bethia. "Ladies." Keturah was still beside the wagon, having another swig. "Trouble is brewing out west, they say there is a new king…"

That was the last Bethia could make of Gazelem's words as the two men walked away. She looked back at Keturah, who now sat eating in the shade of the alley. "I'll be right back," she told her. Keturah waved a response.

Bethia paced quickly to catch up to the caravan masters. Gazelem had led Rezon around a corner to a small tavern. This one did not smell of wine as had so many others. Instead, it had a rich bittersweet aroma that prickled her senses.

Rezon and Gazelem sat at a table separated from most of the other patrons. Bethia was able to enter and sit just beyond them, with an older couple between her and Rezon. The two men had not seemed to notice her, so engrossed were they in their mysterious discussion. A serving girl brought two large mugs to the men.

The girl approached Bethia. "Do you want anything? Or are you sitting like that for a reason?"

"What smells so good?" she asked.

"Our specialty—tejate mixed with honey. Do you want some?"

Father had never allowed Bethia to have tejate, but it smelled so good. Why not? Father didn't know everything, and it was good to try new things.

"It's a drink made from beans from the south," the girl said impatiently. "Do you want one?"

Bethia nodded, while continuing to listen to the conversation between the two men.

"The governor of Shem can barely hold on, forces are at work for revolution. You must listen to me," said Gazelem.

"It's the same every year—war here, war there, it doesn't matter. People always have to eat, they always want good clothes and they always want nice things to dress themselves up a little," said Rezon, as he took a drink. "This tejate is good. You were right, it is the best."

"You are not hearing me. War is coming, and it is coming from all directions. Coriantus of Kishkumen seeks to overthrow the governor of Shem in an attempt to claim all that territory as his own."

"The people would not stand for it. They would stop him."

"They who? Any of the great men you could name are dead. Governor Onandagus is alone. Gadiantons will rule the west very soon, and I have heard they mean to rule here. You need to wake up."

"I never thought you for such a doomsayer. I thought you had a head on your shoulders," retorted Rezon.

"I have good reason to worry over such things. Finish your drink and come with me," Gazelem insisted. "I can show you someone who will change your mind."

Bethia sunk deeper into her chair as she heard the men getting up, one slamming down his mug of tejate. They walked out. The serving girl brought Bethia her mug. It smelled so delicious, but she must leave to follow the men and discover the mystery.

"That will be seven senums," said the serving girl.

Bethia was aghast at the price. Seven senums! That was what she made for a full day of work. She reached into the pouch on her belt and pulled out three senums. "That's all I have," she blushed.

"Get out," ordered the serving girl as she picked the mug back up to be sure Bethia didn't try and take it or touch it. Bethia rushed out the door so she wouldn't lose sight of Rezon.

People were passing each and every way; she couldn't see either of them. She ran a short way down the crowded street. Nothing. She went the other way almost as far as her caravan but still no sign. Maybe it was for the best—Rezon might be upset with her for eavesdropping on things that were none of her business.

The smell of the tejate teased her senses, beckoning her to come and try the most expensive of drinks. The bittersweet scent begged, and her mouth watered. She walked back to her wagon and Keturah.

"Can I have four senums?"

"Sure, you have a dozen more coming I think. What are you going to buy? Find some more silk from the Red Coast?"

"No, I want to try some tejate."

"For four senums? That is the cheapest I ever heard of. Where?" She opened up the locked money box while keeping a wary eye out for anyone who watched her too closely. You could never be too careful with all the robberies lately. That was a large part of the reason for caravans—strength and unity in numbers for protection. Rezon had a dozen men on the payroll who did little but watch out for everyone else.

"Just down the street where Rezon and Gazelem went, but it's not four it's seven," said Bethia, taking the four senums from Keturah.

"Seven, eh? That's the usual price. I guess I'll pass then." Keturah sat down again to play at her bead work. "Do you want to talk to the spirits tonight? Find out your destiny from the stars?"

"I don't know. My father never liked the idea of soothsaying. He said it was a bad idea. It makes me nervous," said Bethia, glancing about for the remote possibility that Rezon might appear.

"Nothing to be afraid of. I could ask Rezon to join us. He likes hearing his fortune told." Keturah grinned mischievously.

"Well, yes, if Rezon is there, I would love to."

"Good. I'll get my things, and we will plan on it in an hour or so."

Bethia smiled and turned away. "I'm going to try the tejate. I'll be back." She walked away, worried at what she had agreed to. She tried not to think of what her father would say about this soothsaying. Or the tejate.

She walked into the tavern and the serving girl frowned at her until Bethia held out the seven senums. The girl took them and walked back toward the kitchen. Bethia sat where Rezon had been a short time ago. She felt such a longing for him, wishing he paid her more attention. He noticed her sales of perfumes and incense, but she wanted him to notice her as a woman.

The serving girl brought her the mug of tejate and said, "I didn't think you would come back. Most of the time people try to steal a taste and run."

"I am sorry. I didn't realize how much it cost, and I didn't want to lose my friends who were sitting at this table."

"Your friends? Gazelem will be back. He forgot his cane," said the girl, pointing to the stone-topped cane resting against the chair. "I'm sure he won't be long. He forgets it all the time and then comes back soon enough."

Bethia waited. She sipped the brown drink out of the white foam on top. It was thick and sweet like honey but with a bitter nut-like flavor, altogether very pleasing.

She dreamed of the future. Rezon would be her husband, and they would have two children, a boy and a girl; not like her mother with so many little ones. Being the oldest, too many responsibilities always came back to her. Two would be perfect. They would have a big home in the hills overlooking Zarahemla. There would be white horses and fragrant gardens. They would go to dances and plays, and they would be the most pleasant, beloved couple of the city, not the despised and mocked couple her parents were. She would name her little boy Rezonihah, as was a popular title for sons named after their father and her daughter she would name...

"Bethia? What are you doing here?" asked Gazelem.

"Oh," she was startled from the daydream and spilled some of her precious tejate.

"Are you alright? I didn't mean to startle you, but I forgot my cane," he said, picking it up and then sitting down across from her.

She looked around for Rezon.

"Rezon went back to his caravan, he has a lot to think about, I hope."

Bethia smiled, a little embarrassed at the spill.

"Here," offered Gazelem, giving her a fancy embroidered cloth from his pocket. "Miss, bring another tejate for my friend."

"Thank you, but no. It's too expensive," Bethia protested.

"Nonsense. You know Rezon talked about you a little."

"Oh?"

"Yes, he did. Says you are the best salesgirl he ever had with so little experience. You know, I am taking my caravan south to Desolation and Teancum, perhaps even Tullan if news is good. I would not mind having you come along."

"Thank you, but no. I have given my word to Rezon," she blushed.

"Loyalty is good, and Rezon is a friend of mine. That is half the reason I am making you this offer."

"If you are his friend, then why would you try and take me away from him?" Irritated, she stood to leave.

"Miss, your new tejate," said the serving girl, placing it on the table.

"I don't want it," snapped Bethia.

"Bethia, calm yourself. I am not trying to upset you, but Rezon is not the man you think he is."

She frowned at him and left, returning to the wagon to sulk underneath the canopy. Why was the world against her happiness? Why did strangers have to try and separate her from the man of her dreams? Gazelem must want her for himself, the pig. If she saw him again, she would give him a tongue thrashing such as her father gave the city council whenever they displeased him. If father could do it to a council of the fifty most powerful men in Zarahemla, she could do it to some lying caravan master.

"There you are," said Keturah. "Come along, it's prepared. We are meeting in Rezon's tent, because it has a hole in the peak to let smoke escape, and I need a small fire."

"A hole in it?"

"Yes, like a Lemuelite tent. Come on."

"Is Rezon going to be there?"

"Of course, says he really wants to know some things, too."

"Is Gazelem going to be there?"

"No, just you and Rezon. Why?"

"Never mind," beamed Bethia.

The tent was circular just like Bethia had heard the Lemuelites make theirs, but this one was made with a patchwork of many fine different cloths rather than the skins of animals. A thin wisp of smoke was exiting the conical top, and Bethia hoped it was Rezon's sweet smelling pipe. Keturah opened the tent flap, and Bethia saw that the smoke came from a tiny fire set smoldering and flickering in a brazier.

Just as she was about to enter, Bethia heard Rezon's voice, and she turned to look for him. He was speaking to Peter, the caravan's black-smith. "What do you mean you can't find any steel?" he asked heatedly.

"I am telling you, there is none to be found in the city, none at all. Everyone tells me that a strange man came through three weeks ago. He bought every piece of exalted copper that could be had, money was no object. And then two weeks ago, a different man came and bought all the steel and iron available, again price and quantity was no object," said Peter. "There has been an awful lot of coin floating around, and it isn't fake. Someone is paying a lot of money."

Rezon kicked at the ground disgusted.

"Folk say that is half the reason we have had such a good couple of days here, is because everyone sold their metals," Peter continued. "Even swords and spears were sold. Crazy as it sounds, we have so much silver now, it would be cheaper to make horseshoes of silver than buy me the ingots of iron I need."

"If only we could make horseshoes of silver. Someone is having a laugh at us," Rezon lamented.

"I feel responsible," the blacksmith said. "I heard there were buyers of iron in Zarahemla last week, and I gave it no thought. There is probably no iron to be had in Zarahemla by now."

"It is not your fault, my friend. I was so excited at how well we were doing that I failed to notice that someone is preparing to rule the market. I'd wager my life that all the ore mines are now owned by a select group of individuals."

"The Brotherhood?" whispered Peter.

Rezon nodded. "I thought Gazelem was letting the fear run away with him, but perhaps there is something on the wind." He turned and looked toward Bethia. "Something sweet, like honey." He gave her a lopsided grin, and her heart melted. "Tell Keturah, I will be there in a minute," Rezon told her as another man came from behind the tent with a sack of silver.

"I will," she blushed again and went into the tent to relay the message.

Keturah grunted in reply as she looked through an open box with powders, elixirs and mushrooms. Bethia looked about Rezon's tent, wondering if someday she might call it *our* tent? There was a bundle of blankets kicked off to the side and a pair of boots exactly like Rezon was wearing at the moment. A dulcimer, lacking a couple strings, leaned against a cushion, and a half eaten joint of mutton just behind. Rezon surely needed a woman's help.

"What will you do to talk to the spirits and soothsay?" Bethia asked.

"I will pour special ingredients into the pot, and we will hold hands and call upon the spirits to come to us and tell us our fortunes. We will be granted visions of the future and be told who our spirit friends are."

"We will hold hands?"

"Yes, that's how it is done."

Bethia's heart leaped. She would hold hands with Rezon, and he would sense her passion. Tonight he would know they were meant to be together. There would be no denying it.

Keturah began sprinkling in pungent brown powders and chanting in a low voice.

"Ladies," said Rezon, popping his head through the door flap. "I, uh, can't make it tonight, I am sorry. I just got word about a possible sale of iron for horseshoes on the far side of the city and I must go. Feel free to stay as long as you want. See you in the morning."

And he was gone. Noticing Bethia's shrunken countenance, Keturah asked, "Do you still want to speak to the spirits?"

"No," Bethia responded, as she plucked a sad tune on the dulcimer with its broken strings.

What Happened in Hagoth's Landing

Miriam's cries were more than Samson could bear. It had been days now since Bethia had disappeared, and still her mother showed no signs of letting up the tears or self-recriminations.

Samson had been at peace with letting Bethia go, but she wasn't his daughter. True it was her choice, but then he went and lied to her father and said he found no trace of her. He felt himself the worst of men, a villain masquerading as a stalwart champion of righteousness, all the while a hypocritical liar. He began to loathe himself, and it grew worse every time he heard Miriam weep.

He went to the decayed side of Zarahemla, to a tavern in the Bowl called Hagoth's Landing. It was named after an explorer who sailed away and had never been heard from again. The place had a low key atmosphere he liked, and he often came here to overhear gossip and news that came from back channels and unclean sources. He drank himself into many burgundy bottles of wine, trying to forget and not feel anything anymore. But the sound of Miriam's tears still came as if they were the ocean hitting the pitiless stones of the distant shore.

"Here now look at this. It's the chief judge's bodyguard drinking hi'self stoopid," slurred a buck-toothed man. Others gathered about and laughed.

Samson ignored them and took another draught of wine.

"I got something to say to you."

Samson turned around, his hand still on his wine bottle.

"Well, the way I sees it, you owe us one," continued the lead man of the half dozen others. They were desperate-looking thugs, the bottom feeders of Zarahemla's underground. "Near all of us have been thrown into prison for a spell, courtesy of your precious judge."

"That so?" asked Samson, as his eye twitched.

"Yea, that's so. Now we got you here all by your lonesome, drunk as a Lemuelite," said the man, patting a makeshift club. The others had various weapons as well—knives and mallets.

Samson smiled and took one last draught of his wine.

"Turn around and face me, or are you a coward?" snarled the buck-toothed man.

The red rage hit and instinct took over. Samson smashed the wine bottle into the man's face and swung what little was left of it into another. He then kicked, punched, bit and stomped until no one was standing but him. Almost a dozen men were on the floor.

City guardsmen came crowding inside led by Captain Lehonti, the commander. "What happened? There's blood everywhere."

"Someone bled," shrugged Samson.

He went back to his apartment near the Judgment Hall and changed clothes. He grabbed a light coat and hat and sent a boy to fetch his favorite horse. Then he went to Onandagus. "I need to go," he said.

"For how long?" asked Onandagus. "As you know, most of my trusted men are gone."

"Don't know exactly, a week maybe."

"And you must do this now?"

"Yea."

"Be careful," warned Onandagus, watching the big man leave.

Samson knew approximately where he was going but no more than that. If anything happened to the girl he would never forgive himself. He rode out of the city's gloomy stink and into the refreshing countryside surrounding Zarahemla, covered with acre upon acre of farmland. Down the southbound road he cut through a long, steep wooded channel. On the narrow bridge crossing the River Melek, he watched where it fed the larger River Sidon. He looked up into the wheeling stars. A cool breeze slapped him in the face, and he didn't feel quite so loathsome anymore.

An Axe for the King

Zelph, hero of the war with Madoni, came to the burned mass of ruins that used to be the temple of Shagreel. He stepped over broken pottery and smashed furniture, blackened from the previous night's fire. Curious instruments of torture and pain were scattered about, giving him eerie sensations. The ruins felt alive and malevolent. If he had ever stood upon unhallowed ground, this was such a place.

Zelph had to stoop and go sideways to enter the vestige of a doorway not made for someone nearly eight feet tall. Strong as any man alive, he was the pinnacle of what the Lamanites considered a warrior's perfection.

"Ah, Zelph you are early. Good," said Balam-Ek, looking him up and down. "You are a big man, perhaps the biggest in all of Mutula next to Tazilacatzin. Once he leaves, you will be the giant of Mutula."

"What do you mean once he leaves, if I may ask?" asked Zelph.

"Yes, go ahead and ask me, but the king or prince...never ask them anything. Truly you are your father's son. Never speak to the king or prince unless spoken to. Your father's unruly ways have corrupted you. A great warrior, yes, but too stiff-necked to be a great servant of the king," said Balam-Ek. "There was a time when men heeded their king's every wish, before the bright god came to our lands from across the sea and polluted the traditions of Father Laman."

Zelph shrugged. He knew all the stories and kept his opinions to himself.

"The Gadianton Grand Master has come bearing news of an immi-nent war with the Nephites. I have dispatched all of my best spies to be sure he speaks the truth. I trust not that viper's word. King Xoltec puts too much credit in what the Gadianton says. I don't know why I am telling you all this but my disdain for Akish-Antum is no secret, and I know I can trust you. Even though I don't like your father, I respect him. He is a man of honor, and I am sure you are as well," Balam-Ek said to the towering warrior.

"Yet we have never spoken before," wondered Zelph.

"No, we have not. You are a phenomenal warrior. I do not like your lack of devotion to Baal, but you are the best man for the job. The Gadiantons could never corrupt you. These traits make you the best bodyguard a king could ask for, like your father, who will be sent north with the rest of Almek's army."

"I had not heard this news yet."

"Of course not. Soldiers are not privileged to hear court proceedings. You ask too many questions; never do so with the king or prince. It would go badly for you."

Zelph nodded, despairing inside at the news that he would be separated from his father. He would remain in the court of a vile king, while his father might die far to the north in Nephite lands.

"Come, Zelph, to the king...to take your sacred oath and be presented your royal ax." They left the ruinous temple and walked across a wide plaza toward the king's hall. "You know the importance and honor of your sacred oath, don't you? I trust that in this matter, your father has not failed to instruct you.

"Yes, I understand the honor and obligation of an oath to the king. And my father has not failed me in anything."

Balam-Ek turned and looked at him while still walking, a wicked grin upon his face. "Of course, I meant no disrespect. It's my nature to poke and pry, to stick my fingers in a wound to see why it hurts."

"Maybe the wound hurts because your finger is in there."

"Never thought of that. Next time I will have to try two fingers."

The king's hall was long, and wider than any room Zelph had ever seen before. It smelled of strange, exotic incense and tobacco. Brilliant murals mixed with jaguar and crocodile skins decorated the walls. Magnificent multi-colored birds strutted on the outskirts.

"Everyone has a designated area to be seated," Balam-Ek explained. "Higher nobles toward the front, lesser ones in the middle and servants and slaves in the back." Despite the order, many nobles thronged closer, arguing and jockeying for position above and beyond their designated stations. "You will stop that bickering, once you are sworn in."

A very small man with an abnormally large head sat near the king, writing down whatever was said. "An Alux, a dwarf, the king's scribe. They have been good luck for generations or so I have been told. His name is Tulum, but you need never speak to him. He is a slave," said Balam-Ek. "It is rude to keep staring though, so stop it." The priest smacked Zelph across the chest.

A slave girl played softly upon a stringed instrument, while another tapped lightly on a strange instrument covered with many tiny pieces of metal, each giving distinct pleasant tones. Zelph thought it was the most beautiful, elegant music he had ever heard. King Xoltec seemed not to hear. He was completely oblivious to it, perhaps from hearing the same tune many times. The king sat with his hand on his chin, sleepily listening to a nobleman with an extravagant feathered head-dress ramble on about robbers who had stolen his crops and kidnapped his daughter. The nobleman demanded justice and a posse to hunt them down.

As soon as King Xoltec saw Balam-Ek and Zelph, his eyes brightened and he dismissed the man with a flick of his wrist. The nobleman bowed and stepped away. Crown Prince Almek, seated beside the king, noticed Zelph for the first time and frowned at him.

"Balam-Ek, you have brought my new bodyguard captain. Excellent. It is Zelph, correct?" King Xoltec said in a jovial mood. "The slayer of Madoni. I am well-pleased. Now Zelph, tell me where is your umbilicus buried and how old you are?"

Confused at being asked this once again by the king, Zelph paused before replying, "I am eighteen sun cycles and my umbilicus is here in Mutula, under my father's hearthstone."

"Good, a local man who will know of our urgent need," said King Xoltec, as he walked to his chambers behind the dais.

Zelph began to ask a question but was cut off by Balam-Ek, who shook his head and gave him a silencing gesture with his long, red-nailed finger. "He is going senile, and he often asks you questions more than once. That does not mean you can ask him anything. Be silent," muttered the priest.

"What is this need he speaks of?"

King Xoltec heard him and stopped suddenly. "Has our situation been explained to the new captain? Do not write any of this down, Tulum," he said harshly to the dwarf, who looked up with sad eyes. A strange little man.

"Somewhat, your majesty," said Zelph, looking for support to Balam-Ek, who now ignored him.

"To my chambers then. Crown Prince Almek, see to the rest of the day's courts."

"But father, the games," he whined like a child.

Zelph smirked. Almek saw and glared hard at the big man.

"They will wait! You wish to be king someday? Act like one today," thundered the king. He led Zelph and Balam-Ek into his private chambers, shutting the door in the face of Tulum the dwarf.

Balam-Ek said, "Zelph, as captain of bodyguards, you are to be near the king at all times until relieved. Because we know your worth and character, you will even sleep in the palace near the king. Times are strange since Akish-Antum has arrived in Mutula. Murders and robberies have more than doubled within the city. It is no coincidence that a dark spirit follows him like a plague."

"He is still a man we can use, but he is not to be fully trusted," said the king, as he lounged upon a fur-covered chair.

The high priest continued his instructions to Zelph. "Never allow the Gadianton and the king to be alone together. Be eternally vigilant. Your very life and honor are at stake. Do not forget that in centuries past, the traitorous Nephite usurper Amalikiah slew noble King Lamoni and blamed it on his servants. They were in turn slain or chased to the ends of the earth. He then took the queen for his own and attempted to supplant our divine right more wickedly than any one man since the days of Father Laman and his cursed younger brother Nephi."

The king nodded at that but said nothing more.

"Your valor in the battle of Lamanihah is not forgotten. You will be given gold and honor. In time, you will be given a woman from the slave's quarters. You will also be supplied room and board for the rest of your days. You are never allowed any wine. A servant of mine says you do not drink, in any case," said the high priest, as he scrutinized Zelph's reaction.

Zelph nodded at that. He fought to remain silent, unhappy about this sudden development. At every turn, things sounded worse. How could he live here and still remain a pure man?

"Zelph, are you listening to me?" snapped Balam-Ek.

"Yes, I am. No wine, sir."

"Speak only when spoken to. You will be given new clothes befitting your new, exalted station. And this." Balam-Ek hefted a wide, double-edged copper ax to Zelph's right hand. It was stout and shone with an impressive sheen; the wooden handle was strong, made of hickory, like his father's staff.

"This and your sword are to be with you at all times, and you are to be with the king at all times. I cannot stress this enough. Be forewarned, the Order of the Gadiantons are up to something, I can smell it. Nothing is of more importance than the safety of the king. Do you understand?"

Zelph nodded, careful not to speak out of turn.

The king coughed. "I often expect assassin's daggers in the night, either Nephite or Gadianton daggers."

"You may have the rest of the morning off, as it will be your last day with your father for a very long time. Gather your belongings and be here at noon," commanded Balam-Ek. The priest saw him to the door then turned and went another way down the wide hall.

The ax was magnificent, probably too heavy to be wielded effectively by most men. Zelph, however, could swing it with grace and ease. Walking home, he felt proud to show it to his father, until all Balam-Ek had said came rushing back like the river free of a broken dam.

Zelph's father, Qof-Ayin, sat and listened long, his brow furrowed as he rubbed his chin in anguish. "I know what we are to do. You will take my place and I will take yours. Better I stay in Mutula guarding a degenerate king. You, whom I myself have trained, can slip away from the army at the right time to build a new life for yourself in a land of peace. Perhaps the land of Grandfather Samuel's other families in the land known as Jershon."

"I don't know where that is, nor if it exists any longer," said Zelph. "The war with the Nephites is coming soon one way or the other. Akish-Antum has seen to that. There may be no peace on earth anywhere."

"My son, there is no peace here, that much we know. You must get away and find something else. There is family in Jershon. Samuel's family was large. I believe we have many relatives there. Go and seek them out."

"I do not wish to go without you," Zelph pled fervently.

"I fear you must. There is a darkness here that means to swallow you whole. I won't allow it, even if it requires my life. I will become the king's bodyguard in your stead."

"No! My father, there must be another way!"

"It must be like this. Be strong and serve the Great Spirit. Pray and be guided."

They prayed then and knew what they must do. Zelph would go and ask the king himself to grant him this great favor.

Zelph approached the door of the king's private chamber. He rapped on the door soundly, and the old king's voice from within muttered, "Who calls? Balam-Ek? Akish-Antum?"

"Nay, it is your servant Zelph, oh king."

"You may enter," called the king.

The stone room was lit by a single torch upon the wall close to an opulent bed of Nephite origin.

"I am done with her," croaked the king, referring to the half-naked harem girl on his bed. She hurried from the room, her long brown hair unable to hide the tears in her eyes nor the welts on her back.

Composing himself to this man he despised now more than ever, Zelph said, "Your majesty, my father wishes to become your bodyguard in my place."

"What of his duties to the army?"

"I would take his place as he takes mine. Long ago he declined your generous offer of being captain of your bodyguard, and he has lived with that regret all these years. I wish to go with the army and win you and your heir much glory and honor. As I have slain Madoni for you, so would I defeat the enemies that would stand against Crown Prince Almek."

The king reached for a sack of wine beside the bed. He drank greedily from it, spilling some on himself and the bed.

Zelph's ire grew with each red drop. The face of the crying slave girl burned into his mind, and he resisted the urge to strangle the life out of the filthy old lecher, but he held still and appeared to be a humble servant of the king.

King Xoltec yawned and scratched himself, then wiped away the droplets of wine from his jowls. He looked hard at Zelph and said, "I will give the decision to Almek. If he wants you as bodyguard, then you and your father may switch duties. After the war ends, you shall return to serve me, and your father may retire."

Zelph nodded. "Thank you, my king."

"So, go now and speak with Almek," said the king, as he continued to slurp at the wineskin. "Remember, it's Crown Prince Almek."

"Yes, your majesty," Zelph said as he closed the door. Outside in the hallway, he punched a stout wooden post. It shuddered and left four huge knuckle marks indented into the wood.

"What was that?" called King Xoltec from behind the door.

Returning to his father's home, Zelph told him of the king's decision. Together they went to seek out Prince Almek.

"I will speak to Almek," said Qof-Ayin "He may listen to me."

Down a small, embanked plaza and past a central ball court, they approached the prince. He was surrounded by his personal ball team and a host of admirers. The prince saw Zelph and Qof-Ayin coming and called out loudly, "Where goes the tiger, the whelp is sure to follow."

Turning to his son, Qof-Ayin said in a whisper, "Do not react to anything he or I say. He will attempt to provoke us. Do not let him."

"Mighty Qof-Ayin and his son the giant, what are you doing here?" sneered the prince, showing off for his entourage. "I asked for no fools before the midday feast." His people laughed.

Qof-Ayin spoke kindly to him, as if he were his own child. "Crown Prince, you know that I have served the king well for over twenty years, and I would that my son serve you as I have served your father."

"What is this? A jest? Did my father send you here to mock me? Be warned I have a new dagger." His group laughed again, but stopped suddenly with a quick turn of his sullen face.

"No jest, my prince. We have come to ask you to allow my son to take my place as your scout, bodyguard and night field commander."

"Replace you? Why?" he gasped with a contorted face of mockery.

Qof-Ayin stepped closer to the prince and spoke with his hand over his mouth. "I have a sickness. I caught it in Lamanihah. It would not do to be close to you."

Stepping backward, Almek shouted, "Stop, stay back!" He narrowed his eyes and questioned, "Why does Zelph not have it?"

"His blood is not as pure as it could be. His mother was a quarter Nephite. This sickness affects only purebloods, I am afraid."

Almek made a hasty decision. "Very well, I suppose he is just as capable as you for these duties. He did slay Madoni, after all. Now get back and do not infect me or my ball team."

"Thank you, my prince," they said, both bowing deep.

As they stepped away Zelph asked his father, "How did you know he would fall for such a shallow, weak story?"

"Almek cares only for himself and his own interests. He caught a bad case of the sickness when he was only twelve summers old. It forever weakened him, and since then he is afraid of getting sick. He will never be as strong as his brother Aaron. Never mind that there is no such thing as purebloods. We are all one blood here, with a common father, Father Lehi. It's the hearts that have the impurities inside."

Both father and son came to the midday feast of the king, held in his palace on the cool westerly side. When Qof-Ayin told the king of Prince Almek's choice, both Zelph and Qof-Ayin hid their feelings, their joy and heartache, about the situation.

"Forget not, Zelph, that once this war is over and won, you will return to be my bodyguard captain," King Xoltec instructed.

"Yes, my king. What of the great ax you have presented to me? Do I give it to my father?"

Biting into a wild turkey drumstick, King Xoltec mused for a moment. "No, I had the Gadianton engineers make it for you. Keep it on this campaign to destroy the Nephites. You will wield it still when you return to serve me."

Mocking laughter came from Prince Almek who remarked, "Yes, once you return, you will serve him all your days, even to the tomb."

Qof-Ayin whispered to Zelph, "You are never coming back here. Promise me."

Although Zelph did not want to be parted from him, they each knew what had to be done. Neither one could deny what the Great Spirit had told them. Still Zelph hesitated.

"Promise me," Qof-Ayin urged, gripping Zelph's mighty arm.

"I promise."

King Xoltec spoke up again. "Something I forgot to mention earlier. Zelph, you will remain as my bodyguard for the next few weeks while I send Qof-Ayin on a mission." Father and son exchanged surprised glances as the king continued, "You, Qof-Ayin, will go immediately to help verify the truth of Akish-Antum's word that the Nephites are amassing at the borders. The other runners and spies are only a day or two ahead of you. We need our best man on this. After this fine meal, you are to go and find the truth." The king offhandedly tore into another piece of turkey.

Zelph was stunned. What would happen now?

"Patience, my son. I will return," Qof-Ayin said.

The Voice of Lilith

The road to Manti was well-traveled and well-kept. Merchants going up and down were often congested in areas near swamps and sharp turns through forests. At these places, Amaron simply took his men overland. They cut through fields or woods and then easily made their way back to the road.

Once, as they cut through a farmer's orchard, the farmer shouted at them to stay off his property and away from his fruit trees. Daniel calmly reached up and took an apple, biting into it in plain sight of the old man, who scowled at them.

"That does not endear the scouts to the citizenry," Amaron chastised Daniel.

"I know, but we had done nothing wrong. He had no right to be rude in the first place," said Daniel. He was taller than Amaron but of a thinner build. A wide grin perpetually split his face as if he knew a secret joke.

Amaron and Daniel had been friends for years, though Daniel was a year older. It had been some time since they had raced about together looking for girls. Amaron missed those times, but the past was the past. He had no regrets at how things change. That's what life is.

Amaron's group consisted of Daniel, Judah, Obadiah, Benjamin, Jared, Lehi, Nephi, Pausanias and Ezra. The first three were old friends who had drifted apart these last few years. Judah's parents had disavowed Onandagus and all who stood with him. Judah did not take sides but neither did he serve Onandagus; his new patron was Judge Levi. He had agreed to come on this mission because the judge had been murdered a fortnight ago, leaving him without a means of income.

Pausanias was another of Judge Levi's personal guardsmen. Amaron did not like the spirit he felt off the man but had no specific complaints against him. Judah had insisted he must come. Amaron reluctantly agreed, but only after Ezra verified that Pausanias was not a Gadianton.

Obadiah, a good friend of Amaron's, had moved across the River Sidon to the city of Gideon, so they rarely saw each other any longer. In a moment of fortuitous timing, they had met when Amaron needed men he could trust. Obadiah had always been a good scout, quiet and reserved. After a beating at the hands of Gadiantons within the Bowl, blinding him in one eye, he preferred to stay out of Zarahemla. He needed work and looked forward to being out in the wilderness again. He felt secure out in the wilds, no dark alleys to get cornered in here. Many feared the wilderness, but not Obadiah.

The next two, Benjamin and Jared, were the younger brothers of Daniel and Obadiah. Amaron did not know Jared, the brother of Obadiah, but he seemed a good lad of sixteen. He kept pace with the others and never complained.

Amaron did not care one whit for Benjamin, Daniel's brother, a drunkard. Since there would be no access to alcohol on the mission, Amaron had agreed to let him come.

Lehi and Nephi were twins who enjoyed juvenile, tiresome pranks.

As for Ezra, Amaron would at times pity him for his hard life, then would remember Helam and get angry again. Amaron hoped that agreeing to retrieve Ezra's cousin was not a mistake. They needed a tenth man, but what if the cousin was a Gadianton stooge like Ezra?

Marching at a steady pace, Amaron let the drums within his head beat a good rhythm to lose himself and let the worries and anger fade away. His thoughts drifted to what their mission might find and accomplish. His group might not learn anything about the Gadiantons. Ezra himself knew precious little of their plans. No need to worry, thought Amaron. Worry profits a man nothing.

"What are you thinking about?" asked Ezra, shaking Amaron from his daydreams.

"Nothing, just watching the roads," he snapped back.

"Do you have any doubts about any of this?"

"No, I do not. Why?"

"You looked deep in thought and worried."

Amaron grunted and said, "Where in Manti does your cousin live?"

"Near the north gate...we should have no trouble finding him. I assure you, he will be an asset," said Ezra. "He is a fine bowman. Are you an archer?"

"No, I'm not very good with a bow. When I was a boy I was alright, but I put it down. Years later when I picked it up again, I had lost my skill." Amaron turned his face away, not liking to admit that he was not well versed with every possible weapon.

"I have never been very good myself."

Amaron cut him off, laughing cruelly. "I know—you are a Gadianton."

"I meant with a bow."

"Uh-huh."

"I am not a bad person," continued Ezra.

"Save it for Helam. Tell him that next time we see him."

"I wish I could take it all back and I could save your friend, but it was the dagger men. Not me."

"Yea, it was," said Amaron as he threw a stone. "Stop talking to me. Say what you need to say about the mission and leave the rest. I don't like you. You are here only because Onandagus thinks you will be useful for the mission."

The others looked at him. He said the words loud and harsh, and no one said anything for a few tense moments. Amaron had always been known for his temper, which was even worse when he was younger.

Daniel was the first to break the tension. "Take it easy, Amaron. He is just looking for a big brother and you are big." He laughed at his own joke.

Amaron scowled and replied, "Let us pick up our pace. We won't make it tonight at this rate."

"We won't make it tonight at any pace, let us find a camp," Pausanias suggested.

"True enough. We will put in another good hour's march, find a good campsite and reach Gideon by noon tomorrow."

They spoke little for the next hour as they went overland like vagabonds, skirting the road's many pointless curves, through expansive forests and up low-slung hills covered in fresh spring growth. Here and there they cut across swamps where the air hung heavy with damp rot. It was nearly dusk as a light rain began to fall.

"Be dark pretty soon," drawled Judah. "I would just as soon find a dry place to camp for the night."

"Let's make camp in the edge of that glen up ahead. The trees will give some shelter," said Amaron, pointing a short distance away from the road's edge.

"Now you say we are on a secret mission, but I gotta ask, we are halfway between Zarahemla and Gideon, not in enemy territory. We oughta have a fire to cook our food," said Daniel.

"Put it in a trench and keep it small. We don't want undo attention from other travelers, but I think we will be alright, at least until we get out into the true wilderness," Amaron replied.

It was a good spot with tall hickories and oaks, even a few stout pines stood low to shelter them on the east side. The glen was protected from wind and would block all but the keenest observer from the road. A trench was dug, and the driest wood available was gathered as the rain dissipated. The near smokeless fire was soon blazing from its hidden trench, and they cooked some venison and corn with wild onions for their dinner. With two men on watch at all times, the others were able to eat and get ready for sleep.

Amaron appointed himself for the first watch. He enjoyed the night. He walked a short distance from the camp to a place facing the road. Putting his back against a wide tree trunk so he would have no silhouette, he waited ever watchful. Never once did he look toward the moon, as its brightness would destroy his night vision.

He thought he could hear faint and fair voices carried across the soft wind. The azure star-flecked night must be playing tricks on his mind. It was coming closer...a woman's voice, no, two women's voices. As they drew near he was able to make out the words that had seemed like a muted droning only a short moment before.

"There must be somewhere we can shelter near, I like not these roads at night," said the first.

"Perhaps we should have stayed in Zarahemla, mistress."

"My business cannot wait," said the first.

"Yes, mistress."

Amaron stared into the darkness at the gathering shadow which now came to fill and give shape to the voices. He drew closer to get a better look at them, still shrouded in darkness. They were two women in incredibly fine clothes, one even fancier than the other. A hulking dark man was right behind them, walking slower than necessary. He had to be a bodyguard.

"May I be of service?" asked Amaron, stepping out into the moonlight.

They froze, visibly startled. The dark man drew a wide curved scimitar and assumed an attack/defensive position.

"Hold," Amaron called to the man. "I am no robber, nor any other threat to you. I am Amaron, captain of the city guard of Zarahemla."

"Oh, my heart," spoke the first woman. "Put away your scimitar, Taharka, finally a guardsman around when you need one." She smiled. The huge dark man was not a Lamanite as Amaron had initially supposed, but an enormous, black-skinned Nubian, girded in the Egyptian style.

"We are glad to finally meet someone on this lonely road. Our chariot axle broke a mile or two back down the road. We worried that robbers might come upon us, so I decided that we should make for Gideon, but it seems to be farther than I thought."

"It is still over ten miles to Gideon from here. Who are you, may I ask?"

"Oh, where are my manners? I am the lady Zoreah and this is my handmaiden Aselin." Both wore long, silken cloaks with hoods, as was the fashion of the day. Zoreah wore gold and jeweled rings on all but a few fingers, Aselin on only one. Each was comely in Amaron's eyes, Zoreah with long black hair and Aselin with light brown hair. The eyes of Zoreah were a brilliant fiery green.

"You have already met my man Taharka. He is very capable and good at what he does, but he is a mute." The big man stood several inches taller than Amaron. He grinned in a menacing way, showing his bright white teeth. Amaron ignored him, not wanting to give him the satisfaction of a reaction.

"You may rest with us in my camp, just within these trees. I have nine more guardsmen with me. You will be quite safe from robbers."

"Really," mused Zoreah. She reached out for his hand. Hers was soft and warm. In the moonlight he could see her bright, scarlet-painted nails and lips. Her sweet-smelling perfume wafted off her body like smoke, almost hitting him in the face with its strong, desirable scent. "Thank you so much, Captain. Come Taharka."

Holding his hand tight, she moved in closer to his body. A fire erupted within him at her closeness. At the same time his still, small voice inside screamed a warning.

Back at camp, he gave her his own bedroll, and Judah's to Aselin. Taharka still grinned his wide, intimidating smile and, like an obedient dog, leaned up next to a tree near his mistress.

Judah came and drew Amaron aside for a moment feigning a jovial smile. He whispered in anger, "What are you doing? You have broken the protocol you demanded of us."

"What are you talking about?"

"You told us not to interact with other travelers, to keep our mission a secret."

"I have told them nothing," Amaron said.

"They know we are a company of ten on a mission from Zarahemla. Any Gadianton worth his blade would guess the rest and know exactly what we are doing. We should wake Ezra and ask him about this."

"I want no help of his," snarled Amaron.

"It won't hurt to see if he knows them at least."

"No, they are women that need our help. It is our duty. Such women could not be robbers."

"You never know, brother," said Judah.

Amaron knew he had broken the very orders he had given his men, on this his first outing as a captain. But these were women in need. He may have saved them from real robbers already. Feeling justified, he mocked Judah, "Stop your worrying, old woman. They are prettier than you."

Judah cursed under his breath and walked back out into the darkness to his post.

Zoreah sat beside the glowing fire, warming her gold-covered fingers. She smiled up at Amaron. He was taken by her beauty. Sitting by the firelight, she seemed to be the most beautiful woman he had ever spoken with. Was this fate for them to meet out here in the wilderness, the perfect opportunity to impress her with his new position and skill?

"I am not tired yet. Come and talk with me. Taharka can take up your watch, he is very effective." The big ebon man grinned as he patted his scimitar's scabbard, and then he ran his finger across his throat and pointed at Amaron. He gave a silent mute laugh.

"Ignore his threats." She gestured for him to sit next to her and patted the ground to further illustrate the point.

She was alluring and yet almost repellent, although Amaron knew not why. Was her thick perfume irritating, or intoxicating? He sat down beside her, confident in himself while giving in to her every command. Her face was framed with short bangs. Deeply red lips smiled.

"You are an interesting man, being a captain of the guardsmen. Out here protecting the...innocent," she said. "Tell me your story. Why are you here? What is there in this dreadful wilderness?" She stared deep into his eyes, and he found himself staring back into the emerald pools.

"This is no wilderness. Many people travel these roads and live nearby on farms or in communes. I could walk an hour in any direction from here and find people. A true wilderness would be Hermounts or southern Desolation," he replied, hoping to impress her.

"I have traveled through southern Desolation, a wretched wasteland."

"You have been there?" He was surprised. It was not a common destination, especially not for rich, beautiful women.

"Yea, I have traveled much in my time. But you are just a youth, and there is much time for you yet. How old are you?" She smiled to take the sting off her words regarding his age.

"I am eighteen summers old."

"Ha, in the darkness I thought you to be older, but your eagerness betrays you. How old do you think I am?"

Not wishing to offend he guessed lower than he believed. "Twenty-five?"

"Close enough. I am thirty winters. Surprised?"

"Why have you traveled so much?" he asked, hoping to change the subject.

"Business. My father is a lord in the west near to Joshua. Here...try some of my wine and tell me of yourself. And why you and your men are out here in this lonely place." She smiled and offered the wine.

"I do not drink strong drink," he said, sliding back a little from her. She smiled and touched his shoulder with soft, sweet-smelling hands.

"It is not strong but fresh, please try it." She spoke in a soft, enticing tone.

He took the skin and drank a small swallow. It was sweet, and he detected no trace of it fermenting. He took a deeper swig. It seemed all right at first, but a strange aftertaste hit him as he put it down.

"It is good, is it not? Now what are you doing out here?" She caressed his cheek then rubbed his shoulder.

He felt a strange sense of detachment, aware of nothing but the fire and the two of them. He wanted to please her. Beneath the bright killing moon, she stared into his eyes. Moving closer, she breathed heavily on his neck. "Tell me, what are you and your guardsmen doing out here in this wilderness. What are you looking for?" She moved onto her knees to bear down on him and look deep into his eyes.

"We are on patrol, looking for Gadiantons. They may be staging a revolution of some kind," he said, slurring just a little.

"That sounds far-fetched to me. But tell me more. How did you hear of this wild tale?"

"That's simple," he said, taking another swallow of the wine, when she plied him. "A traitorous Gadianton rogue told us about it."

"Oh?"

"Yea, he is with us even now, yonder..." He pointed, realizing dumbly that they were now both away from the camp out into the trees. He felt a strange call to return, but she grabbed his hand with a surprisingly firm strength. She took both his hands and made him face her. Dropping her cloak down about her feet, she revealed her bronzed skin with only a simple scarlet girdle over her beautiful body.

"Hold me, my love," she whispered hot into his ear.

How had he not noticed her leading him off into the darkness? Never before had he felt so dazed and confused. She took him in her arms and kissed him on the mouth. Never had anyone kissed him with such hot passion, and he forgot everything.

She pulled away suddenly, looking up at him with deep emerald eyes. "Do you believe the traitor? Do you or Onandagus think the Gadiantons are coming? What about the Lamanites?" she asked, licking her lips. She held up the wineskin to him.

Amaron shook his head and said, "Onandagus? I spoke not of him earlier."

"Yes, you did. You serve him, do you not?"

"Yea, I do. He is the chief judge as well as the head of the priesthood. He is my head." Rubbing his brow, he tried in vain to shake off the confusion and thick head. Stamping in place and blinking rapidly, it subsided for a moment. Standing before him in scarlet glory was a most beautiful woman...what did she say her name was? "Who are you? Why do you ask of my mission?" he asked with a heavy tongue.

She caressed his chest and kissed him hotly once again, clouding his mind over. "Tell me," she whispered into his ear. "How many more guardsmen are searching for Gadiantons...I need to know," she whispered into his ear, her breath hot and sweet.

"Ten captains of ten."

"Wonderful, do you know where they are?"

"We each took one of the ten roads to Zarahemla. I am not supposed to be on this one, but to the west on the old Hermounts trail. On the way to Cumeni."

She smiled a wicked smile and patted his chest before pushing him away. "I cannot believe the luck," she murmured, then shouted "Taharka!" Suddenly the big Nubian was beside them. "We have actually come across the scouts who are supposed to be on the true route. We need not worry about finding the others."

Amaron stared at her. Her voice was different now that she was no longer speaking sweetly to him. Why did he recognize it? They had never met before.

Ezra sat up from his bedroll and saw the girl Aselin as she leaned over the sleeping Daniel with a potion bottle in her hand. A foul-colored spittle hung from Daniel's mouth and chin. Ezra looked and saw Amaron in a stupor beside the woman in the dark. He heard her voice as she spoke to Taharka and knew immediately who she was.

Shouting madly, Ezra warned his new friend, "Amaron! Amaron, what are you doing? Get away! That is Lilith. She will destroy us!"

Amaron thought he heard someone call his name. He looked about in the gloom but could see only a beautiful, sinister woman and a huge, grinning dark man.

"Aselin, why did that one awaken?" snarled Zoreah.

"I'm sorry, mistress, he was the last and I had not yet administered the potion to his lips," she cried in fear.

Who is crying? Amaron sensed a distant danger that drew ever closer.

"I have drugged this one enough for a dozen men and still he stands gazing at me in love," said Lilith.

Amaron continued staring at this vision of loveliness before him, dressed in a scarlet garment, revealing enough to make the sailors of Phoenicia blush. *Who is this woman? No angel was ever this tempting, no devil this lovely.*

"Amaron, my love, take your sword and slay the man you hate. Slay the traitorous Gadianton!" She pointed at Ezra still lying on his bedroll, staring up in great fear. Amaron drew his sword, the dreaded Ramevorn, and held it high over Ezra's quivering skull.

The Dust of His Feet

For two and a half weeks, Qof-Ayin and the other spies kept a grueling pace, traveling farther and faster than ever before in their lives. Near the suspected border of the Nephite lands, the spies separated to better hide in the broad, brown desert. Passing down some low hills near the borders of the Nephite lands, Qof-Ayin saw his first Nephite city.

It sat on the horizon toad-like, a large squat, mud-brown thing atop a wide hill. Towers lined its wall, with a trio of higher towers reaching up toward the unforgiving sun. Scattered farms and fields lay spread around it a mile or two, green and brown lines crisscrossed in all directions from the center. This had to be the city of Desolation, a cruel joke. Who would want to live here? Hardly a tree for miles, just bleak rolling hills with tufts of scrub brush and grass clinging to the hillsides against an ever-present wind.

Nephites are a strange people, thought Qof-Ayin. He had met but a few, who were proud and arrogant, believing themselves superior in all things without having much understanding of the world about them. No wonder his great-grandfather Samuel had to go and teach them.

Gazing about, Qof-Ayin could see no one near, but remained cautious. Moving closer to circuit the area, he found the Nephite city's water source—a murky brown river, wide but not too deep. It flowed well enough. Qof-Ayin moved cautiously across the river to the northwest side. Several farms were near, irrigated by the muddy river, but he had no trouble sneaking past these without being seen. The farmers did not seem wary of trouble or preparing for war.

Teancum was another large city not far away toward the coast of the Sea of Enoch. He decided to travel farther north to the narrow passage and let others investigate the city of Teancum. Being a captain of the army, Qof-Ayin supposed an army would be marshaled at the pass near the city of Boaz instead of these open rolling hills, where men would grow restless under the merciless sun. It was not a good place to let an army sit; the battles near the Black Mountains of Tullan had taught him that hard lesson years ago.

A lazy wisp of smoke curled up to the sky, beckoning someone to investigate. Qof-Ayin smiled at the foolishness of these runners and spies. Several times he had seen small cook fires with the smoke giving away their position. On second thought, he felt ashamed, as he had trained many of these men. They should have known better. Who could be so foolish? Qof-Ayin wondered if it were those who had been to the east of him on the journey, either lean Cahok or stout, sturdy Tzumin; both young and inexperienced, but not half-wits. Something wasn't right.

Knocking an arrow he started toward the smoke, stooping low to the ground. Traveling from bush to bush, he stalked a wide, cautious half-moon circle about the camp, always keeping low of the horizon so as not to silhouette himself. Satisfied that no one was waiting outside the camp to ambush him, he came toward it from upwind. Coming in low and quick, he saw the smoldering fire in the slight gulch surrounded by sage brush. Not the worst spot to camp as far as cover was concerned, but certainly not the best if it rained.

Two bodies were sprawled on the ground—Cahok and Tzumin. Cahok's throat was slit, and Tzumin had three arrows in his back. Qof-Ayin recognized the dogwood shafts with red dyed fletching. He pulled one out to examine the finely crafted, copper tip. His people used only obsidian and bone for arrow heads. This was a Nephite arrow.

Something else wasn't right. His people always retrieved their arrows unless irreparable, and these were fine. These had been shot into Tzumin from close range and with a low pull. Someone stood right over him and shot him in the back while he was asleep, wanting their arrows found. Nephites were a strange people, but this was a waste. It made no sense.

The fire would smolder for several hours to come. Someone had stoked it well only a short time ago, clearly wanting the spot found. Tracks around the camp suggested that at least four men had been here, or rather five.

A blood trail showed where Cahok had tried to run before being struck down and carried back to camp by the man with the heavier tracks. Qof-Ayin's skin crawled at the thought of this sinister set-up and knew he must leave immediately. As he turned to go, a man on horseback shouted to him in the tongue of the Nephites.

"Ho there. Who are you?" A mounted Nephite called to him. Three more riders rounded the hilltop. "I said who are you?" he called again louder.

"It's a Lamanite," said another.

If he ran, they would think him the guilty one. Qof-Ayin lowered his bow to be non-threatening while retaining his hold upon it. These would not be the murderers. There were no horse tracks here, only moccasin and bare feet. Nephites were strange; they never went anywhere without shoes.

The four horsemen were just about upon him when they saw the bodies. "Holy Ashtoreth, this savage has murdered his companions," one swore as he drew his sword. Two more drew their bows and nocked arrows.

The leader remained calm and asked with patience, "Why did you do this?"

Qof-Ayin could not remember his Nephite very well but hoped it would be serviceable. "It was not I. Found this camp. Found dead men."

"Who are you, and why are here in these lands?" asked the leader again, a tall blond-haired, bearded man. His blue eyes were fierce, like a warrior's. Qof-Ayin could respect this man.

"Qof-Ayin, my name is. Grandson of Samuel. I hunt and become lost."

"He's lying! This is some kind of Lamanite twist!" shouted the horseman with the drawn sword. "Cut him down and leave him like the others."

The leader raised his arm for silence, and the rider calmed. "There will be no such thing under my command." The leader dismounted and looked at the bodies. "It seems to me you had a falling out with these men and you robbed them. Those pouches are empty."

"Not my arrows in their backs," protested Qof-Ayin. "See here." He showed his quiver to the leader, who looked shrewdly at this Lamanite and his arrows before turning to examine the ground again.

"No, they aren't your arrows, at least not the ones in your quiver. But there are no horse tracks, just moccasin tracks like yours."

Qof-Ayin did not like where this was going. "I give my word I not did this thing," he said, eliciting the bowmen to pull back a little on their bows as they smirked at his poor Nephite tongue.

The leader spoke to him. "Strange things have been happening in the lands hereabout lately, and I think I know what they are."

Qof-Ayin stared at him with eyes of stone.

"I am Captain Limhi of the city guard, and you are not the first Lamanite to turn up around here lately. Now tell me the truth of your doings here. Your kind doesn't get lost, not this far north anyway."

Qof-Ayin looked at him sullen, saying nothing.

"Do you lie?" asked Limhi.

"No," answered Qof-Ayin.

"Did you know these men?"

"Yes," said Qof-Ayin reluctantly.

"Why did you kill them and make it look like Nephites had done it?"

"I not kill them. I found them before you did. Tracks say they killed by five men. See yourself." He gestured to the tracks, which were plain to him.

Captain Limhi spat at them. "I don't see it that way. You murdered them to stir up trouble against us, and then you were fool enough to stick around long enough to get caught. Throw down your weapons, in the name of the Judge Morihor."

Feeling he had no choice, Qof-Ayin dropped his bow and unbuckled his sword belt. One of the men dropped off his horse and gathered them up while another bound his arms behind his back and attached a rope to his waist. He was forced to follow behind the third horseman. They gave him no water on the three mile march back to Desolation.

It was near dusk as they approached the city gates. These were old twenty-foot tall walls, built of picketed logs then covered in adobe. Most were crumbling, revealing the wood beneath. The gates themselves were new and strong, made of a wood similar to hickory or oak, riveted together with copper.

Inside the open market plaza there was all manner of buying and selling, not that different from the markets of home. Qof-Ayin noticed some fruits and vegetables he was not familiar with as well as a few strange animals. Turning down a side street, they passed what he thought was a church. The doors hung open, broken on their hinges. Dirt and bird droppings covered the floor. The wooden building lurched as it rotted from the inside out.

Scantily clad women lined the street and stared at him. "Who is this strange looking man?" called a brown-haired girl with makeup so dark about her eyes it looked like a mask.

"Another Lamanite we captured lurking about the city. He murdered his companions," said Limhi, looking down at her from his high horse.

"Savage!" she sputtered at him, and threw a glass of something that smelled of wine, although with a foul and foreign scent. Qof-Ayin tried to move away to the other side of the street but was met with more jeering. The women began to throw trash and small stones at him.

"Enough!" shouted Limhi, "I won't tolerate this from any of you. You'll spook my horse."

"See you tonight," called one of the ladies of the night.

"Yes, when I have finished here," laughed Limhi.

Qof-Ayin feared there would be no justice from these people. If he did not return to the palace and serve King Xoltec, Zelph would never be allowed to leave with the army. Limhi dismounted his horse and took the rope holding Qof-Ayin from one of his men, leading the prisoner into a thick-walled adobe structure that stunk of sweat and waste. A guard sat nursing a jug of foul-smelling wine.

"Watch this one, or by Dagon's beard you'll join him in the dungeon. You hearing me, Micah?" shouted Limhi. The man called Micah nodded and took another swig of his wine once Limhi's back was turned.

Thrown into a stench-filled adobe cell, Qof-Ayin took stock of the situation. It was about twelve foot by twelve foot with a single, heavily barred door and a small slit of a window, also barred. A man dressed in rags lay asleep in the corner. He faintly stirred as Qof-Ayin exerted himself on the bars.

After a short time the raggedy old man coughed and awoke. He blinked in the moonlight creeping in through the bars. "I am Abinadab, and who are you, my son? Why are you here?" he asked in a friendly tone.

"I am Qof-Ayin," he responded roughly in his own language.

"Oh, a Lamanite. How fare your people, my brother? I have not been down to your lands in many years," the old man continued, changing to the Lamanite tongue.

A friendly Nephite who spoke Lamanite? This surprised Qof-Ayin. "They are dire times," he replied politely.

"Yea, it's bad all over. Why are you here?"

"They accused me of killing two men out beyond the gates, but I did not. The city guard would not see the evidence for themselves."

"I understand the ways of these men all too well."

"You are old, what could you have done?"

"I told them the truth, and that is more than they can bear," Abinadab said. "I have been preaching repentance to this city for three years now. They have cast me out forcibly numerous times and even shipped me bound and gagged as far away as Tullan." He grew serious, the smile on his face darkening slightly. "But I am commanded to return and preach. This is the last time I'll be cast into prison and beaten, starved and tormented. The Lord has told me it is enough, I am to be freed soon, and then I am to wash the dust of this place from my feet."

"The Great Spirit speaks to you?"

"Yea, he truly does."

"Then he has guided me to you, that I may learn more."

"Yea, he has."

They spoke for many hours, and Qof-Ayin knew the truth of Abinadab's words. Many questions left unanswered all his life were made clear by this sage and seer.

"It is about time," said Abinadab, seeing the brightness of the moon now darkened by cloud cover.

"What time? Have you a plan?"

"No, I only know the Lord will provide something tonight when the time is right."

A whisper came to the window. "Brothers." It was a woman's soft voice.

Looking out the window, Qof-Ayin could see a slender woman reaching up high to hand him a stout rope. "Who are you?" he asked her.

"Don't worry about that, I am here to help. Tie it around the bars well and be ready."

He did so, and standing back from the window, he heard a whip and the grunt of oxen. The rope grew taut until the wall section flew away.

Holding Abinadab back a moment, Qof-Ayin waited for the dust and the falling debris to clear. He helped the old man out over the strewn adobe and iron. The woman stood beside the oxen, whip in hand.

"This way quickly!" she said over her shoulder as she ran. Men shouted from behind the locked door of the prison. The woman led them down a short alley to a stable with four horses waiting.

Another woman came running and mounted the first horse. "We must flee!" she called, racing her mount out the door. They helped Abinadab climb atop his horse, and they trotted toward the gates.

Qof-Ayin feared the gate would be shut at night, but it was open. Yet another woman on horseback was waiting for them just outside. All five careened out into the star strewn night and crossed the muddy river. The shouts of anger and cursed frustration were left far behind. As the wide, golden dawn broke the eastern horizon, they cantered the horses and came to a stop beside the river far upstream.

"My thanks to you, sisters," said Abinadab. He took off his ragged head scarf, and the sunlight reflected off his bald head. Just a hint of fuzzy white stubble grew around his ears and the top of the neck.

They dismounted and watered the horses. Qof-Ayin recognized the women as harlots from the street in Desolation, among the few who had not stoned him.

The first approached Abinadab and said, "We were waiting for the right time; our apologies for your misfortunes."

"You three are the only ones who listened and learned regardless of past sins. Now the Lord's judgment is to be fulfilled upon the city of Desolation. I wash the dust from my feet off that cursed place."

Qof-Ayin watched in amazement as Abinadab sat at the edge of the river, rinsed his feet in the murky river and offered a simple prayer.

"Where will you go now?" Qof-Ayin asked after a moment.

"We will travel north. I have a brother I have not seen in years, and the cities north have just as much need of hearing God's word as this one did. And you, brother, where will you go?"

"South, to my son. There is much I must teach him."

"I understand. Tell your son to keep well away from Desolation. There will be a terrible sickness there for some time."

"I will. Thank you."

"Listen, my Lamanite friend—you will be required to make a great sacrifice, as did Abraham and Isaac. Remember and be strong. May the Lord bless and keep you." With that they departed in opposite directions, Qof-Ayin to the south, Abinadab and his three companions to the north.

Two days later along the trail, Qof-Ayin came upon another dead spy with three Nephite arrows in his back. The next day he found yet another slain spy. He recognized the man's face but did not know his name. His throat had been slit, and a broken arrow protruded from his back. Following the dead man's back trail, Qof-Ayin found a well-concealed camp containing the dead spies' equipment and weapons.

Searching the ground meticulously, he found a Gadianton dagger buried in the dirt and brush, a ceremonial dagger. It all made sense now. Akish-Antum was manipulating the war. There was no war but the one he created.

On horseback, he made good time over the next week, traveling the trackless miles to home. He slept in the saddle or upon the ground, when he let the horse rest. That was when they found him. Three Lamanite-Gadianton braves, one barefoot. Hard and calloused though his feet were, one of them stepped upon the sharp spines of a cactus in the dark and cried out in muffled pain.

Qof-Ayin awoke in an instant. They had meant to slit his throat while he slept, but he rolled hard and fast to his left. They missed his throat, but his arm took a horrible gash. He slashed back at the foes with his simple dagger. He wheeled around and caught one in the heart, twisting the dagger as he ripped out the man's heart. Tumbling to one side, Qof-Ayin rolled as the other two rushed him from opposite sides. He came up sharp and slashed the dagger across mid-thigh of the first attacker. It went deep, a mortal wound. The Gadianton stopped and slowly pitched forward as darkness took him. Qof-Ayin now turned his full attention to the last assassin who, seeing his two dead companions, fled into the night.

Weary from loss of blood, Qof-Ayin bound his wound tight and fell upon his horse as it took him into the night, away from the stench of death.

Through a Rent Veil

The hammering in Amaron's head wouldn't stop. He blinked, and his head throbbed, his strong arm heavy with the weight of his sword Ramevorn, held high and ready over the cowering enemy.

What is that screaming? It won't stop.

"Amaron, no! She is Lilith, the Gadianton's woman!"

Someone was shouting his name. *Who?*

"Amaron, my love. Kill the man you despise. Slay the traitorous fool. Kill him. Kill him now!"

Amaron blinked again at the enemy on the ground before him. The man on the ground stopped shouting, his eyes closed tightly. Ezra could not bear to look death in the face like a true warrior. His arms were folded across his chest, his lips moving ever so slightly.

Is he praying?

"Amaron, kill him!" shrieked the madwoman at his side.

Why should I strike down an unarmed man, who down upon his knees prays for deliverance? Amaron hesitated, staring dumbly at the little man.

"Oh, he is worthless, too much of the leaf in his system makes him catatonic," said the woman. "Taharka, kill them both!"

The mountainous ebon giant pulled his copper scimitar free from its rich leather scabbard and stalked toward the two men, grinning in a devilish delight. Still blinking, trying to clear his head, Amaron heard her give the order and the mute giant approach. Although weakened, he knew the reach of his broadsword. When Taharka was within reach, Amaron wheeled on the ball of his right foot and swung the blade.

It bit deep, and the Nubian smiled no more. Lilith screamed and drew a dagger from her girdle. Amaron faced her with both a dark scowl and naked red sword. She turned and fled into the black night, her servant girl beside her.

"The Lord answered my prayer. He had you save us," exclaimed Ezra.

Amaron looked at the man he had hated and saw now a friend. Exhausted, he lay down and fell asleep.

* * * * * * * * * * * *

Afraid that the guardsmen would pursue and slay her, Lilith ran headlong onto the welcoming rapture of darkness. She ran over thick brambles and fallen logs until she collapsed, never once looking back. She had lost Aselin somewhere far back into the dark trees. She heard the girl calling for her, but nothing on earth would make her reply and risk being taken by that stoic madman of a hero. She cared little for Aselin anyway. If the fool of a servant girl had only given the potion to the traitor more quickly, then Amaron never would have awoken to conscious action.

Taharka was the greater loss to her, far beyond anything a thousand Aselins could ever be. Her bodyguard had been too confident, striding over to the Nephite without his guard up. Fool to approach even a drugged enemy wielding a drawn sword. Since buying him from Phoenician traders, Taharka had been her manservant and bodyguard for ten years. He had been trained by both Akish-Antum and Uzzsheol, the Lamanite tracker assassin.

Taharka was dead and the Nephite Amaron would slay her on sight. There would be no chance for her to turn Amaron to the Order. That cursed Nephite. She would not return to Zarahemla now. It would be too dangerous. The guardsmen might turn back and find her. She could not take that chance. She made for the city of Bountiful due southeast. If she hurried she could make it before anyone heard of her mishap. She wanted none to know she had failed, even if it was the fault of Aselin and Taharka.

Running, she tripped and fell. Darkness engulfed her in thick shadowy arms. As she lay there in the gloom thinking, she noticed that it was almost dawn. The sun would be coming up soon and there had been no hint of pursuers catching up to her. Maybe things would go well on this new day.

Make the best of it, she told herself. She got up and began to walk through the trees toward a road that she knew would take her to the city of Bountiful. There would be plenty of the Kindred in Bountiful to help her. She would return to the Wasp Nest, the lodge of Akish-Antum, her husband.

* * * * * * * * * * * *

When Amaron awoke, it was nearing late midday. The others were awake but still groggy from whatever potion they had been given. Judah had the worst of it; he had been persuaded to drink the most by the hand-maiden.

"I have told them how you saved us by overcoming the poisons. You are a hero," said Ezra. The others all looked appreciative and marveled at the huge body of Taharka lying just outside the camp.

"Don't say that. It is my fault. I let my guard down for a pretty face and it nearly got us killed. I did not look beyond the bend in the river."

"How could you have known?" asked Ezra.

"A good scout knows. I am sorry, I endangered us all. It will not happen again."

"Still, you are the one who saved us," said Ezra.

"Don't," commanded Amaron with a glaring eye. He stood on shaky legs and said, "Let us move on. We are behind on the road and the demo-ness has gone on before us. Let us be wary."

"What do you want to do about that?" asked Daniel, pointing at the body.

"We will bury him," said Amaron.

"But he wanted to kill us," said Ezra.

"I didn't say we had to bury him very deep. Get to it, we must move on."

After burying Taharka, they gathered their gear and began the long hot march to Gideon and Manti, under a blazing, angry sun.

Choose Ye This Day

Within the assembly room of the Judgment Hall, fifty men sat impatiently awaiting the arrival of the chief judge. The white plastered walls were plain, the hard wooden benches ornate. Tension filled the room as these leading men of the nation sweat under a late spring heat wave.

"Onandagus wants us to suffer. He yearns for the days of servitude when the people served the priests and disciples like kings," complained a council man of enormous girth.

"Why do you say that?" asked the young man beside him, scribbling on a scroll.

"The man is a fanatic and too powerful. Chief judge of all the land, governor of Zarahemla, and the priesthood head of his church besides. He opposes the king men because a king would take away his ruling power and give it to someone else."

"So you support the king men?" asked the young man.

"Don't you dare write that down," bellowed the fat man. "What's your name?"

"My name is Simon, a scribe. I am here to record the events for posterity."

"I will tell you this as a member of the Council of Fifty. The program is flawed and needs to be changed, but I do not support the king men. I will not trade a tyrant for a zealous fanatic."

"And who are you, sir, if I might ask? I will not record nor speak of our conversation."

"You don't know, huh," he chuckled. "I am Barkos the Fat, and yes, I am the richest man in Zarahemla. I am the man you have heard of. I own a large portion of the south and west side of town. I own and run the best mail service in all of Bountiful land."

"Yes, but they also say you took advantage of people with your privately owned fire department."

Barkos the Fat glared at him. "Some would say that yes, better to sell their home to me for a pittance and keep their belongings than lose everything. Am I a bad person to make a profit by being prepared? I saw a need. Every Nephite home, every Nephite building is wood and plaster, except a few fools cementing homes out west where they cannot even grow a tree. Do you have any idea how many buildings burn down every year? I thought about it and attached water tanks to wagons and employed an army of men to fight fires."

Simon muttered, "Isn't there more to it than that?"

"Alright, my fire captains will not begin work until the inhabitants first sign over the deeds to their houses," Barkos the Fat said. "Then, I let the people keep their belongings."

Simon had nothing to say.

"Oh no, you can't say anything, can you? Everyone is jealous that I thought of it first. Some tried to do the same. All failed. That is life. I became a member of the Council of Fifty to protect my interests, not to wait on a religious fanatic all day. Where is he?"

The oaken doors swung open, and Onandagus entering seemed surrounded in light. The chief judge took his place on the podium. Close behind was the elderly Ammaron the Scribe, who acted as his secretary.

Onandagus spoke, "I have received dire and disturbing news. The Gadianton robbers are soon to be engaging in a full-blown war against our liberty, our freedom."

A gasp was heard from a large number of those assembled. A few, like Barkos the Fat, guffawed. Several shouted in disbelief and indignation.

"Please allow me to continue. These Gadiantons and king men are behind the strife that will soon infect us. They prepare to enslave us."

"Rubbish!" shouted a man from the back row.

"These king men, some of whom I believe are in this room, plot even now to raise the bladed and bloody hand of the Lamanites. They inflame their longstanding hatred against us, and a battle could be disastrous.

The Lamanites outnumber us ten to one. Preparations must be made. Every guardsman must be called up to active duty and all available men impressed and trained in the basic service."

"You're mad!" shouted the man from the back once again. "You seek excuses to gain power for yourself."

Multiple men shouted him down as a few others grunted their affirmation at what was said.

"We must be prepared. The Lamanites are a warlike people who can surely best us in open battle," called one from the first row.

"Bah!" said a burly judge directly in front of Onandagus. "One Nephite warrior is worth twenty of the armor-less heathen savages."

"Honorable Cezoram is ill-informed. Just one of Onandagus's personal guards is worth more than a hundred Lamanites," said Barkos the Fat.

"I have the floor!" thundered Onandagus, and all was silent once again. He stared hard at Barkos the Fat. "If I want a debate I will ask for it. The next man who interrupts me will be ejected from this meeting."

There was silence for a moment. Judge Hiram stood. "Samson is not present, and your other loyal guardsmen are mysteriously absent as well. How will you go about enforcing your arrogance and contempt for us—this council and your fellow judges?"

A heavy anticipation hung in the air while men on both sides of the debate watched hungrily to see what would happen next. Would the cantankerous chief judge rail against them or would it turn into a Lemu-elite standoff—like two yellow dogs, chained, slavering and barking at one another without either making progress?

"I will enforce his will," boomed a deep bass voice from the open doorway. All eyes reeled to look over at the Titan of a man who entered. Beside him stood a large boy on crutches. The man strode into the hall as if he was its rightful owner and they were but trespassers.

Most knew him; it was Mormon the Elder and his son Mormon the Younger. Big and imposing, he commanded attention. Gray hairs were beginning to show here and there through his thick, red-brown beard, but his broad shoulders and thickly corded arms intimidated men half his age. He was a born fighter, and no man claimed to have beaten him. Many had tried in their time; all met the hard, merciless hands of fate with equal regret.

As Mormon walked in, he doffed his winged helmet of copper and iron and handed it to his son. He did not take off his sword belt as was the custom within the Judgment Hall. He stopped in front of the podium of Onandagus, and with ice blue eyes, he looked over those gathered. "Please allow the chief judge to continue. Any more unnecessary comments and I will throw you out!"

Onandagus continued, "Brethren, gentlemen and citizenry—allow me to introduce my right hand, the former governor of the northern quarter, Mormon of Antum. He is now my reserve lieutenant governor."

"You can do no such thing," they shouted. "You have no right. He has no seniority."

Before Mormon could act, Onandagus thundered again, "I have the authority to appoint any worthy man I choose, seniority or no. It is very clearly stated in the Book of Commandments."

"You are mad. You have no right to supersede us who are the rightful heirs of the city and state. You have no right; it belongs to one of us, the Council of Fifty," screamed Cezoram.

Calm as a summer's day, Mormon walked over and picked up Cezoram by the collar and belt. He walked him to the door and threw him onto the street. Turning on his heel, he said, "Who's next?"

All remained silent.

"Regardless of what you may think of me, I, as chief judge, have the right to appoint any worthy man. Now, on to the real business at hand. Gadiantons, king men and Lamanites are threatening us. My sources have told me that something will happen within months, or even weeks. Most likely the Gadianton Grand Master, Akish-Antum, is aggravating Kings Xoltec, Apophis and Madoni to war with us. This would make him guilty of being a warmonger and under our law, the warmongers and their ilk are to be dealt the ultimate justice."

A man said, "Forgive me, but this sounds preposterous. You speak of war as if it were a possibility. There have been no wars in almost three hundred years. Perhaps we should rethink the punishment for a crime that no longer exists."

"Warmongering is a crime that has not disappeared from off the earth," said Mormon. "The Lamanites still battle the Ishmaelites and Lemuelites with regularity, and they will come here sooner than later. War is the ultimate crime because it is all crimes combined. When you start a war, you are guilty of murdering cities and lands. Thousands of souls are upon that man's head. It is the worst of crimes imaginable."

Onandagus nodded. "That is only half of it. These things happen for a reason, nothing in life is without purpose or meaning. We as a society have let far too many plain and precious things slip from our grasp. Our decadence is causing our decay. We must repent of our misdeeds now and prepare for trying times. Lamanites will come, of that I have no doubt. We should be ready to do whatever is necessary to stop them and save our families. To do such we must have the Lord on our side. Without him we cannot prevail, nor should we."

"May we discuss this?" asked Judge Hiram with a sneer.

"You may have the floor," said Onandagus.

"What sources do you have for these awful things? These sound like lies brought about only to bring strife to our fair city. Lies told to scare us into granting you more power. I demand that you no longer rule over us in fear."

"I seek no power or gain from my office. I receive the same wage as any judge, no more, no less. My hands are calloused from toil in my own fields; I am no burden to my people. I have not taverns full of loose women," rebuked Onandagus.

"This Akish-Antum is a myth, a tale told to scare children," retorted Judge Hiram.

"Many myths are based on truth, twisted and lost through time, but in their own context and symbolism still true."

Members of the council murmured their assent.

"Do not delude yourself. There is no eight foot giant with razor sharp teeth. It is absurd," continued Judge Hiram, with a condescending laugh.

Mormon approached Judge Hiram, closing on him and forcing him to back down. "I have seen the Gadianton Grand Master. Will you laugh and call me a foolish child or a liar? I have seen him in the wilds."

"Did you speak with him? Or merely lurk in the bushes nearby?" Judge Hiram said scornfully. "It could have been anyone. He does not exist."

"Yea, he does, do not taunt me again. He was with a legion of his black-cloaked devils or I would have taken him into custody myself. I regret I did not have sufficient guardsmen with me at the time," said Mormon, gripping the edges of Judge Hiram's table. The smooth fine wood threatened to buckle from his grip.

"Even if such is the case, Gadiantons and Lamanites are no threat to a protected, walled city such as this," spoke a man from the back.

"Oh, I think the snakes are already inside," said Onandagus, looking at Judge Hiram.

"How dare you accuse me!" the man snarled.

"You accuse yourself. I said nothing of you. I wish I had but proof of your villainy."

"You will rue the day you crossed me," raged Judge Hiram. "We will take this matter before the people and see what they have to say. If you are believed by the people, we will do as you suggest. If not, the judges shall unite to depose you. Agreed?"

Onandagus nodded at the challenge. "Yea, I agree, for if the people will not heed me, I have no desire to continue guiding them. I warn you Judge Hiram, the Lord will not allow me to leave until I have fulfilled all of my duties. This meeting is adjourned," he announced, and the council filed out of the Judgment Hall.

Once they were alone, Mormon the Elder said to the chief judge, "The people become more vile every year. If it were not for Ammaron the Scribe's charge of my son, I would not be here. From what I have seen of it, Zarahemla is no more righteous than anywhere else and maybe even worse."

"Judge Hiram will not yet depose me. I was within my rights to appoint you, and announcing it in this way let me see how many are against us."

Mormon nodded. "Most are against us, as when we were young. Remember when I asked the Lord if I could die a martyr to his cause? I still think about that; this world is too ill and needs examples."

"That fills me with sorrow, for when a man of your faith asks the Lord for anything, he generally gets it," said Onandagus.

Unwanted Advice

Bethia was sure that Rezon would soon ask for her hand in marriage. Every day she smiled at him, and he always smiled back. He was so polite to her, the sweetest, kindest man she had ever met. Keturah seemed to think it was all very funny.

In the cool of the evening, after the market had ended on their final day in Manti, Bethia decided it was time to progress their relationship beyond friendly, flirtatious talk. "Where is Rezon?" she asked of Peter, one of his drivers.

"He has gone to the tavern. Why do you wish to know? It is not for you to go," Peter said heatedly, without his usual friendliness.

"What is it to you? I want to talk to him."

Peter frowned at her. "Listen to me. Stay away from the taverns tonight. There's no need to see what goes on there. You are still young, and we all care about you. You'll understand when you are older, but for now do your chores and get some rest. We are bound for Bountiful in the morning." He returned to his duties as if that was the end of it.

It was like her father telling her what to do. Well, no more from him or anyone. "You cannot tell me what to do. I am a grown woman; my mother was married at my age. I am going to…"

He turned on her, and she stepped back twice. "Listen, we all know how you feel about Rezon. It is no secret among the company. You are a naive little girl who does not see what is right before you. You need to stay here and get some sleep. Let things be explained to you another day." He stared hard at her, his long curled mustache quivering and sweat beading up on his shaven bald head.

"What are you trying to say? Is he with someone else, another woman? We shall see if she is half the woman I am!" Bethia stormed off toward the tavern.

"Wait," cried Peter "Don't go, you fool girl." He dropped his tools for shoeing the horses and oxen and followed her.

Tears streamed down her face as she walked away quickly. Peter had a bad limp from an ox stepping on his foot and could not easily keep up with her.

The tavern had been mentioned by several of the people in the caravan. It sounded secretive when they spoke of it, as if they did not want her, the new girl, to know of it.

What does it matter? I will not judge them. I am a modern woman, beyond the constraints my father put upon me.

The tavern was down several back alleys in an unsavory part of the city. Bethia stepped over a number of foul-smelling drunks passed out in the streets. She no longer saw Peter behind her. Composing herself and wiping away the tears, she walked to the door. This had to be the place. The sign out front was small and almost illegible until you were right in front of it, the Brick Back House.

It made little sense. It was not made of brick. She had heard of these types of establishments often enough from her father, how they rotted the society. She had never been to one before, and this one looked especially seedy. She turned the brass knob and entered. Loud drunken laughter filled the air, along with the smell of weak wine and strong beer. It was not a very large room, perhaps twenty paces wide and double that long with people packed in standing shoulder to shoulder. A few meager tables had men crowded around, playing with greasy cards.

Bethia could not see Rezon or his tramp. She would let him know of her feelings and how he wasted himself with this other woman. With her long, raven hair and full lips, she was a beauty to match any woman. Forcing her way in was hard. The crowd seemed disinterested in allowing her to pass. She saw Peter at the door looking for her. He tried making his way toward her through the packed room.

I can hear his laugh. I hear Rezon's laugh. Pushing a little harder she saw him through a gap, his back toward her. Slender tattooed arms draped around him. Rezon was kissing the wanton woman.

"Rezon!" she shouted in angry fury.

He turned, shocked to see her here. And then Bethia saw that it was no woman with Rezon, but a dainty slender man in a dress. At once Peter was behind her, holding her steady.

"Bethia, what are you doing here?" Rezon asked incredulous.

"Me? What am I doing? What are you doing? I am disgusted. Are you mad? I thought you loved me...but this...this—"

"I am sorry you had to see it, but I have tried to be frank and open with you."

She shook her head, the tears coming back. "This is vulgar...you are vulgar and disgusting. I never want to see you again! I hate you!" She squeezed out the door, Peter close behind.

"Someone, get me a drink," coughed Rezon. It was the last thing she ever heard him say.

Peter grabbed her just outside the door. "Maybe next time you will listen when someone gives you advice."

"I didn't ask for advice. I wanted the truth," she sobbed.

"No, you didn't. It was before you all along; you were just too naive to see."

"I can't believe I am such a fool."

"It happens," he said, extending her a beefy arm. "Let us go back to the caravan. You get some sleep. Rezon will not care in the morning, and all can be forgotten."

"No, I can't bear to see him again. I will find another caravan, maybe I will talk to Gazelem. At least I know he is going south, while Rezon goes elsewhere."

"Are you sure that is what you want?"

"As sure as anything. Thank you, Peter. Maybe I will see you again someday but I must leave now."

"Take this." He held out a silver ring. "You lost it back inside. You were wringing your hands so."

She took it and placed it on her finger. "Thank you, truly. It is all I have left of my old life. Tell Keturah goodbye for me."

Peter nodded. "What about your things?"

"I don't care about them. I only want to leave this place. Farewell then." She turned and walked away into the night.

The Rewards of Service

Judge Hiram still fumed over the exchange with Onandagus. Sulking deep within his hidden sanctuary below the Avenue of the Cat, his assistant, Pachus, offered him a goblet of wine. "I have news, Master."

"What news? Anything of value?"

"Mistress Lilith's servant is here."

"Ugh, the Nubian?" Judge Hiram sipped the wine.

"No, her handmaiden, Aselin."

"Did she not leave with Lilith?"

"Yea, she did. But now she is here and looks in an awful state."

"Where is Lilith?"

"She does not know. I have already asked."

"Very well, show her in." Judge Hiram sat in exhaustion, wiping his brow as the doe-eyed girl nervously entered the room. He stared hard at her and snapped harshly, "Where is your mistress and why are you here? What is your message? Be quick about it, I have not time for her games."

"I lost her, oh worshipful master, in the forests between here and Gideon," the girl sobbed.

He was intrigued by the possibility of harm coming to Lilith. "Go on."

"We found a group of scouts loyal to Onandagus. I drugged them while my mistress gleaned information from their captain. They were to be on the route of invasion."

"Then what happened?"

"My mistress would slay them all, but the captain overcame his drugs and slew the manservant, Taharka. We fled into the forest. I lost my mistress and ran all day to return here. I hoped she would be here."

"Was she slain then?" asked Judge Hiram, hopeful.

"I think not. We were deep into the woods when I lost her. I doubt that they followed us as they were all drugged."

"How typical of women, eh Pachus? They run away."

"The captain slew Taharka," Aselin explained, "and as my mistress drew her dagger, he turned on us with such vengeance I could not think clearly."

"We can't have you wandering about, my dear. People may recognize you and grow suspicious. You shall have a hidden room here," said Judge Hiram, rising from his desk.

"Oh thank you, thank you. I will gladly serve you until my mistress returns. I will be silent; no one will even know I am here."

"I know they won't," he assured her. "Pachus."

The club came down hard. Aselin's body went to the hidden room in the basement, to remain forever along with dozens of others the Order never wanted found.

In a Dark Place

Anathoth sharpened his wide, moon-shaped dagger. The beautiful steel had been folded hundreds of times over until it was a swirl of dark blues and grays. Sharpening it provided a relaxing task for him. Hieroglyphs in the old tongue of his forefathers went up and down the blade. The languages had changed much since those days.

It might have been carried by his forefather, Ishmael. He knew legends of their family's beginning from the spoken word that had been told around the council fires from father to son. After ravaging Ishmael's daughters, the Nephite father had caused Ishmael to be left behind to die in the desert.

Nephites were the vile cousins who would destroy you if given a chance. His father had taught him from an early age to strike first, strike hard, and strike deadly, before the Nephites kill you and everyone you love. It is part of their treacherous, deceitful nature. It is in their blood. They hunger for power. *Never give up your freedom, my son, the freedom to have a family and serve your king, your freedom to be man.* He would never forget the words of his father, though the old man had been dead now some thirteen years.

Recently, Anathoth had wondered at some of this. Neither he nor his father had ever met a Nephite. They only knew what others said. All his life, he had fought and slain fellow Ishmaelites, Lamanites, and those lowly nomadic Lemuelites, but never a Nephite. If they were such power-hungry demons, why had they never come here to fight? Now more than ever, some things seemed untrue.

The freedoms his father had spoken of so passionately were a myth. He and his family served only the king, as it had been since his grandfather's time. Anathoth's only thought and care was to his duty and honor. Nothing else existed.

"Anathoth, can you hear me, my husband?"

"Yea, my wife, I can." He put the razor-sharp blade upon a high shelf and walked into the bedroom where his wife, Haza, lay stretched upon her bed. She was breathing heavy, hands clasped across her swollen belly.

"Squeezing pains?" he asked. She grunted in the affirmative. "Should I send for the midwife?"

"No, it is not yet time."

"Would you like some water?"

She held out her hand for the hollowed gourd. He gave it to her half full. He admired her strength but did not know how to say it. She was beautiful with light, olive-colored skin, raven black hair and wide, dark eyes that pierced his soul.

"Do you really have to go? Does the king not know I am near my time?" asked Haza.

"Yea, whether he does or not, I was commanded and I have given my firm, unbreakable oath to him. I will obey. It is my honor."

"Does nothing matter as much as your honor?"

He cut her a sharp glance and came swift to her side upon the bed. "If I had not my honor, I would not be the man you love. I would not be a man worthy of you. I would cease to be."

She wiped away her tears. "Why now? Why must you leave me now? It is too close, and you will be so long away."

He turned to look at the fast fading sunset with a pained heart. "I would change it if I could, but I cannot. Once I finish my duties, I will ask for a position elsewhere, far from this dark place. Perhaps we could live near Cibola or even Angola."

"That is a Nephite city," she said in horror.

"Only for now. If things go as the Gadianton-Second claims, we will posses all that land. Surely King Apophis will reward me a governorship over some of it."

"I would like that. When you are gone, what shall I name the child?"

"It will be a boy."

"How can you be so sure?"

"I saw him in a vision long ago."

"Our son then, he is so close, so ready to come out and meet his father."

"How soon?" he asked, rubbing her belly then kissing it.

"Within a few more days I am sure."

"I leave at dawn's first light to gather our men from the south reaches and meet with the army of King Xoltec the next couple of weeks. I will lead twenty-five thousand of Tullan's finest warriors. It cannot wait."

"What shall I name him? Should he be named for you?"

"No, Haza, he shall be named after my father, who taught me the best that he could all his days and died with honor. His name shall be Joram. Joram Baal."

"It is a good name, a high lord like his father, a general of the king." She struggled to stand, and they embraced a long tender moment. They were interrupted by a slave knocking at the door.

"Great General Anathoth, the mighty King Apophis wishes you to attend him immediately."

"I come," was the stern reply.

As the slave departed, Anathoth went to follow but remembered the knife. As he fetched it, his wife grabbed his hand. Her touch was soft and gentle, but she held him fast. Her deep, dark eyes enveloped his. "Promise me you will be careful. Promise me. I do not wish to raise our son alone, not for all the kingdoms of the earth."

Pulling away, he kissed her gently. "I promise. I love you, Haza. I will return tonight; sleep now." He went into the smoke-filled night. Haza wept at his departure. He could hear her but did not look back.

General Anathoth had become an important and trusted man of the king these last twelve years but had chosen to live in a modest villa near the city's center. Walking to the king's palace was a short route that took him through the wide avenue with its many long reflecting pools. They caught the bright stars on this moonless night and held them in thrall. Staring into them, with the vast dark pyramids behind, he thought for a moment that he was floating in the sky, rising far from this place. Tullan did not feel like home anymore. He was honor-bound to a king he loathed.

Honor is the man. If you have no honor, you are nothing. That is what his father would say. But did Anathoth know who had slain his father? Of course he did, and it did not matter as long as he did his duty to his king, and his son did his duty to his king.

It was a vicious cycle, an ever turning wheel of deceit and treachery. Father had served the former king, Apep, for thirty years, long enough to help forge the Golden Empire of Tullan out of the dust and ashes of the past. He was struck down fighting a host of assassins; in falling he slew nearly twenty men. The killers did not succeed in slaying King Apep for another year.

Once they did, King Apophis took the bloody crown from his father's gory head and put it on himself. The fresh blood poured down his face as he declared a horrible death for the assassins, as well as for his own siblings on whom he lay suspicions.

Anathoth was among the first to swear fealty to the new king. He slew the assassins, but the younger siblings were still babes in arms and children. He made sure he was busy elsewhere, away from those murders that sickened him. He had sworn to uphold the new king and could not go against him. Not then, not ever.

To forget, he threw himself into the nobler service of fulltime warrior, destroying those he knew would have honest blood guilt—robbers and the like. He spilt many a man's lifeblood upon his blade and thanked the great nameless spirit that none were innocent. That was the problem with the war with the Nephites. He had never met one.

Many times he ranged over the red horizon and beyond the borders of Tullan where he could see distant white cities of the plain, cities he had been forbidden to enter. There had been some half-caste adventurers of Nephite or Zoramite blood who had come to Tullan, but these lived the Lamanite lifestyle and were not an example of Nephites.

In all the battles he had fought and won, a belief had crept in that he would be dead by the time he was thirty, but it had come and gone. He found Haza at age thirty-one; she was twenty-three. They would be parents soon, and that changed things. Life was now worth living, for the coming child and for the light in her eyes. Haza sang the song of his soul, and this dark kingdom of Tullan stole it from him. Now that he had everything he ever truly wanted, he stood to lose it all in a war of madness. Tullan knew next to nothing of Nephite battle tactics and abilities.

He would return to take his wife and son far away. Perhaps to the mountains beyond the plains of Heshlon and there he would let the lone memory of this place stand and stretch far away.

"You were missed." It was the bone dry voice of Menares, the ugly old priest. His ratty gray hair and big nose stuck out from his face like the splayed branches of a dead diseased tree. The dirty maroon cloak he wore stunk of vile smoke, burned flesh and singed hair. Congealed gore had stained his hands a violent crimson, looking black in the darkness.

"A general should be with his men," goaded the priest, with a sardonic smile.

"I inspected the men earlier. Everything is in readiness. My duties to my family were greater."

"Greater than your duties to the gods?" he asked in surprise.

Anathoth knew Menares hated him for not bringing home from battle a share of victims for sacrifice. "I need explain nothing to vermin such as you."

Menares' eyes grew crazed a brief moment before he contained himself and said, "You are a strange man to be general of all the armies of Tullan, and yet a man that will not sacrifice to Votan is—"

"Is what?" Anathoth cut him off, an anger building inside stronger than he had felt in years. This man was a serpent on two legs like Belial of old, his presence sickened the general. "Is what?" Anathoth shouted. "A traitor? Shall we ask the king if I am a traitor?"

"No, you are no traitor," Menares said, recoiling a little. "But I think the men would appreciate their field commander demonstrating his thankfulness to the gods. We must give the gods their sacrament, their food, our offerings, the blood."

Anathoth stared hard at this human rodent, trying to burn holes through his skull.

Menares continued, "We owe the gods. It is our duty."

"I owe your gods nothing. They are false creations of stone and fire. I bow to my king and the Great Spirit and none other. I spit upon your vulgar gods of stone!"

"You low-born dog!" the gory priest spat back. "The king has the blood of those gods you revile in his veins. He is the son of Apep and She of the Jade Skirt, the Devourer of Souls."

Laughing, Anathoth answered, "We both know his mother was Adah, the favorite concubine, the tale spinner. So forget this She of the Jade Skirt nonsense. She does not exist and neither do your other gods."

Menares facial features contorted. "I will tell the king of your blasphemy. You cannot get away with this."

"Go ahead, you short impotent mummer!" said Anathoth, loud enough to wake the ghosts on this, the Avenue of the Dead.

"Impotent! I curse a thousand curses upon you and yours by the power of my bloody gods. A thousand curses! Flee if you will, but I am still here and so is your family."

"What did you say?" Anathoth approached in a malevolent stride.

"You heard me." Menares drew his small, sacrificial dagger and held it by his side in the fearful manner of one who has never used a blade against an untied foe before.

They faced one another, studying each other's intent, their wills clashed in their eyes. As Menares drew up his dagger to arc down upon his foe, Anathoth caught it in mid-stroke. It was too easy. Menares twisted suddenly to the side, and the blade bit Anathoth ever so slight across the cheek and shoulder.

Inflamed, Anathoth shouted at him in a tempest of fury, "You are a dead hand, you dream of a night vision by day. You are a starving man at a feast who bites his own tongue to sup upon the flavor of blood. You craven necromancer! To curse me is one thing, but to bring my family into this...for that you shall die!"

The moon-shaped knife met his belly squarely, and the warrior general pulled it out and to the side. Menares had a look of surprise and despair. He tried to speak but all he could say was, "Heresy." Anathoth shoved him backward into the reflecting pool.

The priest splashed ever so briefly and went still in the shallow waters, staring up at his killer and the black star-flecked night. He whispered again, "The heresy, the heresy," and then was silent.

Wiping the blade on the priest's dirty robe, Anathoth put it back in its worn sheath before continuing on to the palace.

Within the opulent throne room, King Apophis sat on his couch of jaguar skins. He wore only his gold crown and a finely spun loin cloth of Zoramite silk. His dark copper skin was offset by numerous golden bracelets and rings. One slave girl fed him grapes and another cooled him with a magnificent, turquoise fan of feathers. The usual twelve guardsmen stood at their appointed places. They were impassive and seemed to see everything and nothing. Three musicians played a light rhythm of flute, drum and harp.

It had a haunting, melancholy feel to it, and Anathoth was surprised that the king would listen to such a piece. He was known for liking loud, bawdy tunes of wenching and battles, not this somber affair.

None seemed to notice Anathoth's presence until the king spoke, "Where is Menares? He was to be here with you." King Apophis stroked the cheek of one of the concubines, and she beamed at him. He looked hard at General Anathoth and waved the girl away with a flick of his gold bedecked wrist.

"I have slain him for wounding me and threatening hurt upon my family."

"For your wounding and your hurt, where have I heard that before," he mused. "He is dead then?"

"Yea, he is."

"It is just as well, he was a foul man. I could hardly bear the scent of him. Now I will need a new high priest, luckily I already have such a man elsewhere."

Anathoth stood still before the king.

"I care not if you believe, Anathoth. The gods know I don't either. However, the men do, and I need you to indulge them."

"Yes, my king."

"Teth-Senkhet, the Gadianton, will travel with you to meet with the forces of King Xoltec. He has told me that sacrifices are planned to keep up the blood lust in the men, to increase their appetite for destruction and savagery. As my herald and commander, I expect and order you to be a part of these things. That means you will follow the orders of Gadianton Grand Master Akish-Antum and his second-in-command, Teth-Senkhet, as if they came from myself; unless of course they seek some way of undermining my power base here. You are the only man I trust enough to discern these things. My other command is for you to make sure that Prince Almek dies before you reach Zarahemla." He waved the musicians and serving girls away. Only the dozen guardsmen remained.

Pulling Anathoth in closer to himself, King Apophis whispered, "The Gadiantons are not the only ones with plans. I have my own, and they depend greatly on you. If Zarahemla can indeed be taken, take it and hold it. If it cannot, then once Prince Almek is dead, return to me at all possible speed. Either way, we will soon be in a great position to rule over all."

Kneeling and performing the Henew Rite, Anathoth spoke simply, "As you command, so shall it be."

"I thank and bless you, my general. Now go home for one last night with your wife. It will be the last for many a moon."

Anathoth nodded. As he turned to leave, the king called again, "And Anathoth, get Menares' body out of the reflecting pool. I won't have it contaminating the water and having the troops say it is a bad omen. Everything is a bad omen with those low-born dogs."

"Yes, my king. How did you know, might I ask?"

Laughing he said, "Ha, my spies see all. Men fear Akish-Antum because they say he hears and sees all with his crystal skull interpreter, bah. He uses spies, the same as I. Several who served him to spy upon me now serve me instead."

"Wise as always, my king."

He grunted at that and said, "Farewell, Anathoth, serve me well."

Who could have seen him? As Anathoth walked down the flights of steps, he stared off into the gloomy black. He could feel eyes upon him, watching with a hungry need. He went down the flight of narrow steps while the shadows played tricks on him.

Anathoth recited to himself silently to renew his oath, his honor: *King Apophis need not watch me. He is my king and I am his sworn servant. I am honor bound to serve him faithfully and I will, even though I know it was he who slew my father.*

He murdered my father, bodyguard of the king, so that he could murder his own and become king. It does not matter nor change the now. My oath is my oath. My honor is my honor, regardless of whom I serve in this world. I have sworn an oath, I will prevail. Still, I know. Warriors have honor, kings do not.

Games of Death

In the weeks that followed, men swarmed to King Xoltec's capitol city of Mutula. All vied to join the army against their hated, yet unknown brothers, the Nephites. Flowing behind the tidal wave of fighting men were their families as well as merchants eager for gain, traveling performers and other camp followers.

Among these, Qof-Ayin came home as well. None noticed him holding his raw, blood-caked side nor the vacant look in his eyes. The poisoned blade of the Gadianton assassins tampered his senses almost beyond reason. Only through sheer will had he been able to guide his horse back home, that and his skill in finding plants to fight the pain and poison. As he rode past the burnt temple of Shagreel, a minor priest recognized him and summoned Balam-Ek.

Balam-Ek looked over the infected wound. "Can you speak?"

"Water," said Qof-Ayin.

Balam-Ek handed him a skin. "Does this mean that the Gadianton spoke the truth? Are the Nephites preparing for battle against us? Have you seen any of the other spies?"

Gulping down the lukewarm water, Qof-Ayin coughed once before asking, "Where is my son?"

"He is in the palace performing his duties as bodyguard to the king, the same as every day. Now, about my questions."

"Yea, the Gadianton spoke truth, the Nephites are a wicked people. They need to be taught, and a lesson is coming. The other spies and runners are all dead, their bodies filled with Nephite arrows or copper-bladed daggers."

"I cannot believe it. They are all dead? I had not thought the Gadianton would be so correct, so true."

"It is so. I could never get close enough to get an accurate account of the Nephite numbers. I was waylaid and imprisoned, then escaped. It will be war one way or another. I know this as I have ever known anything. Now, may I go and have my wound attended?"

"Yes, yes of course. Would you wish for my man here to fetch you the royal surgeon?"

"No, my son is a capable field medic. He will do whatever is necessary."

"Very well then. I will personally see to it that he comes and attends your wounds." The high priest left to tell the news to the king and to send Zelph home to his father.

As the high priest approached King Xoltec, the dwarf Tulum announced in his deep voice, "My lord, Chief High Priest Balam-Ek."

Waking from a midday doze, the king looked at the priest and yawned. "Is there any news?"

"Yea, Rabbanah, there is. Qof-Ayin has just returned, badly wounded. He has requested his son Zelph attend him and his wounds."

"That is fine. Zelph you may go to your father," said King Xoltec. "Tell me my priest, what does he say of the Nephites?"

"Qof-Ayin says that all of the runners and spies have Nephite arrows in their backs and throats slit with copper daggers."

"The Gadianton speaks true, eh?"

"So it seems. I suspected treachery, but if Qof-Ayin, the only one to return alive, is putting his word to it, it must be so."

* * * * * * * * * * * *

Across from the palace was a large plaza and complex with several ball courts and arenas. Here the thousands who had gathered could jockey for position to both watch and participate in the games and contests. A small area was afforded for the royal family and guests to watch without being touched by the masses. Within were Crown Prince Almek, Prince Aaron, Princess Sayame and the Gadianton Grand Master.

With the game over, consequences were due. The winning team captain, Siyach, addressed Crown Prince Almek. "Your majesty, what is your wish for the losing players' lives?"

Two dozen faces looked up at him. The winners knew their place was assured while the losers prayed for the mercy of heartless gods.

"The losers of Midian must die. They will be sacrificed to appease the gods and to thank them for our greatness," Almek pronounced.

"You would slay the losers to thank stone gods for your victory?" asked the Gadianton.

"What? It is our right," said Almek.

"It's a waste. Those men are strong, and this invasion needs the best men you have. Almost seventy-five thousand men have come here wanting to be in this army. I want only the best twenty-five thousand. Let us now choose the best."

"What do you have in mind?" asked Aaron.

"A game after my own heart," said the Gadianton as he leapt down onto the arena floor, where he selected a wooden training sword from a rack of practice weapons. "Who can prove their skill? Who dares show me? I will begin." He stood in the center of the ball court daring all to meet his gaze. Doffing his crimson cloak, he cried aloud for all to hear, "Show me your vaunted skill in battle. Show me!"

Silence reigned as the audience watched.

"Are you helpless as fish out of the sea? Are you something a worm could rule over?"

Angry murmurs rolled over the crowd, and those farthest from his gaze shouted mocking threats. "Do you wish to die? Are you calling our king a worm?"

Laughing, the Gadianton answered, "No, not your king. All of you."

The crowd parted for an immense, dark-skinned warrior. "Tazila-catzin," they murmured.

"Do you challenge me?" asked the behemoth warrior, Tazilacatzin.

"Yea, let's give the people some real sport," replied the Gadianton Grand Master.

Tazilacatzin stood a couple feet taller than even the huge Gadianton. His features were hawk-like, his eyes like obsidian. Neither man seemed afraid.

The mountainous Lamanite gestured for a weapon. A servant was about to give him a wooden training sword like the Gadianton's but Akish-Antum said, "Nay, give him his flint club. I need a challenge."

The Lamanite giant growled at this but accepted his obsidian-flanged club. He swung it around thrice with each arm to loosen his muscles. The Gadianton stood unmoved by the display before him. Then the giant charged.

"I hope he kills the Gadianton," said Almek.

"Tazilacatzin is at the end of all hope. He will die," said Aaron.

Almek turned and frowned at him. "You have been spending far too much time with that Nephite stargazer."

"He is not a Nephite. He is the Gadianton Grand Master."

"All Nephites are liars and cheats."

"Would a liar and a cheat enter into a tournament of death with Tazilacatzin?"

"Be silent, brother. I am immune to his lies and yours."

Aaron sat forward on his chair to watch the duel.

Tazilacatzin, the giant of Mutula, swung devastating blows, unable to connect. He was clearly outmatched and too slow for the panther-like Gadianton. Time and again he felt the sting of the wooden sword as the Gadianton toyed with him.

Roaring, Tazilacatzin swung in fury, backing his foe up against a wall. "I have slain more than a hundred men in combat," he said, sweat stinging his eyes as the sun blinded him.

The Gadianton had the giant right where he wanted him. "I cannot count how many I have killed. You are an amateur when it comes to death." He leapt up and slammed his wooden blade against the giant's temple.

Tazilacatzin dropped to his knees, his body black and blue with bruises on his near-naked frame.

Akish-Antum struck his ribs and thigh hard before asking. "Do you yield?"

"Never."

"Very well."

A quick shot to the side of the giant's neck, and he dropped like a stone.

"Is he dead?" was on everyone's lips.

"He is not dead, merely unconscious. He will revive soon, perhaps a little wiser," said Akish-Antum.

There was relief in the crowd, for Tazilacatzin was one of their proudest sons.

The Gadianton threw down his wooden training sword and gestured with his arms outspread. "Your crown prince, Almek, and I are recruiting the best men to go with us and defend your lands from the Nephites. There are many of you here, but you will not all go. Only the most savage and disciplined warriors may accompany us. We go to conquer, we go for honor and for glory. Who is strong enough to come with us?"

The frenzied crowd roared in unison.

"Then show me," he shouted as the throng went wild.

So the games began. Blood flowed freely on the ball courts, staining them a raw crimson that would not come clean. The crowds loved it.

The young prince Aaron attended every day, usually beside the Gadianton Grand Master, learning what he could of human anatomy and strategy. He flinched the first few times he saw men die, their life blood draining from them. Soon enough, it did not move him except to excitement.

During a lull in the fights, he asked the Gadianton, "How did you yourself become such a great warrior?"

"My inner sword is always drawn to kill nations without pity. Yours needs to be as well."

The boy looked up at him, trying to take it all in.

"I will tell you a part of the great secret. In this life men prosper in accordance with their genius, their strength and cunning. Your people call it the Law of the Jungle. It is the natural way of things."

The boy nodded.

"You will understand more in time, but for now practice as best you can, before the real thing is upon you."

By the end of the week, Akish-Antum and Crown Prince Almek had selected almost twenty-five thousand men to be their new model army —the fiercest, most savage men from all the arena battles. Several thousand dead were taken to a huge pit and buried until it was piled high, making the foundation for a new pyramid of death.

By day and night, Akish-Antum schooled his prodigy, young Prince Aaron, further in all matters of strategy, astronomy, history and the dark arts. He conducted bloody sacrifices to inflame a brutal blood lust within the ranks, and the army began to think of him as their new high priest.

He told Aaron, "These gods of stone are false. They have no more

160

power than anything you project onto them. Use them to control the people and to manipulate whatever it is you wish to accomplish. Sacrifice to the standards, and their weapons will become what they worship."

The doctrines of control were ever ingrained into the boy.

✱ ✱ ✱ ✱ ✱ ✱ ✱ ✱ ✱ ✱ ✱ ✱

Zelph stood back from all these things, feeling helpless in the midst of the maelstrom. Bedridden, Qof-Ayin somehow hung on, despite the poison coursing through his veins and eating away at his body.

"He teaches them false deeds and is building an empire on bloodshed. How much worse can this be?" asked Zelph in despair.

"When I was young, the old men still spoke fondly of the Golden Age of their fathers. The cities were splendid and beautiful, the children happy and all had plenty to eat. Then came the darkness, when the evils of an earlier age were unbound. In the Golden Age, there were neither kings nor beggars," said Qof-Ayin, wincing in pain as he spoke.

"I learned many things from the prophet Abinadab. There is a power much greater than ours at work in all of this. Trust in the Great Spirit and his son Jesus Christ. Believe in him with all your heart, might, mind and spirit, and he will see you through. You are a good faithful man. I will not much longer be upon this mortal coil."

"Don't say such things, father. You will recover and together we can leave this awful place."

"It is not to be. I was told to be willing to sacrifice all for my salvation. I welcome it with a glad heart. You must do the same. I want you to pray on your knees and do not get up until you have an answer one way or the other."

"I will."

"When the time comes, leave the column when near Tullan."

"No, I have overheard that we will not be taking that route. We are instead going near the sea a good portion of the march, then upland past Tullan. There we will meet the army of King Apophis."

"Fear not, my son, there is a plan for you." Taking his son's hand, Qof-Ayin continued, "The wicked have drawn their swords and bent their bows to strike down and slaughter those who live honestly. May their swords pierce themselves and their bows break. Take heart, you have a great purpose."

"Why did you not tell King Xoltec of Akish-Antum's trickery and deceptions?"

"On my journey home, I prayed long and hard. It is the will of the Great Spirit that these things come to pass as the Gadianton is orchestrating them. Without realizing it, he is being used to further the Great Spirit's plan. The Nephites are very wicked at this time and need to be reminded of their God, to repent and return to righteousness. There will be a great round of life. If they do not return to the true God, they will be wiped off the face of the earth. It will be as if they were never here."

"The Great Spirit would not do that, would he?"

"He has and he will again when necessary. Remember the flood, the Jaredites, and countless heathen nations from the land of our fathers."

"So many will die."

"The Great Spirit will receive his own, and the innocent have a place assured. The wicked will be taught the error of their ways on the other side. That is how you teach your children the danger of fire. Are we not the Great Father's children?"

"I understand a little more now. I will go and pray for my own answers. Good night, father."

"Good night, my son."

✴ ✴ ✴ ✴ ✴ ✴ ✴ ✴ ✴ ✴ ✴ ✴

The next morning Akish-Antum gathered the rest of his belongings for the march. Outside his master's door, Aaron stood with a dozen Lamanite servants, who cringed from the unhallowed room. Reaching into an oaken chest, the Gadianton retrieved a number of artifacts. "Aaron, I am leaving these things with you. These are records liberated from a treasury in Lehi and these from the library of Antionum, and these from Zarahemla. Open your mind and learn all you can while I am gone."

Waiting until the servants had left, his arms laden with the Gadianton's belongings, the boy asked, "Master, may I ask why you have such interest in me? I am not blind to your own ambitions. You desire the Nephite kingship for yourself though you do not say this to my father."

"You are a perceptive and sober child, quick to observe. I will tell you." Holding forth his crystal skull interpreter he said, "This interpreter has shown me your future greatness."

"How? I am the least in my father's house."

"Be that as it may, I have seen it and the interpreter does not lie. I know that you and not Almek will be king someday. You will become the greatest king of the Lamanites. I say this not to flatter you but to make you aware of your destiny. I would help mold you to be that powerful king. Be wise, be strong, do whatever you must to win these things. If you do nothing, it will negate the prophecy. There is always a struggle between order and chaos; you must make your destiny come to pass. I will teach you more at another time. Until then, drink deep of the fountains of darkness. Don your crown of glory, before all vanishes like smoke. Farewell."

Aaron stood in awe as the Gadianton stalked from the room.

Fierce Uzzsheol accosted his master in the hallway just before the grand entrance leading to the plaza. "My master, I have slain all the runners and spies, save the one who you know returned here."

"This Qof-Ayin," said Akish-Antum.

"Yes."

"He has said my words were true, and the army is about to march within the hour."

The mohawked warrior continued, "He was captured by Nephites outside Desolation, I know not how he escaped."

"To whom has he spoken since he has returned here?"

"Only Balam-Ek."

"Why did this man support my word?" asked Akish-Antum.

"I know not. I tracked him in the north; he slew several of my men. He was wounded by a poison knife and now he dies the slow death. The only person who has since seen him is the son, Zelph."

"Are you sure he told Balam-Ek nothing?"

"I was hidden in a cloak beside them when they spoke. I heard everything, and I do not believe there was any coded message."

"No, or the king would not have let the plan progress thus far. Perhaps Qof-Ayin means to blackmail us once we are on the move and out of the king's ear," wondered Akish-Antum. "How bad did you say his wound is?"

"He should be dead already. It is strange he still lives. I have never known the poison to take so long."

"Kill both him and his son with unknown assassins."

The lanky, hawk-faced Lamanite bowed and raced off while Akish-Antum pondered. *Why would Qof-Ayin not tell Balam-Ek the truth? It must be that he is waiting to use it against us. There could be no other answer. I must be ready. Things could turn very quickly.*

Akish-Antum made his way to the army column that awaited him and Prince Almek at the grand plaza. Dressed in gilded copper armor, a crimson cloak about his shoulders and a blood-soaked lambskin about his loins, he drew his sword. Pointing to the north, he called to the shouting mass of warriors. "We will burn the Nephites with fire and brimstone. The sword will consume their flesh. Woe to that murdering city full of lies. Our prey is never absent. The sound of the whip, the roar of rumbling wheels and galloping hooves will clamor through the night. Rattling chariots, rearing chargers, singing blades, flashing spears. A mass of the slain, a throng of corpses. There will be no end to the bodies of our enemies!"

His horde cheered, whether shaven-headed Lamanites painted for war or his own corps of Gadianton warriors dressed like himself in copper armor and bloody lambskins. The black and crimson banners were unfurled. Drums and horns beat a steady rhythm of destruction. The somber heavy dirge galvanized the warriors who sang their death song.

King Xoltec and Prince Aaron watched from atop the tallest pyramid. The king was exuberant and shouted his approval at the spectacle, proud that he still lived to send such a force of counter conquest against his hated enemies. Akish-Antum saluted him from his foremost chariot, gleaming like a burning golden tiger, as the column rode and marched out of the city. Aaron wept that he could not join them.

✱ ✱ ✱ ✱ ✱ ✱ ✱ ✱ ✱ ✱ ✱ ✱ ✱

The assassins sent by Uzzsheol could not approach Zelph, who was already beside Prince Almek in a chariot leaving the city. Instead they raced to the home of Qof-Ayin. They entered the unbarred door and saw the former warrior in bed reading a scroll he had received from the prophet Abinadab.

Looking at the intruders Qof-Ayin said, "What took you so long? This poisoned wound is doing your job for you."

They approached with daggers drawn.

"You needn't fear, for I am ready to die. I have said nothing against your master. His secret design is God's purpose in the end." Bowing his head, he began his last prayer waiting for the daggers to fall. The assassins held back a moment as he finished.

"Now do it, I will fall with your knife," he said to the foremost dagger man. Taken aback, the man hesitated.

Now that they were in range of his bed, Qof-Ayin drew out his sword from beneath his blanket. He swung in a wide, graceful arc, taking some of his murderers with him at the last.

Remembering Spirits of the Past

Amaron gazed at the forest, the thick greenery stretching out forever, a sea of trees between his patrol and the first of several destinations. It did not help that the afternoon was so hot and humid. It stuck to the men with an irritating tenacity. Clothing soaked in sweat latched to them like leeches gaining sustenance. The heat made Amaron tired. The drug in his system was slowing him down as well. Still, he insisted that they travel overland through the thick woods and swamps, avoiding all roads. Swarms of biting insects were a constant torment as they moved.

"Amaron, if we must go to Manti to get Ezra's cousin, why not take the road?" asked Daniel as he swatted a fly on his neck, thick with his own blood.

"Those Gadianton dogs are watching for us. They watch the roads not the woods. Isn't that right Ezra?" said Amaron.

"True, the Order does not have the manpower to watch swamps. We will be noticed as soon as we enter the city, eah," said Ezra, breathing heavy. He had a curious way of exhaling at the end of every sentence.

"We do whatever we can do to throw them off our trail," said Amaron. The men grumbled at their wet boots and bug bites but continued on.

"Tell me Amaron," Ezra said. "It seemed like that Nubian you slew really hated you."

"How could you know that? Were you awake?"

"I wasn't at first, but I awoke as the girl was giving the men something to drink. I looked over and saw you kissing Lilith. The Nubian was staring at you both in fury."

"For all I know we had met before."

"How is that possible?"

"You tell me. How many Nubians have you ever seen before?"

"Not very many."

"Neither have I, since few of them live in the Promised Land. Most are typically sailors aboard Phoenician vessels that make port in the bigger cities like Zarahemla, Tarshish, and Bountiful. When I was a youth of ten summers I ran afoul of a gang of Nubian sailors on the south side of Zarahemla, oarsmen and cabin boys of some foreign ship. I could barely understand them, but they made it clear they wanted my fine pony. I kept refusing, so they chased me for it. Their long-limbed bodies were swift, and the half dozen of them almost caught me several times. At first I thrilled at the chase, but as I grew tired of it, I headed home, foolishly thinking it was over." He shrugged and smiled.

"Reaching the safety of home, I put the pony in its stall and brushed it down before going inside to get something to eat. The seven Nubian boys followed me in. To my own home!" Amaron spat. His eyes flashed, still angry after all these years.

"I told them in no uncertain terms to get out and go to hell, but they refused. They said I owed them the pony for making them give chase and run all over the city. They would not leave, so I drew the biggest knife in the kitchen. My threats only made them laugh. Challenging their leader, I advanced and we struggled with the knife on the floor. With all my heart I wanted to drive the knife into his belly, I was so angry that they had invaded my family's home. At that age, it seemed to me an unthinkable act," Amaron said, as they kept up their labored march over the thick shrubbery. Every now and again he would stop and look over their back trail as if expecting to be followed.

"The others were shouting around me, encouraging their friend. Then silence came as I realized they had all gone except the one I was grappling with. My father and mother came home, and my father ended the struggle and pulled my knife away. The young Nubian got up and ran off. My mother was in hysterics at the whole thing. My father told me never to pull a knife as a threat unless I was wholly committed to the task and meant to use it. I had not the heart to say in front of my mother that I had been so committed. I wanted to kill that boy for trespassing. For all I know, that Taharka was one of those boys from years ago."

"Captain, I have a question for you while we are out here in this muck and grime," said Daniel.

"What is it?"

"If we are going to get paid for our losses in the field, might we be able to claim a full crop rather than just half? I lost almost half my crop of corn and two thirds of my barley to that late frost."

"So you would cheat the food stores and tithes from Onandagus?"

No one responded to this.

"Say what you will upon our return. But I warn all of you, blessings will be lost for such an attitude as that."

Daniel scoffed, "Ha, blessings in heaven lost over a full storeroom? I will take the lost blessings and full storeroom anytime."

"Fool," Judah taunted.

"You despise me and damn yourself for that...fool," he snapped back. They hit each other in the shoulder and laughed.

Things were different now, mused Amaron. When he was younger they all went out into the wilderness to train and learn woodcraft. The spirit of the Lord was with them then, but not now. They complained endlessly and conspired to cheat Onandagus. All except Ezra, who did not complain. A better example of soft city folk Amaron could not imagine.

Amaron found it hard to forgive and overlook Ezra for his part in Helam's death, but then Helam knew his job and accepted it always unflinching. In a way, the weaselly little man with the pathetic facial hair had saved them. Seeing him pray was the one thing that shook some sense into Amaron, enabling him to overcome the drug and slay Taharka before he himself was cloven asunder. None of the others acknowledged Ezra's part in that night's event. Amaron had put them all in danger for a pretty face and then had saved them just in time, so it balanced out to them.

Mounting a thickly forested hill, they looked across a mighty valley as they reached the summit. The walled city of Manti sat before them, with its walls thrice the height of a man. The city had been captured and endured many sieges in the past. Once the Christ had come and the wars over, the residents continued to build strong walls and foundations out of tradition.

Tall thick logs were posted in the ground as a stockade, lashed together and stuccoed over. Towers sat along the wall every hundred paces. A small walkway ran the entire distance of the city's perimeter, much the same as

Zarahemla's. Year after year the people of Manti had added to the stucco, giving it strength and fireproofing. It was a beautiful sight from atop the hill.

"I have never seen it from this angle before," said Ezra.

Amaron said, "No one comes up here anymore."

"Anymore?"

"It is considered bad luck. This is Manti Hill where Nehor, the blasphemer and murderer, was hung."

"Why is that bad luck?" asked Ezra.

"I am not saying it is. I have been here dozens of times without incident, but others fear the unknown, thinking old Nehor still haunts this hill and these woods."

"Why would anyone think that?" asked Ezra, as he looked about nervously.

"Because he was hung, suspended between heaven and earth."

Ezra looked perplexed at Amaron's answer, so the burly Nephite continued, "His soul was rejected by both heaven and earth. He is in limbo, he cannot move on to the other side so he stays here. It's what ghosts do, when they can't move on."

"Where was he hung exactly?"

"That I do not know. After he was dead and the flesh rotted away from his bones, they cut the tree down and burned it somewhere on this hill, along this trail."

The thick trees blotted out the sun here and there, shading the forest like tiger stripes as they walked down the hill. Ezra asked, "Do you believe in spirits?"

"Of course I do," said Amaron.

"Do you fear them then?"

"No, they are just spirits. I can respect some, but fear them no, never."

Ezra prodded, "So you have never met any?"

"I have. A few of all types, I would say."

"Are you lying to me?"

Amaron scowled at him.

"I am sorry, eah," breathed Ezra.

"I spent the night at the home of some family friends out to the southeast years ago, near Onidah. It was a very fine home. It had been built near the sight of a battlefield in ages past. I was given my own room to stay in. Now the door and window were shut tight, mind you. I awoke in the night to someone sitting beside me on the bed, up against the small of my back as I lay facing the wall. I felt them get up. I turned over quickly and no one was there," said Amaron, leading them down a game trail with thick grasses on either side.

"What did you do then?"

"I admit it was a little unnerving. Who wants a ghost sitting beside them as they try to sleep? So I went out into the night to sleep in the wagon. A full moon lit up the courtyard. I lay my bedroll on the floor boards of the wagon and lay down to sleep, when something violently shook the entire wagon. No one was there, and it was not me shaking the thing either. I tried to shake it myself and could not reproduce the effect no matter how hard I tried. Remember the courtyard was clear, and I could see in every direction in the bright moonlight. I even got out and looked underneath the wagon to see if there was some sort of trickster about, but there was no one."

Ezra's eyes were wide with anticipation now. "Then?"

"I went to sleep," said Amaron, stepping over a boulder.

"After that?" asked Ezra.

"Yea, what else was I going to do? I awoke sometime later in the night to a deep sound coming at me swiftly, a mournful groaning. My head was on the pillow on the wagon floor, and I had not time to even get up when I felt something intangible moving through the floorboards straight at me. Whatever it was came right up to my face, and I felt a gush of wind as if someone had just breathed cold air into my face. Again, I saw no one."

Ezra shivered and asked, "What did you do? I would have died of fright, eah."

"Nay, I told them to leave me alone and let me sleep."

"And?"

"They did. I stayed there for another week without any further incident. Spirits know how you are feeling. They can read you as easy as any scroll. They knew I was not afraid of them and that their tricks were getting no reaction from me. I felt no fear, no anger. I was no fun to tease or harass so they quit."

Daniel laughed as he chopped a low hanging tree branch out of the way.

"I couldn't do that, I'd be too frightened," said Ezra, still looking over his shoulder.

"I don't think they were evil spirits," Amaron said, "simply those who had not yet moved on. They were like mischievous children. Besides what is a spirit going to do to you anyway?"

"They can make you afraid," suggested Ezra, shielding the sun from his face in a rare spot where it shone through the trees.

"Only if you let them. Your life is what you choose to make of it. Choose not to be afraid." Amaron halted the company and pondered silently which way to go through a fork in the game trail. He stared down the hill, sniffing at the non-existent breeze. He gestured for the men to take the left fork in the game trail, although the right one went toward Manti.

"Why go this way?" complained Daniel. "We're going the wrong way."

"Be quiet," snapped Amaron, as he put his hand on his hilt. Behind the trees, a huge bull mastodon snorted at them and went back to eating the buttercups that grew along the hillside.

"I knew something was down there. I just wasn't sure what it was," said Amaron, continuing down the hill.

"Tell us why you became a Gadianton, Ezra," asked Judah.

"I wanted to be rich. I wanted women to desire me as I desired them. I never had a thought to another way I might get these things because joining the Order seemed so easy. If I was a part of the Order, I was a part of something bigger than myself. I took the oath and I was rewarded for service; others looked out for me until Amaron found me."

"How did Amaron know to get you? That you would talk?" asked Daniel.

Ezra grimaced, "I don't know. How did you decide to go after me, out of all the others?"

"I was told by Onandagus to find you. I still don't know how he knew, I never asked," said Amaron. "I was to look for one of the low ranking, common thief types, someone who could tell us of Gadianton plans. We would never get the information from a high ranking Gadianton, they're too dedicated and have too much protection and twisting of law on their side. Onandagus suggested you. The interpreter stones may have told him about you."

They kept a good pace down the hillside, jumping over fallen trees and over a noisy little brook that fed the corn fields below. Ezra kept close behind Amaron and Judah. When they reached level ground, the trees abruptly stopped and the fields began.

They cut across through the freshly irrigated field until they came to a narrow muddy road. They passed a few farmhouses, with noisy children out front who stared at them before running indoors, except for one curious, brave little towheaded boy who brandished a wooden sword at them. They all laughed to see him behave as such, and he laughed back.

The muddy road soon met another wider road that cut in from up the valley and led straight to the small north gate of Manti. It was called the cemetery gate, near where the townspeople buried their dead. Amaron had not wanted to enter the large eastern gate where traffic to and from Zarahemla would typically come.

Corn was planted to within thirty paces of the city's tall walls and gate, and a single guard dozed at the open gate. Amaron frowned and said, "I have read that in the days of Captain Moroni, a deep ditch surrounded the entire city. It was filled in after the coming of the Christ. Moroni would not have allowed corn to be grown so close to the city walls. It had to be at least a hundred paces away."

"Why was that?"

"So that invaders would have no cover or concealment from the archers along the wall. Good scouts could sneak through this corn and get right up to that dozing guard, slit his throat and take the city. He ought to be flogged for sleeping on duty."

They entered the cemetery gates without the guard so much as stirring. Inside, a boy of perhaps ten in a green shirt was watching the gate as they entered. He ran down the street after he had visibly counted them.

"He seemed to be watching and waiting for some such as us," said Judah.

"Yea he did, didn't he? Quick, Ezra where does your cousin live?" Amaron asked.

"Right down this avenue."

"If the Gadiantons are watching and waiting, should we not return to Zarahemla and tell Onandagus they are wise to us?" suggested Benjamin.

"If so, how could you expect to cheat him, without us actually performing the mission?" Amaron snapped.

Benjamin frowned and said, "I'm here to help."

"Yourself."

Ezra interrupted, "My cousin's home is right here, let us hurry. I will speak to him with Amaron alone, the rest should wait here."

"Stretch out and wait, boys," Amaron told them.

"We will meet you at the cemetery gates," said Judah while Daniel laughed, thinking of an inside joke.

The white stuccoed face of the home was old and peeling, revealing the logs beneath. Ezra knocked on the front door. A scraggly, portly man opened the door with a confused look on his face.

"Uncle," said Ezra as the man examined him, squinting against the sunlight. Amaron could smell the strong scent of wine. "Uncle Reuben, it's your nephew Ezra."

"Eh, Ezra? I don't know any Ezra," said the man, his long white hair arcing about his face.

Looking hard at Ezra, Amaron had a hand on the pommel of his sword.

Whispering, Ezra explained, "Easy, he has been going senile for awhile now." Louder he said, "Uncle Reuben, it is I, Ezra, son of your sister."

A look of recognition washed over the man's face. "Oh, I am sorry. It has been years since I have seen you or your mother. Four, I think," he said, as he rubbed his hands across his dirty brown tunic.

"Six, Uncle."

"Yes, yes, who is your friend?"

"I am Amaron, a captain of Zarahemla."

"Good for you, but if you think I have anything to do with my nephew's delinquencies, think better of it. I have not seen him in years and besides I am a close personal friend of Chief Judge Onandagus."

"No, you're not," contended Amaron.

"I know. But still, I have nothing to do with this one's crimes." He tried to shut the door, but Amaron held it.

"Uncle, this is not about me. I'm reformed; I am helping the law now. We are on a mission from Onandagus himself. We could use a good bowman. Is Sam here?"

Tears came suddenly to the drunken man's face. "Is this a sick joke? What a terrible time for you to come inquire of my son. How dare you of all people come here—a robber, now coming to ask my son to join you."

"Uncle, I am reformed. I am atoning for the things I have done as best I can. I am helping to fight the Gadiantons now."

"It's too late, too late, Sam is gone."

"Where is he?"

"Robbers...robbers murdered him a fortnight ago. Lower class Gadiantons...just scum, killed my boy. Cursed red-caps."

"I am sorry, Uncle."

"You're sorry, everyone is sorry. Your damned brotherhood killed him in cold blood for our corn money. A few lousy senines cost me my son. Go away...go away," cried Reuben, looking away. "I need to drink a little more. There is nothing more to be done or said. All is gone, all is done. The torches have faded away."

Amaron grabbed Ezra's shoulder. "Let's go."

Back at the gates, the others had tied the guard's legs together with a thin twine and were about to let out a loud crash beside him when they saw Amaron and Ezra's swift approach.

"What happened?" asked Obadiah.

"Gadiantons. The cousin is dead. Let us hurry. We need to be on our own route to the northwest of here," said Amaron. He smirked, observing the sleeping guard with twine about his legs as he leaned asleep against the wall.

"But we are only nine men and we need to be a solid ten," said Lehi.

Nephi nodded in agreement. "That's tradition. It's bad luck not to be ten under one."

"It does not matter. We will have to do without a tenth. It is only tradition anyway," said Amaron.

"Humble as a Zoramite, aren't you?" said Daniel, and Amaron frowned at the insult. Zoramites were considered the peak of arrogance and false pride.

"There is tradition for a good reason," said Judah

"Which is?"

Judah shrugged and said, "I don't know. I just know it's tradition and we always get into trouble when we don't follow it. Think about the other night, you broke tradition."

"I know," snapped Amaron.

"What will happen to us if we break this one? That's all I'm saying. Could be real bad," said Judah.

"Let's go. Traditions are made to be broken."

No one liked the sound of that, but they turned and followed Amaron. As they were about to depart out the gate a voice called out, "Stop, stop." It was Uncle Reuben running toward them with a bow and a small pack in hand. "You wanted a bowman," he said. "I am a good bowman, I trained my son."

"We have no time for drunkards," said Amaron.

"I have only drunk the last few weeks since my son was killed. I need a chance to right wrongs. I need revenge. Let me go with you."

"No."

Gripping Amaron's arm, he pleaded further. "Please, please my life is meaningless now. I have no wife and no son. My only family is with you. Ezra, forgive my harsh words earlier. You are trying to right wrongs, please let me as well. I can fight and shoot a bow as good as anyone. I won't slow you down much."

The men looked at one another. It was plain they had their doubts. Reuben was much older than the rest of them, in his late fifties, not in particularly good shape and he smelled of wine. But they wanted an even ten.

"I say let him join us. Odds are this is a fool's errand anyway. Why not have an official fool?" said Daniel.

Amaron scowled at Daniel and said, "Reuben, there is no wine here with us."

"That's all right."

"I may need you to shoot and kill a man."

"If it's a Gadianton, I will have no problem with that."

"But, not unless I give the order."

Reuben paused a long time before answering, "All right then."

"We have a mission, and it is not about your revenge."

"I understand that. Thank you."

"Your life still has meaning. This could save thousands of lives," said Amaron.

"Yes, thank you."

"I guess we were meant to come here after all," said Judah.

"There is always a purpose," said Amaron.

"Thank you again, Captain Amaron," gushed Reuben.

"Just do your best to keep up."

"I will. I will remember for my son, so he will not be forgotten."

"Good. Let's go then. We still have a long journey ahead of us."

They marched out the cemetery gates, the guard still dozing. Daniel, the last man in line, splashed his water skin onto the guard's crotch. He awoke suddenly and tried to stand. Crying out, he tumbled with his legs tied together. "Hey, who are you? Do you have a pass? I am a city guard. You can't do this."

The twine was tied so snug that he could not escape without a knife, which he lacked. He was still hollering after them as they disappeared into the tree line. They were too busy laughing to care.

On the Night of Great Fear

Mormon the Younger put down the scroll he was reading and went to the window. He had a room on the tall second story of the hall, but from this window he could see little. Since coming to Zarahemla, he had only seen the main avenue leading to the Judgment Hall.

The surgeon who examined Mormon's leg deemed it well enough to remove the splints that his father had placed upon it almost a month ago. They then blessed him and the leg felt better at once. There was never any doubt in Mormon's mind that prayer works. His own leg was proof of the Lord's power for those who have faith. At eleven years old, Mormon was well read; his mother had called him an old soul. He liked that; she called him many sweet things that he reflected back on. She had been gone four years now and so much had happened since then.

Father was made governor of the land of Antum, resigning two years later after growing tired of the city's corruption. He had been chief of the city guardsmen for many years before that and said he was able to do more good in the field than he ever could as governor. Then Ammaron the Scribe, his father's uncle, had come to meet him. He visited them for a week and told the boy of a special duty awaiting him. It was overwhelming at first, this sacred charge set before him, to keep a record of the people, to save it for all time as a witness. Mormon accepted, and soon thereafter plans were made for them to move south to Zarahemla to better continue his education.

His father appearing before the Council of Fifty in support of Onandagus had caused quite a stir. Within a few short hours, riots had broken out in the streets. Rabble rousers, his father called them. Onand-agus said it was the king men demanding rights. They cried that they were being persecuted, yet they hoped to tear down the rights and laws in order to establish a king. Others who cared not for king men took to the streets to fight. Thieves and anarchists took advantage of the situation.

Mormon the Elder had gone out into the night with a troop of guardsmen to quell the riots and establish peace. There was no knowing when he would return. A few lit candles gave the boy just enough light to read by as he prepared for sleep. They were dim and near to dying as he yawned and read over a scroll borrowed from Onandagus's library. Intrigued by the story, he fought to remain awake and see what happened next. It was an old scroll that had come into the chief judge's possession years ago from a Greek who had come with Phoenician traders. A tale of Ilian. He read how Achilles had rounded on Agamemnon, lashing out at him, not relaxing his anger for a moment. "Staggering drunk, with a dog's eyes, your fawn's heart. Never once did you arm with the troops and go to battle or risk an ambush packed with Achaea's picked men. You lack courage...you can see death coming."

It reminded Mormon of his hero, Captain Moroni, who he had read about in the old record of histories compiled by his own great-grandfather Nephi. Although Achilles was no Captain Moroni. The rage and strength of Achilles would be no match for the might and righteousness of Moroni. If he had a son someday, he would name him Moroni.

Another candle died, and the room was very dim. He heard a scuffle out in the darkened hall. A heavy tread of sandaled feet was coming up the steps just beyond his door. Many rooms were in this hallway, but none were occupied. No one but his father or Onandagus should be coming here. It was not his father, who wore only stout leather boots that left an unmistakable thump as he walked. These footsteps were accompanied by a strange sloshing sound.

Easing off his bed, he snuffed the dim candle and crept to the doorway to listen. It took a few moments for his eyes to adjust to the new dark. Faint starlight and outside torches gave a weak cold light that illuminated the cavernous hallway, stabbing everything differing slashes of black and gray. He could make out the outlines of the timbers in front of him as well as the stairwell where the man was almost to the top with a sloshing bag. Low to the floor, Mormon breathed slowly through his mouth, waiting to see who it was.

A shadow crept toward him down the black hallway. The man would heft his heavy sack and swing it for momentum, letting it move a few feet as he came down the hall. A thief would be leaving the building, not going farther into it away from exits. As the shadow man neared, Mormon heard the sack making a thick, viscous slosh like oil. No one transported oil in such a sack as this. The man, breathing hard, was now abreast of him in the wide hallway. He stopped and peered into the darkness toward where Mormon lay on the tiled floor. The boy whispered a silent prayer for deliverance.

A voice called soft and sinister from farther down the stairwell, "Thomas, you fool. You are making far too much noise. I can hear you from downstairs. Lucky for you, Mormon and Onandagus are gone."

"Sorry, master," drawled the shadow man.

Mormon wondered whose voice that was. It sounded familiar.

"Have you taken care of the boy yet?" asked the master.

"No, I thought where goes the lion so goes the whelp," responded Thomas, the shadow man.

"You fool, the boy's still here in one of these rooms. Find and kill him."

Mormon fought to breathe as quietly as possible.

"You don't think the fire will take care of him?"

"You are paid to do as I say. Yes, the fire will take care of everything, but I don't want him to awaken and warn anyone from a window. Hurry, fool, and do your job," snapped the man in the dark.

Mormon heard the quick, sandaled steps of the master going back down the steps, while the fool shadow man remained and drew a curved dagger from his waistband. The gleam of the silver blade reflected off the dim light from Mormon's window. Thomas seemed unsure which room to start with, since there were a dozen in this wing alone.

Mormon fought the panic that threatened to grip him. Thomas chose to begin looking in the room directly to the left. Mormon backed further into his own room as silently as he could, trying to think of what to do. He crouched in the darkest corner and decided that when the man entered the room to look upon the bed, then he would run out the door past him and down the stairs to the streets. Mormon's heart beat faster and faster. He had to catch himself from breathing too hard and loud, bracing himself to run as soon as Thomas passed him. He would be ready for the moment, but it did not come. Thomas did not enter as Mormon had expected. There was complete silence from the hallway.

Mormon waited and waited. The minutes seemed an eternity. It could not possibly take this long to search all the rooms. Ever so quiet, he edged to the doorway to see. Maybe Thomas had left already, or perhaps he was struck down by the will of the Lord for daring to defile the Judgment Hall with his very presence.

The heavy sack was still in the middle of the hall with no sign of Thomas. Waiting another impatient moment, Mormon poked his head out the doorway to look around. He smelled sweat and tobacco. He ducked back in the room just as the wide, curved dagger arced murderous intent where his head had been, and embedded itself in the soft pine door frame.

"I heard your breathing, boy!" snarled Thomas, cursing loudly as he realized the dagger was caught fast in the wood.

It was now or never. Mormon jumped back through the doorway to run past the assassin. Instead of the clean getaway he hoped for, he was met with a solid kick to the chest that burst the air from his lungs. He dropped to the ground and tried to get his wind back in time to run. Lying on the floor in a daze, he wondered why Thomas had not yet finished him off. The murderer was still trying to retrieve his dagger from the door frame.

Getting to his feet, Mormon's now splint-less leg ached from the fall. He was about to dash down the stairs when the master's voice called again, "Thomas, you fool, must I do everything myself?" The assassin's master came up the stairs, grumbling oaths to his gods.

Mormon could barely see him, but he noticed the swaying green amulet and the curved sword in the shadowed hand. Doubling back to run past Thomas, Mormon dodged the wild slash of the now rearmed villain. Running down the hall, he came to the stairs that led up to the tower. Mounting these he raced for an escape. His eyes scanned the darkness for another place to hide. He could hear his enemies' voices below.

"Thomas, it's too late for him. Light it all."

"I can still get him, I want to. Let me please," begged the fool servant.

"Very well, but do not allow him to alert anyone. I will start the fire. You have but a single minute, so hurry."

Mormon could hear the racing steps of Thomas coming up the stairway.

"There's nowhere to run, nowhere to hide, boy," called Thomas. "Fire and blood, that's how you will go. Fire and blood."

The stairs wound up and up, without a single place to hide. The white stone tower was taller than it appeared from the outside. Mormon was desperate for a hiding spot. Surely a tower like this should have something like the tales of old with hidden chambers and tunnels. At the top of the interior tower in a small foyer, Mormon spied a short ladder of six feet leading up to the roof. Climbing, he threw back the trap door revealing a small floor and parapet wall. It was square, each straight line facing a cardinal direction. He knew the hall faced due east to the Avenue of the Ram, where the riots were taking place. Guardsmen with gleaming copper armor were down below him on the street. They appeared to be holding a line against a mob of king men. With all of the shouting, no one would hear his calls for help. Staring back at the trapdoor he thought of the only viable option and waited.

"Where are you, pretty boy? Dirty old Thomas just wants a little piece of ya," he laughed. "Come here and get what's coming to you."

Mormon could hear that the man had stopped climbing the stairs but could not see him. Suddenly the wide blade arced through the trap doorway. Mormon waited for the perfect moment before slamming the thick trap door down upon the villain's head, breaking his grip on the dagger. "Arghh! Libnah take you, boy!"

Mormon grabbed the dagger and holding it like a snake, he picked the trapdoor up. The man stared up at him with murderous eyes. "You broke my hand, boy. I was only funning with you. So you owe me one, for my hand. Go on, give me my dagger back and I will just leave off now."

"You will answer to my father and Onandagus. Who is your master?" demanded Mormon.

"Aw, come on now, boy, just give me my dagger or I'll have to cut your heart out." He was cut short by the thunderclap and wave of heat and smoke as the fire exploded all over the hallway far beneath them. The smoke and heat billowed out from beneath and over the top of Thomas. "He lit it and damned me!" the man cried, his eyes wide in primal fear.

Mormon could see the faint orange glow far below at the base of the stairs.

Distracted for a mere moment Thomas made his move, reached over and knocked Mormon off his feet. Falling hard on his back, he lost the dagger as Thomas climbed up and out of the tower. Cursing as he bumped his hand, Thomas reached down and picked up his dagger. He moved menacing toward Mormon. "This is your fault and you'll be paying."

Mormon ran about to the other side of the tower. As Thomas tried to cut straight across to stab at him, he changed directions again until Thomas had the trapdoor behind him. Weaving to and fro, Mormon waited until the assassin was in the right spot, and then he kicked him as hard as he could. Thomas lost his balance and clutched in vain at the air. With a second good kick from Mormon, the man fell through the trapdoor hole, hit the floor and was still.

Putting the dagger on his own belt, Mormon went down the ladder to see if there was any way to escape through the awful smoke and heat. He choked on the smoke billowing up out of the tower as if it were an enormous chimney.

Suddenly Thomas grasped his ankle. "Forget about me, will you? You're going to go to hell with me."

"The gates of hell shall not prevail against me," was Mormon's sole reply as he kicked Thomas, sending the villain back for the final time into a flaming abyss.

Still trapped atop the tower, Mormon had the best possible view of the riots and his own funeral pyre.

A Devil if Ever I Saw One

Samson followed the caravan route from Gideon to Manti and on toward Bountiful. A tejate serving girl in Manti had been most helpful in telling him where Rezon's caravan was bound. He slept fitfully in Manti, anxious to keep on Bethia's trail, but also knowing he needed to allow his horse and himself rest.

Samson knew the roads like he knew the scars covering his body. Early the next morning, he galloped down the main thoroughfare toward Bountiful. He passed through several small towns now laden with costly wares from the caravan.

"Hey, old-timer. Did a good-sized caravan pass through here recently? Led by a man named Rezon?" asked Samson from the back of his horse, the sun looming behind him like a blazing crown.

Shielding his eyes, the old man answered, "Yes, a caravan came through a day ago. The caravan master was a colorful man named Rezon. Why do you ask?"

"I'm looking for a friend," said Samson. "Thanks for your help."

"Are you alone? Watch out for robbers. They are thick in these woods as of late."

"Thanks, I'll keep an eye open."

Riding as swift as he dared push the horse, Samson found the caravan by late afternoon. A pair of armed horsemen accosted him as cantered up behind the slow, groaning wagons. One of the men nocked an arrow, the other readied his spear.

"Just hold on there, what's your hurry?" said the archer.

Samson raised his hands. "I want to talk to Bethia. Is she here with this caravan?"

"Bethia? I don't know any Bethia," said the spear man. The archer still had his arrow nocked at Samson with a half a pull on his draw behind it.

"You going to put that down, or do I need to make you eat it? Is this Rezon's caravan or not?" Samson snarled. He had little tolerance for weapons pointed at him.

"This is Rezon's caravan but I don't know any Bethia," said the spear man.

"Wait, there was a Bethia," said the archer, lowering his bow. "She's not with us anymore. She left back in Manti."

Urging his horse past them, Samson called out, "Rezon! Come and speak to me!"

"You can't shout at our master," growled the spear man, raising his weapon. Its brazen edge was dangerously close to Samson's face. A butterfly came and landed on the edge, flitting its wings.

"Aw, look at that," said Samson. The spear man averted his eyes, and Samson grabbed the spear a foot down from the point with his right hand. He pushed the man off his horse with the butt-end of his own spear. He then swung it backwards, hitting the archer in the chest and unseating him as well. "I don't take kindly to idle threats," said Samson, dropping the spear on the ground.

Several men rode up, one wearing a bright colored jacket. "I am Rezon, what is the meaning of this?"

"You had a girl, Bethia, with you since Zarahemla. I want to know where she is."

"Why should I tell you?"

"Because I'm asking you. I am Samson, a friend of hers."

"You don't look the sort," said Rezon.

"Lord, is this how it's got to be?" Samson asked, looking skyward.

"I may be caravan master but I am no lord," said Rezon.

"I wasn't talking to you."

"I will not tell you anything about Bethia, so you had best leave," Rezon said, gesturing to the archer with a drawn bow, on the ground behind Samson.

"Don't slow me down," Samson threatened.

"Are you too stupid to see I have an arrow at your back?" Rezon grinned smugly. "You better leave."

"You can't put a man up against a wall and not expect him to kick. You gonna tell me where she is?"

"No."

"Alright, I warned you." Samson clicked softly into his horse's ear. It kicked its back legs at the archer, throwing the man back against the trees, and then it lunged forward. Like a tiger, Samson leapt from its back, taking Rezon down with him. Before the handful of men could do anything, Samson was up with the caravan master squeezed inside his arms like a rag doll, a knife at his throat.

"You going to tell me where she is now?" he said, clicking for his horse to return.

"She's not here. She left the caravan in Manti after she saw something she didn't like," Rezon sputtered, his face turning red.

"That's not what I asked." Samson squeezed all the tighter in his brutal bear hug grip. "Where is she?"

"She joined Gazelem's caravan. Didn't she?" Rezon looked to his men. Several nodded. "They are southbound for Desolation."

"Why not tell me that in the first place?" growled Samson.

"You looked like you might wish her harm."

Samson pushed Rezon away and sheathed his knife. He glared at the men as he mounted his horse.

"Do you wish her harm?" Rezon asked him.

Samson lit one of his rolled tobac cigars. "No, I don't wish her harm. I came to keep her out of trouble."

"Who are you anyway? What is she to you?"

"I'm her father's bodyguard."

"Your name is Samson?" asked one of the men.

Samson blew a cloud of smoke out his nostrils and grunted in the affirmative. He then wheeled his horse about to look directly at Rezon. "If I find out you lied to me, I'll be back and cut you into a thousand pieces." Kicking his horse's flanks, Samson trotted back toward Manti and was gone.

"That man there is a devil if I ever saw one," said the spear man. "Samson is the bodyguard of Onandagus."

"Onandagus? The chief judge and governor?"

"The very same," said the spear man, spitting at both the ground and memory of the brutal giant.

"So Bethia is the chief judge's daughter? Get Isahias up. Is he alright?" Rezon pointed at the fallen archer.

"He's out cold, probably has broken ribs from that horse kick," said the spear man, as he jostled the fallen man and struggled to lift him.

"Get him into the wagon, and let's get moving again. Bethia better be with Gazelem or I am going to need a lot more men," said Rezon. He felt his throat, where Samson's knife had pricked him.

Open Your Eyes

O pen your eyes, Bethia. There is a lot more to life than some fancy-lad," said Gazelem. He cracked the whip on his oxen to get them moving down the southbound road.

"I gave him my heart. I put it right in front of him and he scorned me," she said, letting her hand brush through the green leaves of a low-hanging branch. The leaves were cool and fragrant, reminding Bethia of her mother's orchard.

"He didn't scorn you, since he never accepted you in that way. He asked me to warn you, and I tried, but you wouldn't listen." Gazelem played with his long curling mustache as he spoke.

"I was so sure that it was right," she whined.

"How do you know that? Warm feeling in your gut, or was it what you wanted to happen? I can promise you it wasn't in the stars. I've known Rezon a long time, and the stars were never right on that boy. You're a spiritual girl, Bethia. Did you pray about it?"

"I didn't, because I think I was afraid of the answer."

"Well, you're with us now. Enjoy the caravan lifestyle. There's still a wide world out there and lots of time for you to get things figured out."

Bethia looked back at the long winding train of wagons, men and beasts. "You have more guards than Rezon did," she said to change the subject.

"Bigger caravan. Most of what we're carrying is wine, some furs from the north and a load of copper ingots I bought cheap from a merchant up in Antum a month ago. I forgot I had them and now with the price of ore the way it is, I am guessing that by the time we get to Desolation and Teancum, I will make a very healthy profit." Gazelem looked at Bethia sitting on the bench next to him. "Besides, there's a lot more Gadianton robbers than there used to be. I can't take any chances."

"My father says the Gadiantons are bolder now than ever."

"Yea, they surely are. When I was a lad, they were only rumored to exist. Some people thought the Gadiantons were a myth made up to scare us."

Bethia nodded. "Yes, I remember hearing those old stories."

"Then they began to strike at caravans like this out in the wilder lands. Now, even in the city you might be held up, if they think they can get away with it. A lot has changed this last generation. Life is more dangerous now."

"Maybe you just remember things that way," suggested Bethia.

"Maybe. I know my grandfather didn't have guards for his caravan, but my father did. Something has changed us as a people. Listen to me going off like that preaching blowhard Onandagus."

"I have heard him preach many times. He is not that bad."

"I suppose. How did you hear him so much?"

"I've lived in Zarahemla all my life. It was unavoidable. But I choose my own destiny now."

"Of course, and why not? We'll be in the city of Antiparah in a few hours, and I expect you to sell for me as well as you did for Rezon. You have quite a future before you, Bethia, mistress of the caravans, queen of wine kegs, princess of perfumes," he said, laughing aloud as he whipped the oxen.

She wasn't sure anymore that this is what she wanted. It was different before, when she dreamed of being with Rezon.

Gazelem noticed her frowning. "Here now, I was only having a little joke. No need for that look upon your face. It will all work out. There are more men than Rezon in the world." He watched, waiting for her to look at him. "Like me," he said, howling with laughter and pulling on his mustache. "Come on, I'm a handsome fellow."

"You're not funny," she said, wondering why she had ever left home.

"Yes, I am. You have no sense of humor," he retorted.

"Wake me when we get to Antiparah," she said and crawled into the back of the wagon.

"Alright," responded Gazelem. "Duchess of dregs."

"That's enough!" she snapped. He chuckled and tugged at his mustache.

Antiparah wasn't as big as Manti, and theirs was the only caravan in the city square. Although it was late in the day, they set up their wagons and booths. Some came around to buy their goods, but it was a slow evening.

"We'll be busy tomorrow. Don't worry," Gazelem told Bethia.

"I'm not worried. I know how the markets go. Thank you for taking me in and for retrieving my things from Keturah's wagon. I didn't want to go back there."

"Think nothing of it. Your temporary misfortune is my gain," he replied before leaving to see to the others.

Bethia prepared her bedding inside the wagon and ate a bit of amaranth and strawberries. Never before had life been this haphazard and unstructured. She could hear her mother's voice chastising her for sleeping in a wagon in a city square.

Traveling on a day later, they came to a wide river.

"Where are we?" she asked Gazelem.

"This is the Hermounts River, one of the biggest after the Sidon. We'll take the ferry and then make our way toward Desolation," he answered, pointing at a crossing with wide flat boats.

It took the better part of the day for the entire caravan to cross the river, considering that they had more than twenty wagons, fifty horses and two elephants. While Bethia waited for the others to come across, she hiked up a long grassy hillside.

From the top she could see a wide rolling prairie covered with bison. Mile upon mile, the huge, grazing animals bellowed and moved like they were part of the landscape itself. She had never seen such a vision. The sight was truly magnificent. Looking off to her left, Bethia saw almost a dozen strange men, coming toward her, calling out in a foreign tongue. They were dressed in animal skins and carried bows over their shoulders. Their straight hair was as dark and long as hers. They smiled at her, and she turned to run back down the hill.

Gazelem came up beside her, looking pleased and twirling his long mustache. He raised his hand in greeting to the strange men, and they returned the gesture.

"Who are they? Lamanites?" she asked.

"No, they are Lemuelites, sons of old Nephi and Laman's brother Lemuel, nomads of the plains. They knew we would be crossing the river soon, and they want to trade for some basic supplies. They are friendly, even if they look fearsome."

The men smiled and spoke with familiarity in a fluid language that Bethia could not begin to understand. Gazelem introduced them to her. "This is Yeasues, a chief. He keeps telling me that he will be king over all the Lemuelites someday. I just laugh and tell him that's fine as long as he only trades with me."

Yeasues was short and lean, no taller than Bethia but still thick with muscle beneath his open bearskin shirt. He had a determined, hard face. He nodded to Bethia and said something briefly to her while pointing with his turtle-shell baton.

"What did he say?" she asked.

"He wants to know if you are for sale."

She stepped back shocked.

"I'm just fooling around," he laughed. "He said hello. The Lemuelites are not the barbaric brutes you have heard about back in the city. They are good people and more honest than most Nephites." Gazelem spoke again to the Lemuelites and led them down the hill to the caravan.

They spent the afternoon looking over the goods and trading both fresh bison meat and gold nuggets for numerous articles of the caravan, but they were especially pleased to buy kegs of wine. Bethia found them to be enjoyable company despite their language differences. An older shaman told her a fanciful story about the sun god for whom Yeasues was named. She felt strangely sad to say goodbye to Yeasues and the Lemuelites. As they were about to depart, Yeasues handed her a turquoise necklace and spoke a few words to her. It was heartfelt, she sensed, whatever it was.

"What did he say?" she asked Gazelem.

"He said if you ever want to leave the caravan, you have a place in his lodge," laughed Gazelem.

"What did he really say?"

"That's what he really said. He said he could tell you are a strong spirit and he likes that. Spirit of the bear, he called you."

"What does he call you?"

Gazelem grinned and said, "He says I have the spirit of the weasel."

As they continued on their journey south, the caravan folk remained aloof and unfriendly, which furthered her loneliness as the days wore on. She missed Keturah.

One night, everyone gathered about a small bonfire that cast orange lights upon their faces and hands. A few strummed upon stringed instruments, and one thumped upon a skin-drum. A man extended Bethia a wineskin. It smelled stale and sour, but she put it to her lips and drank. It overflowed and ran down her chin.

As the music and fire lit up the night, Bethia danced. Her head felt numb to the loneliness until it washed away completely. She thought she had never had so much fun in her life. They joined hands and danced in a circle around the fire until she retched and fell over, to everyone's amusement. She had to sit down. Her head was spinning and the voices made little sense. Trying to get up, she couldn't walk or even crawl. Some of her new friends tried to pick her up, and she felt them tugging at her arms and legs as if unable to move her.

"What is this? Let her go!" demanded a familiar voice.

Bethia felt herself swept up in strong arms, cradled like a child in a colossal embrace. "Hello Samson," she slurred. "Are you gonna take me home to father?" she asked before all went dark.

★ ★ ★ ★ ★ ★ ★ ★ ★ ★ ★ ★

The morning light brought the worst headache Bethia had ever felt. A horrible taste stained her mouth and burned just a little. She was inside her wagon, while Samson sat on the buckboard a few feet away. "You been there all night?" she asked.

He grunted in the affirmative and handed her a water skin. "Yea, and now we ought to be heading back," he said. "You have had your little adventure, but your mother is worried sick about you. You need to come back."

"What about father?"

"He misses you, too. I have to tell them about you. I don't want to hear your mother crying anymore, and I don't like lying to your father."

"Tell them, but I am not going back. I have a new life here, new friends."

"I saw your new friends—that bunch of idiots laughing at you drunk."

"You drink, you smoke, you do all kinds of things father says are bad."

"I got my reasons," he countered. "Besides I'm older. What business is it of yours what I do?"

"Why should I go back with you? I have a life here now."

"Look, I can't lie to your father anymore. We need to go back."

"No, I am not ready, I'm not done. Tell them I am alright but I am staying. Your guilt is your own matter." Bethia held her head as the ache flared again.

"That's how it's gotta be, huh? I help you and you hang me out to dry?"

Casting her eyes down, she said, "I'm sorry, you did help me. What if I write a letter to my mother, telling her it's all my choice and to please accept my choice?"

"Maybe," muttered Samson. "But I need to know that you're going to be alright. Last night gave me no confidence."

"You and my parents have to let me go. I have to find my own way."

Samson thought for a long moment. "I'll let you stay, but you must write a letter home every week. You can afford it now that you're working. If we don't have a letter from you every week, I am coming to get you."

"I promise," she said, leaning forward to hug him.

"It's alright. You be more careful and tell your new friends I'm sorry. I thought something else was going on when I first rode up. I'll get going as soon as you write your letter."

Bethia wrote a long letter to her mother and a short one to her father. She then handed them to Samson who blew on the wet ink and once dry, placed them in his saddle bags.

"Take care," she said as he mounted his horse.

"You too," said Samson. He then rode out of the city square.

Once he was gone a number of the caravan folk came out. Bethia realized they had been curiously absent.

"He's gone," said one, and then the others appeared.

"Bethia, you need to let us know that such a man looks after you," said Gazelem with an odd firmness.

"Why? What are you talking about?" she asked surprised, as she climbed out of the wagon.

"He thought we were up to no good with you last night and made us pay dearly for it," snapped Gazelem. He had a splinted arm and a black eye. Many of the caravan men had splints or bruises; one had a bandaged head and another was on crutches.

"I'm sorry. Do you want me to leave?"

"No, but please don't ever drink with us again."

Tower of Strength

ire! Fire! The Judgment Hall is on fire!" screamed a frantic man.

This news took awhile to register with young Captain Gidgiddonah. The gathering mob pressed upon him throwing stones or worse, and he could not lose concentration for even a moment. He and his brothers in arms continued holding the line as Onandagus had charged them. Earlier that afternoon, when Governor Onandagus had announced the coming war, many fellow judges and members of the Council of Fifty had gone to the streets calling for his resignation. They wished to appoint a king who would have the ultimate power to make law and order to protect the people.

Fools or villains, thought Gidgiddonah, to trade freedom for security. As Mormon the Elder had pointed out, no matter how much these king men called for reform and change, they had not disclosed who would be king.

Mormon spoke to the guardsmen in the shield wall beside him. "It stinks of Gadiantons. They hope to get Onandagus to step down, and then they'll spring a monster on us. It would doom us as a nation to be subject to such a king. Stand tall and true. I am with you against these scoundrels."

"It is futile to stand here and take this unjust abuse," said a guardsman on Gidgiddonah's right.

Gidgiddonah ignored him. Complaining did not change anything. Although he had just met Mormon earlier this afternoon, he knew this was a man to respect, unlike Commander Lehonti. Lehonti was an older, vainglorious man who had wanted to retreat at the first sight of the gathering mob. Onandagus had told him he was relieved permanently and could retreat to his own home and there display his quality. "Mormon, you are now in charge of all the guardsmen," Onandagus had declared.

"No rest for the wicked," Mormon the Elder laughed as he donned his thick winged helmet and dared the king men to move him.

As the darkness grew, the mob became bolder. Their slings increased the speed and accuracy of their rocks. The guardsmen warded off the projectiles with their copper shields.

"Enough of this," said Mormon. He pulled a stout club and waded out into the fray, knocking heads and hands. The guardsmen joined their new headstrong commander.

Captain Gidgiddonah had said, "Yea, now there is a true man. He leads from the front." Surrounded by more than twenty king men, Mormon had bashed some amount of sense into their thick skulls.

"Judgment Hall is on fire!" shouted Gilhi, a young, new guardsman. "What do we do?"

Mormon turned scowling at the hall, eyes blazing as he muttered, "Treacherous dogs must have had a man inside. Gidgiddonah, can you handle the rest of these good citizens?"

"I will do my best."

"That's all I ask."

Taking every third man with him, Mormon the Elder rushed inside the gates as those who remained tightened the gap, protecting the grounds from the king men. The mob gained courage and surged forward at Mormon's departure. The guardsmen were hard pressed to keep them at bay. Cudgels struck skulls, and fresh blood flowed freely on the Avenue of the Eagle. Some of the men were tempted to draw their swords in this ruckus but were ordered to refrain unless drawn against with blades. Knowing this, the mob did not draw blades, increasing instead their rocks.

Battling as furious as sheep dogs and wolves, the two groups reached a point of impasse. The mob began to back off as they saw the fires licking out the windows of the hall. The white stuccoed walls were blackening. The impenetrable tower itself had smoke belching out the top like a furnace. From somewhere out in the distance a horn blew a low note, and the mob began to fade away. Gidgiddonah was confused at this develop-ment, wondering if the horn had called them off. He heard a familiar, unsettling voice behind him.

"Captain Gidgiddonah, come quickly. I need your help."

"What is it, Judge Hiram?" He despised the man. "I cannot leave my post, sir."

"I think I know where the arsonist is."

"Yea, and how is that?"

"I was in my personal chambers with a servant when I first heard the fire starting. It went swiftly as if with oil. In the thick smoke I saw a man run past. I gathered my scrolls and went to the hallway, when he ran past me in the gloom. I watched him, and even now he hides within the barn of Onandagus on the southeast corner."

"Did you see who it was?"

"Nay, I did not, but you must hurry. He cannot remain there for long." The fire was worsening, and the mob had almost completely disappeared. "You must hurry," said Judge Hiram.

"Barak, you're in command. Keep a company of ten at all the gates," Gidgiddonah commanded.

A company of ten followed Gidgiddonah, who followed Judge Hiram through the courtyard toward the southeast corner. The barn stood off by itself on the other side of Onandagus's personal fields and gardens. The ten surrounded the place and, breaking into several pairs, they advanced on the doors at each end while Gidgiddonah kept a close eye on the judge.

It was pitch black inside with the smell of oil and wine heavy in the air. Lanterns hung on the first inner posts. Judge Hiram lit those with a torch. Inside, they followed the strong smell. A man lay in a stall holding an empty leathern sack that smelled like oil. Unconscious, he reeked of alcohol.

One guardsman held a spear at his chest as another rolled him over. "It is Gershom, one of the chief judge's assistants," he said.

"Yea, it is indeed. I cannot believe this." Gidgiddonah knew the man from church. He did not drink, and he was not a man who would be in such a state for any reason. Raising him up to sit, they could not rouse him. "He has a large bump on the head, and the wine is on his clothes, not his breath," said Gidgiddonah. "He is not a wine bibber, this is suspicious."

"You claim he doesn't drink. Bah! Everyone does," said the judge, standing in the doorway.

"He does not. I know him."

"Apparently he does, besides being an arsonist."

Gidgiddonah slapped the man's face a time or two, and he mumbled something unintelligible. A bucket of water was tossed upon him, and he began to awaken. The captain helped pick him up and take him outside. A crowd had gathered near, some looking to be of the mob.

"Here is the hero, Captain Gidgiddonah. He has captured the villain who has burned our Judgment Hall. Now, who is it but Gershom, Chief Judge Onandagus's own man. You craven dog! You will burn for this," proclaimed Judge Hiram, working the crowd up into a fever pitch.

"Yes, your head will roll!"

"Traitor, anarchist, villain!"

Gidgiddonah interceded. "This doesn't make sense. There will be order! We will find out if he is indeed the arsonist."

Judge Hiram cried all the louder. "Hail Captain Gidgiddonah, our hero! Let us hang Gershom now."

The crowd surged forward, with bloodlust in their eyes. "Yea, let us hang him now," they cried out in unison.

Gidgiddonah drew his sword. "Stay back! He will receive the law the same as anyone. He will be judged by the chief judge, and then we shall see."

"How can that be fair? He is the chief judge's man. Let another judge him," said a man in front of this new mob.

"Yea, yea." cried another.

"Judge Hiram is judge, let him decide," shouted another.

"Judge Hiram is justice," cried various members of the crowd.

Gidgiddonah thought their praises and calls ridiculous.

"Put away your sword, noble Gidgiddonah, captain of tens and their tens. You have done your duty, now let me do mine," said Judge Hiram, acting valorous.

"Nay, Judge, I shall not. I believe this man to be innocent. If Onandagus cannot fairly judge him by being his master, then neither can you, as you are a witness against him."

Judge Hiram's face darkened and his wrinkles furrowed in anger. He spoke slow and deliberate for the captain's ears alone. "You fool. Can you not tell which way the wind blows? The smoke of Onandagus's destruction is all around you. You are given a chance to be a hero and have a place among us, but it is all for naught. You choose instead to lose everything!" He turned and again addressed the crowd, "The arsonist will receive a fair trial and hang for his crimes."

The crowd cheered and began to disperse. It is far too convenient, thought Gidgiddonah in suspicion and disgust.

✳ ✳ ✳ ✳ ✳ ✳ ✳ ✳ ✳ ✳ ✳ ✳

At the top of the tower Mormon the Younger paced back and forth from end to end, doing his best to stay far back from the trap door where the heat seared him. It was too far to jump and live. Looking down and to the west, he thought he saw his father directing men with buckets of water. It was hopeless. Such a pitiful amount of water could do nothing against a dry wood structure already boosted with oil. A loud crackling and rumbling crash sounded far below at the base of the stairs. Even more sparks flew up and out of the hole. Mormon worried that the stone tower would collapse.

I do not want to die. My life has only just begun. Ammaron the Scribe told me I must keep the record, and that I have a long hard life set before me. This has not been very long yet. What am I to do?

The floor on which he stood was hot, smoke seeping through some few cracks here and there. Tar which had waterproofed the flat roof was now bubbling and sticky, giving off a noxious fume. Stepping to the parapet, he knelt upon the stone. It was cool in comparison and the air somewhat fresher.

Deliver me, oh Lord. Here I am on the edge of life. Deliver me that I may serve you all my days—that I can do and say all that is before me. I will walk this world until the hair on my head is white as snow, so that I will have the time to do your service. Deliver me in the name of thy Son, Amen.

Though the wooden structure within burned and was destroyed, the spire remained steadfast as a tower of strength. It stood with no stone loosened from one upon the other.

✳ ✳ ✳ ✳ ✳ ✳ ✳ ✳ ✳ ✳ ✳ ✳

"Has anyone seen my son?" asked Mormon the Elder, asking everyone he met as he watched the fire consume the inside of the Judgment Hall. "Omni, have you seen my son?"

"Nay I have not, the fire erupted so fast I scarcely escaped myself."

Mormon pushed him aside and moved on, shouting for Mormon the Younger. He knew it was useless to call within the chaos; the fire roared and a hundred men were shouting. Some watched the fires while some fought it, futile as it was. The bucket brigade had given up as soon as Mormon himself had quit to look for his son. Flames leapt out of all visible windows. There was nothing to be done.

Barkos the Fat appeared with a dozen of his retainer firemen and a horse drawn wagon of water.

"Away with you, we have no need of your kind of help," said Onandagus.

Barkos replied, "I will donate generously to the hall being rebuilt."

"No doubt, as long as it is named after yourself."

"Nay, only to have back our hall, the pride of the city as far as architecture went. I would see its swift return," Barkos insisted.

A guardsman approached the chief judge. "Sir, Captain Gidgiddonah has a prisoner, a man that Judge Hiram claims started the fire. The mob wanted to lynch him, but the captain will not allow it."

"If the man was condemned by Judge Hiram, he must be innocent," Onandagus said.

Barkos the Fat cocked a curious eyebrow.

"So, says the captain, sir," said the guardsman.

"Please have Mormon deal with this right now, soldier."

"I would sir, but he is growing irate searching for his son."

"Have Gidgiddonah hold the man securely while I attend to Mormon." Onandagus went looking for Mormon while Barkos the Fat followed close behind. It did not take long to locate the howling giant. Onandagus looked into his weary eyes. "Calm yourself, my friend. I will help you."

Mormon removed his winged helmet from off his sweat-drenched head. Somehow, over the crackling flames they heard, "Father, up here. Father!" Stunned, they looked upward and saw the boy clinging to the edge of the tower, vaguely illuminated against the azure sky by the sparks within the smoke.

Mormon turned to Onandagus. "What do we do?"

Barkos spoke up. "I have an idea. Fetch a good bowman and a stout piece of rope."

"Do it," Onandagus instructed one of the guardsman nearby.

Barkos continued, "Attach the rope to a good arrow and send it over the top of the tower, careful not to hit the boy, and avoid the smoking trapdoor or the rope will burn."

The archer nodded as he tied the rope to a stout arrow and began to gauge the wind. They shouted up to Mormon the Younger. "Secure the rope to the parapet block and then slide down carefully." He nodded that he understood.

The archer let the arrow fly, the weight of the rope almost stopping it from making it over the top. Mormon managed to grab it as it arced over. The rope went slack, and he secured it to the large parapet block. The men on the ground yanked a couple of times to be sure it would take the weight. In a moment, Mormon was hand under hand hurrying down the rope. He froze once, looking down, but his father called to him and gave him courage. Down on the ground, he raced into his father's waiting arms and held him tight. This was a night he would not easily forget.

"Thank you for your help, Barkos," said Mormon the Elder.

"You are welcome," he replied with a grin. "Perhaps we can help each other a little more than we had previously thought."

"Are you allying yourself with us?" asked Onandagus.

"I am. Better you than the king men. An attempt was taken on my life tonight. I need to be allied with someone, and the enemy of my enemy is my friend," Barkos the Fat laughed. "I will do whatever it takes to help defeat these king men and retain our liberties."

"We are glad to have you. There is much to be done."

Marchers of Doom

The mighty marchers of doom trampled the brown earth beneath their sandaled feet. The heavy din of men who smote their shields and sang lusty ballads of war echoed. Among them was Zelph. They marched from the emerald forests surrounding Mutula and Lamanihah to the sparser oasis of Dagon and Ashkelon, the cities of the Red Coast. Taking a wide circuit of Tullan by staying between it and the coast, they avoided the high desert and Black Mountains of Fire. The drum never ceased and neither did their pace, but not a man fell behind.

These soldiers had forsworn their lives and honor on what they would accomplish. The strength of their nation rode proud on their brawny, painted shoulders. By night, they sat around campfires and delighted in tales of blood and debauchery under a cold moon. Before the sun had risen they would be on the move again. Always at the head was Akish-Antum and Crown Prince Almek.

The prince was as far away from home as he had ever been. These new experiences caused him both fear and boldness. He sought to overcome his inexperience with bravado. "My army shakes the earth beneath their sandaled feet. Who can stand against us?" he said with arrogance.

Akish-Antum looked at the boy prince seated across from him on his gilded chariot. "Careful, my prince. Though the torrents and thunders are weapons, they do not win the fight themselves."

"And what does...stargazer?" Almek said, his last word dripping with disdain. He had no use for scholars and philosophies. As his father's heir, he considered such things beneath him. His dreamt up wisdom had no real life experience behind it. Theories of life abounded within him, but taking few words of advice from anyone, his knowledge and intelligence were damned.

"The mind, my prince, the mind," said the Gadianton as he tapped a gauntlet clad finger to his copper, tiger-faced helm. Weary of speaking to the young man, he urged his mount ahead. The prince scowled at him.

After a month of marching they approached the Nephite borders. It was here that Akish-Antum changed orders. Soon there would be no more singing or drumming, and no more cook fires. Raw flesh would suit them better in the war to come and increase their savagery. He had a perimeter of guards always on patrol, forever careful that the Nephites would not become aware of them. This would be the last night of celebration.

As they made a camp about the edge of the border, Zelph asked, "May I go hunting, my prince?"

"You may go for an hour or so I suppose. I would that you bring me back an antelope. All of it."

"Yes, my prince." He knew that Almek would not eat it, but he had learned to take the prince literally. Two weeks ago when Almek asked for a deer, Zelph had brought back only the meat. The prince screamed at him for leaving the bowels in a pit and ordered him to go back and retrieve them.

Zelph must endure until the time was right. He hoped it was tonight. He walked almost four miles from camp, well beyond most of the revolving scouts. Being a captain of King Xoltec's army allowed him the luxury of going out beyond their reach; he would use it to his advantage tonight.

Finding a small hollow he knelt to pray aloud, "Oh, Great Spirit, how long must I remain here? Will you forget me, or may I go away from here never to return? How long will you turn away from me without answer to my prayer? How long will I have this pain in my heart and have my enemies exult over me? Please allow me to keep walking tonight, away from here. Give me an answer, Great Spirit, please." Silence reigned a while longer.

He knew the Gadiantons had murdered his father by now and were seeking to start a war between Nephites and Lamanites for their own power and gain. They would set up a puppet king to rule the Nephite lands, with Akish-Antum being the real power behind whoever ruled as king.

Zelph waited another few moments before deciding to continue walking until directed further. *I will not return to the army. I will walk this earth until I find what the Great Spirit wants of me.* As he walked on, he heard an audible voice. "Zelph, Zelph you are to return to the army and continue with them for a little while longer." It was a warm voice that gave him no fear. Looking about, he saw no one. *Surely the Great Spirit who moves in all things has answered my prayer, and I will do as he has asked me. Thank you, Lord, for answering my prayer.*

Traveling back toward the camp he came across a young antelope. He nocked an arrow and said, "Brother Antelope, I slay you now so that I may staunch my hunger, and continue doing the service of the Great Spirit. Please forgive me."

He released and slew the antelope. Approaching it, he said, "I thank you for giving your life to me, and I will honor you." Slinging it over his shoulder he carried the body back to camp, arriving just in time for the usual laughter and debauchery of camp life. Prince Almek had given the last few skins of wine to the men as well as bringing some camp followers from the nearby Ishmaelite town.

Girls danced to the sound of drunken laughter. Zelph noticed a strong contingent of guardsmen not allowed to join in the festivities, cursing for having drawn up guard duty. Under any other ruler or general they may have revolted at not being allowed their own debaucheries; but with the Gadianton Grand Master, fear ruled them into humble submission. Akish-Antum would leave nothing to chance.

When Zelph brought the antelope before Crown Prince Almek, he said, "I do not want that dreadful thing. Away with it." He directed his attention back to a trio of dancing girls.

Zelph carried it behind their quarters and began to clean and dress the body. He would still eat tonight. "Great Spirit, do not forget me. Have mercy on me as I fade away here. Heal me, oh Lord, my innermost being is tormented. How long will I have to suffer here?" He ate a light meal of the antelope and then went to sleep in his tent, angry at himself for agreeing to leave his father.

By dawn the dancing girls had gone home. Akish-Antum arrayed the army in the pattern he wanted for the remainder of the journey. Gadianton scouts would continue on ahead of the column, watching for any signs and making sure the path was clear. The Nephites must not learn what was coming their way until it was too late. Zelph wondered how such a large army could snake its way through enemy territory without being seen. But then again, with as much as the Gadiantons seemed to know and control things, was it really enemy territory?

The column would be split into commands of ten by ten. The men would be split into groups of ten spearmen, ten archers, and ten swordsmen and likewise repeated. This way, Akish-Antum explained, in case of a Nephite attack, they could best work in concert to repel them and support each other's strengths and weakness. The Gadianton said he hoped they could make it as far as the borders of the River Sidon, within a day's march of Zarahemla before being detected. By then it would be too late for the Nephites to defend themselves. This all depended on the Gadianton scouts finding clear paths on seldom traveled roads. Nephites could be on any road at any time, conceded Akish-Antum, but they could be dealt with. They would be captured and slain on the altar of choice, whether Baal, Moloch or Votan. The warriors cheered at this, their blood lust insatiable.

It was well before midday when the riders came. The clouds billowed overhead on this hot and dry late spring morning. Scouts rode up hard and spoke to Akish-Antum. "Grand Master, there is a goodly force approaching quickly from the southwest."

"Nephites?" asked Almek.

"No, they are well-armed Ishmaelites of Tullan," answered the scout.

Akish-Antum signaled a halt and bade everyone rest for a moment under the hot sun. Soon the army of horsemen and marchers became visible from the distant hills; black shapes wavering in the red heat plumes of the white hot desert, walking mirages with glittering spears and golden shields. These were tall lean men, copper-skinned of a slightly different shade than the men of Mutula. They wore more armor, bracers and greaves of hammered, embossed copper. They also wore copper and leather head plates with cotton bandannas to shield them from the merciless sun. Their loins were draped in bright green and black kilts. Sharp daggers were at their sides and long spears in their hands.

The army was led by Teth-Senkhet, second-in-command to Akish-Antum. As they approached, he spoke to Teth-Senkhet. "How went your journey? You are a little later than I had hoped."

"We had a small sandstorm to deal with a week ago in the high desert, but we are here now and ready for your orders," replied Teth-Senkhet, who even in the heat wore a black cloak with gold trim.

Prince Almek frowned at them. "Who are these men who intrude while my army waits and sweats under the sun?"

"Patience, my prince, these are our welcome allies, the warriors of Tullan." Turning back to his second-in-command, Akish-Antum asked, "Who is their field commander?"

"It is the tall one there. Anathoth." Teth-Senkhet pointed to the lead horseman who now dismounted to approach them.

The man's sharp face was outlined by his Egyptian style headdress. He wore the same greaves and bracers as his men. "Hail Akish-Antum, Grand Master of the Northern Gadiantons," he said, his arm upraised in the Lamanite fashion of greeting.

"Grand Master of the North, how amusing," Akish-Antum said under his breath.

"King Apophis of Tullan is not yet agreeable to renouncing his claim," Teth-Senkhet explained. "His men will obey us and yet still not acknowledge our divine right."

"Very well, but let us keep the armies separate. I want no fraternization that could jeopardize our plans," the Gadianton Grand Master whispered to his second before shouting to the Tultecs, "Hail Anathoth, General of Tullan, servant of Rabannah King Apophis!"

Prince Almek glowered at the Gadianton calling anyone besides his father Rabannah. Zelph stood near to Almek, as was his charge at this time. He sized up this Anathoth and his black stallion with his fine steel bow and full quiver and judged him a capable warrior. He also had a broad scimitar slung across his back in a fancy decorated scabbard. Anathoth sent his spear into the ground before him as he approached the prince and the Gadiantons.

Akish-Antum dismounted his chariot and clasped hands with the general. "We are unified, are we not?"

"We are," said General Anathoth.

The Gadianton stood head and shoulders taller than the warrior, but the Tultec did not seem the least bit intimidated by him. Akish-Antum then began to speak in a tongue that neither Almek nor Zelph could understand. Anathoth answered him in kind, and Almek was all the more infuriated by not understanding the interchange.

"This is not right. I should be privy to all matters of this war. What are they saying?" the prince shouted.

"They are agreeing on who commands the army of Tullan," said Teth-Senkhet. "It's simply a formality of transferring authority from King Apophis to Akish-Antum. It is their way."

"What are you talking about?" Almek shouted at Akish-Antum.

"Patience my prince, I am negotiating the order of the army."

"That should be my place. It is my army."

"Don't you mean your father's army? I will tell you what I have done—I am placing Anathoth and his men in the front."

"In place of my honor?" whined Almek.

"No, they are better armed than your force, and they have more experience as well. Anything that happens, they will be the first hit. You will be safer back here. Fear not, you have not lost your command by any means. All is the same as it ever was. Now we simply have a bigger army in front."

Almek frowned but did not reply.

"You still command your own army, Prince, but I will command the army of Tullan since you don't speak Tultec. Agreed?"

Almek scowled and cried out, "Let us move on then, and get some wind in our faces instead of this accursed sun."

The Gadianton nodded and waved Anathoth on, who rode his horse hard ahead at the lead of his twenty-five thousand men.

Zelph, close to Almek, was surprised as the prince motioned him to board his chariot and stand next to him, bidding the driver to get off. Zelph stood beside him, expecting to be pushed backward for the cruel prince's childish amusement.

Instead Almek said, "Zelph, you have traveled more than I and received good battlefield counsel from your father. What do you know of Tullan? Is it true what Akish-Antum says, that our armies cannot beat theirs in a fair fight?"

The big man was suspicious. Was the prince baiting him only to torment him further? "Do you really seek my counsel on these things?" asked Zelph.

"Yes, I do."

"They are hardy fighters who use a disciplined method of fighting learned from Zoramites. It is based upon old Mulekite techniques. On an open battlefield, I believe they could best us. However, in the forests and jungles we could split them up and break their vaunted phalanx techniques."

"Why do we not go out and destroy them, instead of leaving them between us and the Nephites?" said Prince Almek, whipping the reins on his chariot horses.

"I am sure that is part of the Gadianton plan," said Zelph. "It is in the best interest of the Gadiantons to have us fighting Nephites rather than each other. There is no profit for them when we fight each other, and I don't believe they want that. That they even organized a joint coalition between us denotes their intent."

"Yea, I seem to remember my father and Balam-Ek saying something of this awhile ago, but the wine, the dancing girls...I was not paying attention when I should have. In this grave hour, I now realize how much time I have wasted. I am not ready for war. It is good you are here. I can use your true counsel as opposed to Akish-Antum's self-serving designs. It is good my father has Qof-Ayin, and I have you." He looked away a moment. "Forgive me, Zelph, for my cruelty to you. When I conquer Zarahemla, you will be richly rewarded."

"Thank you, my prince." *It will not happen. I will not be there. Great Spirit, remember me, show me what I must do to avoid this war, this bloodshed. Great Spirit, remember me.*

That night they made camp after crossing a slow-running, mud-brown river. Akish-Antum had the army sleep in fourths at all times. A full quarter of the men were awake and ready for battle. The Gadianton Grand Master warned the men against being spooked by lights or shouting that could come from out in the darkness. Tales had already been told of possible Nephite tricks, and he would not have his plans thwarted. He told them that they were now within the Nephite lands and to expect the worst if captured and taken prisoner.

Lamanites offered their war prisoners as a sacrifice and appeasement to the gods, a quick and honorable death. Nephites, however, tortured their prisoners for years before slowly burning them alive or feeding them piece by piece to dogs. Such an end would not allow a true warrior entry into the hall of the gods, but would make him a slave for all eternity, an administering servant to the Nephites in their own paradisaical glory. Or so Akish-Antum told them while on the march. A few Gadiantons would laugh at these tales as they circulated the camp, swearing they were all true.

All through the night Akish-Antum received reports from runners and spies about the route ahead. No one ever saw him sleep. Zelph thought of him as the shadow on the light of the world.

The Coward's Bravery

For the past three weeks Amaron and his men stalked through the back roads and trails far west of Zarahemla. They ventured as far as the edge of the ruins of Ammonihah, the Desolation of Nehor. Beyond these were the plains of Heshlon and the wilderness of Hermounts. Ezra said he was reasonably sure that the Lamanite attack would take place further south of Ammonihah.

Amaron told his men, "Let us go south and loop back to Zarahemla in a wide, easy, half-moon maneuver overland. If we find nothing in the next couple weeks you can all be released since it is almost summer. I will not keep you any longer beyond this journey."

All agreed to this except Reuben, Ezra's uncle. "I want to kill Gadiantons," he bellowed.

"Easy, uncle. He who lives by the sword shall die by the sword," said Ezra.

"It's better than on your knees like my son was forced to. I will have my righteous revenge by heaven's throne!" said Reuben, spitting as he talked.

Ezra grimaced and begged, "Don't say that."

"I will say it. We Nephites have a God-given duty to slay the enemies of God, like Lamanites, Gadiantons, Lemuelites, Ishmaelites, and Nubians."

"That's enough, Reuben. Shut your mouth," said Amaron. "Let us keep our discipline and politics separate. Now, we cut through that swamp yonder, ascend the hills and make camp for the night."

"Why not go the way we came? It will be easier and we can make those hills in half the time," said Ezra, rubbing his sore legs.

"A scout learns never to take the same trail twice, to avoid ambush. By always taking a different route, we confound the enemy at every turn," Amaron explained. "With an undesirable trail, we can better avoid detection and trouble."

"The Gadiantons will have scouts of their own, and I believe the route will be here in our own territory. I don't wish to die confronting them, eah," Ezra said fearfully.

"No one does."

"I admit I'm a coward who wants redemption. I have sinned many times."

"Everyone has."

"I never prayed until Onandagus had me pray with him, you know, to begin my repentance process."

"And?" Amaron questioned. "Get to the point."

"I pray constantly in my heart now for what I fear will happen to me on that last day." Ezra stared off into space.

Amaron put his hand on Ezra's shoulder and looked him square in the eye. "You can't live in fear, nor should you do what's right out of fear. Do your best with us. You desire to learn much and that counts for a lot, even if you are city folk," he smirked.

"Thanks."

They snaked their way through the murky green waters that went from ankle deep to their chests. Amaron kept them together and free of the many serpents. On the other side several hours later, they stopped to remove ticks and leeches. They ascended the hills and were hiking along a small creek when nightfall was almost upon them. They found a spot where in times past the creek had washed out a good-sized cavity in the rock but now stayed just abreast of the ledge. It had a clean little overhang to keep them warm and dry.

"This will shield us from the rain that I think may come in the night," said Amaron. "Let's get a small smokeless fire going to dry our clothes and boots. If we put it under the rock face no one will be able to see it."

The tall thick trees blocked out the night sky. The slivers of the moon stabbed through here and there giving its cold light and striping the forest floor. Ezra stared at the fire for a moment then looked out into the impenetrable night. Judah rigged up a rack of sticks to dry their boots and socks. The men ate a light meal of venison from a deer they had killed a couple of days before and chewed on corn cakes that Reuben prepared on a small skillet. He burnt them a little, but everyone wanted something besides two-day-old dried venison so they didn't complain about the burnt cakes.

"Daniel and I will have the first watch," said Amaron, munching a corn cake.

"Could I be on first watch?" Ezra asked.

"I don't care...Daniel?"

Daniel nodded, as crumbs rolled down his chin.

"Let the fire die down to coals, and each watch will maintain the fire throughout the night just enough to relight if necessary," said Amaron finishing his cakes.

"Why let it die? We have kept it going all night thus far," asked Benjamin.

"I have a strange feeling. Something is telling me that it is close. We must be careful from here on out. Good scouts could come down this gully and spot even our sheltered fire."

The last flames began to flicker and disappear in the dying coals, until a warm orange and gray glow remained.

"Ezra, you and I will keep watch, eyes wide in the dark," said Amaron. They walked a short distance into the darkness as the others stretched out on their bedrolls.

"Something else troubles you, what is it?" asked Ezra.

He asks questions like a woman sometimes. It is a strange feeling to hate someone and yet feel indebted to them; to pity them while growing tired of them. I must grow beyond my anger; it is all in God's hands. Things often do not happen how we wish them to. I cannot put my trust in any arm of flesh, not even my own, only the Lord. Everything is his will not mine, not mine.

"Amaron?"

"What? Oh, I am sorry, just thinking. Yea, I am troubled. Things are not like when we were younger. My friends have changed. This mission is not what I planned at all. I do not like the attitude of the men. I wish things were as they used to be, but that time is gone. It exists only in memories and dust."

"I am sorry for the part I have played in your troubles. I never wanted Helam to die."

"I know. You have said that many times, and it is my own fault for being a vengeful man. There is nothing that can be done to change anything now. I must move beyond my weakness."

"We're supposed to be on watch, but can we talk a little while longer?"

"Yea, go ahead. The others are making enough noise for the Lamanites down in Tullan to hear."

Ezra said hesitantly, "What have you done to atone for your wrongs?"

"I have never done anything to speak of. I do not drink wine nor smoke the tobacco. I have lain with no woman and told no lie. These things are the root of my arrogance, I suppose. I know it and am working on it. Pride comes before the fall, or so I have been told."

"What can I do to atone?" asked Ezra.

"I am not the man to discuss this with. I was baptized and made a member of the Church of Christ at age eight. I am the eldest of my father's sons and have always done my duty and scorned those who did not. Perhaps you should ask these questions of the chief judge."

"He said I should speak to you of such things."

"Does he mock me?" said Amaron, his ire raised for a brief moment. "No, I suppose it is to make me think. When we teach others, it helps to make things clear in our own minds."

"My life was never good. I never knew my father."

"I am no fortunate son," Amaron retorted.

"In some ways you had better opportunities than me. I learned on the streets to take what I needed with no thought of consequence. It is how many are taught now. There is no responsibility. You are lucky you had the family you do."

"It is not luck, I do not believe in luck. It was meant from before the beginning," snapped Amaron.

"What do you mean by that?"

"In the beginning, the Father in heaven asked his greatest sons how the earth should be. The eldest son said we should have freedom to choose. It is how we could best learn and progress. The other said we should all be forced to do what is right, that we might all return to heaven after having been on the earth. I am not good at this," Amaron scowled. "I am no missionary."

"Please go on, for it rings true to me."

"There was a war. In it, there were spirits on both sides along with those who chose to wait and see which side would prevail. They all fought one another. They did battle in ways I cannot describe."

"I have never thought much on these things. I would like to learn more."

"Tomorrow. We need to be silent now and keep watch. I am surprised at myself for telling you any of that. It is not the kind of topic I usually speak of." They sat a moment longer in the dark until Amaron was sick of listening to Ezra's erratic breathing. "You take a position over by those rocks and keep an eye out, especially to the east. I will go by that fallen log and watch our west and north."

Ezra nodded and went to the rocks. The others were settled for the night and most were asleep, tired from the long wet hike earlier that day. Gradually the threatening clouds moved out, and the bright moon shone through the trees. The wind blew down the gully, and a deer moved swift and silent a hundred yards to Amaron's right. He watched and wondered at what made it move so quickly and with so much fear. Something must be out there. Wiping a sweaty hand on his buckskin trousers, he hefted the hickory handle of his war hammer. It felt good in his hands. He would not draw his sword until necessary. The moon might glint too much off its razor-sharp edge.

Some moments passed and still he heard nothing, although he thought he saw a big shadow making its way down the gully. Always the shadow seemed to stay in thick darkness, was it really there? It moved with grace and agility in an easy zigzag manner, almost hypnotizing. He began to think it was a trick of moonlight through the trees, until the wind changed and the shadow stopped dead. A low, deep growl escaped as it bounded behind a huge boulder with one terrific leap. Amaron caught sight of a massive tan leg in the moonlight. Turning toward Ezra who was near to dozing, he warned, "Hsssst!"

Ezra yawned at him and mouthed silently, "What?"

"Lion."

"Here?" he gasped and craned his neck at the maw of surrounding darkness.

Inching toward Ezra and the camp, Amaron watched the boulders. "Yea, a lion. Big one, too. There are plenty of ravenous beasts near the wilderness of Hermounts."

"Where is it now?"

"Behind those rocks. Make your way back to camp and wake the men. It knows we are here, but it may leave. They don't normally like to fight men if they can avoid it."

Ezra nodded and began to inch back toward the overhang, feeling his way since he would not turn his head away from the rocks where the lion lurked. Fast as fear, the lion roared its challenge, and jumped over a huge stand of rocks. It ran a short distance to another dark collection of shadows.

Amaron drew his broadsword with his right hand and held the war hammer ready in his left. Scanning the darkness, he waited anxiously.

"Where is it?" asked Ezra.

"I don't know."

The men stirred. "What was that?" Reuben asked, rubbing his eyes.

"Get up and ready your spears," Amaron called over his shoulder. "Reuben, your bow."

"I cannot shoot well in the dark," said the old man, still trying to rouse himself.

"You're worthless," muttered Daniel.

"Hey, when the light comes I will—" said Reuben. The beast roared again and cut him off in a hurry. It had circled the camp.

"It's fast, could be a maneater to be this bold. It must know there's a group of us. It's aggressive; be ready for anything." Amaron scanned the darkness.

Ezra twitched, watching every which way, eyes wide with fear.

Judah approached with his spear poised. "Where is it? I don't see anything."

"Be still," Amaron warned. "It is stalking us. Don't move anywhere without backup."

They clustered a little more now, waiting. The silence in the darkness seemed to stretch on without end. Ezra moved farther into the camp and threw more wood on the fire.

"Don't anyone look into the fire. The lion won't come from there anyway," said Amaron.

Ezra's fire grew quickly and was crackling loud; he had thrown all the wood for the night onto it. Amaron felt sure that the men looked into the flames for the primeval, false comfort it gave them from the creatures of the night. Their night vision would be destroyed, rendering them useless if this fight went anywhere. The huge cat was still out there. He could feel its presence, watching, waiting, and ravenous to devour them. It could sit and wait, then slam them to their deaths. Amaron had seen the saber-toothed lions swat bison with their paws and break legs and ribs, before puncturing the thick bodies with their long, curved teeth.

A vicious snarl ripped through the still of night. With near blinding speed, the lion with its dagger-like teeth pounced upon Judah, blind-siding him and taking the hapless man to the ground. The instant Judah screamed Amaron moved to aid him, as did Daniel and Reuben, each with an arrow nocked. The lion roared again and disappeared into the night.

Judah had deep claw gashes across his chest. He was in shock and quivered uncontrollably. They cleaned his wounds and sat him next to the fire.

"It's still out there feeling us out for a weakness," said Reuben.

"You bet your fat backside it's still out there. That curelom muncher is hungry, and it's got a taste for Judah's flesh," Daniel said with a smirk.

"Shut up," mumbled Judah. "It did not get a taste."

The beast roared again. Amaron remained a short distance from the camp, his back to a thick tree, waiting and listening. "Where are you?" he whispered. "Come taste Zarahemlan steel." He moved a short distance to another thick oak. A low groan came from behind, Amaron swung ready to drive Ramevorn hard, but it was only Ezra carrying Judah's spear.

"Don't do that!" Amaron snapped.

"Sorry, I wanted to help."

"Be more careful. It will try to sneak up behind us if it can. That's a cat's way."

"Like it did with Judah?"

"Yea, he is blessed it did not get him worse."

"Those fangs, they were huge," said Ezra, shuddering.

"Yea, they stab and kill with them, or swat you with their paws. They can strike hard enough to break a man's leg or neck. We have seen them out in the Hermounts wilderness leap upon a mammoth and bury their long fangs in its back until it drops dead." A roar sounded this time much farther away, somewhere near the peak of the next hill.

"Did it leave?"

"It seems so. It must have decided we were not worth the trouble. I would still prefer to hunt and kill it, because man-eaters should not be allowed to roam anywhere near our settlements."

"Maybe it will get some Lamanites for us," offered Ezra.

"Maybe the Lamanites sent it to get us," joked Daniel.

"Let's go back to camp—" Amaron was cut short as the lion leapt upon him, pinning him to the ground. As it moved to stab its saber-like teeth into Amaron's neck, Ezra sent his spear into its ribs. The spear head sank deep all the way to the knot of eagle feathers Judah had placed inches below the brazen head. The lion cried out in pain and rolled off Amaron, convulsing and spitting. It glared at its attacker, powerless to move toward him. It took a half step and collapsed, its eyes still following the skinny man who had driven the spear.

A second roar rang out as another huge cat leapt out of the shadows toward the unconscious Amaron. Ezra was now weaponless, his spear still embedded in the first lion.

The others stood frozen near the fire. Ezra was on his own. Raising his arms above his head, he screamed at the cat, "Get outta here or I'll kill you, too!" The savage lion roared at the little man and took a step forward, its sinister green eyes fixed on him.

"Go, go get away from here!"

The lion stepped forward again until it was almost on top of Amaron, who lay deathly still. It roared its challenge and looked to its fallen mate, sensing that the little man had no weapons. It took another step forward, its gruesome head lowered ready to leap. Amaron's war hammer swung upward like a striking serpent, its curved spike sinking right between the lion's eyes. The beast dropped like a stone.

"You all right?" asked Ezra.

"Yea, I am."

"I feared you were gone. You had not moved in all that time."

"I would be dead if it weren't for your bravery. You gave me time to regain my senses and let the cat walk into a trap." He rolled onto his side and took deep breaths for awhile before struggling to his knees. He looked at Ezra and said, "I thank you for your courage."

"You're welcome."

"It's time for someone else to take over the watch. I need some sleep."

Tongues of Fire

How can a heart be so black? Why does he watch me so? His intelligence is the abysmal depth of despair upon me, it is so cold.

"What are you thinking about, Zelph?" asked Prince Almek as he tossed a spent and fatty morsel of meat into a small brazier burning low blue flames before him.

"Nothing, my prince," Zelph replied.

"Don't claim you weren't. Come now, I need all your thoughts and counsels."

"I was only thinking that Akish-Antum stares at me. I know not why."

"Take heart, big man. He stares to unnerve me, not you. You are my bodyguard; and I expect that should the need ever arise, you would do better than me at slaying the dreamer—that cursed stargazing sorcerer," he muttered, looking at his scarred hand where the shattered obsidian blade had cut clean and deep. A bizarre spiderwebbed scar tore itself across the universe of his hand.

"I would do my best," said Zelph, fingering his own dagger.

"I mean, if you have to."

"Of course, my prince."

Almek scowled at the fire in the brazier. "We shall see what happens upon this journey of conquest. I don't trust him. Grand Master of the Gadiantons he may be, but he is still a Nephite dog. It is the Nephite way to usurp our birthright and betray us and being a Gadianton only compounds the treachery. It always comes back to the

216

birthright, I am sure of it."

"We should be brothers," responded Zelph offhandedly.

"What? You and I, perhaps; my father did get around but you look just like a bulkier Qof-Ayin."

"No, I meant Lamanites and Nephites," he said, regretting that he had said anything out loud.

Almek's face darkened and he threw down his wine glass. "Do not speak of such things. Such thoughts are well and good for philosophers, poets, and priests, but I am grounded in the real world, and I tell you there will never be peace between us. Not until we stand upon their graves and bury their memory from off the face of the earth so that no one will know they ever walked this land. When their very existence is denied a thousand years from now, then I will be happy."

"That is a long time to wait for satisfaction."

"It will be worth it," said the prince, tossing a small amount of his wine into the brazier. The fire flared up briefly at the alcohol fuel. He sat watching the flames, fascinated at their devouring power. It took a few moments for him to come back. Zelph stood by quietly watching.

Almek straightened in his chair and continued in a heated, haughty tone. "I have heard the tales, the fables, the myths, that the Nephite forefather guided us here from across the great deep, bah. He eventually sought dominion over his elders. They would not stand for his trickery and stole away into the wilderness to retain their liberty. Father knows the names of the lands and peoples across the sea. I care not. They have no meaning in my life. What does he call them? Row-mans, and before that it was the Baby-Lonians. No, we are not brothers and should not be. The Nephites have my scorn and can have the sharp end of my sword. That is all I care to give." Almek drew his sword and held it high toward the rising red sun. Its golden hilt shone bright as scarlet death in the morning light.

Zelph said nothing. He had heard all this dogma before many times, but his father Qof-Ayin had taught him the truth of those ancient bygone times. Their ancestor, Samuel the Prophet, had left a written record for his children. In time it had passed to Qof-Ayin, and he had read the account to his son Zelph, who had believed even as a boy. His father bowed to no gods of stone, he knew who his God was—the Great Spirit, the Ancient of Days.

Two riders in mud-caked cloaks came up hard and fast, their mounts frothing heavily. Wiping his brow, one dismounted and approached Zelph and Almek.

"My master, where is my master?" said the first, not yet realizing he was addressing the prince.

"Here," said Akish-Antum as he strode forward from out of the western darkness. "What news?"

Almek frowned that the scout had not addressed him as my prince. Most of the Gadiantons did not show him the respect he deserved.

"Ill news, Grand Master. The Nephites have four score men heading this way. There are too many for us to handle. If they should spot the column—"

"Silence!" thundered the Gadianton Grand Master, as he struck the scout, knocking him backwards. Akish-Antum rubbed his chin for a moment. "Anathoth!" he shouted. General Anathoth came forward, sharp spear in hand. The Gadianton spoke to him in a language unfamiliar to Zelph. General Anathoth and three hundred of his warriors then marched down the road.

"What was that?" asked Prince Almek.

"I took care of a problem, my prince. Anathoth will handle it swift and clean. No word of our approach will escape. We must be especially careful now. It will be more difficult to avoid Nephite townships and farms. We must slay more than a few to mask our approach," said the Gadianton, cold as the frozen north wind.

"I have no problem with that. But I make the final decision, is that understood?"

"The Tultecs only answer to me. They would not acknowledge your commands. Trust me, my prince, we all serve but one purpose," said Akish-Antum, flexing his hand underneath his gauntlet. The bright, copper hand had several sharp spikes with the fingers ending in claws, the inhuman hand of a monster.

It disgusted Zelph to be near the man. He only wished to be away from here. *Why am I here, what am I doing with these wicked, bloodthirsty men? Great Spirit, I am to serve you. How can I do that here? Please answer me and guide me soon.*

Within the hour they passed through a wooded glade covered in red gore. The copper smell of spilt blood hung thick in the air against the wet white sage. It had been quick and decisive. Anathoth and his men were completely unhurt; the Tultecs did not have a single casualty. It must have been lightning quick and deadly.

As the royal chariot passed over the crimson ground, Zelph prayed. *Great Spirit, how long must I remain? Please hear my prayer and deliver me.*

Akish-Antum, standing in the glade beside a few of his men, spoke to Uzzsheol, "You are sure none escaped?"

"None now live."

"How many were there?"

"Forty two, Malachi cannot count."

"Good. See to it that the bodies are hidden as well as can be expected."

"Yes, Grand Master."

In all his eighteen years, Zelph had never felt afraid of any man, but something about the Gadianton Grand Master made his skin crawl. It was as if a primordial evil hung over him and radiated outward. The man stared at him as though reading his thoughts.

Great Spirit of my fathers, help me escape from here.

After the massacre in the glade, Akish-Antum demanded an extra heavy march. He wanted as many miles as possible between their camp and the glade.

"You are not a gambler, are you Akish-Antum?" said Prince Almek.

"No, my prince, not when I can control the outcome. So, I am no gambler. I fix everything," said the Gadianton with a mirthless laugh.

Zelph sat near the prince, but he would not join in the conversation. He had no desire to speak with the company of Gadiantons, especially when the talk drifted to women and all manner of debauchery. Each man swore by the throne of heaven that his were the worst of stories, and each in turn said they could best what came before. The talk overflowed with riotous laughter at the climax of each story, growing in intensity from the increased drunkenness.

"Let me tell you my miraculous story of debauchery and buggery!" one named Samos said slurring drunkenly, and the laughter and arguments arose all over again.

Zelph went within himself to avoid listening.

Akish-Antum drank deep of his wineskin and proclaimed, "The sacred virgins of Isabel in Tennen-Isis are the best. I will see if I can capture you one, my prince, once things are done in Zarahemla. They can—"

He was cut off by Zelph who could handle no more. "May I go hunting once again, my prince? I long for some fresh venison."

"We move again at dawn, and we need you to be rested for the morrow," said Almek.

"I shall be ready," Zelph answered, walking away into the darkness. He noticed the Gadianton Grand Master motion to Uzzsheol. *He will surely have me followed. I must be cautious. Great Spirit, please guide and direct me. Help me. Deliver me from my enemies.* As Zelph walked away from the dim lights of the camp's few cook fires, he looked low and over his shoulder and saw the lanky form of the hawk-faced Gadianton tracker behind him. *Great Spirit, my God, please help me. Open a way, I know you can.*

At that moment a dog ran from a tent and began barking and growling at Uzzsheol. He stopped short to draw his tomahawk from his belt, taking his eyes off Zelph for a moment. A dozen men came from their tents to see what caused the dog to bark.

"Who are you to come to our tents at this late hour? Are you a thief?" demanded one.

"Nay, I am not," said Uzzsheol the tracker, annoyed that the snarling dog was not called off.

More men began to congregate around them. Several shouted at Uzzsheol who, now silent and angry, tried to push his way through. A burly Lamanite shoved him and Uzzsheol pushed him back. It escalated to a wrestling match. As they rolled on the ground, the dog nipped at his legs until he kicked it and sent it yelping in pain. He drew his big knife and slashed the burly man's left ear off. Another man grabbed a spear, and the tracker crouched ready to fight all two dozen men if need be.

"Enough! What goes on here?" shouted Akish-Antum, whose appearance caused most of them to slink off into the shadows.

"This man is a thief. My dog caught him, and he cut off my ear!" said the man clutching his bloody head.

"He is no thief. He is my servant and you had one ear too many," laughed the Gadianton, as the man retired to his tent holding his bleeding head.

Uzzsheol looked about, but in the gathering darkness he had lost Zelph. He had no idea which way the big man had gone.

* * * * * * * * * * * *

Zelph kept a good pace until he was miles from the camp. The army was heading northwest to go the long way around the Narrow Pass, so he would go northeast and skirt around the mountains above the Narrow Pass. He kept going until he passed out from exhaustion some time near dawn.

He awoke near midday to a bright and warm sun. The trees flowed gently in the wind, and white wild flowers surrounded him on all sides amidst a sea of grass. *This place is beautiful; I will thank the Great Spirit for guiding me here.* He knelt and prayed aloud, "Great Spirit, if this is the course you have set before me, guide me that I may find what you would have of me. Help me provide for myself that I may eat. I will go where you lead me. Thank you, Lord."

As he looked up, he saw a large buck standing nearby, gazing at him. He drew his bow and nocked an arrow, but the buck ran from him. Giving chase, he ran for miles with the buck always staying just out of reach. Yet if it went too far ahead, it would wait for him to catch up. This strange game went on for some time, until the buck came to a cool stream in a small grove and stopped. A small waterfall made a music all its own here. Zelph was about to shoot the deer when he heard a man's voice.

"Hold your arrow. I have food enough for both of us." The man was quite a bit shorter than Zelph, with a full beard and sparse gray hair. He stroked the buck's neck like a pet.

"Who are you, that the animals fear you not?" asked Zelph.

"I am a disciple of the Lord. One who will tarry until his return," said the man kindly.

"I have heard a little of you three."

"And I have heard of you as well, brother. I know your concerns and fears, and I am here to tell you that your father is a good man and has need of you to do his work in the temple of Zarahemla."

"How can you know that? Does my father still live?"

"Not in body, but I have spoken with him."

This puzzled Zelph. "How can I go to Zarahemla? The Nephites will kill me."

"Some would try, yes; but the Great Spirit's plan will not be stopped. You have a great faith and a great purpose to fulfill for yourself and for your family."

"I don't know what I should do. I was told I have family in Jershon, but I do not know the way. Nor do I speak the Nephite language."

"Do you believe in the Great Spirit with all your might, mind and strength?"

"Yes, I do, but..." stammered Zelph.

"Which is it?" queried the disciple.

"I believe. Nay, I know that through him all things are possible."

The disciple looked at him and said, "We all must be tested. As your father made the ultimate sacrifice for you, you will also make a sacrifice someday. Today you will be tested. Come with me."

"Are you going to test me?"

"No, you will test yourself. In this life we are here to prove to ourselves who we are, not prove to the Great Spirit. He already knows." The disciple led Zelph to a small cave beside the waterfall. They entered the tunnel and walked inside for some distance until it was completely dark. "You may stay here and pray," he instructed Zelph. "When you have an answer, come out and I will introduce you."

Unsure what that meant, Zelph decided to obey. He knelt and prayed. At first he was angry, thinking he was wasting his time. He had a very long journey ahead if he were to stay ahead of the army. Then he realized such an attitude profited him nothing, and he chose to think only of that which was uplifting and beneficial to himself and others. Soon enough, he felt ready to go and see what the disciple wanted. It was night. He had been inside the cave much longer than he had thought.

"How do you feel?" asked the disciple.

"I am fine, thank you. I had no idea that so much time had passed."

"More than you know," said the disciple. "I have something for you...a stone." It was a glossy, yellowish stone about half the size of a hen's egg. "This is your personal Urim and Thummim, an interpreter stone. With this you will have the tongue of fire. You will be able to speak and understand all languages, a most useful tool for your missions."

"And what is my mission?" Zelph wondered.

"He will tell you."

"Who is he?"

"I will introduce you now, to your Lord."

"I am not worthy of such an honor," said Zelph, bowing his head.

"You are more worthy than you know. Your faith has proven it. There is a great work for you, and it begins now. Come, let me introduce you."

* * * * * * * * * * * *

The next morning as Zelph looked into the pool of water in front of the cave, he was astonished at his reflection. His black hair had turned light brown, even white at the edges, and his skin significantly lightened, from a mahogany brown to a paler shade of white. He looked exactly the same but with an older, wiser look about him. He appeared to be well beyond his eighteen years.

I should not be surprised by this. Who could look upon the face of the son of the Great Spirit and not be changed? A change so obvious that all can see. A change that will make me cursed in the eyes of some, just as the evil spirit Ahtmar foretold. But that which the Great Spirit chooses to give I cannot refuse.

The disciple offered some last bit of counsel as he bid Zelph farewell. "Seek out Onandagus, the prophet. He will guide and direct you. Farewell, my brother."

They clasped hands and Zelph, now the white Lamanite, continued on his journey northward to Zarahemla.

The Vision Serpent

I t is time," whispered High Priest Balam-Ek to the king. "He is young, yet you know as well as I that things are happening and we need to prepare."

The royal hall was almost empty. Aaron sat next to his elder sister Sayame and disliked being talked about as if he were not there.

The lean old king stood high and held his scepter aloft as he proclaimed to the few gathered, "Arise, my second living son, Aaron. It is time to begin your journey and find your way."

The small, twelve year old boy stood up, unsure of what was about to take place. He approached his father and knelt before him.

"He is too young," pleaded Sayame, his willowy, older sister who had practically raised him since their mother had died at his birth. Sayame and Aaron often wondered if their father had ever forgiven him for that.

"Yea, he is young, but his elder brother, my heir, goes to war and glory for my house. Almek will succeed me soon enough, and his brother must be ready for his duties as well," said the king.

According to tradition, Aaron was two years too young. Most initiated boys began at fourteen years of age. At only twelve, he would be the youngest initiate ever. King Xoltec was never one to be mindful of tradition. He had sought to break his people of them whenever possible. Any traditions similar to the Nephite ones, he had crushed. All of the Nephite holidays and celebrations had been banned and replaced with new ones on different dates and with different meanings.

"Balam-Ek, begin immediately. Aaron, you will serve your brother.

It is your destiny." The king dismissed the hall and turned his attention to the dancing girls as they entered the hall. The musicians began their exotic sounds of strings, drums and bells. King Xoltec's head swayed in time to the music as he watched the girls' belly-dancing.

Sayame felt disgust. Here was the man who had carved out an empire in the same forests where their ancestors had barely scraped a living. He had united petty tribes and kindreds together and had slain dozens of other chieftains...all to be the one great king. He had been the most feared ruler of all Lamanites, and now he wasted himself on drink and dancing girls. Is this the end result of power? Is this all that it comes to? Better we had stayed in our tents in the wilderness, than live in cold palaces of stone, thought Sayame. Out in the forests there was a simple true existence, hard but honorable.

✶ ✶ ✶ ✶ ✶ ✶ ✶ ✶ ✶ ✶ ✶ ✶

Following the high priest to the house of sorcery, Aaron felt at ease. What was it Akish-Antum had told him? That he, not his brother would be king, that he had seen it in his interpreter, his crystal skull of doom. *I must prepare to make my own destiny. Drink deep of the fountains of darkness, don my crown of glory, before all vanishes like smoke. Akish-Antum is my Master. He sees more than Balam-Ek, but I will learn what I can from this high priest.*

"Much is expected of you, Prince Aaron. You must know how much your family is depending on you. You have spent time with the Gadianton Grand Master, Akish-Antum. He is not to be trusted. Your father knows that. It is part of the reason that you are to begin your training early. I warn you, some things will hurt, some things will be dangerous. But I will not allow you to die. Remember that you must always master your fear. You must slay your own fear before it slays you. You must conquer the fear that kills with your own mind which is your greatest weapon. I will help you sharpen it."

Balam-Ek led him to a room inside the temple that Aaron had never seen before. The priest pulled open a double door set into the floor. Inside was a dark pool of water with steps on one side leading into the murky depths.

"Why have I never been here before? I thought I knew the entire city," said Aaron. "Is this a baptismal font? I thought father outlawed those."

"It is not a font; look deep into it if you can. You cannot see the bottom. It is an initiation pool which we use to test our priestly initiates," explained Balam-Ek.

"Do we both go in?"

"No, it is a test for you alone. I did mine at fourteen years of age."

"What must I do?"

"Dive deep within the dark water and find the true way out, for you cannot come back out the way you came in," said Balam-Ek.

"So there is another passage out?"

"Yea, there is, but you must remember to dive deep for the obvious way is false and will only lead to more troubles."

"Very well, I am ready." Aaron took off his sandals, his golden necklace and other princely trinkets and stepped into the warm water. It had a strange but familiar odor to it. The deep green water relaxed him. Taking the second step in was fine, as well as the third, but there was no fourth—it went straight down.

As he came up for a gasp of air Balam-Ek laughed and said, "You must dive deep, the obvious way is false. Do not let fear kill you."

Aaron dove back into the dark abyss. Running his hand along the sides, he could tell that it was a smooth stone box going down and down ten feet or more. His lungs were ready to burst when he found the passage. It was only sixteen inches wide and opened up to another room with bright lights above it. As he raced upwards to catch a breath and to tell Balam-Ek how easy it was, he noticed long dark shapes above him in the water. Crocodiles!

He turned to go back the way he had come, but the original passage was dark as Egypt. Balam-Ek had shut the door on his entrance. He needed air. He must go up for air and exit the pool of crocodiles. Pushing himself upward from the bottom of the pool, he shot for the surface. A long reptilian figure moved closer in. Aaron emerged from the water and gripped the slick side of the pool, face to face with a growling, snapping crocodile sitting on a wet ledge beside the pool. Another narrow ledge had even more crocodiles lounging upon it. The walled enclosure holding the beasts was more than six feet above the water's edge; Aaron could not possibly reach it.

Balam-Ek stood above him and laughed. "It would be a shame for me to tell the king that his second son is a bigger fool than his eldest."

"Do you mean to murder me?" coughed Aaron.

"Ha, I told you the obvious is not the way."

Aaron backed away from the crocodile's ledge. It inched closer toward him.

"Best watch out for that one," said the priest. "He's a biter."

The pool was larger than he had first thought. The crocodile grinned at him and slid into the water.

"You must dive deep, the way is never clear."

Aaron dove again, hating Balam-Ek's laughter. Something tore at his side and he kicked, feeling his foot push against the scaly body. He dove deeper to the bottom, unable to see anything in the murky water. He ran his hands along the stony edge of the pool. He couldn't hold his breath much longer but didn't want to return to the surface, fearing he would attract a crocodile attack. His hand brushed an open space in the stone work. He no longer cared if it was the first opening or not. Perhaps there was still some air trapped beneath the doorway.

Climbing inside, he pushed up and bumped his head on a stone ceiling. He again despaired, until realizing that the tunnel curved before turning up once again. Lungs aching and ready to burst, he wanted to take in a mouthful of water and end it all. Breath, he needed a breath. Any breath, even a crocodile's kiss. Then his head broke the surface. Too tired to fight off a crocodile, he opened his eyes, fearing the worst.

Balam-Ek stood above him extending a hand. "You did well. I have lost more than a score of junior priests this way; but if they cannot prevail, I don't want them." The massive priest pulled him out with ease and gave him a small towel.

"I thought you said you would not let me die!" Aaron shouted in accusation.

"So I did, and you did not," laughed the priest.

"What if a crocodile had been swifter than I, or what if I had not found the passage?" Aaron looked at his ripped shirt where the croc had nipped it. He bled a little from the deep scratches.

"Your wound is not deep. You are fine," said the priest, examining the scratches. "I would have made you stay in and find the passage, even if I had to spear all the crocodiles myself. You are, after all, no junior priest." He laughed again. "Get dressed in these new robes and meet me on the north patio. This is only the beginning."

"But what of my wounds?"

"Nonsense, they are shallow and will only enhance the evening." The priest walked away, and Aaron wondered what would come next. He had succeeded where others, older boys with more experience, had failed and died. Perhaps he *would* be king someday, as Akish-Antum had said.

On the patio, musicians played as a dozen dancers frolicked about to a bizarre, unrecognizable tune. Each of the dancers was dressed to imitate a certain god. Balam-Ek was the black tiger of Baal. Aaron recognized Nu-Bak-Chak from the royal court as Moloch the bull god; he did not recognize the other dancers, although he saw that they were dressed as many of the Lamanite gods.

The most important twelve gods were all represented. Votan, a noble looking man and warrior. Taloc, the rain god who looked like a man with a curiously long nose and other strange disfigurements. Shagreel, the mighty sun god. Libnah, lord of the white land, jackal-headed god of death. Elkanah, a raptor-faced god of the sky. Set, the great serpent of the world. Korash, god of the south and the oceans. Mahmackrah, the lion-headed god of power and royalty, who rules fire and the north. Buluk, god of war and sacrifice, a warrior covered in tattoos. Finally there was mighty Kuhtuli the death god, who appeared as a grotesque tentacle-faced dragon.

"It is the last night of the waning moon, let us retire inside for the ceremony," directed the god Baal.

Inside the house of sorcery, the ceiling was painted a very dark azure, and the torches on the wall reflected tiny lights on the ceiling. Jewels set in the ceiling as stars captured the false light and reflected it back in the form of constellations. Aaron recognized Venus, for its pentagram trajectory had been mapped out for him many times before this. On the walls were stone representations of the gods. What was it Akish-Antum had said? What good is an idol? An idol of stone and wood is only an image, a source of false reliance. It cannot save anyone on their day of reckoning. Use them to rule the people, but never fall into the trap of venerating them yourself.

The drums started before the pipes and strings, enchanting ancient music that stirred a passion within his breast. Suddenly it stopped. Baal approached and whispered in his ear, "Ma'at-neb-men-aa, Ma'at-ba-aa." He gave Aaron a gold cup with a green liquid inside it. "Drink it," urged the god.

Aaron hesitated a moment longer.

"Drink it," he commanded more sternly.

It tasted foul, like crushed fungus and human blood. Knowing Balam-Ek, it would be blood, but this was not the time or place to ask. He left a little in the cup.

"Finish. It won't hurt you but helps with your journey. It is made from the sacred mushrooms," said the god.

The music started again. The musicians carried a wild rhythm, the drums beating, the pipes blowing and the strings strumming with a furious dirge of descending chords, loud enough to wake the real dreaming, sleeping gods. It was wonderfully mad and like nothing Aaron had ever heard before. Surrounded by dancing gods, Aaron stood like a carven statue as they surged about him in a wide semicircle.

The god Set pulled a large orange and brown snake from a crate and danced furiously with the serpent coiled about his shoulders. Mighty Kuhtuli knelt on the ground and sang a hideous song in a requiem of madness. Everyone was caught up in the frantic beat of the maddening music. Faster now and ever faster, the dance went on, with Aaron joining. He danced on and on. Candles on the far side of the room quickly melted down and dwindled in pools of cooled honey-wax upon the floor of stone. His legs and lungs ached, yet he danced. The drums throbbed, some of the gods collapsed, and still they danced upon the floor, twisting and writhing like broken stricken rabbits—the kind you left to die without wasting an arrow.

Buluk, the tattooed god of warriors, lay on the ground twitching. Jackal-faced Libnah, god of death, stood still amid the dancers, wild-eyed and occasionally shouting unintelligibly. Votan was drawing a thorned rope through his own bleeding tongue. At the sight of that Aaron wanted to retch, the green drink settling on his stomach in an unpleasant way.

"It is time!" shouted Baal. The music stopped and the room seemed to stop moving. Baal again whispered into Aaron's ear, "Ma'at-neb-men-aa, Ma'at-ba-aa." He gripped the boy by the shoulder and shouted to the other gods, "Now it begins again, the cycle set forth by our fathers of old under the cosmic serpent so long ago."

"Under the cosmic serpent so long ago," chanted all the gods, even those Aaron had thought were unconscious or dead.

Aaron was ushered out of the room, down a long dark tunnel. A door was thrown open. Baal forced him to sit on the floor of what seemed a huge expanse with no windows and no light. Drawing a knife, he cut Aaron ever so slightly across his left and then his right hand. "Write down upon this parchment your name and title, your ancestors' names, then write down your questions, dreams, hopes and fears."

Baal stood over the boy as he numbly did as instructed. The cuts did not hurt and Aaron felt that he actually liked the sensation of his own warm blood in his hands. There was no sense of time and Baal did not seem impatient, no matter that Aaron scrawled in large fluid characters across several sheets of parchment, his fingers streaking the glyphs, and then beginning to hurt. "I am done," he said. He licked his sore fingers, the blood relaxing and sealing the tiny wounds.

Baal took the papers, placed them in a large brass brazier on the floor and lit them on fire. The parchments smoked lightly, and the god shut the door tight. A lock dropped into place.

"Why am I here?" Aaron asked, his head still swimming.

"To have your vision," answered Baal.

"It is too dark. I am blind."

"You will see."

"But if I am blind, how will I see?" There was no longer any reply. "If I am blind how will I see?" he whispered to himself.

Though initially it had been dark as pitch, it gradually changed from black to dark purple to blue to a deep blue gray. No, it was smoke billowing out of the ether, far beyond anything the smoldering parchments could have produced. It came from the walls and the floors surrounding him. Out of the irrepressible darkness came a figure—a green-scaled serpent. It slithered up before him, and Aaron saw no boundaries of any kind, not even the earth beneath him. He heard a rushing of waters as the serpent grew in size until it was the size of the mightiest tree in the forest. It was as tall as his father's pyramid.

It spoke to him, "Behold, Son of the Prophecy. Wrath is coming to the world of men. In storm and tempest he comes, he rebukes the sea and dries it up. Mountains shake before him, rivers move before him, who can survive him?"

"Who are you speaking of, oh great vision serpent?" asked Aaron.

The head of the serpent drew back and the mouth of the serpent retched open and a man stood within it. "It speaks of you, of you, of you," said the man. He was dark of skin and complexion but had cold, light eyes. He wore a turban, and he wore the skins of animals unknown to Aaron. Strong he was, with a savage manner for one who stood so still. His short beard was trimmed; he had an arrogant, imperious face, and yet he gazed proudly on the boy.

"Who am I, to bring wrath to the world and who are you to tell me such things?"

"I am your forefather of old. I am Laman, Father of all the Lamanite peoples. You are my greatest son, for you will destroy the seed of my hated brothers, the Nephites. You will wipe all trace of them from the face of the earth until it will be as though they never existed. You are my wrath, my revenge!"

"How can you be here? You died centuries ago!"

"A son of perdition never dies; we wait for the unmaking and will thwart it if we can." With that, the serpent closed its jaws over the man and seemed to swallow him.

"Oh mighty serpent, is the man your servant, or are you his?" asked Aaron.

The green vision serpent looked sly at him and hissed, "Perhaps thou art the same as he, not my servant but slave he be." It slithered backward and disappeared, the mist vanishing with it.

The disappearance sucked the air from Aaron's lungs as he collapsed in a writhing euphoric heap, weak and aching. At last Aaron knew the truth. He was the one, the son of bloody prophecy, the fulfillment of dreams and revenge.

Pale Stranger

Zelph felt strong and vigorous. He had traveled far over rough terrain with thick forests and wide rivers with no fatigue upon him. He had met and talked with the Son of the Great Spirit. When he looked at his own hand he saw the paleness, almost a glow, to his skin. It was no dream. He kept a good pace, hoping to outdistance the army of Almek by several days. The army was cautious for fear of being spotted, but Zelph had no such worry. He was on a divine mission and the Great Spirit blessed him.

This land of the Nephites was indeed beautiful; he loved the numerous lakes and rivers. He saw many farms with men working them, but they paid him little heed. They all have their own work to do, what matters a tall stranger; and from afar I probably appear to be one of them, he thought.

These lands also contained many caves. Near the entrance of one he faintly saw the Gadianton mark on its stone face. Had he not so recently been with the Gadiantons and learned their ways, it would have seemed only a curious weathering on the rock. Knowing they might be nearby, he kept an eye open for trouble.

On the fifth day of his desertion, he awoke and crawled out of the brush wickiup he had made for himself. Drinking from a cool stream, he ate some of the amaranth and honey the disciple had given him and finished the last piece of salted meat brought from camp. Walking down a narrow gully, he smelled something amiss. He stopped. The birds had stopped singing, and all was deathly still. He dropped low and got his back up against a thick tree.

A rough voice called out, "Come on out of there, big fella. We want your valuables, not ya life and we will be on our way with a thank ya very much, so come on outta there."

Zelph gave no reply. It was then he realized that the man was speaking Nephite, and he had no problem understanding.

"I have ten excellent archers ready to shoot ya down if ya try to run away. Ya best come out now. It's your valuables we want, and we will be on our way. Don't make me angry."

A new voice, firm and humorless, called out from across the gully. "Ah, but what if I want *your* life, robber?"

Peering out from behind his tree, Zelph could see a lean, dark-haired Nephite with a short, trim beard prodding a robber with his sword. Other men, dirty and unkempt, were pushed out of the woods at the hands of a band of organized warriors.

"Come on out; we have these rascals," the dark-haired man called out to Zelph.

When the lead robber tried to scramble up and away, the man kicked him back to the ground. The lead robber looked about fearful, his long greasy hair hanging out of his odd red cap. The dark-haired man, apparently the leader of the Nephite band, knocked the red cap off his head and trampled it underfoot.

"I have rights under the judge's law," said the robber, trying to grab his cap.

The Nephite leader stepped on his hand this time. "When you became a robber to prey upon good folk and innocent people, you gave up the right to flaunt your liberty that spits upon ours."

Zelph did not quite understand all of this but he had a good feeling about the dark-haired man. He came out toward him.

"My sword, you are a big fellow. My name is Tobron, captain of these ten. It seems we have come upon these robbers just in time. They meant to rob and murder you," he said, looking intently at Zelph. "What is your story and why are you in this forsaken place?"

"My name is Zelph, son of Qof-Ayin, great-grandson of Samuel the Lamanite. Perhaps you have heard of him? I understand he visited these parts a long time ago."

Some of the Nephites snickered. "We have a comedian," said one of them.

"You are no Lamanite," said another. "Look at his skin."

Captain Tobron stared Zelph up and down. "Yea, he is a Lamanite, though the palest one I have ever seen, and with ice blue eyes."

Zelph had not looked at his own eyes. It had not occurred to him that they could have changed as well. All his life he had been dark of hair, skin and eye. The scouts of Captain Tobron milled about him now to peer closer. Even the robbers being held in place on the ground with a foot or spear head craned their necks upward to look at him.

"What are you doing here, Zelph? It's a long way to Jershon where your people dwell in Nephite lands," said Captain Tobron, referring to the pacifist Lamanites who had been given a holding of lands in exchange for renouncing war.

"I seek to go there, but do not know the way," answered Zelph.

"How can you not know the way home? Are you that lost?"

"I have never been there."

Surprised, they realized that he was a Lamanite from the far south, where there was strong animosity toward the Nephites, and where there was preparation for the first war in centuries.

"Then where are you from?" said Captain Tobron warily.

"Far to the south, from the city of Mutula, ruled over by King Xoltec. I need to speak with the prophet Onandagus in Zarahemla as soon as possible. Can you help me?" asked Zelph, extending his broad hand.

"Yes, yes, I can." Captain Tobron shook hands with Zelph. "But you need to speak with me as well. After all, that's why my men and I are out here."

"You are seeking me?" asked Zelph.

"Not you so much as your Lamanite brothers, and the Gadianton dogs who lead them."

"What of these here you have already captured?"

"These scum are wanderers who I have tracked for the last few days almost as much by smell as their trace," said Captain Tobron. "The dangerous ones blend in much better, only scum like this waylay people out in the wilds."

"Please sir, ya are mistaken," spoke the lead robber. "We meant no harm. We were simply starving and thought, hey, that looks like a big well-fed man. Perhaps he has a little something to eat on him. We weren't going to hurt him." The robber chief grinned through yellowed teeth.

Captain Tobron scowled at him and put his sword to his throat,

234

making him wince before removing the blade.

"What is the meaning of their red caps?" asked Zelph.

"Their Phrygian cap is a symbol of their supposed freedom from under the judge's law. Some judges will not prosecute men who wear them, others will. For me, it is a good indication of who is a Gadianton, or at least a king man. Chief Judge Onandagus has outlawed the wearing of the red hats during public demonstrations because they are used as a badge among rioters, a way of identifying among themselves who not to stone."

Zelph was curious now, realizing that things in the Nephite land would not be as simple as he initially expected. Motioning for him to follow, Captain Tobron led Zelph along with his men over a hill and into a gully where the group had left their horses.

"Why are you out here by yourself then, Zelph?" asked Captain Tobron. "You are part of an invading Lamanite army, are you not?"

"I was, but I have left them behind and now seek Onandagus."

"Why should I trust you? You might be a scout or a spy."

"Or worse, an assassin," added one of the captain's men.

"I am not a spy or assassin. I left to escape my fate as a bodyguard to the king. I was with the coming army, true, but I could not be a part of it. They are being led to ruin by the Gadiantons. It is not right to have such a war for conquest and bloodthirsty ways."

"How many are in this force?"

"Over fifty thousand, mostly marchers but some chariots, a train of supply wagons and a small cavalry."

Captain Tobron stopped and his lips moved inaudibly as he counted.

"Do you disbelieve me?" asked Zelph.

"I believe you. This is precisely the reason we are out here, to find the army as it approaches and slow it if we can. How far behind are they?"

"Not more than a day or two. But they are not coming this way...they are routing northwest to go around the Narrow Pass, up alongside the wilderness of Hermounts and then come straight across to Zarahemla. As the prince's bodyguard I overheard a fair amount of military planning, and I was a captain in the king's army."

Captain Tobron thought for a moment. "Stand up," he commanded the lead robber, who held his red cap in his hands like a beggar.

"Well, it seems ya are very busy with such important news for the judges, we will just be on our way, and thank ya, we have learned our lessons," said the red-capped robber attempting to walk away. "My thanks, good captain." He bowed and turned to go.

"Hold it," Captain Tobron commanded.

The robber chief stopped and turned. "What? We said we was sorry."

Captain Tobron went to him and hit him full in the face. "You insult me. Do you take me for a fool? I know your kind, Gadianton, you will hang when the chief judge hears your case."

"Hang?" gulped the youngest robber, looking to another. "But you said the brotherhood would protect us."

"Shut your mouth, Noah!" snapped the third robber.

"Oh yes, you will all hang for your crimes of besieging travelers and murdering innocent people in cold blood," said Captain Tobron, directing his words to the youngest one.

"Never!" cried the red cap. "He is bluffing. We will be released, just stay true to the oaths that the Gadianton Grand Master gave us."

"Stay true to the oath, and you will perish," said the captain.

The younger robber, Noah, continued to sob. Zelph judged him to be a couple years younger than him, a boy of fifteen, already initiated into this dirty band of robbers.

"Look at where you are," said Captain Tobron to the boy, holding the red cap out before him. "This holds a bloody bitter future for you."

"I will talk," stammered the boy.

Pulling him aside from the others, the captain asked, "What do you know?"

"Your oath!" shouted the red cap to the boy. "Your throat will be slit ear to ear, your entrails slung over your left shoulder."

"Silence that man," commanded Captain Tobron. One of the soldiers hit the robber chief over the head and began tying him up, another gagged him with his own cap.

A robber shouted, "Noah, don't tell them anything. You know what awaits you if you talk. It is far worse than anything some holier than thou judge can do to you.

Coming at him, a warrior scout hit him so hard, teeth flew from his mouth. "Murderers, you are the cancer of our society. Worms in carrion!" He spit at the fallen robber. The robber knelt on the ground, bleeding and weeping, as the other scouts bound and gagged him. Zelph stood by silent and immobile.

Captain Tobron said to him, "I am sorry, my friend, our tempers can get away from us, but these have been hard times for all of us on account of these robbers. My own father was murdered by them."

"I lost my father as well," said Zelph. "They are no friends of mine. The Gadiantons infest the lands to the south like vermin and they have subverted our peace, our way of life."

The captain nodded. "So we both know of their evil all too well." He turned back to the boy robber. "Talk to me. You do not have to hang like these two if you help us."

"What will happen to me?"

"That is for the judge to decide." Captain Tobron looked at him and gestured to get on with it.

"I do not know where to begin," said the boy robber.

"Why did you join them?"

"That one is my brother, Muloki. He said that if we did not raid and take what we wanted we were not living. To work and farm is for the weak and stupid, he said."

"Do I look weak to you?" asked Captain Tobron.

The boy ignored the question. "He said who are we to toil and work by the sweat of our brow when the world is ours for the taking? I myself have only been with them a month or so. I am an apprentice. I have never killed anyone, I swear, I shot my arrows over people's heads. They are the ones who murdered. Aha and Muloki are the real killers, not I. They have slain a dozen men since I joined them."

The two gagged robbers were now silently screaming underneath their gags.

He continued, "What do you know of a Gadianton raiding party with many Lamanites?"

"Only a little, Aha said we need not bother helping them. There was more profit to be had in raiding across the countryside while the war is going on near Zarahemla. It's Akish-Antum and the city robbers, that's all I know of it."

"Very well, bind him and take them to Manti," commanded Captain Tobron.

"Please sir, there is one more thing."

"What is it?"

"Do not send me before just any judge. Deliver me to Chief Judge Onandagus."

"And why is that?"

"Because many of the judges are Gadiantons, and they will surely slay me for breaking my oath. Only Onandagus do I know for certain is not one of them, for they are always complaining of him. They hate him. With him, I know he would judge me for my crimes and naught else."

"What about these two? What would you have me do with your two compatriots?"

"Allow them to be judged by any other judge; they will not be condemned for they have broken no oath," explained Noah, seeming more confident.

"Why not have all three of you together before Onandagus?"

The boy stiffened and hesitated an odd moment. "Because they would lie to slight me, as I have broken my oath."

"I think I will spare him your lies. You all will go to Manti to stand before Judge Alma." The captain turned to one of his men and said, "We must return to Onandagus to report on these events. The white Lamanite and I will ride with all possible speed back to Zarahemla. Omnias, you are in charge. Be sure to get these Gadianton dogs to Judge Alma. Farewell, brothers."

He and Zelph mounted horses and began the long ride to Zarahemla. They kept a good pace through thick emerald forests and by deep green rivers, reaching the city of Manti by dusk. Zelph was taken by the beauty of the countryside surrounding Manti. He liked the gray stuccoed walls of the city, until he realized that the walls were a necessity because of the aggression of his own people. He felt ashamed.

Zelph's companion interrupted his thoughts. "We will get some food here and trade horses. These are in dire need of rest. I have more from my own stables. We should be in Gideon by this time tomorrow. We will also get a good meal from my wife."

At his home, Tobron explained to his wife that he must return quickly to Zarahemla with urgent news. Soon enough, they had fresh horses waiting for them. His wife made a meal of corn, buffalo steak and beans. She rolled it all up in tortillas and made extra for them to take with them. Outside, he held and kissed her for a long moment before mounting his horse. He leaned down and kissed her again. She held his face for some time.

"I love you. Stay close to Uncle Joshua and your father," he said as he wheeled his horse around. He did not look back as he rode away. They rode swiftly out the east gate toward Zarahemla, keeping on the well-traveled road until well after dark.

"We had best let the horses rest and graze for now," said Tobron. "We should catch a little rest ourselves."

"Should we keep a watch?" asked Zelph.

"We will be alright. My horses will keep a good eye out for us. I have trained them since they were colts."

Zelph had never heard of anyone training a horse like that before, but he believed him. He could feel a kinship with this man who was a friend of the one he sought, Onandagus. "Where did you get such a fire to fight Gadiantons?" he asked, as they took their bedrolls off their saddlebags. "I sense it was not just your father's murder."

"I am their enemy because they are an enemy to my people and my God. They delight in the shedding of blood, thinking they possess some great secret when they are only maggots in carrion. They feed off the misery they themselves induce. Nephite society is crumbling and many do nothing. It makes me wish to fight all the harder for my children's sake."

Captain Tobron directed Zelph into a copse of trees for them to camp for a few hours. The oaks, elms and pines were alien to Zelph in this new land. Still it felt like home more than Mutula ever did.

Zelph rolled out his blanket upon the tall grass and asked, "You mention the Gadianton secret. What is that?"

"I know their secret...I have been fighting them long enough. It is to turn life into property, all life, people, animals, trees, everything. Nothing is sacred to them, because it is all property to be bartered with. They will even barter men's souls if they can. Lord knows so many poor fools have already done that, some don't even realize they have chained themselves to the hold and keel of the devil's ship. They row for their new master who carries them further and further away from home." Tobron paused and looked out at the stars.

"Even in my city of Manti," he continued, "always a good city, the vices grow. The mind-altering mushrooms are everywhere, called sacred by some, but I trust not the thing that dulls men's sense and destroys their life's ambitions. There are men in Manti, former friends, who cannot get by a single day without that all-consuming need. And don't even get me started on the harlots." He paused and looked sheepishly at his new friend. "Forgive my rants, Zelph, I am a man who has seen too much. Someday soon I will take my family away from Manti and go somewhere safer."

"Where is that?"

"I don't know. I wish I knew. Yet, one cannot live with his head buried to the ills of the world. There must be a balance somewhere, and I am trying to find it. We have talked of building an Order together somewhere to the east." He pointed through the trees toward the band of stars in the east.

"An Order?"

"Yes, a United Order where family and friends can work together to build up God's kingdom on earth. We can worship together and not deal with the wickedness all around us here. The time is ripe. If we do not do something soon, we run the risk of our children having nothing to do with the gospel. The evil of men is more prevalent now than I ever remember. It is getting harder to do the right thing," said Tobron, casting away a twig. "Something evil is on the wind...it calls."

"I understand all too well," said Zelph.

Captain Tobron looked away to the night sky before rolling over into his wool blankets. "If we have the speed of the Lord on our side, by the end of tomorrow, we will be in Zarahemla and you will meet Onandagus, the best man I know in all the world."

A Grim Road

This is a grave turn of events. How could this have happened?" demanded Prince Almek. His forehead contorted wide avenues of new wrinkles, trying in vain for an answer he could accept.

"He seeks even now to go to the Nephites and warn them of our plans. He is a traitor," said the Gadianton Grand Master, "just as his father was at the end."

"Nonsense! Qof-Ayin is no traitor, and neither is Zelph. He would not betray me. Couldn't your tracker find any trace of him?" asked Almek, grasping for any kind of explanation other than this one proposed by the Gadianton—that Zelph was a traitorous deserter.

Rubbing his strong chin then cracking his knuckles, Akish-Antum said, "Uzzsheol lost the tracks over thirty miles away from our camp."

"Lost them?"

"Yes."

"How, a river? How could he lose them? Ravenous beasts? The Nephite army?"

"No, the tracks disappeared at a rock face," answered Akish-Antum.

"Is your man that unskilled? Zelph must have climbed up the rock face. I am appalled at your tracker's failure that you are trying to pass off as Zelph's treason."

Akish-Antum choked back a laugh. "Uzzsheol can track a fish through the sea. He could follow a cloud blindfolded. He has stalked tigers from your jungles that go from tree to tree. Men are nothing in comparison. You would sooner lose your head from off your shoulders than Uzzsheol

241

lose someone's tracks. No, something happened. His tracks vanished."

"That's impossible," shouted Prince Almek.

"Even so, if Uzzsheol says the tracks are gone, they are gone and not a man on earth can recover them."

"Can I speak with him?" Almek asked with a hint of annoyance in his tone.

"If you wish," Akish-Antum responded, equally annoyed. Stepping out of the big maroon tent, he returned almost immediately with the hawk-nosed Uzzsheol and the general of Tullan, Anathoth.

"Why is he here?" muttered Almek.

"He commands legions. He must be privy to all scenarios and possibilities in the field," said the Gadianton Grand Master.

Although Anathoth could speak the Lamanite tongue perfectly, he felt no need to let the foolish prince know that. He looked on as if unaware of the tension. Teth-Senkhet, the second-in-command of the Gadiantons, entered with a scrolled map under his arm. Almek's Chief General Tubaloth, an imposing warrior of renown, followed him in. General Tubaloth, a hard-faced man, bowed to his prince and stared coldly at the others.

Teth-Senkhet unrolled the map before them on Almek's ornate table. "Show us, Uzzsheol, where you were," he said.

Scanning for a brief moment, the mohawked warrior traced his gnarled finger along their trail and over toward the steep and craggy hills that Akish-Antum had led them around. It was beyond the legendary narrow pass. "Here we traveled around Nephite cities, and here I followed the big man. He walked twenty miles in the night over rough ground, I respect his stamina."

"Get to the point," said Almek.

Uzzsheol stared at him a moment before continuing. He did not speak much, so for someone to accuse him of rambling was odd and rude. "He stumbled twice then went to sleep. When he awoke he chased a deer, a five year old buck, for ten miles. He came to cliff face and stream of water and disappeared. The deer drank water and went into forest to sleep."

"Go on," snapped Almek.

"The big man is gone from this world. He has powerful medicine, some spirit came and took him somewhere else," said Uzzsheol, grim as ever.

"Impossible. You lost his tracks at the cliff face. Did something else get him?" babbled Almek.

"I did not lose the tracks. They stopped, something spiritual took him."

"Are you afraid of spirits? Is that your excuse?"

"I am not, but I respect them," Uzzsheol said without emotion.

"Anything else?"

"Yes, I did see another man after this. He was short with balding hair. He said I would not find the big man, Zelph. He told me I should repent and join the pacifist Lamanites who dwell in Jershon, or be unmade."

"And?" snarled Almek.

"I looked away to grab my tomahawk, that I might slay this man, but he was gone and left no track either. It was a place of deep medicine. He was a trickster, that one."

Almek scowled at him before exploding, "No, you're a drunken idiot! You lost Zelph's tracks and made up this ridiculous story when the Nephites probably have him as a prisoner."

"Shall I now?" Uzzsheol asked Akish-Antum, fingering his long flint knife.

The Gadianton shook his head. General Anathoth had his own hand on his sword's pommel while General Tubaloth glared at them both, holding his spiked club.

Prince Almek was the only person oblivious to the tension in the room. "Get out of here, you drunken cumom follower," he yelled at Uzzsheol.

"I hear and obey," said Uzzsheol. The tracker turned and left the royal tent, his face a mask of stone. General Tubaloth snickered; calling someone a cumom follower insinuated that they were of the Lemuelite horde, those who followed the migrations of beasts.

"Prince Almek, you have neither ears to hear, nor eyes to see," said Akish-Antum. "There were no Nephite tracks leading Zelph to flee from our camp some twenty miles. He is a traitor, and if we should see him again he must die."

✼ ✼ ✼ ✼ ✼ ✼ ✼ ✼ ✼ ✼ ✼ ✼

General Anathoth wondered at what would possess a seemingly devoted warrior to betray his prince, his nation, and his people. He had never spoken to Zelph, but a true warrior knew another true warrior on sight. He had also heard tales of how not long before, Zelph had helped to take the rogue Madoni and slay him. Such was not the act of a traitor.

No, something more had happened. He wondered about the mysterious stranger who had told Uzzsheol to repent and then disappeared. There are strange unexplainable things in the world. Anathoth had heard of them, but he had never experienced them himself.

Anathoth also noted that Zelph was the only man besides himself who never drank wine or let himself be seduced by the sensual debaucheries like the rest of the camp. He appeared to be a man of honor and respect, regardless of what the Gadiantons said. If Zelph had been able to speak Tultec, Anathoth might have spoken with him. He himself spoke Tultec, north Lamanite, Lemuelite, Western Nephite, Zoramite, and the language of the Islanders. He probably could have understood Zelph just fine but he had never made the time. What did it matter now?

Long and hard is the road to conquest. I serve my king to my utmost but this does not seem right. Long have I served with distinction and a fullness of honor and duty to my king and to my people, but this sneak attack on the Nephites seems weak and wrong. I have always defended the borders of Tullan, my country, and exacted retribution when necessary. I am not afraid to fight when it is right. So why does my heart tell me Akish-Antum is lying?

Those Nephites we ambushed and slew were not real warriors. They were drunk and in a stupor. It was as if Akish-Antum wanted us to find an armed party of Nephites to show the truth of his story of their aggression, of his lie. They fought as a scared rabbit that found itself in a new field dropped from an eagle's taloned clutch. There was no honor in it. Someday if my son were to ask me if I had ever slain any Nephite warriors, I would have to say no, as of now.

"Why the long face, General Anathoth?" asked the hulking Gadianton Grand Master.

An eerie feeling swept over Anathoth as if the Gadianton had a wave of cold air forever about him. "Those men I slew a few days ago, there was no fight in them, no honor for me."

"Ha, what can I say? They were foolish and drunk. It is the Nephite way to be a slave to their lusts."

Prince Almek was nearby and nodded approvingly. "They are dogs," he agreed, without looking General Anathoth in the eye. "You did good work in dispatching our hated enemies."

"I must return to my men. We march soon?" Anathoth asked.

"Yes, within the hour. Break camp!" called Akish-Antum above the din of the camp.

As Anathoth walked from Prince Almek's tent he could hear the Gadianton Grand Master laughing his twisted laugh, that awful deep bass sound of a demon's drum reverberating out of the darkest abyss. *What did Zelph know that would cause him to leave? I should know what Zelph knows.*

A brawny warrior over a span taller than Anathoth approached. It was Lib, an Ishmaelite captain. He had the blood of the ancients in his veins. He possessed six fingers and six toes on each appendage. The extra digits did not hinder him; in fact amongst the Tultecs, he was the best with the spear and the jagged, flint-lined club. "My general, the men are ready. How soon do we march?" asked Lib.

"Within the hour, I should think. I am impatient, but first we wait for the Gadianton scouts to tell us of the road ahead."

"Yes, my general. A horseman of theirs has just returned."

"I will see about it, have the men ready to take the lead."

"Yes, General," said Lib. He saluted his general and turned to go.

Lib would follow me anywhere. I would have thought Zelph would stay with Almek anywhere. I need to know what Zelph knows.

✱ ✱ ✱ ✱ ✱ ✱ ✱ ✱ ✱ ✱ ✱ ✱ ✱

Prince Almek felt a great loss without Zelph. In the last couple of weeks he had felt that he had the truest friend of his life regardless of his prior abuses; and now that friend was gone.

As a replacement, he had a young captain with him constantly. Siyach the Wise, he was called by his fellow officers. Just a little older than Almek, at twenty seasons, he had become a favored warrior of King Xoltec for various missions requiring unorthodox thinking. The young captain had excelled at all tasks given to him while in the army. He had a knack for thinking ahead that had saved his skin a few times in wars with the loathsome Lemuelites and Tultecs. He was also the head captain of Almek's ball team, and he never lost.

"Siyach," asked the prince, "what happened to Zelph?"

"I do not know, my prince. It does seem that Zelph betrayed us, but I know him as well as any man in the army. He always had a good solid head on his shoulders but was strange and aloof. Maybe things got to him. I have noticed many times on campaign that he and his father did not associate with the others or the camp followers."

Prince Almek grinned. "Those things I have heard many times. If

Qof-Ayin were any less a warrior, I think others may have questioned his masculinity. No, they are of that old breed who cares about morals. Zelph spoke of righteousness a few times, but I never listened. It never mattered to me."

"I think only the Coatl knows the truth of Zelph," said Siyach.

"Yea, but if it turns out that he has betrayed me and we should ever see him again, I will slay him myself," spoke Almek, as he stabbed a dagger into his wooden map table.

A black clad horseman rode up to the command tents and dismounted from his frothing mount, joined immediately by Teth-Senkhet and Uzzsheol. They all approached Akish-Antum. "What news? Ahab, see to his horse. What news?" asked the Gadianton Grand Master.

The horseman coughed and spoke. "A caravan is coming down the road, so large that it cannot be dissuaded by our few scouts."

"How large?"

"Over twenty wagons, fifty horse, two elephants, well-guarded and armed. I know there are many barrels in most of the wagons," said the scout.

"Wine," smiled Teth-Senkhet.

"Is it supplies for a Nephite army in the south?" asked Prince Almek, now approaching.

"Nay, nay it is a great merchant train," said the scout.

"What else do they carry?" asked the prince.

"Trade from Hermounts and Tennen-Isis. Copper ingots from the north countries. The train is bound for Desolation and Teancum, I am told."

"That is good. It will not be missed for some time," said Akish-Antum. He motioned to Ahab, who had just returned from taking care of the scout's horse. "Summon General Anathoth immediately." Ahab raced off and in a moment the Ishmaelite general was there, spear in hand.

"Now, a challenge for you if you wish to limit your men," said Akish-Antum.

General Anathoth looked at him sideways, with an irritated frown.

"This caravan has numerous guardsmen, too many for my scouts. You must deal with them. Their wagons have a good deal of plunder to warm our bellies and lighten our moods."

"I am not a thief," said Anathoth coldly, turning to go.

"Ha, what is it you Lamanites say? If I cease to raid, I cease to be."

"I am an Ishmaelite."

"It makes no difference," laughed Akish-Antum.

"You are under orders," Teth-Senkhet reminded him.

The general nodded. "Are we to take any prisoners?"

"No, unless someone serves a true purpose," said Akish-Antum.

"Very well, I will do as you command." As he turned to go, he spit at their feet.

Teth-Senkhet was ready to rage, but Akish-Antum merely laughed mirthlessly. "Easy, we know how he feels...he wears his precious honor for everyone to see. We will watch and wait for him to break."

"Why not let some of my men attack the caravan?" asked Prince Almek. "My men are capable and hungry, too."

"As I was saying, my prince, we shall all share equally in the spoils. Let Anathoth and his Tultecs risk losing a few men. Besides, I am pushing him. He is bristling under his yoke. If I do not show him who is master here, he may rebel at a more critical time. I need to know he will always do as ordered. King Apophis said he was his most trusted servant and general."

"He may be, but Apophis is not here," Prince Almek pouted.

"True. All the better to keep a handle on this one, to better cripple the other later."

✳ ✳ ✳ ✳ ✳ ✳ ✳ ✳ ✳ ✳ ✳ ✳

General Anathoth rallied his spearmen and bowmen into two equal units of a hundred and fifty each. He lined them up on either side of the brushy hillside along the road, having them take the best cover possible. The trees were sparse here, and the bushes small, but if the caravan guards were inattentive this early in the morning it could be quick and painless. Anathoth did not want to lose a single man if he could help it.

The archers were instructed to shoot each armed man in the caravan as they themselves were lined up. This was a good spot in the road. It ran between two low-slung hills; his men would be shooting down at their prey. Several would roll boulders down to the road, not to fully block it but to provide a distraction.

Anathoth had finished surveying the layout of the ambush when someone spoke behind him. "This is a good spot," said Akish-Antum. He wore his own full plate, exalted copper armor and tiger helm with dagger-like teeth lacquered in gold.

"I can do without your help," said Anathoth, annoyed at his presence.

"Of course you can," said the Gadianton.

"Your flashy armor may give us away."

"I won't be seen until it is too late, I assure you," said the Gadianton Grand Master, grinning through his razor sharp teeth. He stepped up and backward, fading into the undergrowth.

For such a big man he moves like a panther, silent and swift, thought Anathoth

As they waited, the sun began to heat the men as they crouched beside the road. Biting flies buzzed and sucked blood. Soon enough, Anathoth heard the creak of the wagons as his men waited in silence. One of the mammoth elephants trumpeted as the caravan rounded the bend, right into the trap. General Anathoth had never seen an elephant before. He hoped that they would not be too formidable a beast to slay, that they would be more like cattle than like a fierce or attentive dog that protects its master.

As the caravan completed its circuit around the corner, Anathoth counted them—a dozen horsemen up front, laughing and talking, unaware of their doom. They were followed by several wagons fully laden with another dozen horsemen behind them. It was not a bad defensive system, if their guards had been aware. As the last of them rounded the bend, the general marveled at the brown woolly mammoths. Each had a rider and carried extra large saddlebags.

When the caravan was in position, his designated men rolled the haphazard distraction of rocks and logs. It stopped the train in its collective tracks and made a number of the wagons back into each other. It was exactly what General Anathoth wanted. They were trapped. Sounding a war cry and whoop, his men loosed their arrows in a wide merciless rain of death. Each guardsman was hit and fell. Women screamed while a few men in the wagons attempted to break off and run for safety. These died with arrows in their backs. Fully surrounded by the copper-skinned men and bloody screams, the remaining Nephites were swiftly cut down. It was over in an instant. Warriors were upon the wagons with their sharp scimitars, killing the women as quickly as the men.

Mighty Lib pulled a beautiful girl out of the back of one of the rear most wagons and decided not to slay her. Her long, wavy black hair and blue eyes caught his fancy. He knew he was too ugly for the likes of her but, for just a moment, he held her in his arms. Throwing her over his shoulder, he ignored her kicks and cries for help. Her struggles were as nothing to his great strength.

There was an odious cry of victory from Anathoth's men, excited by the spoils of this ambush. Over half of the caravan was loaded with succulent wines from the southeast Nephite lands.

Striding up to General Anathoth, Lib dropped the girl at his feet. "A prize for you, General," said the giant in his twisted speech. "Once I saw her beauty, I knew she must be for one such as you. I decided not to slay her but grant her as a gift from your men to you."

No longer screaming, she had hateful fire in her eyes. "Why?" she asked. "Why, why, why, why?"

"What does she say?" asked Lib who spoke only Tultec.

"She asks why we did this," said General Anathoth with pity.

"Ha! It is life," said Lib. "She is yours." He strode back down the low hill to claim other spoils for himself.

Looking at the weeping girl in the light blue shift and sparkling girdle, Anathoth spoke in broken Nephite. "Remove your gold and jewelry and give them to me."

She was quick to comply, handing him her earrings and bracelets.

"The ring too," he said.

She pulled it off and gave it to him. He put these in the pouch that hung from his wide leather belt. "I am Anathoth, a general of the army from Tullan."

"You are from Tullan?" she asked.

"Yes, but for your own good, do not speak again unless I ask you to. I will not hurt or violate you, but if it is not clear that you are my slave, worse could come upon you. You understand?"

She nodded, wiping away the tears.

"You will ride on a horse behind me, or in my chariot and sleep in my tent. Remember, I am your only hope here, so do not betray my trust or you will be dealt with harshly." She looked over at the wagons as they were being torn apart. "Was your family there?" he asked with concern.

"No, they are in Zarahemla."

"Why were you here? What is your name?"

"My name is Bethia. I ran away. It was stupid, it was foolish."

He just stared, revealing nothing, and she turned her face away.

"You may have a chance to see your family again, soon enough."

"How?" Her eyes, still damp with tears, were wide and bright.

"We are bound for Zarahemla even now."

"Zarahemla?" she gasped. "But why? You cannot raid it as you would a caravan. Are you not just Gadianton robbers?"

"Nay. Well not all of us are."

"But why Zarahemla? You could not possibly take the city. My fa—I mean Onandagus, would hang you all."

He smiled at that as they rounded the bend in the road, revealing the full size of the army to her. "There is not enough rope in Zarahemla to hang all these men."

She stood amazed at the thousands upon thousands of Lamanites and Ishmaelites arrayed in line upon line. "What is all of this? What is happening?"

"It is an army," he said, raising his sword to the watching warriors.

"For what? What are you going to do?"

"Conquer," said Akish-Antum, striding up beside them. He seemed to look right through the girl's very soul.

"But Zarahemla's high wall, and its guardsmen, and the prophet Onandagus will stop you," she said, full of urgent fear.

"No, he won't," laughed Akish-Antum. "This army will take Zarahemla and I will drink Onandagus's blood," he thundered as he walked away toward his chariot. He turned once more to stare at the girl, but just as quickly, looked back to his gilded chariot and drove his team away.

"Please, no," she whispered.

General Anathoth looked at her and said, "It cannot be stopped. This army has but one purpose, and it is grim."

The Baptismal Undertow

The new, makeshift assembly hall thundered with accusations and threats. Gathered in a large tavern with a wide-open banquet hall and tiered floors radiating out from its center, the members of the Council of Fifty and Judge's Council argued. Smoke from many pipes filled the air and the smell of sweat was heavy. Those who were warriors stood ever ready to spill blood. Hands on hilts, they waited.

"Order! I will have order. Everyone will have a chance to speak in turn," said Chief Judge Onandagus. The room slowly quieted. "Now, I accede that the accused, Gershom, is a secretary of mine and some lawyers argue that as such, I cannot fairly be the judge of him on this case. So be it, but I can still call upon anyone else to do it, someone proven to be unbiased."

A large number of men yelled out, and Mormon the Elder was sure he could hear a few yelling for Judge Hiram to be judge of the case. Onandagus heard it too. "If Judge Hiram is to testify against Gershom, son of Joseph, then he cannot hear the case. This is one of our oldest laws. I stand in the way of nothing." The mass of men stood and shouted in chaotic gnashing and confusion. Mormon the Elder rose from his chair and glared at them; the room quieted briefly.

"I am not the only one accusing him," shouted Judge Hiram. "Captain Gidgiddonah is he who captured the culprit."

"I don't believe he is guilty," shouted Captain Gidgiddonah as he stood to refute Judge Hiram.

"Rich man's son!" blustered a man from the back. "You can't tell us what to think."

"As if my dead father has anything to do with this case," muttered Captain Gidgiddonah in response, bristling as he looked at his worn shoes and the tattered edge of his cloak. "How dare they; am I not my own man?" he said to Mormon the Elder under his breath.

More shouting ensued, with people on both sides screaming at each other. Mormon the Younger sat close behind Chief Judge Onandagus and his father. On his other side sat Samson, the chief judge's colossal bodyguard. The huge man was chuckling, as he sat with his brawny arms folded across his chest and feet stretched out. He had just recently returned from the south, and whatever news he had brought had both relieved and infuriated Onandagus.

"What is so funny?" Mormon the Younger asked Samson.

"Looks like we got ourselves a Lemuelite standoff," laughed the bodyguard.

"What's that?"

"It's when you got a couple of idiots who'll never agree or back down. They're too scared to fight it out, but they sure talk like they will. It's called a Lemuelite standoff, but anyone I ever knew who fit that category lives right here in Zarahemla." He chuckled again as the arguments became louder.

Chief Judge Onandagus banged his staff on the floor, and it echoed across the hall. "I will have order or I will make this a closed court."

"You cannot do that. This affects all of us," shouted someone in the back. "The Judgment Hall was burned!"

"As was my governor's home and the temple," countered Onandagus.

"Bah! A temple for a forgotten religion of fools," said Palal, a stout man in the back.

"Throw that man out. Gilhi, Barak," commanded Mormon the Elder, motioning to his two trusted guardsmen.

The stout man with jewel-encrusted fingers came from a wealthy and proud family. He struggled against the two strong guardsmen. "I am Palal, you cannot do this." He pulled away from them, but they retained their grip on his silken shirt, tearing it. "You tore my fine shirt. Your thugs have ripped my shirt," he shouted at Onandagus. "You will have to pay for that."

Mormon the Elder signaled for the two men to throw him all the way out. They pushed and pulled him from his seat and threw him out the door. He tumbled across the cobblestones, and his fine mica and pearl necklace ripped apart, scattering its many finely chiseled pieces all over the street. He knelt to pick them up and then tried to reenter, his torn shirt exposing pale white skin. Embarrassed, he turned to go while cursing them over his shoulder. Gilhi and Barak looked to Mormon the Elder who nodded, and they ran after him. He began running, only to trip and fall in the dirty street. The laughing guardsmen stopped and returned to the meeting.

After this, the assembly began to quiet down. Ammaron the Scribe copied down everything said to the best of his ability; a pen and ink were at his side and the scroll stretched out before him. A wide brass book was also close at hand, the one he had been using to teach Mormon the Younger. It was the Book of the Judgments, Statutes and Commandments. The Judgments were those laws that came down from the chief judge. The Statutes were those which were voted upon by the whole of the Council of Fifty and the Commandments were those which had come down from the Lord God through the prophets. Mormon the Younger had to learn the differences between all of these, from even the most obscure of cases.

"As chief judge, I may appoint any to hear this case as I see fit and that shall be our newest, youngest judge, Nemuel," said Onandagus.

The young man stood in surprise. "I am honored," he said.

Stepping down from the podium, Onandagus gestured toward it. Judge Nemuel had only recently started shaving a weak beard, but he had a strong chin. So far as Onandagus knew, he had nothing to do with the Gadiantons or with Judge Hiram.

"I call this case to order," Judge Nemuel began. "I will do my duty to God and to the Nephite nation. This case is to determine the possible guilt or innocence of one Gershom, son of Joseph, in the fire of the Judgment Hall. Nothing else is permissible, save that which determines his guilt or innocence. Accusations of others will only be permitted in the circumstance that the witnesses testify that it was not Gershom who caused the fire. So be it."

The case had begun. First, Judge Hiram began with his already well-known story of his own heroism at barely escaping the flames from his ground floor quarters. His green amulet of judgeship swayed hypnotically from his neck as he spoke in condescending tones. He also swung his arms about in exaggerated movements. Samson chuckled as Judge Hiram spoke. Several times Judge Hiram turned to look at him, and the big man would sit still a few moments longer before something else would set him off.

Mormon the Younger watched the amulet and remembered its sway. Judge Hiram was the leader. He caused the fire. "He did it," Mormon said aloud. Samson snorted at that and taking his thin pipe from his mouth, narrowed his eyes at Judge Hiram. The brutal gaze of the strong man was lost on no one.

The judge turned to look coldly at the boy but went right on speaking, "As I was saying, and young Mormon must be agreeing with me, I did follow a strange man through the smoke filled hallway and out to the shed. It was Gershom," he proclaimed, pointing at the accused.

"No, I did not agree with you. You did it, you and another. You called him a fool, he called you master. His name was Thomas," shouted Mormon the Younger, much to the surprise of his father and Onandagus. Samson just smiled.

"Order, order! You will wait your turn, young Mormon, or you will be ejected," said Judge Nemuel.

Mormon the Elder took his son by the hand and led him out of the court. "You will tell me here and now and not in front of those murderers— what is going on? Why didn't you say anything earlier about this master business?"

"I forgot most of it as I climbed down the rope. I only remember now because of the green stone amulet, swaying around his neck."

"Are you sure? Most of the judges wear those."

"No, it was him. I recognized his voice. Besides, how many other judges were even there that night?"

"I don't know, but it won't be that hard to find out once we look at the records of the day. Ammaron the Scribe should have those back at his home," said Mormon the Elder.

"He was ordering a man named Thomas to soak the hall in oil, and to find and kill me. I forgot much when I got down and touched the ground," said the boy. "But it was Judge Hiram who fired the hall, as the one called Thomas chased me up to the top of the tower. We struggled and I kicked him; he fell down into the fire to his doom. His bones would still be in the bottom of the tower, whatever is left of them."

Captain Gidgiddonah was outside with them now. Wiping away his son's tears as he recalled his ordeal, Mormon the Elder said, "Captain, go and search the ash and ruin at the bottom of the inside of the tower for a man's bones...maybe you can find something."

"As you command," spoke Captain Gidgiddonah, as he turned and hurried to the remains of the tower.

Looking his son deep in the eye, Mormon asked, "Can you testify of these things to the face of that man while he is in the same room with you?"

"Yes, father."

"Good." He clasped his son and patted his shoulder hard. "We will get these devils yet. Let us go back inside."

Judge Hiram had finished his spin on the events and had requested witnesses to testify. Over a dozen men testified that Gershom was the man in the barn. Resting his case on that, he sat down in good spirits. For the next hour, Judge Nemuel heard Gershom tell how he was struck, covered with wine and then put in the barn. The accused brought forth witnesses of his good character. Nothing, however, could prove he wasn't guilty.

It was deadlocked, when Onandagus himself got up. "If I may, Gershom was seen going from the fire to the barn by one man only, not two or more. We have a witness, young Mormon, who says it was not Gershom who started the fire, but Judge Hiram and another man. But again we have only one witness for that, or do we?"

Judge Hiram guffawed and looked annoyed. "If I did this horrible thing, then where is this mysterious accomplice, hmmm young Mormon?"

"Here!" shouted Captain Gidgiddonah. He approached the podium with a broken, blackened skull and a bent, black, curved blade.

"That belonged to Thomas, who tried to kill me with it," said Mormon.

"I found them without too much trouble. They were near the top of the debris, as if this Thomas fell from the top of the burning tower," said Captain Gidgiddonah. "This looks like a Gadianton sign on the blade right here. I have this troop of ten men behind me as witnesses, that I, or we, have only just recovered this evidence from the ruins of the tower." He gestured behind to a dozen guardsmen, who nodded their assent. He brought the blade to Judge Nemuel, who examined it, turning it over in his hands a few times.

Thinking for a few moments, the presiding judge said, "In light of this new evidence, it is apparent to me that the accused man, Gershom, did not start or cause this fire. At least not so it can be proven beyond the shadow of a doubt, as there is only one true witness against him. Neither can I charge Judge Hiram, as there is only one living witness against him as well; unless there is anyone else who can step forward and help determine these matters once and for all."

Judge Nemuel then turned his full attention toward the formerly accused. "Gershom, it is your right to send charges against Judge Hiram if you wish. If you do not, then this case will be officially closed in relation to the fire, until more witnesses can be found to come forward, which I doubt will happen."

There was silence for a few tense moments. Gershom looked at Onandagus, who nodded vigorously then he looked at Judge Hiram who frowned. Lastly he looked toward his wife and son and said, "I do not press charges."

This brought a loud outcry from both sides. Men shouted back and forth, arguing why it should or should not have been pressed. Judge Hiram's frown curled into a wicked smile. Judge Nemuel banged his staff, ending the case. He stepped down, deferring the podium back to Chief Judge Onandagus.

Onandagus was visibly furious, but he held silent a moment to bang his own staff and declare, "This meeting is adjourned." He stalked over to Gershom, who sat with his head in his hands. "Why Gershom? Why didn't you press charges?"

"I am sorry, sir. I could not put my family in jeopardy. Even if we win, we lose. There would be retribution. I must resign myself from your service, and I pray that they forget about me when I am gone."

"No, it doesn't have to be like this. We need good men, we need you."

"I want to believe you, but they burnt the Judgment Hall, they destroyed the temple and they tried to make it look like I did it. There is no safe place for me, and I cannot risk my family. I am sorry, but I am done. I resign and will leave Zarahemla in the morning. You are a good man who can do great things, but I am a small man who cannot fight fate. Farewell," said Gershom. And he left with his wife and family.

Onandagus went to the door after him and shouted, "Gershom, there is no fate but what we make!" The man would not turn around, but acknowledged that he heard by giving a low underhanded wave. Turning to Samson, Onandagus said, "Keep an eye on him. Make sure none molest him as he and his family leave the city." Samson grunted, dumped his pipe ash outside, and followed.

Mormon the Elder walked up to Judge Hiram, put his hand on his shoulder and held him down on his chair as he squeezed. He whispered menacing, "You got off today, but remember there is going to be a reckoning, and you will be repaid in kind."

"So will you, my good general," he said, attempting to pry Mormon's hand off his shoulder, which he never could have done had Mormon not allowed it. The judge then got up and skulked away.

Captain Gidgiddonah approached Mormon and Onandagus in the now deserted hall. "There is another problem in the city. You asked me to watch for signs of king men."

"Yes," responded Onandagus.

"Well, I may know who wants to be king."

"Who?"

"His name is Mazeroth the Baptist," said Captain Gidgiddonah, pointing out the doors toward the ruins of the Judgment Hall.

"He is here in Zarahemla?" responded Onandagus.

"Yea, he is right now. As I searched for the skull and dagger of Thomas, Mazeroth was outside the walls, proclaiming God's judgment on the wicked government."

"So, who is he? He is not half wrong, and he is a Baptist you say?" asked Mormon.

"The man is a crazed fanatic, but I cannot believe he is with the king men," said Onandagus, pacing to the door.

"Why not? Because he is righteous?"

"Hardly, he is called the Baptist because he baptizes people."

"And?" replied Mormon the Elder impatiently. "I baptize people. Sounds like he could be one of us."

"No, he is not. The old scoundrel has a small army of dedicated followers who assist him in forcibly baptizing people against their will. As he does so, he proclaims he is saving their souls for all time and that is the end of their obligation for good; they are done, no more works, no more faith. Overall his plan is akin to the devil."

"He forcibly baptizes?" asked Mormon the Younger, disbelieving.

"Yea, he does. He is a false priest, a Nehor, in my book."

"Can we jail him for such behavior?" asked Mormon the Elder, following Onandagus outside.

"If he forces anyone to be baptized against their will, yes. We must jail him and any of his followers who interfere, which they will. Although this is the worst time to be dealing with more riots. Where is the man now, Captain Gidgiddonah?" asked Onandagus.

"He is still in front of the Judgment Hall on the Avenue of the Eagle."

"Very well, go and watch him, for trouble will arise soon enough. We shall gather all the available men for the coming riots," said Onandagus, leaving the hall with Mormon the Elder.

Gidgiddonah went to watch the spectacle and as he neared he noticed that Mormon the Younger was beside him. "I want to see this," the boy said.

"Alright, just watch out. If anything starts up, hurry and get out of the way."

A crowd of hundreds had already gathered to hear Mazeroth the Baptist speak. Normally these streets would have been full of merchants and vendors, but the merchants had packed up and moved on so as not to lose their products to a mob. The streets sloped up to the edge of the wall of the Judgment Hall grounds. The man stood next to the walls to better look out over the people, and to be seen and heard by them.

Mazeroth the Baptist was skin on bone with long white hair and a long venerable beard that reached to his midsection. Tall for such an old man, he stood without any stoop to his back. He wore only white. His voice was deep with a sinister urge.

"Too long, people of Zarahemla, have you stood by and let the devil lead you about by the nose and heart. I am here now to baptize and save you all. I will heal this broken land. Come to me of your own free will or I will be forced to expel the devil from your hearts before you are forever damned like the Lamanites. I will come to all of you, if I must." His deep, hollow voice rang out in a fear inducing wave.

A few in the crowd dared to jeer him, even though he was thronged about by his own fanatical followers. "You say you will save us?" asked a man.

"Yea, it is not me, but it is done through me. Will you accept?" Mazeroth boomed.

"I will." A young man stepped forward.

Tall, lean Mazeroth held a glass of water in his bony hand and mumbling something unintelligible to all but himself, dipped his fingers and flicked them at the man. A few drops hit his face and ran down his cheeks, not even moving the dirt thereon. "He is saved. His soul is done, and he has no more need of life." The man looked puzzled at that but walked on.

"Who shall be next, who will be saved from eternal damnation?" cried Mazeroth.

Some in the crowd still mocked him, and his followers gathered to surround the doubters. They brought four young men before Mazeroth.

"You have cursed the everlasting God and I, his chief servant," said Mazeroth, to the four men. "But, I forgive you and will still grant you peace." Dipping his fingers, he flicked water on the four of them, as they struggled to escape the hands of their captors. As the water hit their foreheads they ceased struggling, and one began to weep.

"That is crazy," said Mormon the Younger to Captain Gidgiddonah.

"Some people are more susceptible to things than they like to let on," the captain responded.

The followers released the men, and Mazeroth announced in a loud voice that carried out to the crowd, "You are saved, now go and do what thou wilt, for there is no more earthly responsibility in you."

Mormon the Younger could take no more. He struggled through the people and inched his way closer. Captain Gidgiddonah noticed too late and could not reach him to hold the boy back.

"You are no man of God. You do not teach the people the gospel. You only tell them what they want to hear to uplift yourself. You don't even hold the priesthood to baptize people," said Mormon the Younger, staring hard at the wizened warlock's face.

Mazeroth's pursed lips and impassive face became a toothy cruel snarl. "I hold all I need to hold," he said, motioning to his men to grab Mormon. "Now hold him still, and I will baptize this mouthy whelp."

Mormon struggled in vain against the grown men who held him fast. Mazeroth's men were strong; they lifted him off the ground each holding an arm or a leg. Mazeroth dipped his fingers in his glass of water. "I will save your soul, my son." He began to mumble his strange incantation. Mormon strained against his assailants to no avail. The old man came closer, his long bony fingers coming out of the water to baptize the boy.

A golden gauntleted fist struck Mazeroth across the face, sending him reeling. It was Mormon the Elder in full armor. The false prophet sat on the ground missing teeth and bleeding from the mouth.

"No one baptizes my son but *me!"* shouted Mormon the Elder, as Mazeroth's men let go of the boy.

"Stand down!" commanded Captain Gidgiddonah. Two dozen guardsmen stood behind him with brass studded cudgels. The fanatics fell silent and still. None dared to move against Mormon the Elder, not daring to even help old Mazeroth up.

The gaunt old man stood and said to Mormon, "You would stop the work of the Lord of this earth?"

"This earth right now? Yes, I would. Yours is not mine," declared Mormon the Elder. He stood strong, his volcanic blue eyes burning into the old man.

"Still, I will baptize even you," he said, dipping his fingers in his cracked near empty glass.

Mormon drew his sword, the stout, wide blade forged by his fathers of old. Oziasrowa its name was, the Strong Arm of Jehovah. It was rarely drawn without someone paying dearly for it. "I think not. You are going to be taken prisoner for disturbing the peace of the city. There are already more than a hundred complaints against you for forcibly baptizing people."

"You are Mormon, the former Governor of Antum," said Mazeroth.

"Yea, I am."

"I have heard of you. I tell you the end is coming, and you must prepare. Be baptized and live for the day. There is nothing more to do. We are but helpless souls adrift on a black sea of infinity; our only hope is to grab hold of that tiny life raft of the Savior and cling to it as we drift into the nothingness. Mark my words, all this you fight for so admirably is for naught. At the end of the day and age, it is nothing, it is forgotten, dust, the dross of a fallen people. I read the stars. I know what is coming, there is no way round." The crowd stood silent watching the two square off. Angry as the people were at Mazeroth and his thugs, they were taken in by his words and were afraid.

"This is not the golden age," said Mazeroth.

"This is not a storybook page," responded Mormon.

"This is where the sword rules the pen," continued Mazeroth.

"This is where the king kills the men," said Mormon.

"So you are an educated man, who knows the old songs of a forgotten land across the sea."

"I know history and art and law," said Mormon. He had not yet put his sword away.

"I am only telling you what I know. Time is short. Join me, abandon this hopeless thankless post. No one cares what you do here. You could die next week and be forgotten by the next. No one cares, a black sea we float on. Don't drown, join me, hold to the Savior's ship with me and he shall take us to a lighter place. Nothing else matters, all is dust." Mazeroth held out his bony hand, and seemed sincere.

A woman in the crowd said, "Take it."

"Take it," called out more people in the crowd. They were all taken in by Mazeroth's words. "Take his hand. He wants peace, we all do." Men and women openly wept at the old man's request, so moved were they by his words.

"You lie. I know what honor and duty are. They matter to me, no matter what other people think or say. And I already have a place assured for me on the Savior's ship. When the time comes, I will be moored to the greater stars of Kolob."

"You are a simple man, too simple to understand."

"I know this—that I have had enough of your rhetoric. You are coming with me. Bind his hands," commanded Mormon.

The guardsmen, Gilhi and Barak, grabbed Mazeroth and had little trouble in subduing the old man and getting his hands tight in a flaxen cord. He scowled and cursed, "Sons of Mahmackrah. Why do you do this? I am a prophet like Abinadi and Samuel."

"You are nothing like them. You are brother to Nehor and Korihor," said Mormon the Elder.

"Bah! Ye dogs, if my hands were free I could show you what powers I have," he said as the guardsmen pushed him through the crowd.

"If any of his servants follow, arrest them as well," said Mormon to Captain Gidgiddonah.

Taken before the makeshift courtroom of Chief Judge Onandagus, Mazeroth sneered with contempt. "You think you can judge me? I am above man's law. I am your prophet. Do you hear me? Let me preach and baptize in peace."

"Mazeroth, you are a man who takes one piece of the gospel and holds it so tightly that you lose your grasp on everything else, including your sanity. If you teach neither repentance nor works what good will baptism do anyone?" asked Onandagus. The old man just glared at the chief judge. Onandagus continued, "It is everyone's free will to accept the gospel or not; how can a forced baptism save anyone?"

The courtroom was full of the remaining members of the Council of Fifty as well as any others who could force their way in past the guards to watch.

"I only know that it does," responded Mazeroth.

"Then you know nothing. You are a deceiver who has only helped to cripple and drown the weak souls of this nation in the devil's undertow. I command you to repent in the name of the Lord," thundered Chief Judge Onandagus from his judgment chair. His eyes flashed at the man before him.

Mazeroth grinned at him. "I will not. I have done nothing wrong. You have no authority over me. Give me a sign that I should do as you say."

"Such things do not bestow faith and are not how the Lord works."

"Show me anything that I might know you are right and I am wrong, something unique on this earth that will back up your claims. Show me a seer stone that would work for me or a miracle of the heavens. Show me a changed man pure in heart like white driven snow, a blind man that can now see. You can't, can you? Very well, I will show you my power and you will be forced to recognize me as your spiritual head."

"Want me to give him a kick in the head?" asked Samson, stretching from his chair behind the chief judge.

Onandagus frowned at him and Samson smiled and backed down. He lit his thin pipe, amused at Mazeroth's posturing. Mazeroth now gestured wildly in the air, calling out unfathomable words and holding his eyes closed so tight he shook. Nothing happened. He stopped a moment and started over, and still nothing happened.

"I am weary of this. Captain Gidgiddonah, throw him in a cell," said Onandagus.

As he was being led away Mazeroth cried out, "I am being tested, but you, Judge Onandagus, you show me nothing. A sign, any sign, give me a sign and I will repent, you dogs."

At this moment Captain Tobron of Manti and Zelph rode up to the new court and came inside. "Chief Judge," Captain Tobron called out, "I have important news."

Mazeroth the Baptist turned and looked at the eight-foot tall white Lamanite. Astounded he said, "How did you change your skin, Lamanite?"

"I did not of myself," Zelph replied. "I have met the Son of the Great Spirit and was changed."

Mazeroth fell to his knees. "I believe! I believe you are my sign. Forgive me, Lord! Someone needs to rebaptize me."

To Dream a Fiery Dream

In the morning Amaron decided they would rest a full day for Judah's sake, fearing his wounds may become infected. They hung the big cats upside down from stout branches that could take the weight and let them bleed out. With good knives they skinned the tawny lions. Amaron preferred using a small blade that had both a straight and serrated edge.

Ezra quickly picked up the concept of skinning. "It is easier than I thought it would be."

"We're not done yet. Watch how you tear that piece there," instructed Amaron. "Bring the knife in against the muscle tissue smoothly. If the blade is sharp enough, it will glide." Watching the little man cut, Amaron asked, "How old are you, Ezra?"

"I am going on nineteen summers, but I look older than I am, don't I? It's because when I was a baby I almost died from a sickness. It made me small, and wrinkled my face a bit."

When they finished skinning, Amaron fashioned a necklace from the cat's claws using some rawhide from his pack. He made a push dagger from one of the lion's long curved teeth. Upon seeing it, everyone wanted one. Amaron had the ten draw lots with reeds of differing lengths.

Daniel lost and said in anger, "When would I ever need to use such an ungainly weapon anyway?"

No one paid the remark any mind, understanding his disappointment. Amaron gave one to Judah, another to Reuben, and the last to Lehi. The others tried to barter with the winners to get the daggers.

"These lion hides would make fine leather cloaks," said Amaron, "if we were able to tan them."

"What do we need?" asked Ezra.

"A lot more salt...we have almost none. Without the salt to cure them, they will stink and go bad."

"What if we could get some salt?" said Ezra, excited at the thought of a lion skin cloak.

"Where? There is no town close enough to us. I too would like a lion skin cloak, but not enough to haul a stinking hide through this heat and humidity. The flies are already bad enough," said Amaron. "I hate to waste these skins, but we have no choice."

"Are we to remain here the rest of the day?"

"Yea, why?"

"Let me see if I can find salt from a nearby farm or something."

"I don't know what you could find. There are few salt mines in these parts, and not many farms. Antionum isn't very far away, but no one lives there anymore. I don't want you to get lost," said Amaron smirking.

"Well, I would like to see what I could do just the same. My feet are not as sore as they used to be, so I could use something to do today. Who will go with me, then?" Waves of indifference from the men washed over Ezra.

"We have marched enough, so thank you, but no," said Daniel.

"Uh, Uncle, will you go with me?" asked Ezra.

"What? Yea, yea I will go with you, better than sitting here all day. And if I see any Gadiantons I'm gonna be shooting 'em," Reuben replied.

"Let's go then," said Ezra, pulling Reuben along with him. The older man was still fascinated with the saber-toothed push dagger Amaron had made and given to him. He kept twisting it over in his hands.

Ezra led him along the precarious brushy trail. Although Amaron did not think they would find anything, he decided to thoroughly wash the lion hides in the swift little creek next to their camp.

Once at the bottom of the gully, Ezra took their bearings and decided to go west around the swamp and then return to this spot from the east.

"Nephew, we won't find anything," said Reuben, swatting at blood-sucking flies.

As they marched alongside the swamp, it grew hotter than the day before, and with it the humidity increased, making them sweat profusely.

"It should be too hot for the mosquitoes and flies," complained

Reuben, swatting all around himself.

The swamp met a wide lake, forcing them to turn and go up a thickly wooded hillside. Struggling to get through the dense underbrush, Ezra was about to heed Reuben's plea to turn back, when it opened up on a jagged ravine. "What caused this, I wonder?" said Ezra.

"The excessive rains this spring, a month or so back. They eat away at the earth sometimes. Looks like there is a way across right over there," pointed Reuben.

They went uphill a little further until the ravine widened and leveled out. Here it was only about ten feet deep, but almost twice as wide as it had been farther downstream. A tiny trickle of a stream coursed through it, smaller than the one by their camp. Easing down the steep embankment, they dropped to the bottom. They crossed over and when Ezra was almost halfway out, Reuben tugged on his foot. "Look at that."

Behind them and just up the ravine as it bent around the hill was what appeared to be a great stone doorway. It was visible only from this angle.

"No one could live here, could they?" asked Ezra.

"I don't see how. This ravine is freshly cut, only a month or so ago. See, there are tiny, young plants growing within," observed Reuben. Slowly approaching the doorway, he drew his bow and nocked an arrow.

"What are you afraid of?" Ezra asked.

"I don't know, it just seems strange is all. I got a weird feeling."

Rough uncut stone had been placed together with such perfect precision that it was as if it had been masterfully fit from a mold. It formed a corbeled arch over the doorway. The door itself seemed to be basalt stone with massive metal hinges green with age. It was a couple of feet taller than they, and almost six feet wide. Roots dangled from tiny cracks within the cyclopean masonry, attesting to its grand age.

"Do you think we can move it?" said Reuben.

"Do you think we should? It looks ancient, and it could be dangerous," remarked Ezra.

"You are the one who told Captain Amaron we would find something."

"Yea, but I thought perhaps a farm we could barter with, not an ancient tomb."

"Maybe it's not a tomb but a storeroom. It could have salt, wheat and corn inside."

"It looks too ornate for a mere storeroom," said Ezra.

"Should we look inside or leave it alone, then?"

"I don't know." But curiosity got the better of Ezra. "Let's see if we can even budge the stone." Putting his bow down, Reuben got beside him and each pushed to move the stone door. Even with their combined strength, it barely inched to the left.

"Let me get something for leverage," said Reuben. He walked away a short distance, scanning the ground for anything useful. He found a branch almost six feet long and a few inches thick toward its base. Wedging a piece in the narrow opening, they were able to move the stone door another few inches, enough to put a thicker piece of the branch in farther and repeat the process. It took each man straining with everything they had to open it about six or seven inches.

"I think there are stones wedged behind the door, and that's what we're pushing against," Ezra suggested.

"Well, reach your scrawny hands in and move them," said Reuben, wiping sweat from his eyes and brow.

"What if there are snakes in there?" Ezra's expression was ashen from the straining and from his innate fear of serpents.

"'*What if there are snakes in there?*'" Reuben mocked. "No, I can feel cool air from inside. It would be too cold for them. They are all out in the swamps."

"Alright, alright," said Ezra, getting down on his knees before the door. He reached around and felt behind it, stretching as far as his shoulder would allow, only half the distance of the door's width. He pressed close and could feel the dry coolness from inside. The floor within was worked with smooth flat stone.

"What's blocking the door?" Reuben asked.

"Just a second, I can touch whatever it is—feels like sticks. Here, I have some." As he pulled out the debris, he dropped it in horror. They were bones, human bones. "Arghh!" He got up and wiped his hands furiously on his torn silken breeches.

"Calm down, it's a tomb then, ain't it? What did you expect? You were the one who said it was too fancy for a storeroom," laughed Reuben.

"I didn't expect that."

"Any treasure has probably been washed away in ages past. Still, we could look, eh, nephew?"

"I don't know. It seems wrong."

"Seems? Ha, of course it is, but what did you think? Looking in a tomb was a noble idea?"

"You agreed to it," countered Ezra.

"Yea, I did, but I didn't think it was alright. Still, I have no compunctions about stealing from the dead. They won't use the gold, and I can," laughed Reuben. "I'm more concerned about how much I can carry without the others suspecting anything. I don't think we could ever find this place again."

"Let's go back and talk to Amaron about it," said Ezra.

"Alright, we can share with him, but only him."

"What are you talking about? There might not even be anything in there."

"Oh, yes there is. You disturbed some poor soul's bones, some poor Jaredite is up in heaven or down in hell saying, 'Hey, my bones is moved, lemme at him who disturbed my grave!'" Reuben laughed.

"Have you really quit drinking?"

"Haven't had a drop in over a month now."

"Alright, let's go get Amaron."

＊＊＊＊＊＊＊＊＊＊＊＊＊

As Ezra walked into camp, he drained the last of his water skin. He spoke to Amaron alone. The others were spread about the campsite dozing from the midday heat.

"We found a tomb, I think." Reuben lagged a short ways behind but nodded in agreement as he arrived.

"A tomb?" Amaron responded.

"Yea, it looks very old. Do you want to take a look?" said Ezra, ready to turn around and go back.

"Did you go in? Where is it?" Amaron asked with curiosity.

"Near a freshly cut ravine between the two big hills a little off to the north. It is deep and seems to have washed out the tomb," replied Ezra. "There were letters or glyphs on the threshold, but I couldn't understand them."

"Let us go and investigate then." Amaron put on his sword belt and grabbed Judah's stout spear.

Returning to the tomb seemed quicker than before. It felt stranger than ever, with an eerie feeling of being watched surrounding them like an enveloping mist. The door was high for even Amaron, who stood a foot and a half taller than Ezra.

"It is Jaredite. See these glyphs? They did not write as we do," said Amaron.

"Can you read it?" asked Ezra.

"I might if it were Lamanite or Ishmaelite, then I could get the gist of it. But these marks I have never studied." He reached out his hand to feel the cool, gray stone. "I don't know what it is, but there is something about this tomb," he said warily.

"We felt it too," said Reuben.

"But still, you tried to open the door."

"Uh, yea we did."

"Let us push the door shut, I don't think we should disturb it," said Amaron.

"I, uh, got these from within." Ezra pointed sheepishly at the few bleached bones laying a short ways from the doorway.

"Put them back, and let's shut up the tomb."

Ezra gingerly picked up the bones and placed them back behind the door. Each man exerted himself on the stone door and it began to shut. Amaron pulled a quill and ink as well as a small scroll from his pouch, to write out the glyphs on the doorway. "I will show these to Chief Judge Onandagus. He will know what they say and whose tomb this is. Another good storm could collapse these ravine walls and fill this in, so that no one would know it was here."

"That's a shame. There is probably a lot of gold in there," said Reuben.

Amaron glared at him. "Do you realize what you said? Desecrating a tomb is not the way an anti-Gadianton should behave."

"But, what if it is not a tomb? What if it is an ancient library or storeroom?" said Reuben.

"You saw the bones, Reuben. They don't keep those in libraries," smirked Amaron. "I recorded these signs for Onandagus to interpret. If it is worthwhile and there is no war, let us return to see what we may."

"I'll mark some of the trees so we can remember this spot," said Reuben.

"Fine, but don't be too obvious about it. We don't want anyone else noticing and following them."

"What should I do then?"

"Make random cuts about two feet from the bottom, we will know what they are but no one else will." They walked back to camp while Reuben made his marks on various trees.

* * * * * * * * * * * *

As evening came on Amaron fell into a deep sleep. The night blew in and clouds covered the sky, wiping away any remnants of the bright sunny day from earlier. He was awake and yet asleep. He found himself standing before the tomb, and it was neither day nor night. The sky and landscape was a charcoal that went on for eternity. All the forests and swamps were swept away as if the tomb were on a flat, lonely plain. The door was open, and a tall majestic man stood within. He wore a long white robe and had a golden crown upon his head. It was set with brilliant jewels the likes of which Amaron had never seen.

The king's eyes burned, and his voice was as a roaring wind. "Son of a once great but now fallen people—behold, vengeance cometh speedily upon the inhabitants of this nation. A day of wrath, a day of burning. A day of desolation, of weeping, of mourning and of lamentation cometh. And as a whirlwind it shall come upon all the face of this nation, and upon thy house shall it begin and from thy house shall it go forth. First, it shall come to those among you who have professed to know the Lord and yet have not, those who have blasphemed against the Lord and those who love not their fellow man. Now is the day when the sands have run out on this people. Thou hast been shown and thou must heed or be burned as stubble. When the chosen of the Lord is shown thee, thou shalt sustain and serve him. Always be true, a sword of justice and mercy thou art. Be true and the gates of hell shall not oppose thee, Lion of the Lord. Be true. I am Orihah; I have spoken to you on behalf of the Lord. Be true."

Amaron felt himself taken up by the physical hand of Orihah and from on high he looked down on all the lands he knew. He could see the wickedness of his people, a wickedness he had seen many times and yet had not fully perceived. The fires of many cities lit up the night sky. The nation of the Nephites was at an end.

"It will be just as it was with my people. The unrighteous will be wiped from off this Promised Land. This vision is for thee alone. Be silent about it, be true, be the sword of the Lord when called. Be ye ready for the sacrifices of all those who are righteous. The Lord will not suffer his servants to be ground under the heel of this people's wickedness longer than they can bear. You are to help ease these burdens. Be the Lion of the Lord," proclaimed Orihah. Then he let go of Amaron's hand.

Amaron found himself back in his bedroll, on familiar ground as dawn broke. The fire crackled next to him, warm on this cool morning. The mists from the swamp seemed like smoke to him, like the fires of doom called down upon a wicked people. He felt it billowing all around him. "It was a dream," he said.

"What?" asked Daniel.

"Nothing, it is nothing. Have you made any tea yet?" Daniel grunted in the affirmative. "Good, let's have some and be on our way. We have a good long way to go to get home."

Prayers, Oaths and Curses

Within the palace of King Xoltec, weak candles burned, giving off a pale light. Incense filled the room with its sickly-sweet aroma. King Xoltec and Balam-Ek, the high priest, needed to discuss Prince Aaron's vision.

The prince waited impatiently for them, his mind wandering. A bat swooped into the room, chasing down a moth before flitting back outside into the night. The eyes of the boy followed the bat, thinking he himself was like the moth, seeking light and glory only to be snatched up by swift, winged death.

"So speak, my son, what did the Vision Serpent tell you? What is your destiny?" asked Xoltec in unusual humor.

Aaron looked at the floor lost in the intricate limestone patterns. The Vision Serpent had said that it was he, not his brother Almek, who would be the great king of the Lamanites. Aaron, the younger brother, would be Laman's revenge. "I...it was not important," he stammered.

"Not important, nonsense," boomed King Xoltec. "You had a vision, did you not?"

Yes, father, but..."

"But what? If you had one, it is important. The Vision Serpent speaks the truth; it speaks of destiny and duty. Duty to your brother," Xoltec said, swinging his scepter about absentmindedly.

Balam-Ek rose from his stool. "Prince Aaron, you have been endowed with the sacred priesthood of Baal. You are being trained in the arts of war; you have a mission set before you. Even if you are young, the youngest

I have ever endowed and trained, you must be ready. It has been done and cannot be undone. You had a vision, and you have an obligation to tell us —your king and your father, and your priesthood head and your friend. Tell us what you were told."

"I do not want my father to be angry with me for what I have to say."

"Why should I be?" said King Xoltec. "Duty is destiny, and your destiny is your duty."

"Yes, but..."

"But nothing. Speak to us, your elders, of your vision so that we may better understand the gifts of the spirits and the will of the gods," shouted the king.

Balam-Ek encouraged the boy. "You have overcome the crocodile pit and danced the dance of the gods. You have drunk the divine nectar. You are one of us. Speak of the vision's message."

Aaron finally spoke. "The Vision Serpent said to me, 'Behold, wrath is coming to the world.' I asked of whom it was speaking...it said it was I."

"The Vision Serpent said this?" asked Balam-Ek, as Xoltec's face darkened.

"No, the man from inside its mouth said this."

"An ancestor? Who was it, do you know?"

"It was Laman, our father of old."

"What did he say next?" prodded the high priest.

"He spoke of me and said that I would bring wrath to the world. That I would become his greatest son." Watching the doubt on his father's face he added, "I speak the truth before you. He said I would destroy the seed of his brother Nephi, our enemies the Nephites." Aaron hoped this last part would ease the anger he sensed was building.

King Xoltec stared a moment at his youngest son and the fires of hatred burned in his cold heart. "Liar! Blasphemer. You who are nothing, less than the dirt under my feet. You are as dust," he screamed.

There was madness in his eyes, a dark light that flickered with malevolent fury. Throwing his wine goblet across the room, it clanked and clattered to the floor, spilling the wine. He strode to his youngest son. "Trust no god and trust no woman, my father taught me. Both will rule you if they can, and take you in the darkness when you are not looking. You are the same, but oh, I am wise to you." He started beating Aaron, hand over fist like a furious ape.

Balam-Ek watched immobile for a short moment before interceding and putting his hand on the king's shoulder. "My king, please. What if the boy is telling the truth? At least as he understood it."

King Xoltec kicked the boy once more in the head. Glaring hot fury, he turned to Balam-Ek, ready to strike. The high priest smiled and removed his hand, unafraid. "What do you mean? The boy is a liar, anyone can see that. He mocks my dreams as he seeks to steal his elder brother's honor. He is just like the forefather of the Nephites...the trickster Nephi who sought dominion over his elder brothers, our forefather Laman!" King Xoltec panted, out of breath. "His Nephite name has cursed him to be a new reincarnated Nephi seeking to steal honor from his elder brother. Crown Prince Almek, my eldest son, is the Laman of tomorrow, not this vile usurper with the cursed Nephite name."

"You must have honor for anyone to steal it," said Balam-Ek, under his breath.

"What?"

"Nothing, my king."

"I know his heart, and it does not have my blood. No, it is evil. He was born to a dark star. His mother, my most beloved wife, was consumed by him at his birth. I was a fool not to have him slain and left to the beasts. It was Qof-Ayin who stayed my hand, my righteous hand of vengeance. He said if I loved her so much I should not take out my anger on the innocent child of her womb. I know not why I listened to him." King Xoltec scowled at the prostrate form of Aaron on the floor.

"It was for Sayame."

"What?"

"It was for Sayame, your daughter. She asked that you spare him, don't you remember? Qof-Ayin held the boy while your grief was calmed. The princess begged you. I remember, I was there," said Balam-Ek.

"And now you too seek to spare this demon-son's life?"

"My king, I exist only to give counsel. Aaron was initiated through me. He danced the dance, he drank the drink, he dreamed the dream," said the priest with an expectant look on his broad, bearded face.

"Has the whole world gone mad?"

"Rabbanah, I only serve, and I am telling you, Aaron has a purpose. What it is, I do not know, but it would anger the whole pantheon of gods for you to slay him. They have a vested interest in him. I am sure he spoke the truth as he understood it. Perhaps he misunderstood."

"Perhaps he is a liar," thundered the king. Aaron still lay curled into a ball on the floor. Bruised and bloodied, he was barely awake. Balam-Ek could see he was breathing but otherwise motionless and silent. Aaron had never known how close he came to death at birth. It gave him a new appreciation for the dead Qof-Ayin and his sister whom he loved so much.

"Well then, what could it mean? How could he be the wrath of the world? He is lying. He is not half the warrior his brother is," shouted King Xoltec, throwing his arms in the air as he paced. "I am tired of this and I don't want to think on it anymore. I retire to my chambers, send a slave girl."

"Which one, my king?"

"I care not."

"It shall be done," said Balam-Ek, watching King Xoltec stumble off.

The boy whimpered in a faint sad way that reminded the priest of a trampled dog. Kneeling over him, Balam-Ek spoke, "How do you feel, my prince?" He shook him a little, and Aaron struggled to prop himself against the wall and sit up. His face was smeared with blood and an eye swelled. His head ached from the last kick his father had given him.

"I won't hurt you, my prince. I am your friend, your counselor, your priest. Are you well enough to walk, to speak?" Aaron shook his head, realizing he could not speak. The words were in his head but would not come to his mouth. "You should have lied, you know your father well enough by now. You know his devotion to the idiot Almek."

Aaron looked at him angrily, as if to say, "I did what you asked me."

"It's alright, we shall calm his nerves. I will have two slave girls called to bring him more wine and settle his nerves for the night. On the morrow, you had best say you were mistaken. No matter what the Vision Serpent really told you, say it was of your brother Almek's greatness, not your own. Do you understand?"

Aaron nodded and Balam-Ek patted his head and helped him to rise. The boy slumped again only to be forcibly picked up by the stout priest. "Can you speak now?"

Aaron again shook his head.

"Let me look into your eyes," said the priest. He stared for a moment forcing Aaron into better light at the far end of the room. "You seem alright except for your speech which should return to you soon enough. You should have lied; I thought you would. If there is anything a Gadianton is good at, it is lying."

Aaron looked sharply at him and shook his head, mouthing silently.

"What, you're not a Gadianton? I thought perhaps with as long as you studied with Akish-Antum...I thought he would have taught you to lie by now. It is his trade."

Aaron struggled to stand, bracing himself up against the wall.

"You are hurt, but full of spirit. Perhaps I should have pledged to serve you rather than another, but what oaths are made and done, cannot be undone."

Aaron wondered who the priest meant. Someone besides his father?

"I will see that Sayame cares for your wounding and your hurts. Come," said the high priest as he led Aaron down an adjoining hall where Sayame waited. Aaron had the feeling that she had been eavesdropping on them for some time.

"I am here my brother, what happened?" she said.

Balam-Ek looked at her and said, "Care for him gently, Princess Sayame, for he cannot speak."

"He cannot speak? What did father do to him?"

Balam-Ek looked down at the beautiful, willowy girl and without responding, he walked away into the deep night.

Aaron could not express to his sister the cryptic things Balam-Ek had said nor what his Vision Serpent had said.

"I will care for you until you recover, my brother. I will never leave you, as our mother left us with that madman." She held him close and wept in the darkness. "I will never leave you, never, ever. Together we will go to the high places where you will rule."

He held her as tight as he could with broken fingers.

She prayed aloud, "Goddess of wonders, see through my eyes. Heal my brother, that he may fulfill his destiny. Hear me, hear me, Zilonen, and if not...let me fly far away from here on a burning star."

Aaron wished he could respond to her, but he hurt too much to make even a sign. In time he knew, he would learn all there was to rule. Laman's design would not be thwarted. He would do all that Akish-Antum had asked of him and more. *I am the wrath and when I am ready there will be our revenge. I will cleave my path through their armored bodies like a sickle at the harvest. No one to hold my ark steady but mine own hand. I will take this entire vast land, and it will be one under my terrible reign.*

✴ ✴ ✴ ✴ ✴ ✴ ✴ ✴ ✴ ✴ ✴ ✴

Sayame cleaned his wounds and bandaged his cuts, put tobac leaves upon his bruises and sprinkled holy oils over his brow. A fever took hold soon thereafter, and she sat by him every day, wiping him down and muttering prayers. The slaves were chased off and not allowed near the boy prince, all tasks were hers alone. She burned sacred incense to cleanse the room of evil spirits and when she thought he was asleep, she wept.

Why him? The only pure soul in the world, why should he bear the burden? My brother is the one who will someday redeem us and let us triumph over our enemies.

"Anything I can do for you, Princess?" asked Balam-Ek, startling her.

"I asked to not be disturbed," she said icily.

"Of course you did, but it has been a week. Either the boy is going to pull through or he won't. You can't change anything at this point. Think of your own needs."

"How dare you! Priest though you are, it is not up to you to bandy about words as if he is nothing special. He is the prince, and he will be made whole. He will rise, and my father will sorely rue the maltreatment of his son." She stood and pointed at the door.

Balam-Ek grinned. "Of course, Princess. I thought you needed to know, but I will come back another time and tell you of your father's plans for your marriage." He ducked out the doorway.

She gasped and chased him out into the hall. "What are you saying? I demand you tell me this vile news!" she cried.

Smiling devilishly, Balam-Ek began, "I was not supposed to break the news yet. If I tell you, you are to say nothing to anyone yet. Do you swear to remain silent about this news until your father brings it forth first?"

"I swear by Zilonen, I will be silent. What is this marriage? I won't have it... whoever it is, I will not have it!"

"Your father has confided in me that he means to marry you to the Gadianton Grand Master, as a means of securing a permanent alliance with that host," said Balam-Ek, glancing furtively down the hallway.

"Why are you telling me this?"

"Princess, it is no secret how much I despise the Gadianton. Why would I wish such a delicate flower as you upon this monster? I serve the king and I want a strong secure lineage for our royalty. At this point nearly anyone would be a better match, don't you think?"

She frowned at him. "I want no man. No man!"

"Of course, I am not trying to push anything or anyone upon you, just making an observation. Have you seen how Nu-Bak-Chak looks at you or even General Tubaloth? They could be fine suitors don't you think?"

She screamed, "Votan's heart! I will take the man who thinks he could marry me to the grave!" Running back to Aaron's room, she slammed the door.

Balam-Ek remained in the hall, alone and smiling. Time to go and tell King Xoltec that his daughter planned to run away and marry the Gadianton Grand Master. A similar reaction would ensue, with neither willing to speak directly to the other. No matter how difficult or unpredictable some people could be, once you found their strings they could be played upon to create gloriously discordant music.

Finding the Higher Ground

In Zarahemla, the public outcry at Mazeroth's arrest was soon put down. Two dozen or more of his followers were arrested and imprisoned. These actions by Mormon and Onandagus averted the riot from getting worse. Many rabble-rousers were less inclined to risk being thrown into prison after seeing the swift judgments that befell their comrades. The prisoners were housed in a three hundred year old jail built before the sign in the heavens.

Mormon the Elder lamented that night. The situation in the city was getting worse every day. He wondered why he was here. Should he leave and go on to the peaceful east? No, he must stay for his son's education and the call of duty. Zarahemla was more than ten times the size of Antum. When Mormon was a boy, Zarahemla had been a beautiful, peaceful city. Now it was a corroded shell of its former self. When he moved his family away from Antum, they had been the last members of the Church of Christ, the last who respected the old ways. He took it upon himself to burn the temple of Antum down so that it could not be further vandalized. It was the only time his son had seen him shed a tear since his wife died.

"Commander?" The voice brought Mormon back to the present.

"Yes?"

"Is something troubling you?" asked Gilhi, the guardsman.

"No more than usual, Gilhi," he said, shifting the weight on his wide sword belt.

"I want to let you know that the rioters are all secured. I am amazed at the construction of the holding cells, they are so old and yet so strong."

"Never underestimate what our forefathers knew over what we in our day know. It would amaze you the things I have found out," said Mormon.

"I do not doubt you, sir," said Gilhi. Barak, another young guardsman, appeared behind and nodded in agreement. At just over fifteen, Gilhi was the youngest man allowed to become a guardsman. The older guardsmen told him that he had seen more action these last few months than they had for the last few decades. It was an exciting time to be a guardsman.

"At the end of your shifts, be sure you are relieved by competent guardsmen we know and trust," said Mormon. "I will return. Watch and pray."

"Watch and pray," repeated the two guardsmen.

It was a quick brisk walk from the jail to the Judgment Hall. Already workmen had cleaned much of the burned debris away. The stone of the tower and most of the walls still stood while the insides had been gutted by the voracious flame.

Mormon saw Onandagus and his men standing under the canopied roof of the garden walkway. The white lattice-covered wood was over-grown with grape vines, still remaining as a place of peace. Onandagus was conversing with the big white Lamanite as Captain Tobron and Samson stood watch and kept the curious away. The chief judge would answer nothing until he himself knew everything. Captain Tobron and Samson parted for Mormon and then closed ranks as yet another spy crept closer to inquire about the white Lamanite. Samson stomped his foot at the man, who turned and fled. Samson was almost as big as Zelph, and all in Zara-hemla knew to give him a wide berth.

Mormon stood with his brawny arms across his chest. "Well?" His bushy, red brown beard flowed in the breeze. His ice blue eyes burned into Zelph who, having nothing to hide, chose not to be intimidated.

Onandagus introduced them. "Mormon, this is Zelph, son of Qof-Ayin, great-grandson of Samuel the Prophet. He brings dire news, a confirmation of all our fears."

Zelph extended his hand and Mormon extended his own and gave the bigger man an iron handshake. The white Lamanite gave as good as he got, and the two let go with satisfaction on their faces and red hands.

"Akish-Antum, the Gadianton Grand Master, has manipulated the

Lamanites to war. Even now they march here," Zelph said.

"Here?" exclaimed Mormon. "I had expected if such a thing were to occur, they would assault Desolation or Teancum first."

"They avoided all other cities so that they might better surprise you here, near the center of the land. They hope for a quick easy victory through surprise and deceit. They went around Desolation and the Narrow Pass. I could not be more than three or four days ahead of them at the most."

"How many are there?" Mormon asked.

"Fifty thousand Lamanite and Ishmaelite warriors, and untold numbers of Gadiantons who are helping to sneak them through deserted and little known roads."

"Rumors on the streets make it sound like there could be a legion of Gadiantons inside the city already," added Samson.

Onandagus spoke to Mormon, "It cannot be a coincidence that they are striking this month."

"No, it can't. So many followers of the church are to be here this holiday weekend to give thanks and commemorate the landing of Lehi upon the Promised Land. They must hope to murder us all in one fell swoop," said Mormon, unconsciously holding his sword hilt tight, ready to pull it forth. "They would be able to end the line of priesthood they so despise, end the very way of life they loath, end the right of choice and liberty."

"We could spread word for the followers of Christ to stay away, but the Gadiantons would find where many reside and slay them eventually. I fear we must make a stand here and now," proclaimed Onandagus. "Perhaps this is the endgame where we must stand and fight or be blasted from this Promised Land as the prophets of old have foretold."

"If that is how it is, I shall make an end of it," declared Mormon, drawing his sword. "There are enough good men at arms between here and Gideon. Let me muster them. They will heed the call. I will not allow the few innocent to be harmed by these devils."

"Very well, we shall put out the call for everyone to come unto Zara-hemla and be protected within its walls. You, Mormon, shall ride west and gather all that you can. I will send Captain Gidgiddonah to Gideon, he has family there. Captain Lehonti can go to the village of Joab just north-west of here. There may be some good men there as well. Captain Tobron will go to Manti and alert the captains there," said Onandagus. "Before you all go however, I will have you assist me in conferring the holy priesthood on our new brother, Zelph. He will be one with us."

"Are you sure? He has only just arrived. Meaning no disrespect to you, Zelph, but I don't know you," said Mormon. "And how does a Lamanite from the south speak such perfect Nephite? You sound as if you were born here."

Zelph pulled a small brown stone from his medicine pouch. "One of the Three gave me this. He said it gave me the Tongue of Fire, that I would understand all languages. It is to help with my mission."

Mormon still looked suspicious.

"It is all right, Mormon," said Onandagus, gripping Zelph's massive shoulder. "He has been baptized by water and fire with the three disciples and has been introduced to our Lord. He is clean, he is pure; he has been changed."

"I see the skin but thought perhaps you were born different."

"I was not born like this. My hair was black, my skin a deep copper. I am changed, true, but more so on the inside. I understand more than I ever did before, and I am ready to progress on my mission."

Mormon nodded as he and Onandagus laid their hands upon his head. Captain Tobron and Samson assisted as well as witnessing. Afterwards they all went their separate ways. Zelph and Onandagus were the only ones to remain in the city that night.

"Now accompany me, dear brother Zelph, as I will try to awaken a sleeping people of the mortal danger that threatens them," said Chief Judge Onandagus.

Zelph followed out onto the streets of the city, where the Avenue of the Eagle met the Avenue of the Ram. It was a wide, busy intersection and a host of people were already there. Many stopped when they saw their chief judge getting ready to speak. He stood upon the upturned cart of a friendly merchant.

"Hear me, oh people of Zarahemla, we have little time. The Lamanites and Gadiantons will soon be upon us. You must repent or we shall be wiped out as a people. A grave day of judgment is at hand. It is a day of doom for the wicked among us. We must repent and turn our lives around and come back to the Lord."

Many people stopped to listen, but few understood or were prepared to heed. Many scorned Chief Judge Onandagus as he stood before them. Their hatred of his perceived goodness was their driving force of will.

They cried out, "Old fool!"

"Our walls are strong enough to withstand the naked savages. Who can defeat us?"

"Our steel and iron is greater than those barbarian clubs of stone. We are the greatest nation in the world; no heathens from far away could ever defeat us."

Onandagus stopped for a moment and Zelph said to him, "Perhaps I should ascend the wall and speak to them as well."

"Do what you can, my new brother."

Zelph went toward the city gates to speak and help to spread the word. Onandagus continued, while the crowd gathered, larger but no friendlier. Judge Hiram appeared at the forefront, watching with eyes set in a blaze.

"Repent, repent, for the army of doom is at your very doorstep seeking to enter and devour whomever it may. I wish that you were all my children that I could usher you inside to my arms and protect you from this ravenous beast," continued Onandagus over their calls of disdain.

"Silence you doomsayer!" cried Judge Hiram. "Again, with your tales to frighten children—we won't be afraid of your lies anymore. Be silent I say. We will not be fooled into being slaves of your false religion. Rule your own house with fear but do not seek to rule ours."

Onandagus continued undisturbed, "Repent and prepare, my people. Hold to the Iron Rod of God's salvation. Able men of righteousness should prepare their families and then report for duty to help guard our city."

"Nay!" cried Judge Hiram. "You are a teacher of lies and false traditions. Stop trying to frighten us into obeying you. We are wealthy and happy, let us be."

A few men up front, however, listened to Chief Judge Onandagus and began talking of going to help defend the wall. Judge Hiram shouted at them as well, "Do not listen to him. He is a false prophet. Go back to your homes. No one is coming to harm us." Some in the crowd began taking sides in the debate.

Onandagus addressed Judge Hiram. "If I am a false prophet tell me of any false prophecy I have ever given. Tell me, dog, of my ever cheating any man or telling any lie. No, you cannot, for I am spotless before the likes of you. I have wronged no man and unlike you, I have cheated no one; so be silent and let these people, my people, judge for themselves what they will do." Stepping down from the cart, he approached Judge Hiram and whispered into his face, "You child of hell, your time is going to come. You cannot serve the lord of pain and expect to go unrewarded, unpunished. Now begone."

Judge Hiram fell silent at that and slunk back into the alleyways.

Zelph stood upon the walls of Zarahemla and spoke as Samuel his father of old had done, "Behold, I am Zelph, and I do speak a word of warning to this people. Hear me, and do forgive my weakness with words. Although the Lord has put these things in my heart, I am but a man like you. A sword of destruction will fall upon this people within four days. Blessed are those who repent for they shall be saved. Nothing will save this people except repentance and returning unto the Lord. If this great city will be saved it is because of the few righteous within it. Join with them, repent and hearken to the words of the Lord God. I pray you will heed me and this destruction will be averted."

The public speeches worked, and within hours those few who listened became a large body of men gathered to help with the watch and the repairs on the wall. The weak spots had been a concern for some time. The gate frames were reinforced, and a new gate of steel was added to the main west door. The thick wood was reinforced with bands of hardened steel. The wood itself was treated with a fire retardant mixture that Onandagus created from oils he alone knew. Mormon the Younger was a constant companion to the chief judge on these projects. The many uses of chemicals were especially fascinating to him. Onandagus also showed the boy the secret process of hardening copper, and the boy embraced this newfound knowledge with great zeal.

In two days Captain Gidgiddonah returned with a greater number of people than those in Zarahemla who had listened to the prophet. He had able-bodied men ready to fight, hunters to guard the walls with their bows, farmers and city men alike willing to be trained for war, all to preserve their land. For every man there were at least three or four more who accompanied them—wives, elderly parents and children.

Captain Lehonti also brought in the entire village of Joab save for four old men who would watch the bridge over the River Melek, one of the routes into the city that might be used for the invasion. If necessary, the four old men would fire the bridge to slow down the enemy.

Mormon did well in the cities to the west. A stout fighting force of some two thousand souls came with him as did their families. With so many people coming into Zarahemla, many of those who had been apathetic began to wonder if Onandagus were not right in his warning speeches. The citizens of Zarahemla remembered and retold the tale of Captain Lachoneus and Giddianhi the Gadianton, when in ancient days the Nephites had gathered all to the center of the lands to protect themselves from the robbers. These stories were spread about so quickly from person to person that by the fourth day, most of the citizens in Zarahemla believed and supported Chief Judge Onandagus over the hostile Council of Fifty, led by Judge Hiram.

"Now at least the people seem to believe, even if only because they think everyone else does," said Mormon.

"Does it matter?" asked Captain Gidgiddonah.

"Yea, it does. Men need to know for themselves and not be sheep. I will say nothing I do not study out and learn for myself. If you study and research you can discern the things of this world and beyond. But if you simply lay back and let things come to you as they will, where is your experience coming from? You cannot dream up wisdom. It takes work and time."

Captain Lehonti, the old captain of the guard before Mormon, had been silent for some time now, as he puffed on his frog-pipe, a cloud of smoke rising above his head. It had taken all the courage he could muster to come and ask forgiveness of the chief judge for his embarrassing handling of the riots weeks ago. He had apologized because he could not stand the thought of war coming to Zarahemla and being left out of it.

"Well, shall we establish a standing army to combat these Lamanites or just wait for them to annihilate us?" said Captain Lehonti, grinning as he rocked back in his chair. "Do you have any ideas? Onandagus said it was up to us though I don't know how much we should include the pale Lamanite."

"Zelph is with us. He will not allow innocent blood to be shed. He has so sworn," snapped Mormon.

"Fine, fine I just don't want him with my ranks," sniffed Captain Lehonti.

"He can command under me," said Captain Gidgiddonah. "Besides, he may have more combat experience than all of us. Is that not so, Zelph?"

"I do have experience in war," Zelph said softly, almost in a whisper. The Lamanite had been in the far corner of the room, unknown to Captain Lehonti.

"What did you do? Throw a boulder at another savage?" sneered Captain Lehonti, gaining arrogant courage at Zelph's quiet tone.

"I would watch my mouth if I were you," said Mormon chuckling. "He is a lot bigger than you."

There was no anger in Zelph's eyes. "I was with my father Qof-Ayin as part of King Xoltec's army sent to put down a revolt in the city of Lamanihah. A nobleman named Madoni had declared himself a god king and begun sacrificing many people from the northern part of the kingdom. We went to deal with him. The city was protected by a strong gate and wall as this city is. My father had a plan of assaulting the city head on while I led a small group of able warriors up and over the back wall. We broke into the palace of Madoni where I did slay the mad king. King Xoltec was to reward me by making me his bodyguard for life. With my father's help I came with this invading army to thus escape my fate."

"Fate? What do you mean?" asked Captain Gidgiddonah.

"Once King Xoltec dies, and he is an old king with ambitious sons, his court will be buried with him. It is doubtful that I would have escaped. Even if the new king had chosen to retain me, it is our tradition that bodyguards do not have families."

"Why is that?"

"So there is no one with a place in their heart above the king. I did not wish to be the end of the family line. I want to have many sons and daughters."

"Seems you are in a perfect position to be a back door man and spy," Captain Lehonti scoffed.

"You just don't know when to shut up," said Mormon, slamming him in the chest. "Let me decide whether Zelph is a spy or not. They could've found a less conspicuous spy, don't you think? So before you go on flapping your fool gums, stop and think."

"I apologize."

"Good," said Mormon, as though it had never happened. "Zelph, I will have you with Captain Gidgiddonah and our infantry force. Captain

Lehonti, you will be in command of one wing of the cavalry. Do we have any elephants available?"

"Too few to matter as yet," answered Captain Lehonti.

"It appears we will come under siege. If they strike elsewhere besides Zarahemla, we must be able to move quickly and attack. Zelph, can you please refresh us as to how these Lamanites are armed?"

They discussed the Lamanite army long into the night. Zelph spoke of its strengths and its weaknesses, its tactics and strategies. As they were preparing to leave, Onandagus arrived. "Zelph, will you come with me?" he asked.

"Of course."

They left the singed room of the hall and headed to an untouched section, one of the only spots the fire had not blackened with smoke. Onandagus took hold of a curious stone in the wall and twisted it to the right. A passage door swung open, heavy upon its hinges. "I am sending out warnings to members of the priesthood order. Come with me, I have something to show you."

Samson appeared at the doorway to join them, twisting the stone to shut the door. A tunnel stretched out before the three men, its inky blackness extending for a greater distance than Zelph could judge. It went to the east toward the river, which gave him his only sense of direction. Lamanites generally avoided caverns, as it was believed they were the entrances to the underworld and the home of various demons and spirits.

"Let us go on then," said Onandagus.

Samson led with a tin lantern. They soon passed stacks of records and other curious records on hewn stone, relics of dusty ages past unknown to Zelph.

"Some of these are records of the Jaredites," said Onandagus. "We can look upon them another time. These tunnels are a secret that few know of, but I felt inspired tonight to let you know of them for some purpose." They continued walking until they were up to their ankles in cold water. The water continued rising until it was up to their waists. Zelph felt nervous but said nothing. "It is alright, the waters will recede soon, we are almost to the end," said Onandagus.

The tunnel ended at another stone door that looked the same as the one they had entered. Putting a torch down, Onandagus repeated the stone twisting motion and a lever pulled the door open. Cool night air greeted them. The stars twinkled overhead. The great river Sidon splashed against a waiting boat. "Greetings, Diomenes," said Onandagus.

"Greetings, Judge. Where do you wish me to ferry him?" said a lean man who stood aboard.

"Down river to Nephihah is fine, Samson knows where to go. Thank you for coming on such short and late notice."

"It's alright. A job is a job," Diomenes shrugged. His vessel was anchored near a large rock that matched the tunnel door. Zelph was not completely sure he could find the right one again.

"With everything happening, are you sure this is the best time for me to be playing messenger? Couldn't someone else spread the word?" asked Samson as he threw the pouch of letters into the boat.

"There will likely be Gadiantons watching for that pouch and hoping to stop the word being spread. There is no one more capable than you, my friend, to see that it gets through. Be careful, Samson." The big blonde haired man merely grunted and waved a low wave.

Chief Judge Onandagus and the white-skinned Lamanite stood on shore until the ship disappeared down the dark river. "Do you send word to others because you expect the worst?" Zelph asked him.

"The messages go to Jershon, the land of your people, the people of Ammon, to tell them of what is happening here and halt any who may be coming for this week's holy celebration. If they don't cross over the Sidon, I think they will be safe. The messages also tell of you, their long lost brother. They will want to meet you soon."

"I wish to see them as well."

"As soon as we can. There is always a purpose and once the Lord deems it, we will go together to that peaceful land to the east, across the great river." He closed the stone door, and they walked back through Zarahemla's deep underground tunnel.

Tenth Man Down

Amaron worried about his men who continued to grumble and bicker like spoiled children. The weeks had passed, and the scouts were only a few scant days from home. The mission was almost over and still they had nothing tangible to report to Chief Judge Onandagus.

"Those farmhands we spoke to are probably just a bunch of liars looking to make names for themselves," said Daniel.

"Aye, they knew nothing of value," agreed Lehi. "That funny looking one, that farmer, Gish, said he thought the disappearances were just men walking out on their families."

"Gish is a fool," said Judah.

"Don't call anyone a fool. Contempt of them will damn you...Fool," laughed Daniel as he punched Judah in the shoulder.

"Fool," said Judah, punching Daniel back even harder sending the other away in a stumbling motion. To call someone a fool in direct violation of scripture warning was a favorite pastime among the scouts.

"There must be some grain of truth to the rumors," suggested Amaron. "Something has them scared. People have gone missing. Something strange is coming over the land." He moved to the edge of the small, unnamed lake near their camp. Staring at the sliver of moon just beginning to rise over the gnarled trees, he thought again about the dream he had weeks before. He had not spoken of it to anyone. He did not want to be called a hero or a visionary.

It was early evening on a lightly clouded day and cool for the first few days of summertime. The camp was next to an oval-shaped lake where

Amaron had camped at a few times before. It was peaceful and still with good clear waters. He went further way from the camp to be alone with his thoughts. A forgotten road meandered past the lake on the north shore.

Having found no trace of the Lamanite attack force, Amaron would head them back to Zarahemla on the morrow. He worried that they would miss out on the action in the city, where they would surely be needed. They had been away long enough, and tensions were running high. The men argued with one another constantly over petty things. The brothers Lehi and Nephi were at each other's throats, and none seemed immune. Amaron caught himself several times ready to blow up at insignificant matters. Only Ezra seemed undisturbed. Strange little Ezra, growing his wisp of a mustache and beard.

The sudden thunder of horses startled him. More than a dozen riders bore up quick with dark earth-toned cloaks and unfriendly faces. They looked the men over before one approached the campfire. His mount stamped at the ground impatiently. Amaron stood silently by the lakeshore. Something told him to remain still although it was his duty to address a fellow captain. The riders had not noticed him, and a still small voice said to keep it so.

"Who are you and what are you doing on my lord's land?" barked the lead bearded one. They were well-armed and outnumbered the scouts of Amaron almost two to one.

Judah took it upon himself to answer. "This is a public road so far as I know, and I have been on it several times before."

"I asked who you are!" demanded the man, spitting as he spoke.

"We are scouts in the service of Governor Onandagus, Chief Judge," said Ezra. "Who are you to claim this land and road for your lord?"

"The governor's men, eh? That's all I needed to hear," said the bearded man as he wheeled his horse away.

Amaron, silent as a ghost, stood motionless, curious at their rudeness.

"Take them, brothers!" cried the leader as he charged his horse at Judah with his saber in a murderous arc. The horsemen quick and vile turned again with blades drawn, and with their stout, curved bows, began savagely attacking the unsuspecting scouts. Reuben and Lehi dropped, slain where they stood, and then Judah, still weak with wounds from the lion. Daniel grabbed a spear to fight back but was laid low by a number of arrows. Ezra tried to run, but the bearded captain cut him as he ran past.

Amaron, running out of the darkness, charged the enemy horsemen. "Gadianton dogs!" he shouted as he threw his war hammer at the nearest target. The man was hit and went down, his head caved. The horses spooked, throwing a rider who was then trampled by his own mount. Amaron ran at them with his broadsword raised in a savage fury, deftly slaying a man and his horse with a cruel swing of Ramevorn. Another tried to run him down, but he dodged and sheared the man as he rode past. A third attempted to charge and met with the same fate as Amaron plunged his broadsword through the Gadianton's armored breastplate. Now panicked under Amaron's furious onslaught, the Gadiantons urged their mounts to hasten away.

It looked like every one of Amaron's men was down upon the ground with grievous wounds. Amaron dropped and knelt on the bloody ground next to his men, his friends all. He cradled Obadiah's gashed head. He was gone with nothing more to be done. Judah still laboriously breathed but had a rattle in his chest. Amaron knew it would be only short moments.

"Watch and pray, that's what we did, right?" whispered Judah.

"Watch and pray," Amaron repeated.

Judah looked up at the friend of his youth and said hoarsely, "Warn the people, tell them." He heaved and was still.

"Am I cursed that people near me die at the hands of the Gadiantons?" spoke Amaron to the ghosts. "The dogs will be back, I must hurry." He gathered food and supplies, cleaned his sword on a fallen Gadianton and hefted his war-hammer. He was about to retrieve a bow when the drum of horse hooves returned. Amaron left the bow lying there as he had not yet gathered any arrows. He retreated to the lake's edge and hid among the tall brown cattails.

The fleeing horsemen had returned with new, hungry warriors. Amaron saw a score or more of lanky, sharp-faced Lamanite warriors running alongside the mounted Gadiantons. Their bows were drawn with vicious-looking obsidian arrowheads as they fanned out to control the campsite. Amaron marveled at their efficiency. One came dangerously close to his hiding spot in the reeds. The Lamanites were subservient to a particular captain and seemed scornful of the mounted Gadiantons. The Lamanite captain had long black hair and wore more copper armor than the others. He held a long, brazen spear in his left hand as he gazed over the slaughter.

"I told you we needed help, General Anathoth," said the mounted Gadianton captain. General Anathoth grunted and looked over the bodies. He picked up one of the saber-tooth push daggers Amaron had made and showed it to one of his men.

Amaron could not understand what they were saying. It wasn't the Lamanite tongue, possibly Ishmaelite. A second group approached. The captain of this second group, a man with a mohawk and numerous scars on his body, knelt and examined the ground. He wore only buckskin trousers and moccasins, a long knife and tomahawk at his waist. His upper body was covered in scars and tattoos. A great snake slithered its way across his back, jaws agape ready to pounce from his skin.

"What do you see, Uzzsheol?" asked the mounted Gadianton.

The tattooed Lamanite scanned the ground a moment longer before answering, "Eight dead, one more dying there." He pointed to the profusely bleeding Daniel. One of Uzzsheol's men slammed a spear into Daniel and he went still. "But there is another, one more Nephite. Not the dozen you said attacked and killed your men." His voice had no emotion.

"Yea, there was, a dozen or more. They must have run off at our approach," sputtered the Gadianton. "Where's that little one I cut?"

"There were not that many, I count ten or eleven. Ten. The last one looked at his slain brothers then hid on the lakeshore. He is probably in the reeds." He pointed roughly to where Amaron was hiding.

Amaron had only a fleeting glance at the Lamanite, but knew he would never forget the malevolent scarred visage. A hawk-like nose jutted from his face and diverted attention from the scars and pits. Cold dark eyes that had seen hell flashed towards him.

Angry a tracker had discovered him so soon, Amaron slid silently into the deep green waters, adjusting his knife and sword as he went in. The war hammer's wooden handle slapped against him in the water. He had not gone far when he had to undo the leather straps of his exalted copper breast-plate, as the heavy metal threatened to send him to the bottom. It was one of his prized possessions and worth many senines of gold. He would need it once he climbed out and had to fight again, but it was sink or swim. Underwater, he swam as far as he could, until his lungs were ready to burst. Slowly, he let himself rise up, eyes and nose first like a crocodile. A good distance from the shore, he watched them.

The Lamanite warriors were beating the reeds in an attempt to flush him out. As soon as Uzzsheol appeared, however, they stopped and looked out into the lake. "He has gone into the lake." Uzzsheol shrugged.

"We need to find him," demanded the Gadianton as General Anathoth stood by. "Akish-Antum has gone to great lengths to launch this operation. He will not allow it to be ruined this close to the end."

"I will bring the tenth man down for the evil eye and kill him," said Uzzsheol without a trace of emotion. "He will not escape. I will skin him for you, Hadad, to keep you warm on lonely cold nights."

The other Lamanites chuckled at this but the Gadianton captain, Hadad, bristled and began to ride away. "Just find him," he called as he rode off, followed by the other mounted Gadiantons. General Anathoth and his score of warriors continued up the road away from the lake towards Zarahemla, while Uzzsheol's wolf-pack of Lamanite trackers remained behind to find the tenth Nephite.

"Gulam, Paron, Musook," said Uzzsheol, pointing three warriors to the left of the lake. "Nimrod, Tecotl, Menah." He pointed to the right, and three others raced off. He waded into the lake with a dozen others, his tomahawk raised ever ready for the death blow.

Amaron went down again and began swimming for the distant shore. He rose up again for another breath and heard shouting. A few arrows were sent after him, but in the darkness they missed. The Lamanites would surround the lake and wait for him. His only hope was to reach the opposite shore and disappear into the woods. He swam as if he were on fire. The shoreline was thick with trees and shrubs to better hide his landfall. The lake had a few jagged peninsulas of rock near the mouth of a small stream that fed the lake. Making for it in the dark, he had a plan.

Every so often he would stop to catch his breath and watch how close the Lamanite torches were to his planned exit. They were slowed by the undergrowth, and Amaron thanked God for small miracles. This had been a wet spring, making the foliage a good obstacle. Touching the lake-bottom, he struggled to be silent, walking up the mouth of the stream. He took big deep breaths, trudging out of the mud and onto the sturdy, yet slippery rocks of the creek. He would walk up the stream as far as possible to mask footprints from the tracker. Hopefully, in the dark they would not spot the smudged moss, and they would surround the lake all night, waiting for him to emerge. He slipped numerous times and this made him feel like a fool.

The night air was cold, but he knew to keep moving and he would soon be warm. A hundred yards up the creek he moved off the rocks and onto the matted grasses of a game trail. It went up a slight hill. At the top he stopped to look and listen. He could make out faint shadowy shapes running around the shore where he had just been. He had got out just in time. Some of the Lamanites weren't even using torches; they were running back and forth onshore like dogs that had lost a scent.

As he passed over the rise he heard a bloodcurdling shout—"Aiyeeee!" They had found his trail, but how? Cursing the gods of the Lamanites he began to run. They must have seen his tracks on the mud of the lake bottom. There was no other explanation. It didn't matter now. He had only a few hundred yards on them, and they weren't tired and soaking wet as he was. Coming up against a narrow defile, he began running along it in an easterly direction. He could not see the bottom of the gully in the dark. A dead tree had fallen across it just ahead of the next rise.

Suddenly, the warrior was upon him, crying out and attacking with his scimitar bared. Drawing his own blade, Amaron blocked with his sword on the Lamanite's arm and then swept upward. The near headless attacker dropped to the ground. Another warrior was just as quick with an obsidian flanged club. Amaron let the sword sweep out from his center, and he ripped it across the man's breast. The warrior stepped back and looked at his own bleeding chest. The wound was slight, a mere scratch but he howled in a fury. They slashed at each other a few more times until Amaron kicked the warrior, knocking him down long enough to pierce his heart. Kicking him into the defile, Amaron looked at the dead tree spanning the ravine.

Testing it for strength he ran across, as an arrow struck the tree branch beside him. Turning around and going low, he saw one more warrior with a drawn bow. The Lamanite looked down at the defile and then the tree. Amaron stayed low out of sight and took a rock from the ground. He threw it and struck the man in the shoulder and sent him off balance. Amaron then grabbed the end of the tree trunk and rocked it so that the man fell off into the ravine. It was not very deep, but Amaron heard him moaning down in the blackness. The tree was too heavy to move, so he left it and ran on up a low hill.

There were few clouds in the sky, making it a chilly night. The hills leveled but the forest thickened. Stopping to gather his bearings and listen for signs of his pursuers, Amaron waited. Hearing nothing but the night, he wondered if he had lost them already. No, that hawk-faced Lamanite was too good a tracker. Knowing he must keep moving, he ran for maybe a mile in the moonlight, until he heard the steady tromp of sandaled feet on hard-packed earth, the sound of fifty thousand men marching.

Amaron stealthily made his way closer. In crossing the lake and running through the forest overland, he had inadvertently made his way back to the road, perhaps a mile or two up from his campsite. He watched from a short distance of about ten yards as a vast procession of Lamanite warriors marched in rows of ten. Someone had organized them similar to the Nephite armies of old. These were certainly more disciplined than the Nephites now. They wore little armor, but were very well armed. The foot soldiers all carried scimitars, spears, small bucklers of leather and long knives or axes. Next, a row of pike men marched, these all carrying fifteen foot pikes and a quiver of a half dozen javelins on their backs. They had short swords at their belts. Then a row of archers went past, their quivers holding at least fifty arrows apiece. They too carried the short Lamanite sword.

The rows repeated themselves again and again. Judging by their speed, Amaron guessed that a thousand men passed in front of him in only a few short minutes. The groaning of poorly greased wagon wheels broke the monotony of night. The wagons carried enough food and supplies for an army of tens of thousands.

"Watch and pray," he muttered.

Last of the Wilds

A maron wondered where to go before the tracking Lamanites could catch up to him when an opportunity came. A swarthy man in a dark robe jumped out of a wagon and walked almost directly towards him, apparently to relieve himself.

Watch and pray.

Amaron relieved the red-capped Gadianton of all his worldly cares by breaking his neck. He took the foul-smelling cloak and put it on, but he could not bring himself to wear the hated red cap. He placed it in his pocket and picked up the limp body, slung it over his shoulder, carrying him back to the road and the creaking wagons. He went right up to a slow-moving wagon and flung him in the back.

The drowsy driver looked back and said, "What's his problem?"

"Too much wine, he went to the woods and fell down. He's drunk. I picked him up before the master sees him," said Amaron with a drawl.

"Good we gotta look out for our own, don't we?" said the sleepy driver. Amaron leapt up to the wagon seat beside the driver. The man looked at him. "You're big enough to hunt bear with a switch. I don't recognize you. Are you from the Manti order?"

"No, Zarahemla," muttered Amaron, not looking him in the eye.

"This sure is gonna be something, isn't it?"

"Yea," responded Amaron, seemingly disinterested.

"Come on. You fooling me? You realize how rich we'll be when Akish-Antum is made king? The rest of us will live like kings, huh? Kings among men, and to think my father said that the Order was a bunch of conniving back-stabbers. He said that when I was just a boy you know. He was wrong to stand in the way of progress and the change that's coming. Ain't nothing on earth gonna stop this army, the days of the Nephites spitting in our eyes is over. We will rule," spat the man. He took a long look at Amaron. "You say you're from Zarahemla?"

"That's right, been there almost all my life until this."

"I guess that explains it, and I thought I knew everyone in the baggage train," said the driver, turning his attention back to his oxen.

The bumpy ride was beginning to rock Amaron to sleep. He had been awake for close to two full days. He dozed fitfully for a few moments before rousing himself enough to watch for another spot to leave the road and continue on. He wondered if the column would rest any time soon. When it stopped, he would walk out into the bushes to pretend to relieve himself like the Gadianton he had killed. He should not wait much longer. Someone might try to rouse the man and discover his neck was broken.

The pale moon was well into the sky now and threatened to reveal his identity. Too many Gadiantons might recognize him. Watching for a good spot, he was about to exit the wagon when two lanky, shaven-headed Lamanites came jogging up alongside. One carried a torch and the other scanned the ground. They stopped a moment at one spot, and Amaron turned his face away as his wagon creaked by them too slowly.

A horseman rode up and stopped beside the trackers. "What is it? What are you searching for now?" he bellowed. Amaron recognized the voice as the bearded captain, Hadad, from earlier.

"The Nephite swam the lake, he crawled upstream, very sneaky. We found one set of tracks he running through the woods. He found road, he found army. He is marches with them now. We look for where he leaves road," said one of the lean trackers. His broken speech belied his utter disdain for all things Nephite.

"Impossible," snarled Hadad. "Where is Uzzsheol?"

"Here." The tall warrior with the savage hawk face walked up silent as a ghost.

"How could a Nephite march with the army? He would stick out like a Lemuelite tongue. We would spot him."

"No. You are a fool, Hadad," snapped Uzzsheol in his barbarous accent. "One man walked into the woods to make waters, the Nephite warrior struck him down, carried him to the marchers. He is in disguise,

even now. You have too many men for us to search everyone. He'll probably leave the road soon, we'll find him."

Amaron could faintly hear Uzzsheol's words as the wagon creaked out
of earshot. They were watching for a sign of his leaving the road. He must
come up with another plan. The two tracking Lamanites continued up the
road, watching for a sign as they outdistanced the wagons. Uzzsheol and
Hadad stopped and talked as the wagons disappeared around the bend.
Spying a good spot, Amaron was about to leap off the wagon onto some
gray stones. The old man driving the oxen did not seem to be aware. He
wouldn't be able tell them anything; just a man, big enough to hunt bear
with a switch.

"What are you doing? We are about to stop for the night. Just wait,
and we can have another drink," said the driver. He must have thought
Amaron wanted to dip into the wine vats in the back.

In a short moment the column stopped and the driver, like all the other
wagons, prodded the draft animals to the far side of the road. Lamanite
warriors milled about everywhere, sitting down against trees or stones,
anywhere to rest their feet. Many took off their sandals and caressed their
swollen toes. Considering how many had been tracking him at the lakeshore, Amaron guessed more were still behind him watching the sides of
the road.

"Come on then, quit dawdling," said the old man. "Let him sleep," he
pointed at the broken-necked man. "You carry the barrel for the command
tent. I gotta feed the oxen." He motioned to the wine barrels in the back.
"Get going."

Amaron picked up a barrel, heavy and full. "Where is the command
tent?"

Scowling, the old man looked at him like he was the biggest fool he
had ever seen. "Look at that, big as a church and empty as one too. Right
where it always is, almost at the head of the column. Hurry up! You are
keeping 'em waiting, hurry!"

With the barrel over his shoulder, Amaron kept his head down and
walked down the road towards the front. He could not reasonably leave
the road anywhere along the way now; Lamanite warriors surrounded him,
dozens thick, all staring greedily at the barrel of wine. After almost a half
mile, he saw several tents up ahead looking regal and fine with expensive
trim and ornaments. Hoping he might leave the barrel and fade away into

the night, Amaron brazenly decided to try and give it to the first servant he could. "Here is the wine, for the masters," he said to a swarthy, bald man.

"You fool! Do you not know the second-in-command when you see him?" snarled Teth-Senkhet.

"A thousand pardons, your eminence," said Amaron.

"Take it inside," said Teth-Senkhet, gesturing to the largest maroon tent.

Amaron complied, and Teth-Senkhet followed behind, gesturing again toward the rear of the tent. A serving girl was slicing joints of meat and heaping them on silver plates. "Can I leave this with you?" Amaron asked her.

"Do I look like I can pick that up?" she said, not looking at him.

"Well no, but I have to go."

"You are here to give them wine, don't try and add to my duties. I have enough to do, thank you very much. And try and touch me again and I'll stick this knife in your gullet."

"I didn't touch you. Where are the cups?"

"The *goblets* are in that chest, just like they always are, you should know that." She finally looked at him. "Who are you? You're not the usual slug. Where is Samos? Not that I care."

"He had to take a needed rest. Do I have to serve them?"

"Yes, you do. I am giving them the meal, you give the wine."

He pulled the goblets from the ornate chest and looked over to see how many were needed. The girl glanced back at him and signaled for seven. Pulling out seven goblets, he gingerly filled them, sloshing a bit of wine onto the swept dirt floor of the tent. Amaron gazed at the seven men seated. The fine, black-cloaked Gadiantons with their weapons of steel or exalted copper, the Lamanite prince in ridiculous feathered headdress and crown, and the shrewd Ishmaelite general with roving eyes taking in the others. Clearly they did not like or even trust one another.

With his sword and hammer hanging at his side beneath the stinky black cloak, Amaron considered his next move. His sword reminded him of duty and opportunity. Should he, like Teancum his ancestor of old, slay these evil men in their tent here and now? He thought of pulling his blades out and slaying them as they sat, sure that he could take half of them before an alarm would sound. He would take the rest afterward then die a great martyr, a hero who cut the heads from the hydra of evil. First, he would let them drink the wine, then strike as they became preoccupied with the food.

The Gadianton and Lamanite leaders sat around an ornate table as the girl placed the meat before them. Amaron followed suit and put the goblets beside the plates, trying to look inconspicuous. The Lamanite prince sneered at him. "Your new servant stinks, Akish-Antum."

The Gadianton Grand Master ignored him, listening to General Anathoth explain about the Ishmaelite tactics used against Lemuelite nomads.

"I said your servant stinks," said Prince Almek even louder.

"I suppose your servants are as fragrant as the lilies of the field," said Akish-Antum laughing, and going back to the conversation with General Anathoth.

General Tubaloth, Almek's lead general, was not amused. He said, "We have a standard for those that serve the prince. The Nephite serving girl is almost too much, but your foul smelling troglodyte is too much. Send him away, I like not his spirit."

"Bethia is not my serving girl. She belongs to General Anathoth; and she is a fine specimen who knows her place," said Akish-Antum. "As for my wine-man, Samos does his best." Noticing Amaron, Akish-Antum narrowed his gaze. "Who are you? Where is Samos?"

"He fell ill, I was sent to replace him," answered Amaron, keeping his head low. His left hand stayed inside his cloak, fingering the war-hammer's handle.

"Ill? Samos is a horse, send him here immediately," ordered Akish-Antum.

"Yes, master," said Amaron, turning to leave. He contemplated wheeling about with weapons drawn and slaying them all, when Uzzsheol entered the tent. His warriors followed close behind. Uzzsheol stared hard at Amaron and fingered his knife.

Bethia placed a plate of warm bread before Akish-Antum and as Amaron was about to pounce and slay, the Gadianton grabbed Bethia and forced her onto his lap. She struggled to escape his grasp while he laughed. "Why so wild? You could be my queen."

Amaron could not cut him down without harming the girl. Uzzsheol still stared at him.

"She is my slave. Let her go," said General Anathoth, cold like the wind of the northlands.

Akish-Antum relaxed his grip on Bethia and turned his attention to Amaron in the doorway of the tent. "I said to go and get me Samos," he shouted as Bethia still struggled.

Amaron and Akish-Antum locked eyes.

"I said to let my slave go." General Anathoth stood with his hand on his sword hilt.

The Ishmaelite general was fast. If Amaron moved to slay the Gadianton, this man would slay him in turn. The tracker Uzzsheol remained glowering beside him, ready to pounce. Amaron realized there were too many variables to kill the Gadianton Grand Master right here. He stared back at Akish-Antum.

"Let her go!" demanded General Anathoth.

Amused, the Gadianton, still holding Bethia's wrist, yanked her toward himself, then pushed her away and laughed. "Relax, Anathoth, we are all friends here in this tent."

Amaron left the tent.

"Who was that anyway?" asked Akish-Antum.

"I don't know, worshipful master," said Teth-Senkhet. "I trusted he was sent instead of Samos."

"You trusted? Uzzsheol bring him back, I did not recognize his face," said Akish-Antum. "Something is amiss." The tracker nodded and went out into the night.

"Can I just eat without these nightly parlor games?" exclaimed Prince Almek.

Outside the tent, men were arrayed in all directions, some standing and talking, some sleeping, some slouched against trees and brush. Uzzsheol looked for the tall, dark-cloaked wine-man. His own trackers and warriors sat rolling dice made of bone. "Where did the wine-man go?"

They looked puzzled at the question. "What wine-man? Aren't we seeking the Nephite tenth man?"

Uzzsheol grunted and swore. "Nimrod, go and find Samos and the other tall wine-man, who was sent to replace him." Nimrod nodded and went down the road, back to the wagons. He disappeared quickly in the inky blackness. Musing that perhaps there had been nothing unusual about the tall, smelly man, Uzzsheol joined a quick game of rolling the dice.

General Anathoth finished his meal and excused himself from the company he loathed, bringing Bethia with him. They walked to the front of the column where the Tultecs encamped. Lib greeted him and held the tent flap open for them. Bethia followed the general inside then sat upon a purple silken divan.

"That pig!" she shouted. "Saying I could be his queen."

"It's over, let it go," said Anathoth.

"Why are you with them? I know you hate them, you don't believe in any of this."

"As I have explained to you many times, my son is now two moons old. I cannot let him grow up knowing his father disobeyed the king. I will not have my son, Joram-Baal, grow up dishonored because I was not man enough to do my duty. You are a girl who does not understand honor and duty. If you did, you would not ask me every night."

"I know that you are a good man and will be a good father. I had to run away to realize what I had back home with a father like you, a good man overwhelmed with responsibility and duty. Yet he would never turn from his beliefs to please anyone else."

"I do what I do to please no one but myself!" General Anathoth fumed.

Lib looked inside the tent flap, smiled at what he perceived was a lover's quarrel and closed the flap.

"I didn't mean it like that. My father will not deny truth nor do what he knows is wrong even if the whole world were against him."

"Why do I have the feeling that the whole world is against him?"

"Because it's true and there are few that support him. I should be there uplifting him, rather than causing him and my family worry."

"I cannot fight my fate."

"What fate? We choose what we will do in this life. I am here with you because I chose to run away. It was not fate. I chose it, and I have to live with it."

"Lib chose to spare your life. Was that not fate?"

"I don't believe so. We choose the strings that all weave together to form the tapestry of being."

He shrugged and took up his spear. "You are a good daughter, Bethia, and your father should be proud. If it is up to me, I will spare his life when the time comes. Who is he?"

"Just a man, no one special."

"I will think on the things you have told me and if the Great Spirit allows, perhaps my destiny can be changed, where I can keep my honor and still do my duty. Only the Great Spirit could accomplish these things. Get some sleep. We will be moving again in a few scant hours," said Anathoth, going out into the dark of night.

✻ ✻ ✻ ✻ ✻ ✻ ✻ ✻ ✻ ✻ ✻ ✻

"Samos is slain!" shouted Nimrod to Uzzsheol. "Someone broke his neck and stole his cloak."

Uzzsheol's joyless eyes flared. He pulled his tomahawk and barked commands to his men, gesturing for them to scatter in all directions and find the tall dark man.

Hearing the commotion, Akish-Antum exited his tent and cursed. How could a Nephite have gotten so close? He had looked the man in the eye, and he would never forget him. Almek, wine goblet in hand, came up beside him while General Tubaloth followed Almek, to stay close to his prince.

"Now do you see, Prince Almek, how crafty the Nephite devils are?" said Akish-Antum. "An assassin crept into my tent and could have poisoned us all."

"Where is he? He could be hiding anywhere among us now," said Prince Almek, looking nervously about the chaotic camp.

"He is gone into the forest by now. He is gone, but Uzzsheol will find him."

✻ ✻ ✻ ✻ ✻ ✻ ✻ ✻ ✻ ✻ ✻ ✻

Amaron needed to put some distance between him and the blood-thirsty trackers. He tore off the reeking Gadianton robe but kept hold of it. He had a plan. They would find his trail, but he would not make it easy for them. Time and again he doubled back in rough, thick areas hoping it would discourage and weaken the resolve and attention of his pursuers. He had run for perhaps an hour or more when he found a promising spot between two trees. After digging a shallow depression, he used his knife to sharpen a number of stakes, careful that their chips went only into the hole. He covered over the trap with a few branches and some grasses, then hung the filthy robe on a low hanging branch next to the trap. He ran on in a serpentine pattern to confuse the trackers. It was an old trick Captain Lachoneus had taught him, so that crafty enemies could not cut you off.

Amaron was half way up a thickly wooded hill when he heard a scream coming from the area of his trap. They had found his trail sooner than expected, and he must do more to slow them down. Finding the right type of sapling, he yanked it back and secured it precariously with another branch. He attached a few sharpened spikes with rawhide strips to make this a good second trap. The branch holding the sapling barely restrained it. The first scuffle of feet would release the deadly spring. He raced down the hill hoping to gain some good distance. Getting to the top of the next rise would give him a good lead, and from there he could get a good look at them. He heard a howl of pain and much cursing. At the top of the hill, he waited next to a stand of thick shrubs. His keen eyes spotted a trio making their way down the hill. He could easily handle three men. Crawling quickly through the brush he raced on, going between fallen trees and other obstacles to worry his followers.

At the bottom of the wooded hill was a swift stream, about a foot deep and ten to twelve feet across with a heavy late spring runoff. He crossed in an obvious wide manner to a well-chosen spot where he would make a stand against his foes. He selected a few good stones and waited. Sword drawn and sling ready with a stone, he sat ready to revenge himself with a bloody fury. *Watch and pray.*

Their arrival took longer than expected. The sun was beginning to rise behind him. One mohawked Lamanite and two with shaven heads, all in buckskins, appeared ever watchful—the wolf pack of Uzzsheol. *Wait, one of the devils was Uzzsheol.* The scarred warrior looked upon the stream and the woods beyond. The look on his face was cold and yet full of anticipation. Amaron sensed he was excited about the hunt. He would end that.

Sending one of his warriors across the stream first with a drawn bow, Uzzsheol and his companion drew their bows. It was a cover and move system not unlike what Captain Lachoneus had taught Amaron and the other scouts. Once all three were across, Uzzsheol examined the trail again.

Amaron wound up the sling and let the stone go with terrific force. It hit a man; he hoped it was Uzzsheol. Without their captain they would be easier pickings. Besides, he thought, the world would owe him a favor for ridding it of such a devil. It had, however, hit another, knocking him senseless. Taking cover behind boulders, Uzzsheol and the other tracker abandoned the fallen warrior. Arrow nocked and ready, they waited for the Nephite to make a move. Uzzsheol's man tried to better his position and outflank Amaron, but he was waiting, sending another stone. It struck the Lamanite's head, sending him to the black abyss.

Uzzsheol shot his copper-tipped arrow at Amaron, just grazing the edge of his right shoulder. Amaron crawled through some brush to change positions, and lost his sling. "Baal's devils, where did I drop it?" he muttered.

After a few tense moments, each of them watching the shadows, Uzzsheol cried out, "It is a good day to die. Come and fight me, Nephite. I am honored to face you. No one has ever before lain so many of my braves low." He stood in the open without his bow, holding his massive knife and spiked tomahawk, trusting that Amaron as a man of honor would not hit him with the sling. The other Lamanite remained senseless on the ground next to him.

Standing and drawing his broadsword, Amaron strode out to face Uzzsheol. As he came into the open, the wounded man recovered enough to grab his bow and arrow. Amaron froze, ready to dive into the underbrush. Before the warrior could loose a shaft, Uzzsheol hit him in the neck with his tomahawk, killing him in an instant. Amaron was shocked by this savagery to one's own man.

"This is between us two," said Uzzsheol in his cold, emotionless way. "Tell me your name, that I might boast of it in the campfires to come."

"My name is Amaron, son of the scribe, and you will never boast of it," he roared as he slashed at the Lamanite.

Agile and quick, Uzzsheol sidestepped and struck back with his dagger. Amaron blocked and kicked at the same time as he pressed in. Uzzsheol sidestepped again and actually chuckled. It was the only show of emotion Amaron had seen from him. Amaron's broadsword arced at the tracker's chest again as he heaved himself backward, narrowly missing being eviscerated. Amaron overextended himself in the attack, and Uzzsheol stepped inside his area. The broadsword was useless now for so agile a foe, and Amaron dropped it to catch the dagger that raced at him in hungry anticipation. Uzzsheol threw back his tomahawk to split

Amaron's skull, but he caught the Lamanite's grip with his left hand.

As they struggled face to face, Uzzsheol said, "I have given my word to the Evil Eye, my master. As proof of my dedication, you will die! I will give him your head!"

"Tell him...in your frozen hell...that you failed."

In the contest, Amaron proved the stronger and craftier. He shoved the Lamanite back hard, tripping him on the body of the dead man. In his fall, Uzzsheol swung the tomahawk and it glanced across Amaron's left arm, bruising him. Each man struggled against one another for the big dagger.

With the tomahawk gone, Uzzsheol reached into his hair and produced a tiny finger of a knife. Amaron still held against the big dagger and did not see the tiny blade in his foe's left hand. Feigning extra exertion with the right hand for the dagger, Uzzsheol jabbed the little knife four times into Amaron's chest with the speed of lightning. The tiny blade could not get very deep as Amaron strained against Uzzsheol's reach, but the quick jabs inflamed a wild rage within his breast.

Eyes reeling, Amaron head-butted the man and shoved him away. As Uzzsheol went down, Amaron had better control of the dagger and, sweeping it at his enemy he slashed off his nose and cut his shoulder, then ripped it across the chest in a zigzag motion. Uzzsheol struck the rocks beneath him, the pain and shock rendering him unconscious. His nose had been sheared off, and he bled profusely from his face, chest and shoulder. If the tracker wasn't dead, he soon would be.

"Watch and pray," Amaron slurred, spitting blood from smashed lips. Binding his own shallow wounds and girding his sword, he took one of their bows and quivers and continued his journey to Zarahemla, to warn Onandagus of the evil that was coming.

end of book one